To Sue

Pedro

and the

Magic
Marbles

Best Wishes

David H. Worsdale

DAVID H. WORSDALE

Black Lacquer Press & Marketing Inc.
3225 McLeod Drive
Suite 100
Las Vegas, Nevada 89121
USA
www.blacklacquerpress.net

Quantity sales. Special discounts are available on quantity purchases by corporations, associations, and others. For details, contact the publisher at the address above.

CONTENTS

CHAPTER ONE

END OF TERM

Pedro lived with his Mother and Father in a yellow painted cottage in the village of Marbleville. It was called Marbleville because of the Marble Mine, situated just outside the village.

Pedro's mother Mary was a very cheerful lady of medium height with bright red short curly hair. She didn't go to work but did spend a lot of time in her garden, which went round three sides of the cottage. She grew lots of vegetables, which she sold at the village Saturday market.

Tom, her husband was quite a bit taller than her, about 6ft. He had dark brown straight hair, which he kept quite short. He was very fit which he put down to all the manual work he had always done during his life, be it on some of the local farms when he first left school or in the Marble mine. He had worked there since just after Pedro was born.

When they were first married Tom and Mary had shared a house with his parents, but when the opportunity of a job at the mine came, because it also included a house he decided to take it. They stayed with his parents until Pedro was born and then set about making the new house their home. The house they were first given was a bit small but after only a few months at the mine, the cottage where they now lived became vacant so they moved. It was a lot bigger than the first one they had and also had a much larger garden, which pleased Pedro's mother with her love of growing things.

Pedro, at the age of ten was nearly as tall as his mother. He had inherited her red hair but it was not as bright as hers. He was quite a bright, intelligent boy, but not as clever academically as other children of his age at school.

Most of the men in the village worked in the mine digging out pieces of rock which, when carefully cracked open could contain a pretty glass marble. The rocks were sent to the surface where a team of men sorted and graded them according to their size and shape. This team of sorters was made up mostly of men too old to go down into the mine.

Not all the rocks mined contained a marble but most of them did. The marbles, once they had been sorted, were placed in baskets and sent to another building where they were polished and graded before being packed off to the big towns to be sold in the toyshops. Each marble was graded according to the pattern it contained. Some had two lines of colours in them, some had three and some had just one or none. They were graded according to their main overall colour. There were also some odd shaped marbles but as they were not completely round they were discarded as being of no value and therefore not sellable. They were all dumped in the mine's rubbish tip which was just a short distance from the mine.

The owner of the mine was a bad tempered man called Mr. Bilk. He made the men work very hard in the mine, but at the same time paid them very little wages. No one could remember the last time they had seen him smile or could ever recall him saying a kind word to anyone. The mine had been in the Bilk family for as long as anyone could remember. Mr. Bilk lived in a big house on top of a hill overlooking the mine and every day would stand at his window counting the men as they reported for work. He would make a note in his book if any man was missing, and at the end of the week would take some money out of that man's wages for not being at work, even though the man may only have been a bit late and had arrived at work after Mr. Bilk had stopped looking out of his window.

Mr. Bilk also owned all the houses in the village where the men lived with their families, so as well as working for him, they also had to pay him for their homes. Most of the men working at the mine did so because they could not afford to do anything else. If they stopped working at the mine then they also lost their homes.

One thing Mr. Bilk had started doing however, was that at the end of each working day, every man in the mine who had children was allowed to take home with him two pieces of rock they had collected that day. The men gave the rocks to their children to break open and if they contained a marble then they could keep it. Nobody could understand why Mr. Bilk did this, but as he did very little else for the miners or any of the other people in the village they accepted it gratefully.

As his father came through the garden gate at the end of the day, Pedro would be waiting for the pieces of rock his father had collected in the section of the mine where he worked. Pedro would have had his tea before his father got home so he would sit on the back door step chipping away at the pieces of rock, leaving his father to eat his meal in peace.

"Thanks dad", said Pedro, "I hope they have marbles in them as good as the past few days".

"That's just what he said yesterday, and the day before," Pedro's father said to his wife as he washed his hands at the sink.

"You know what boys are," said Pedro's mum, "It doesn't take much to please them. Come along and have your tea Tom, it's all ready for you."

By this time, Pedro was sitting on the step chipping away at the first piece of rock very carefully bit by bit, so he would not break anything that might be inside. He used a special little hammer made for him by his grandfather the last time he and his grandmother had visited them. It was supposed to be used for tapping in the small nails on his model railway track but Pedro found it just as useful for opening the rocks. As all the outside pieces fell away Pedro could see that there in the middle was a lovely round marble, just as nice as the ones he had found for the past five evenings. He started on the second bit of rock and when he had just as carefully removed all the outside bits there was again a lovely marble with four nice coloured stripes running all the way through. He picked up the piece of cloth his Mother had given him and started to polish his marbles until they were really shining. 'Wait until the other children at school see these two,' thought Pedro as he continued to get the marbles even brighter.

Every day at school all the children would show one another their marbles to see who had the best ones. Pedro was pleased because for the past week he knew he had the best ones. The ones he had found the past few nights had all had four coloured stripes running through them. The marbles of most of the other children all had only two or three stripes in them and some only had one or even none at all. Every-one now waited to see if Pedro turned up with another one of his 'Special Ones' as the children had begun to call them. One of the boys had even offered to swap ten of his marbles for just one of Pedro's, but Pedro would not part with any of them. For once in his life he had something no one else had and he wanted to keep it that way for as long as he could.

Pedro kept his marbles in a soft cloth bag his mother had made him, and each marble in turn was wrapped in a piece of cotton wool she had also given him.

Of course he had to keep them out of sight when he was in the classroom or else the teacher would take them away from him and at the same time scold him for not paying attention to the lesson.

Pedro hated going to school, but that was mainly because all the other children made fun of him because he was not as clever as they were. This made him sad and miserable, but his father told him not to let it worry him as one day he would be able to do something that none of the other children would be able to do, and then they would stop poking fun at him. Having the 'Special' marbles was a bit like that thought Pedro, and that was why he would not swap any.

The end of the summer term was getting close, and that meant that all the children had to do tests to see how much they had learned. Pedro was nearly always bottom of his class and this also upset him a lot. No matter how hard he tried he just didn't seem to be able to remember a lot of what was being taught. At the beginning of every new term he promised himself that he would try to pay more attention to his lessons so that he would be able to do better in the tests. That would really please his mother and father, who, although they were disappointed at his test results, never made him feel bad about it.

"Just as long as you have done your best, that's the main thing", his mother would say.

The end of the school term also meant the start of the summer holidays, which in turn meant that his grandparents would be coming to stay with them as they did every summer. No one in the village could really afford to go away on holiday because of the poor wages the miners received but there were always lots of things do to in and around the village. Pedro enjoyed very much the long walks his grandfather would take him. He knew an awful lot about the countryside, and the birds and wildlife, which could be found in the surrounding area. Pedro and his grandfather would go off early in a morning with sandwiches and a bottle of drink his mother had prepared for them and they would spend the whole of the day just walking through the fields and woods. Sometimes they would take one of the other boys with them, but really Pedro enjoyed it more when it was just him and his grandfather.

One other main reason that Pedro looked forward to the end of the school term was that it was his birthday during the long summer holiday. This year he would be eleven and so that meant he only had one more term at his present school before he had to go to the big school in the nearby town.

When the day for the tests arrived, he tried to tell his mother that he was not feeling too good hoping that she would say he did not have to go to school, but his mother knew what the problem was and said he had to go.

"Just do your best with the questions, Pedro and you will be alright," she said. "Maybe you will surprise us all and come top of the class" Pedro knew his Mother was only trying to cheer him up, but he did make a silent promise to her that he would try as hard as he knew how.

At school the children were all talking about the tests they would be doing that morning so no one asked about any new marbles they may have found. Pedro was so worried about the tests that he had forgotten to mention to the other children that he had found two 'Specials' again. He had brought just the two from last night's pieces of rock and they were safely wrapped in their cotton wool and in his jacket pocket.

The teacher called the children into the classroom, and told them to sit at their desks, and not to talk. Then she went round and gave each child a test paper, laying it face down on the desks, telling them not to turn them over until she told them to.

"Don't start until I tell you", she said. "And I don't want to see anybody looking at the paper of the person next to you. You may copy down a wrong answer if you see their answer is different to yours. I want no talking during the test. When you have finished and you have checked to make sure there is nothing more you can do, get up quietly from your desk bring your paper and put it on my desk then leave the classroom and go and wait in the playground until the rest have finished. You have one hour to answer the questions. Right, you can turn over the papers and start now."

Pedro looked through his paper and studied the questions very carefully. He picked out the ones he thought he could get right and decided to do them first. There were twenty questions in all and he thought that he could answer at least half of them. If he managed to get all those right at least he wouldn't be bottom of the class, he thought. He started off by answering the questions he felt sure of, and then looked at the ones he knew he would have trouble with. By this time a lot of the other children had finished the test and had gone outside to play. When the teacher announced that there was only a quarter of an hour left he still had eight questions to answer. It was getting near to the end of the time and Pedro and two girls were the only ones left in the classroom.

"Only five minutes left", Pedro heard the teacher say. Pedro looked at the last few questions left unanswered on his paper. He had been wishing with each one he did that he knew the right answer. He finished the last question just as the teacher said time was up. He gave his paper to the teacher and went outside to join the other children.

The children were all playing football so he took off his jacket and put it with all the other jackets and joined in. After about half an hour they all got very hot and decided to sit down for a rest. Of course, as soon as they were all sat together, the talk got around to the latest collection of marbles. Pedro went to collect his jacket so that he could show off his latest two bright marbles.

He very carefully took the little bag out of his pocket, and reached into it to get out his two marbles. He opened out the cotton wool they were wrapped in as all the children crowded round to have a look. When he took the marbles out and laid them in the palm of his hand to show everyone he could not believe his eyes. Lying there were not his two lovely coloured striped marbles but two very plain ordinary ones with not even one stripe.

"Someone has swapped my marbles for these plain ordinary ones," shouted Pedro, very close to tears. The other children just looked at him and said he must have been mistaken and had brought two ordinary plain marbles to school. Pedro knew different, however, because ever since he had started finding the 'special' marbles, he had put all his plain ones away into a separate box and had not even taken them out to look at them. None of the children would admit that they had taken Pedro's marbles, and they were still arguing about it when the teacher came out to see what all the noise was.

"Come into the classroom Pedro, I want a word with you," was all she said, and turned around and walked back into the school. Pedro followed her into the classroom wondering what she wanted him for. 'Certainly not for arguing', he thought. The children were always arguing and none of them had ever been called into the classroom for it before. He stood in front of the teacher's desk and he could see she was quite angry.

"Pedro!" she said sternly, "we all know here at the school that you are not the brightest boy we have ever had, but there is no need to cheat with your tests. You have got nearly all the questions right; and in fact you have come second in the class. Now I know you are not that clever, so I can only suppose that either you saw the questions last week when I was preparing the tests and then found out the answers, or else you looked at the paper of Peter who sat next to you knowing that he always gets good marks in the tests."

Once more that afternoon Pedro was very nearly in tears as he listened to his teacher. He started to tell her that he had never once looked at Peter's paper during the test, but his teacher just held up her hand for him to remain silent. Her next words made Pedro's legs turn to jelly, and he really started to cry.

"You will go straight home now Pedro, and when I have finished at the school I will be round to see your parents about this".

Pedro ran out of the classroom and out of the school not even bothering to collect his jacket, which he had left on the grass when his teacher had called him. When he arrived at his house his mother was in the garden working on the vegetable plot. She looked up as Pedro came through the gate and she could see immediately something was wrong. He ran straight up to her and threw himself at her sobbing his heart out.

"What on earth is wrong Pedro?" She asked him, but he was so upset that in the end she had to speak very sharply to him to stop him sobbing and try to tell her what was wrong. When she finally heard what had happened at school, she was a little upset that the teacher had accused Pedro of cheating without first finding out if there was a good reason why he had done so well in the test. For all anyone knew, Pedro could have really tried hard that term at school, and got all the questions right on his own.

"Pedro," she said, "I know you would never tell lies to either me your father or to anyone else for that matter, so I am going to ask you, did you cheat with the test in any of the ways the teacher suggested?"

"No! No! No!" replied Pedro, once more starting to cry, "All I did was answer the questions with what I hoped were the right answers. I never looked at Peter's paper once, honestly I didn't. In any case Peter was one of the first to finish and had left the classroom while I was still answering the easy questions".

"Alright" said his mother, "now stop crying, go and wash your face and we will sort this out when the teacher comes to see you father and me later".

Pedro went up to the bathroom and washed his face and hands ready for tea. While he was there he heard his father come home and heard his mother explaining to him what had happened. When he went downstairs and into the room where his father was he was beginning to feel frightened because of what he might say to him, but all he said was that his mother had explained what had happened, and that they were not going to discuss anything else about it until later when his teacher arrived.

"So sit down and have your tea Pedro. I am sure you are telling the truth about all this but we must hear what your teacher has to say about it."

Although Pedro knew he had not cheated on the test, he was still a bit frightened as to what the teacher would say when she came to the house later. He just hoped that none of his friends had been listening outside the classroom door when his teacher had called him there. He would hate it if they all thought he was a cheat and stopped talking and playing with him.

Pedro ate his tea in silence but not really feeling like eating. He asked to be excused from the table and decided to go outside into the garden to find something to keep himself occupied until Miss Richards, his teacher arrived. All the trouble over the test, and then the worry over what his father would say had put all other thoughts out of his mind. As he passed through the kitchen on his way to the garden, he noticed that the two pieces of rock his father had brought home that evening were on the shelf above the sink. He thought that perhaps he had better not ask if he could have them this evening because of all that had happened.

Seeing the pieces of rock brought his mind back to what had happened in the playground, when he had got out his two new marbles to show the rest of the children. That also made him remember that he had not brought his jacket home when he ran from the school. His mother would certainly be cross with him for leaving that behind, so Pedro decided he would go to the school after Miss Richards had been to the house, to see if the jacket was still there.

He sat down on a log in the garden trying to work out why the two marbles he had taken out his pocket to show his friends had been ordinary ones and not the ones with the bright stripes in. The only thing he could think of was that while he was playing football, someone had gone to his jacket and changed them over, taking the good ones for themselves and leaving two plain ones in their place. Even as he was thinking this he knew that could not have happened because his jacket was being used as one of the goal posts and he had been the goalie, so would have seen if anyone had gone near his jacket.

All this waiting was making Pedro very restless, so he decided to go to his room just to make sure he had not taken plain marbles to school that day by mistake. He was certain he hadn't because he remembered that the evening before, when he had finished polishing his new marbles, he had put them straight into his jacket pocket ready to take to school next day. He also knew that, including the ones he had polished the night before he now should have sixteen of the special ones. He got out his box of marbles and counted them. Fourteen! That was how many were in the box so he knew he was right and that he had taken two good ones to school with him. So someone must have swapped his for two plain ones. He knew that he would never find out who had done it so decided that in future he wouldn't take any of his special marbles to school. Instead he would take some that he had had for a long time. They were not as good as the others and they only had three stripes in them. He knew it would mean that he wouldn't have the best marbles when the other children showed theirs but he would know himself that the ones he had at home were better than any the other children had.

He stayed in his room for quite a while, just looking at his collection of marbles and every now and then picking one up and giving it another polish.

"I wish the teacher would hurry up and get here," said Pedro to himself, "Then we could get this thing all sorted out". Just as he said that he heard the garden gate open and footsteps on the path leading to the front door. He heard his mother go to the front door to welcome Miss Richards to their home. He decided to wait in his room until he was called down. He could hear his teacher's voice and now and then either his mother's or father's but couldn't make out what was being said. After a while his father came to the bottom of the stairs and called for him to come down.

He walked into the living room. His father was sat down in his chair by the fireplace, and his mother and Miss Richards were sitting at the table. All of them turned to look at him as he entered the room, which made Pedro start to feel sick. He was sure they were all going to start on him at the same time.

"Sit down here at the table, Pedro" said his mother gently. "We have listened to what Miss Richards has had to say about the situation. We have told her that we don't think you cheated when you did the test and she herself has made it quite clear that she was most surprised to find herself thinking you had, as you had never done that sort of thing in the past. If at any time you didn't know anything you either asked or just left it. However, it does seem unusual that on this occasion you came so high in the class when she marked the papers".

Pedro looked across the table at the teacher. She smiled at him and said, "We want to be absolutely fair about this Pedro, and so, what I have suggested to your parents is that you take the test again." Pedro's heart started beating faster at the thought of having to do all that writing again. Miss Richards saw the look on his face and said, "Don't worry Pedro you won't have to do it at school. We can do it right here in this room. I have given your Father a set of the questions with the correct answers and your mother has your actual test paper with the answers you filled in this morning. I will just ask you the questions and you can give me the answers. We can then all listen to your answers, and we can all check them with the papers we have. If there is a question you are not certain of, just say so and you can go back to it just as you would at school. I will put a little mark against those questions and ask you later." Pedro looked across at his father who was studying the paper he had in his hand. His father looked up and saw the worried look Pedro's face. He gave Pedro a smile of encouragement and said, "Don't worry Pedro. Just answer the questions carefully and you will be fine."

This cheered Pedro up a little but he still didn't like the idea of doing the test in front of his parents. Miss Richards asked him if he was ready and when Pedro told her he was she started to ask the questions. It seemed to Pedro that they went on forever. There were just a couple he asked to leave to go back to otherwise he just gave answers as he thought were correct.

"How many feet in a mile?" asked Miss Richards. When Pedro heard that question he knew the test was nearly over because he remembered that that question was one of the easier ones he had done that morning before going back to the more difficult ones he wasn't too sure of, and that it was towards the end of the test.

"Five Thousand Two Hundred and Eighty" said Pedro confidently.

Miss Richards asked him two more questions which he answered with equal confidence, and then she told him that that was the end of the test.

His mother reached over and patted his hand and gave him one of her kind smiles.

"Go into the kitchen and get yourself a glass of milk while we are checking the papers," said his Father.

Pedro practically ran from the room, he was so pleased it was all over. He poured himself a glass of milk, and then decided to fill the kettle and put it on to boil as he was certain his mother would offer his teacher a cup of tea before she went home. He also put two biscuits in his pocket because he was also just as certain that if he had got a lot of the questions wrong then he would be sent to bed without any supper. He looked up as his father came into the kitchen. "Go back into the living room" he said to Pedro, "Miss Richards has something to say to you."

Pedro could see no indication on his Father's face as to how well he had done with the test, so he just nodded and did as he was told. His mother smiled at him when he walked into the room and got up and walked towards him. She leaned over and gave him a big kiss on the cheek and held him close to her. When she stood upright again, Pedro looked across at Miss Richards. She was also smiling at him.

"Well Pedro," she said, "We, or should I say I, owe you a very big apology. You gave us the very same answers; including the wrongs ones, that you put down on your paper this morning. It appears you had been paying attention to what had been taught this last term after all. If you hadn't known a lot of the answers this morning and had looked at Peter's paper, you would not have been able to remember all the correct answers this evening. It was evidently all your own work and I am truly very, very sorry that I accused you of cheating. I hope you and your parents will realise that I had a genuine reason for being concerned and speaking out like I did, and only hope that you can find it in your heart to forgive me."

Pedro could not believe what he was hearing, but at the same time was very glad the way things had turned out. He gave his teacher a smile and just nodded, unsure what to say. He knew he hadn't cheated, but at the same time did not realise he had paid so much attention to the lessons that term.

At that moment his father came into the room. He patted Pedro affectionately on the head and said, "Well done Pedro, you were right, you didn't cheat. Now off you go into the garden and play for a little while. Oh, and today's rocks are on the kitchen table for you."

Pedro, feeling very relieved, left the room and collected the two rocks on his way to the garden, crossing his fingers that his father had managed to bring him the same good rocks as previous nights. Chipping away very carefully so as not to damage anything that might be inside, Pedro was soon in his own little world again where all thoughts of tests, teachers and cheating were far from his mind.

At last Pedro had chipped enough of the rock away to be able to see that indeed inside was yet another bright marble with four stripes, but this time they were all the same colour, a lovely bright blue. Also this marble was a lot smaller than any of the other ones he had found, and the stripes were thinner and closer together and all in a straight line, whereas the other marbles he had found so far had the stripes running across in different directions. He carefully removed the remains of the outside rock taking great care not to damage the marble. When he had removed the remaining pieces of rock he carefully put the marble to one side and set about opening the second big rock.

He was so excited wondering what he would find, and had to force himself to stay very calm as he set about the task of chipping away at the outer coat of rock. His patience was rewarded when he eventually reached the marble inside. This one also had four nice bright blue stripes just like the other one, all close together and running in a straight line. Something told Pedro in his mind that these latest two marbles were even more special than the ones he had previously found. Pedro wanted to dash inside the house, and tell his Father what he had found, but as Miss Richards was still there he decided to wait until she had gone. Instead he contented himself with clearing up the mess breaking the rocks open had made and then set about polishing the new marbles. He had never seen anything like the ones he had got that evening. He loved the ones he already had but they had all got different coloured stripes, whereas the new ones all had the same colours. He made up his mind there and then he would not be taking them to school, or even mention, them to anyone.

As he continued to polish his new marbles, he heard his parents and his teacher making their way to the front door. He put his marbles down carefully and made his way round the side of the house to the front garden to say goodnight to Miss Richards. She gave him a nice smile and although she didn't apologise again about what had happened, he could tell by the way she looked at him that that was the case. "Goodnight Pedro," she said. "I will see you at school in the morning. Don't worry about the other children, they know nothing about this." she reassured him. "Oh, and I have given your jacket to your Mother, you left it in the playground when you ran home."

Pedro thanked her and wished her goodnight, then stood with his parents as they watched Miss Richards walk down the road towards the village. She lived at the other end of the village next to the school. The school was owned by Mr. Bilk as was the house she lived in. It was included in her salary as teacher. She was the only teacher at the school who lived there. The other four teachers at the school either lived elsewhere in the village or came from the nearby town. Some of them only came on a part time basis as they also taught in the big school in that town. A music teacher called Mrs. Pelley came once a week, and there was also a Mr. Carter who taught history. He also took the children for games and sport and came to the school two or three times a week. Mrs. Burns taught geography and Miss Wilson taught math and English. Miss Burns also taught science if there were enough children there who were interested in the subject. These teachers all came to the village school under an arrangement made between Mr. Bilk and the Head teacher of the school where they normally taught.

Pedro and his parents went back into the house and his mother told him that as it was getting a bit late it was time to clear up his things, and have a wash before having a bit of supper and going to bed. As he tidied up Pedro remembered what Miss Richards had said about his jacket so after he had cleared everything up and as he went upstairs to have a wash he collected it and took it up to his room. When he got there he checked the pockets just to make sure he had not been mistaken about his marbles before his teacher had called him into the school. He took out the two marbles and saw that there had been no mistake; he clearly held in his hand two plain glass marbles. He put them into the box with rest of his ordinary ones. He also picked up the two marbles he had been polishing when his teacher had arrived and put them in the other box where he kept his 'specials' not noticing that one of the marbles only had three stripes in it.

CHAPTER TWO

THE ARRIVAL OF PAUL
AND GRANDPARENTS

The next day Pedro went off to school quite happy knowing that there were only two more days left before the start of the summer holidays when the school would be closed for six weeks. He was also happy because that meant his Grandparents would be coming to stay with them. They normally stayed for about four weeks and it was the best time of all for Pedro. Not having a lot of money meant that like so many of the families in the village, Pedro's parents could not afford to go away for a summer holiday but having his grandparents to stay was a lot better in his opinion. Sometimes they would all go off together for day trips, and other times Pedro would go off, just him and his Grandfather, and spend the day wandering along the lanes and over the fields just looking at all there was to see. His grandfather was always very keen to tell Pedro anything he wanted to know about what they saw. He explained how different birds made their nests in different trees or bushes depending on what type they were, or how foxes lived in places called dens, or lairs and badgers lived in sets. The last time his grandfather had visited them he promised Pedro that on his next visit he would ask Pedro's mother if he could take him out one night to see if they could see any badgers or foxes. He said he would try to remember to bring a spare pair of binoculars so Pedro could get a good look at what the various animals did.

When he arrived at school, Pedro just went in as normal as his father had advised him to. None of the other children said anything to him; in fact they were very pleased to see him. At least one half of the group was.

"Come on Pedro!" James shouted, "We need you in goal, we are two down already" Pedro quickly dropped his jacket on top of a pile marking one of the goal posts and a grateful Freddy, who had been the goalkeeper, happily let him take his place. "Watch out for that boy in the yellow jumper," warned Freddy, "He's pretty quick with the ball"

"O.K. thanks," replied Pedro. He looked to see the boy Freddy had been talking about. When he spotted the yellow jumper he didn't recognise the boy at all. 'Must be another boy from the village,' thought Pedro. The big school in town had already broken up for the holidays so Pedro thought that perhaps he had just come down to the playground to join in the games.

"Look out Pedro!!" Looking up Pedro could see that the 'yellow jumper' was heading towards the goal with only one defender between him and the Pedro. The defender did his best to stop him but the boy managed to slip past him and take a shot at the goal. Luckily for Pedro, it was not a very hard shot and he was able to save it quite easily. The boy in yellow was the first to say anything after the cheering had died down.

"Well saved," he said," I can see why they wanted you in goal."

"Thank you" replied Pedro. Playing in goal was about the only thing at school he was good at and was always pleased when he was picked for it. Just then the bell sounded for school to start so he collected his jacket from the pile. The other boy did the same and he and Pedro walked towards the school together.

"Are you from the school in town?" Pedro asked the boy.

"No," the boy replied. "I have just come to live here. My name is Paul and I have come to stay with my granddad. He lives in the big house up there on the hill."

By this time all the children were going into the school so Pedro did not have time to say anything else. He just hoped that the look of shock he could feel on his face at the news of who Paul was had not been noticed by him. As they entered the classroom Miss Richards asked them all to take their places.

"Good morning children." She said when they were all seated.

"Good morning Miss Richards" they all replied.

Pedro saw that Paul was standing beside Miss Richards. "This is Paul," she said to them all. "He has come to live here in the village with his grandfather and will be joining our class after the summer holidays. His grandfather thought it would be a good idea for him to come and meet you all for the last few days before we break up. That way he won't feel such a stranger when we all come back after the holidays. I know he is a few years older than most of you, but he has been quite seriously poorly over the past two years and so has missed a lot of schooling. His grandfather thought it would be best for him to attend here at least for the next two terms to enable him to catch up a bit." Miss Richards looked around the classroom then said to Paul. "There are four empty places, so just choose whichever you would like. We can sort you out properly next term." Paul walked towards the middle of the classroom and chose the empty desk next to Samantha.

"Right," said Miss Richards, "first things first. All the test papers have been marked and I am pleased to tell you that you all passed so very well done to you all." She deliberately avoided looking at Pedro and he on his part did not look up as she made the announcement.

"I know you will all want to know who came top and how many marks you all got, that is understandable. The important thing is that it doesn't matter who came top or bottom, but that you all passed which shows that you have all been paying attention to what has been taught you the past term."

She went on to tell them what they would be doing for the last few days of the term.

"Today we will spend time finishing off the various things you have been doing in art and hobbies so that they will be ready for you to take home on Friday." There was a quiet buzz went round the classroom because the children all knew that there would be no more serious lessons. Miss Richards continued,

"Tomorrow Mr. Carter will be coming to the school and will take some extra games lessons. Mrs. Burns will also be with him. Mr. Carter wants to take you boys for a football trial. The school in town has challenged this school to a game of football to be played during the holidays and Mr. Carter wants to make sure that this school can put out a good team."

Again she waited for the chattering to die down then said, "You young ladies have not been forgotten. Mrs. Burns will be hoping to get a couple of teams together, which will also play on the same day. She is looking for a netball team and a hockey team. Those of you who are not chosen for any of the teams will not be left out. You will be required to be general helpers on the day, handing out programmes and looking after the guests and parents who we hope will come to the occasion. It should be a very enjoyable day for everyone, and I am sure that those who are chosen to play for the school will do very well."

Pedro was hoping that his grandparents would still be here when the day arrived because he was really hoping that he would be picked for the football team.

"Just a couple more things to tell you before you go away to the arts and hobbies room," said Miss Richards. "This afternoon I will be going to see Mr. Bilk to tell him the results of the tests and while I am there I will ask him if he will be willing to provide trophies for the winning teams in the games and also, as you have all done so well this term, I will ask him if we can finish the term on Friday at lunch time instead of having to wait until the afternoon."

"Bet he won't agree to either of those," said Sam from the back of the class.

"Now, now," Miss Richards said, acutely aware that Paul may have heard the comment. "That was not a very nice thing to say Sam"

She cast a quick look in the direction of Paul but could see no sign that he had heard the comment or had realised the implication of it. As far as she knew, no one else but herself knew he was related to Mr. Bilk. "Now, off you go to the hobbies room."

The next two days just couldn't pass quick enough for Pedro and the rest of his class. They seemed to spend an awful lot of the time just doing 'nice' things, not real lessons at all. Still, the fact that they were not doing ordinary lessons would make the days pass more easily. He wondered what the point was in Paul coming to school each day till the end of term. As far as Pedro knew, he was the only one in the class knew just who he was, apart from Miss Richards. All the teacher had told them was that he had come to live with his grandfather but hadn't said who his grandfather was.

Pedro's house was at the far end of the village just passed the bottom of the hill where Paul's grandfather lived.

Paul was waiting at the bottom of the hill as Pedro walked to school the next day, so none of the other children saw where he came from. The first day he just talked about things in general, about who lived in the village and the names of the families and their children. Pedro saw no problem in answering his questions, as they seemed to be O.K. As they entered the school yard one day James joined them as they walked to the class room and asked Pedro if he had had any of his good marbles lately.

"No, I haven't" replied Pedro. In fact since the incident with his teacher and the fact that they were not doing much at school, checking the rocks his father brought home each night had sort of taken second place. The night after his teacher had been to his house the rocks his father had given him had only contained plain marbles without any sort of stripes in them.

"What's this about good marbles?" asked Paul eagerly. By this time they were at their classroom so they had to stop talking about marbles and go to sit at their desks. As he sat there Pedro had a funny feeling about the way Paul had wanted to know about his marbles. All the other children knew about his "special" marbles and didn't really ask him much about them too often, but the way Paul had asked and had looked at him made him feel a bit uneasy. He decided then and there that he would not tell him too much about things, especially him being who he was. He certainly would not let him know how many he had or let him see them.

After Miss Richards had called the register she went on to explain that most of the arrangements for the mid-holiday sports day had been finalised. The names for the various teams would be put on the notice board after lunch and all the children would be given a copy to take home together with an invitation for all parents and friends to come along on the day and enjoy themselves.

"Mr. Bilk has generously provided five trophies for the events being held and has also agreed to provide the bulk of the refreshments," said Miss Richards, " but if any of your parents would like to bake cakes or make extra sandwiches then they will be very welcome to do so. We want to make it a fun day to be enjoyed by all" There was a general buzz of excitement went round the class room everyone wondering who would be on the various teams. Miss Richards clapped her hands to regain their attention and said, "You will all be pleased to know that Mr, Bilk has agreed that we can close the term at lunch time tomorrow Friday and start our holiday then." This announcement was greeted with a cheer from all the children so that she again had to get their attention to tell them that in return for the extra half day, all the children were expected to help in the morning to make sure all classrooms were left neat and tidy before they left at midday. That way, she explained they would be nice and clean and tidy for the sports day when all visitors would be invited to look round the classrooms.

Normally at the end of a school year everything was taken down off the walls ready to start a new term but this year because of the open day they were having, it had been decided to leave everything as it was so all parents could see just what the pupils had been doing. All the children were then divided into groups of six and each group were given their different tasks. Pedro was glad he had not been selected with Paul's group. He was still not too happy about the way Paul had questioned him about his marbles. He made up his mind there and then not to tell him too much. He also hoped that the other children would not talk about his marbles either.

The rest of the day passed off quietly enough with all the children just finishing off any of their projects so they could take them home that evening. The sound of the bell at the end of the school day was greeted with a few cheers. After the cheers had died down, Miss Richards told them that they could come to school next day in whatever clothes they wanted. "Tell your parents what you will be doing," she said, "That way you will be able to wear older clothes which won't matter if they get a bit dirty with the cleaning etc. you will be doing. Don't forget also to tell them you will be home lunch time." She then went on to say that they would all be given a letter the next day explaining about the 'Sports and Open' day being held during the holidays. There would also be a request with the letter inviting any of the mothers who would like to contribute on the day by making cakes etc.

There was lots of exciting chatter as all the children made their way out of school and home. Pedro noticed that Paul was walking with a group of boys ahead of him. He was glad about this, as he didn't feel like talking about his marbles again. About half way home just before they all reached the turn off which led to the hill where his Grandfather lived, Paul said goodbye to the boys he had been with and waited for Pedro and his friends to catch up with him. When they did Paul singled him out and said, "Hello Pedro, the boys have been telling me about your striped marbles. It would be really great if I could have a look at them sometime. Perhaps I could come round your house during the holidays and see them."

Pedro didn't quite know what to say. "O.K." he replied, "But I don't know when I will be in. My grandparents are coming to stay and I spend a lot of time going out with my granddad."

"O.K. but I'm sure we will be able to arrange something." With that Paul said goodbye and turned to go up the hill and Pedro ran to catch up with his friends to ask them what Paul had been saying.

They told him he had been asking about what sort of marbles had been found at the mine lately and who had the best ones. They said they had told him that as far as they knew, he, Pedro had been the one who seemed to have had the best although one other person, a girl called Sally, had showed up with some funny looking ones as well. They also said that Paul hadn't asked anything about what stripes were in the marbles and they hadn't told him. Just that they were nice ones.

As they said this Jimmy turned round and saw that Paul was walking up the hill. "What's he doing going up there?" he said pointing out to the others where Paul was going, "There's only one house up there and we know who lives there." Pedro then went on to tell them all that Paul had told him earlier that he had come to live with his Grandfather.

"No wonder he wanted to know all about the marbles." Billy said. The boys carried on to their various homes agreeing between themselves that they would tell Paul as little as possible about any marbles they all had. They also promised Pedro that they would not say anything about his special ones. They all wished that they had some like Pedro but it was just Pedro's good luck that his father worked at the spot where the pretty ones were being found. Maybe later on their fathers would be moved to a different part of the mine and then it might be their turn to get striped ones. Pedro said good night to his friends and carried on up the main road. His house was a bit further on than the rest of his friends.

As he was walking along wondering what he would do about the "Paul" situation, a bus stopped next to him and he heard his name being called. He looked into the bus and saw his father by the door. "Jump on Pedro," his father said, "I am going to meet your grandparents at the station so you may as well come along as well." Pedro climbed on the bus and as he sat down his father explained that he had had a message from his father that they would be coming to see them earlier than they expected and would be arriving on the 5 o'clock train. The news that his grandparents were arriving that very day put all thoughts of Paul, School and marbles right out of Pedro's mind. He really loved it when they came to stay and once they got here he always wished they could stay forever. His grandmother and grandfather were the nicest people he knew apart from his own parents and never seemed to get upset about anything. They always taught him that he should treat other people as he himself would like to be treated no matter what another person had said or done do him. They also said that things had a habit of working out for the best and if anyone was nasty or cruel to another person, then eventually they would get their just deserts.

Pedro had always tried to act on this advice, but found it hard, especially when some of the older boys from the local town had sometimes come to the village and tried to stop him and his friends from playing their games. How could you think nicely of someone who just came and took your football away and never brought it back, or pinched the bell from your bicycle?

His father telling him they had arrived at the station brought Pedro out of his deep thoughts. He leapt off the bus and ran to the barrier looking down the track for the train. "About another five minutes yet," his father said, "Why don't you go and stand up on the bridge and then you can see it as it comes round the bend by the river."

Pedro was off like a shot and raced up the steps to the bridge. Two other children were already there, looking up the line in the direction the train would be coming from.

"Hello Pedro," they both said, "Who are you meeting?" Pedro explained to them that he was here to meet his grandparents who were coming to stay for a few weeks.

"My granny is coming too," said Sally, who was in the same class as Pedro. She went on to say that her granddad would not be coming as he was still away at sea, but would try and get down before the end of the holidays. "What about you Simon?" Pedro asked the boy, "Who are you meeting?"

"I've come to collect my dog," said Simon. "Remember last week when he was running in the field and got caught in a trap? Well, he had to go away to the Vet to get his leg fixed and the vet has put him in a special box and the guard on the train is looking after him for me. I am just hoping the box is not too big for me to carry onto the bus."

Don't worry," said Pedro, "Me, and my dad will give you a hand to carry it."

"Thanks a lot," said Simon.

Just then they heard the whistle of the train as it came round the bend by the river, and stood gazing as it made its way into the station and came to a stop. The three children rushed down the steps of the bridge and on to the platform, Pedro looking for his grandparents, Sally trying to see her Granny and Simon looking for the guard's compartment to collect his dog.

Pedro's Granddad was the first off the train and gave a big wave to Pedro before turning back to the carriage door to help his wife down onto the platform.

"Hello Granny," said Pedro as he rushed into his grandmother's arms. His grandfather had re-entered the carriage to get their cases. When he got back out again he gave Pedro a big hug, then stood back to take a good look at him. "My, but how you have grown since we last saw you," he said, "I swear you must have grown another six inches. You'll be as tall as me soon."

"You always say that Grampy!' replied Pedro.

As they all made their way to the station exit, Pedro remembered Simon who had come to collect his dog. He looked down the platform and could see that he had indeed collected his dog and that the Guard had put it on a barrow for him and was pushing it along the platform with Simon walking alongside him trying to look in to the box to get a glimpse of his pet. Everyone stood together waiting for the bus to come round to the station: Pedro with his father and grandparents, Sally with her grandmother and Simon with his dog in the box which the guard had placed on the ground. "I hope I can get this into the bus," said Simon.

"You shouldn't need to," said the guard. "I have a note here from the Vet who brought your dog to the train. It says that on arrival your dog can be taken out of the box and allowed to walk on his lead. Just don't let him jump up at anything or do any running around for a few days. Here, let's get him out for you and then I can take the box back into the station to be put on to the train to be returned to the Vet."

When he was released from the box, the dog made as much fuss of Simon as Simon did to his pet. The guard gave Simon the note telling him that there were a few more instructions from the vet as to how the dog was to be looked after for the next few days. He said the vet had told him to pass on the message that he would be in the village in two weeks time and would call in then to see how he was getting along.

Sally arrived to join the group having found her grandmother and as they all waited for the bus together Pedro introduced everyone to his grandparents and likewise Sally did the same. They all made a fuss of Simon's dog, who loved the attention he was getting. When the bus arrived they all got on while Pedro's father helped the driver to put the luggage in the boot of the bus. They were the only passengers on the bus so there was plenty of room. Simon was the first to get off and said goodbye with the promise to Pedro that he would call round to see him the next day. During the journey Pedro's grandfather had invited him to come on a walk with them in the next couple of days and Simon said he would have to ask his mother if he could. Sally lived in the middle of the village by the post office. When the bus reached their stop Pedro's father lifted her grandmother's luggage out of the bus and quickly carried it to the front door of Sally's house. As the bus set off again the driver looked at Pedro and said, "I know where you live young man. You live in the yellow house at the end of the main street, the one with the pretty flowers. Every time I pass by there your mother seems to always be doing something in the garden." Although the actual bus stop was a little way from Pedro's house, the driver stopped right outside his front gate, saying that as there were no other passengers on the bus there was no problem dropping them off right at their home. They all thanked him, retrieved their luggage from the boot and waved him goodbye.

"I can see what he meant about the garden," granddad said as he walked up the path to the house, "it is a real picture and smells lovely."

Just then the front door opened and Pedro's mother stood there holding out her arms to welcome her Mother, and Father-in-law.

"Welcome! Welcome, to our home." she said as she gave each of them a big hug. "Come in, Come in." She really was so excited to see them both.

They all went into the house and Pedro's father carried their cases through to the little room at the back of the house. It had once been a sort of utility room but as his mother had got older and found it difficult to climb stairs he had converted it into a small but comfortable bedsitting room ideal for his parents to use when they came to visit. At other times Pedro used it as a place to set up his model railway track. This was pushed under the bed out of the way during his grandparents' visits. There always seemed to be so much to do when they were there, so things like railway layouts took second place.

Pedro's mother than told them all that tea was ready so they all went and sat at the table. As they ate their meal they just talked about things in general, each one eager to hear all the latest gossip from one another. "How's school coming along young man?' asked Pedro's grandfather, "Still playing in goal for the football team?"

"Yes I am" replied Pedro, thankful that he had been asked about football and not any of the other lessons. His grandfather turned to Pedro's mother and said, "You certainly keep the garden all nice and tidy Mary. The bus driver was saying on the way up here that he often sees you at work there." Pedro's mother could feel herself blush at the compliment, but was secretly pleased that here efforts in the garden had been noticed.

The conversation eventually came round to the mine and Pedro's grandmother asked her son how things were. "Not too bad at the moment mum," he said. He then went on to tell his parents about the strange thing that Mr. Bilk had started to do in letting all the workers with children take home a couple of rocks at the end of each shift.

"He must be up to something Tom," his mother said. "Old Man Bilky never did anyone any favours without a reason and I doubt if his Son is any different. Just like his father he is and his father before that. He'll have some evil scheme in his mind you mark my words."

Tom's mother was the same age as the present Mr. Bilk and had gone to school at the same time as him. Her husband, Pedro's grandfather had come from the next village and they had met many years ago when they were both still very young, and attended the same school. There had been no school in his home village so had attended the one in Marbleville. He had started work at the mine when he left school so they continued seeing one another. Pedro's grandfather had been training as an electrician so his work was mainly on the surface. He had to go down into the mine occasionally but not very often. Pedro's grandmother also worked at the mine in the offices. She had been one of the secretaries working for Mr. Bilk's father. He could sometimes be just as bad tempered as his son was now, although he had always been quite pleasant to her and to the other girls who worked in and around the office. It always seemed as if the workers in the mine received the bad tempered side of him but as jobs in those days were very scarce it was a case of just getting on with things. She also helped to look after Mr. Bilk's mother who was getting quite frail and could not do a lot of the things she used to be able to do. In those days the Bilk family lived in the old Manor House. It had been in the family for as long as anyone could remember. A part of it was sectioned in the earlier days and used as a school before the present one. It was because the house was so big that old Mrs. Bilk could no longer manage the upkeep of it all and had asked her husband to see if there was a young lady working at the mine who might like to help her with the things she could no longer manage. Knowing that Pedro's grandmother came from a good family he had no hesitation in asking her if she would like the position. He told her that she could work there most of the week instead of in the office. She had liked the idea and so Mr. Bilk had taken her along to meet his wife. They got on very well together and old Mrs. Bilk counted her more as a friend than helper. She told her quite a few things over the years, each time stressing upon her to keep them to herself.

One day when they were alone in the house, the old lady gave her a large envelope. It was sealed with blue ribbon and the knot was covered in wax to make it secure. "Take this my dear, and keep it in a safe place where no one can find it. It contains lots of things about the mine, the marbles and the goings on there over the years. Keep it sealed until it is time to open it. You will know by instinct when the time is right. Read what is in there and you will know just what to do. No one else but me knows what is in there, although I am sure others suspect such documents exist. Should they get into the wrong hands then someone could just as easily use the information the wrong way and cause upset to lots of people, much more than has been done already over the years. I hate to say it but especially don't let Cedric get hold of any of the things I will give you. I know he is my Son but I think he is being influenced by that manager my husband has put to work in the mine. I don't really trust him and told Alfred so when he told me he was giving him a job. He is from a different side of the family. There has always been friction between the two sides, mainly because our side of the family has the ownership of the mines. It was once owned equally by all the Bilks, but many, many years ago we were told that there had been some sort of family argument and when one female from the other side of the family passed away she left everything to one of her cousins on our side, and there has been a bit of a family feud ever since. From information I have managed to gather over the years this appeared that was not the complete truth. In fact it was when I was talking to your own grandmother a few years ago that a completely different side of the story came out." She then gave her a little box, again wrapped and tied with ribbon and again with the knots sealed with wax. In the middle of the wax seal was a very small indentation. "When the right time comes, someone who I trust just as much as you will provide you with the means to release the wax seal." She implored Pedro's grandmother to take extra care of what was in the box. "The five little things in that box could cause a lot of pain and upset if they ended up in the wrong hands. There has been enough damage done over the years and I would hate it to happen all over again. I will rest in peace if I know that those silly bits of round glass could be used for what they were intended, just children's playthings." Pedro's grandmother was about to say ask if she didn't think she was too young to be given such responsibility but it was as if she old lady could read her mind. "I know what you are thinking and that you wonder if you can do this but believe me, I have come to love and trust you over the years you have been helping me and there is no one on this earth I would rather trust with this task." It was just as if the old lady wanted someone else to know what had been going on at the mine.

Pedro's grandmother assured the old lady she would do just as she had been asked and would tell no one about the envelope, not even her family and that the box she had given her would also remain secret. "There may come a time when you will need to open that little box, and when that time comes you will know in your heart when it is the right time to do so." the old lady had said.

That day Pedro's grandmother had taken both items home and had put them in a secure place and vowed she would never tell anyone about them unless, as the old lady had said, the time and circumstances became necessary to do so. Over the next few months the old lady gave Pedro's grandmother a few more packets and envelopes, all sealed with wax. She now had 10 packets in all, some large and some a lot smaller and some which felt as if they had more than just paper in them. She marked them with large black numbers feeling that the old lady had given her the envelopes in order of their importance. As usual, the old lady requested that she keep them safe, again saying that when the time arrive that Pedro's grandmother judged they should be opened, then they were to be opened in numerical order.

The old lady eventually got so bad that she could no longer stay on in the house. Even with the help that Pedro's grandmother could give, it was not enough. Mr. Bilk had her put in a home where she could get proper attention. Pedro's grandmother visited the old lady as often as she could but one day when she arrived to see her, she was met with the sad news that she had passed away. The matron in charge of the home asked her to come into the office. When she got there she was given two large bags and a carved, circular wooden box about five inches in diameter and about six inches in height. It was very much like the one she had been entrusted with a few years ago but was much larger. At first glance it appeared to be three boxes on top of one another, but on closer inspection, although each one seemed to move ever so slightly it was impossible to separate them. It was decorated with circles and rings and flowers. On the lid were three flowers with large petals. In the centre of each flower was a hole. Each flower had a different size hole, and a thin line of a different colour surrounded each hole. One red one blue and one yellow.

"Jessica asked me to make sure that you got all this," said the matron. "It was with all her personal things she had when she arrived." She asked Pedro's grandmother to close the door and then took out a book from one of the drawers in her desk and gave it to her. The book was a bright red one and had a strap fixed to it, which was fastened with a lock. "She also said to give you this. She was adamant that no one but you should have it. It is a diary she has kept over the years and she also said that the key to open it was on a hook behind the mirror in her bedroom. She said for you to try and get the key and then you will be able to open the diary. She said it would explain a lot of what had gone on in the past and what is in there would tie in with rest of the papers she had given you over the years. In there also, would be instructions explaining how to open the box. There is also a larger square box under her bed which she would like you to take out of the house and keep safe until the time was right and again she said you would know when that was.

She told me that in the event I could not pass it on to you then I was to try and get the key myself and do what I thought was best with what the information I would find in there. I am really glad to be able to pass it on to you," matron said. "I think it must be something really important and while I am honoured to think she trusted me enough to deal with whatever is in there I really am glad to be able to hand it to you. She said that she thought you were one of the most trusted and loyal friends she had ever known, and although she could not put her finger on it, she had a strange feeling that a lot of what had gone on in the past and was contained in the packages was in some way connected to you. She also asked that when all was revealed you would not think any the worse of her for the actions she had taken over the years. She also said one more thing I could not understand." Matron went on to say that over the past few weeks as the old lady got a bit weaker she kept referring to someone or something called 'Ishe' and kept repeating 'where Ishe'. "I had no idea at all what she meant," Matron told her, "then the night before she passed away, she called me in to tell me about what

I was to give you, and say to you. She looked at me and said quite plainly, 'Tell Joan Ishe will help when the time comes.' What she meant by that I have no idea. That was the last thing she said to me before I settled her for the night. The next morning when I went to see her she had passed away." The matron told her that she looked extremely at peace with the world.

Joan told the matron that she couldn't think what 'Ishe' might be or who it might be. She had never heard the old lady mention it to her before.

The matron went on to say that she had only known Jessica Bilk a few years when she had sometimes been called to the house to help with her medical needs, but she had struck her as a very nice, open friendly sort of person. "Not a bit like the male side of the family if I may be so bold," said matron. Pedro's grandmother agreed saying that not a lot of people in the village liked the male Bilks, but because of the situation with the employment, then it was something they had to just accept.

Pedro's grandmother had easily been able get hold of the key from behind the mirror. She had gone to the house with the two bags of clothing and had been asked by Jessica's husband Alfred if she would be so kind as to sort his wife's clothing out and make sure they were given to the home where she had been so well looked after in her final months. That request had made it easy for Pedro's grandmother to locate the box and take it to her own house. She had managed to get it to her bedroom without anyone seeing her.

Once she had cleared all the old lady's clothes and taken them to the nursing home, she went up to the house one more time to say goodbye to Alfred Bilk. He thanked her for all she had done for his wife and said that it had been his wife's wish that if there was anything in the house she would like as a keepsake then she could have it. He said he knew she had always admired the Grandfather clock, which stood in the hall at the bottom of the stairs and would she like that. He said his wife would have been glad knowing that it was in good hands. Pedro's grandmother said she would like it very much so the next day Alfred Bilk made arrangements for it to be delivered to her home. The house wasn't really big enough for the clock to stand in the hall so her father had moved her wardrobe in her bedroom and the clock was placed there. That was the last time she had been in the house and the last time she had seen old Mr. Bilk. Of the two Mr. Bilks she had known so far, he had been the nicest as far as she was concerned. He was sometimes a bit abrupt and didn't always treat his workers as well as he could have but Pedro's grandmother put that down to the fact that he had found it hard to come to terms with the disappearance at sixteen of his daughter from suspicious circumstances. He had become withdrawn after her disappearance and even found it hard to discuss things with his wife. He had felt responsible for his daughter going missing but didn't really know why.

Pedro's grandmother had known the Bilks' daughter although she had been a few years older than her. She had gone missing with two friends just after she herself had started at the school. She remembered the whole village had spent days searching for the pair but no trace was ever found of either girl. A little while later, her best friend Rebecca had also just vanished and once again, despite an intensive search by the whole village, no trace of her was ever found. Pedro's grandmother, looking back, suspected that old Mr. Bilk had maybe thought that she would be a sort of replacement for his wife for their daughter. The old lady had never really spoken much about her daughter's disappearance but did refer to it on occasions when she was talking about funny things that had happened over the years. With the death of his wife, Alfred Bilk moved away from the area and handed over the running of the mine to a manager who had worked for him for many years. He was to look after the mine until his son was old enough to resume responsibility as the new owner. He never returned to the village as far as anyone knew, and about three years after his wife passed away news came that he had also died.

A couple of years later and while the mine was being run by the manager appointed by Alfred Bilk, the old manor House burnt down. The only person living there at the time was the manager and he never could explain to the authorities as to what might have caused the fire. Alfred's son Cedric had been sent away to live with relatives just after the disappearance of his sister and went to a school a few miles away. He visited the mine and village occasionally but never stayed very long, only returning to live there when he took over the ownership of the mine.

Over the course of the next few months she read the diary and just could not believe what was in there. It bothered her a little that she had been chosen by Jessica to be the keeper of the secrets but at the same time considered it an honour and made a silent promise to Jessica that she would do all that she could to carry out her wishes. She had found the instructions on how to open the box but did not fully understand them.

When Cedric the present Mr. Bilk, became old enough to take over the running of the mine, he persuaded the uncle he had been sent to live with, to purchase the house on top of the hill overlooking the mine using the money his father had left him. That house became the Bilk family home. He married a lady called Amelia who he had met whilst living away from the village and they set up home in the big house. They had one child James.

Cedric Bilk treated the staff so badly that a few of them left including the manager who had looked after the mine for six years. Pedro's grandmother, who had returned to her old job in the offices following the death of the old lady, just did her job and kept out of his way. As far as she could tell, Cedric hadn't really changed much since he was at school and she had learned even back in those days just to keep out of his way. He had been a bit of a bully but because of who his father was, and the fact that most of the men working at the mine relied on their jobs for a living and their homes, the children he bullied dare not stand up to him. His own son James had showed no interest what so ever in the mine and had left home as soon as he could get a job in another town. He was only six years old when his mother passed away with a mystery illness so had been brought up by a series of older women his father had employed to look after him. He had spent a lot of his time on his own as his father always seemed to put the interests of his mine before family. That was the main reason he ignored his father's pleas to work in the mine and left as soon as he was able.

Pedro's father leaned over and gave his mum's hand a quick squeeze "Don't worry mum, I'll just do as I have been doing and get on with my work. It's a bit hard sometimes but at least I have a job and am able to provide for my family. Just wish the pay was a bit better then we could afford a few nice things."

By this time everyone had finished their meal and Pedro's mother started to clear the table. "Let me give you a hand with that," said grandmother.

"Certainly not," replied her daughter in law. "You sit and relax. You've had a long journey. It won't take long to do these dishes and Tom will give me a hand. When I've finished I'll make us all a nice cup of tea and we can all go and sit in the garden. It's such a lovely evening."

"Alright then if you are sure, I'll go and unpack the cases and hang our clothes up to let the creases fall out," said grandmother.

Pedro and his grandfather made their way outside and Pedro showed him how he carefully tapped at the rocks his father brought home for him to crack them open so he could get at the marbles inside. There were about eight rocks that needed opening. With all that had been going on at school and getting ready for his grandparent's visit he had not been doing much with the rocks lately. This time the rock he opened once more contained one of the smaller marbles he had found a few nights ago, but this marble, had four green spots in it. It was a smaller marble like the one he had previously found, the ones with the blue stripes. This one was exactly the same size as the one with the stripes very close together. He could hardly believe what he was seeing. His grandfather offered to polish it for him while he opened the rest of the rocks. The other rocks all had similar marbles in them. There was one small one with green stripes in it and the rest were all like he had found originally with four stripes of different colours. Pedro and his grandfather both polished the marbles to get all the dust off them and Pedro went and got the box where he kept all his marbles. He found a separate one to keep the four small ones in.

"That's a good collection you've got there," said his grandfather. "I haven't seen any like that since I was working at the mine and that was many years ago, long before the terrible accident in one of the shafts. You need to show your grandmother, she knows all about the different shapes and designs because at one time she worked in the part of the mine where they graded them all before they were sent off to the various shops to be sold."

By this time Pedro's mother was calling them to tell them that the drinks were ready and to come along while they were still hot. They all sat around the table and Pedro put his box of marbles on the ground beside his chair. His grandfather had carried the box with the smaller marbles in and placed it on the table. "Young Pedro's got a fair collection of marbles there Joan," he said to his wife as he sat down, "I told him that perhaps you would have a look at them for him as you used to do a lot of the grading when you worked at the mine."

"Grampy has been helping me to polish them," said Pedro as he put his box on to the table. He pushed the box across to where his grandmother was sitting so she could have a better look. "These are my best ones, the ones with the four stripes, although I did find some smaller ones and one of them only had four dots." he explained to her. "They look nice," said his mother. This was the first time she had seen them as Pedro kept them up in his bedroom. She reached into the box, picked one up and said, "This one only has three stripes Pedro. You must have put it in here by mistake." She kept hold of the marble so it wouldn't get mixed up with the good ones again. Pedro for his part looked into the box and was trying to work out and remember just how many four striped marbles there should have been altogether.

Pedro proudly laid out all his marbles for his grandmother to look at. As he was doing this his mother said, "Let me clear away all the cups and saucers and then you will have plenty of room." As she got up she winced in pain and stood still for a minute. Her mother in law noticed this and asked if she was alright. "Yes, I'm fine really," Pedro's mum replied. "I just twisted my ankle a bit yesterday getting off the bus from town. I just wish it would hurry up and get better. It's more annoying than anything else." After a couple of minutes it felt fine and she carried on clearing the table and took the tea things into the kitchen.

Pedro by now had laid his marbles out in order of their colours for his grandmother to look at. His father also showed some interest. This was also the first time he had actually seen all the marbles he had been bringing home. "Can you tell me anything about them granny?" asked Pedro.

"I certainly can," his grandmother replied, "but I think it will take a lot longer than we have this evening. It's getting quite late now and will soon be time for you to go to bed. I am quite tired from the journey so I think it will be best if we have a look at them again tomorrow. Is that O.K. with you Pedro?" Although Pedro was disappointed, he knew his grandmother was right. It had been a long day for them all and even now he was up later than he would normally be. Besides he was only at school for half a day tomorrow as it was the end of term.

"That's fine granny," said Pedro, "and anyway I will be home just after lunch time tomorrow as it is the last day of term." He began to collect all his marbles and place them back into the box unaware of the look passed between his two grandparents. Just then his mother came back out into the garden. "Here you are Pedro," she said and went to hand him the marble she still had. As she gave it to him she looked down at it and said with surprise, "Oh! I thought it had three stripes in, I must have been mistaken."

"How's your ankle Mary.' asked grandmother. "It's fine thank you." She replied, "It just hurt a little bit as I stood up earlier, must have been because I had been sitting down so long." Again there was a look which passed between the two elderly people but which went undetected by everyone else.

Soon everyone was back inside the house and Pedro said good night and made his way up to bed. As he lay in bed he went to sleep wondering just what his grandmother would be able to tell him about his marbles the next day. He also made up his mind that he would say nothing to anyone at school, especially Paul, who he had started to have more than just a funny feeling about.

CHAPTER THREE

MR. BILK'S ANNOUNCEMENTS

Pedro was up bright and early the next morning. His father had already left for work but as he came downstairs he could hear someone talking in the kitchen. It was his mother talking to his grandfather. "Morning young man." he said, "I was just saying to your mother that if it was O.K. with you I would walk part way to the school with you and stop at the shop to get a couple of things your mother needs." Pedro thought that would be great. "Just let me know when you are leaving and I'll be right with you," said granddad.

"Come and get your breakfast Pedro," said his mother. "Granddad had his, with your father before he went to work. He is going for a look round the garden until you are ready to go." She put his breakfast on the table then said, "By the way, your dad put three more pieces of rock on the table outside. He found them in the pocket of his jacket. He hadn't worn that jacket since the winter so he reckons they must have been there quite a while. In fact he said can't remember wearing it during the time he has been working at the location he is now, so it must have been when he was working at level four. He hopes that any marbles that are inside will be alright for you."

This bit of news excited Pedro and he could hardly wait to get outside and open up the rocks. He finished his breakfast and then remembered that today he didn't have to wear his uniform, just ordinary older clothes. He had forgotten to tell his mother the previous night with the excitement of his grandparents arriving. He asked his mother what he could wear that didn't matter if it got a bit dirty and explained why. "Best put your older playing clothes on," said his mother, "the ones you wear when you help me in the garden. Although they are old they still look alright so it's not as if you will look scruffy."

Pedro got changed and then went out into the garden to find his grandfather to tell him he was nearly ready to go. He found him looking at the three pieces of rock his father had put there. "I haven't seen that shape of rock for many a year," he said. "If I remember rightly, that sort of rock had really funny shaped marbles in them but no one thought they were worth polishing and sending away so they were just put with the rest of any rubble that came out of the mine." Pedro went and got his little hammer to start to crack open the rocks but just then his mother called him to remind him of the time so any thought of starting to crack open the rocks would have to wait until he came home again.

He and his grandfather said goodbye to his mother, and grandmother, who by now was up and having her breakfast and set off down the road towards the school. As in the previous two days since he had arrived in the village, Paul was waiting for him at the bottom of the hill. "Hello Pedro," he said 'how are you?"

"Fine." replied Pedro, and introduced Paul to his grandfather, explaining that he and his grandmother had arrived the previous evening. "They managed to get here a bit earlier than we had expected which is great," continued Pedro.

All three carried on walking towards the school and Pedro was very glad his grandfather was there as it prevented Paul from asking about any of his marbles again. Soon Freddy and Simon joined them and again Pedro introduced his grandfather. He only had to introduce him to Freddy because Simon had met him at the station the previous evening. "How's that dog of yours?" he asked Simon. "Fine, thank you Sir. He had a good night's sleep but woke up very early this morning. I was out in the garden with him by six o'clock. My mum had to put him back in the house and close the door as I left for school or else he would have followed me down the road."

By then they had reached the shop so grandfather said goodbye to the boys and told Pedro he would try and get back to meet him when school came out if that was O.K. "Course it is Grampy!" said Pedro, "we will be out about twelve thirty." With that the boys carried on to school. Pedro stayed with the main group of boys not wanting to be singled out by Paul to be asked any questions.

As they got to the school and entered the playground, Miss Richards was there and called Paul to come into the classroom for a quick chat before school started.

"Wonder what that's about," said Freddy. A few of the boys went to play a quick game of football but as it was not a proper game Pedro's services as a goalie were not required.

Sally who said her father had brought home some really funny shaped rocks the previous night, joined Pedro and Freddy. She hadn't had time to open both of them but the one that she had opened had the same kind of funny shaped marble she had shown the boys a few weeks previously. Pedro then told them both about the rocks his father had left out for him that morning and how his grandfather had remarked when he saw them, that years ago when that shape rock had been found the marbles inside had been considered worthless and so had been discarded. "Well I am not going to throw them away!' said Sally, "they are a bit like your marbles Pedro, different."

"Quite right," replied Pedro. He then remembered what his grandfather had said and asked Sally if she knew where in the mine her father was working. "Was it area four?"

"I don't know but I can ask him when I get home." She said.

"Better not mention any of this to Paul" said Freddy to Sally, and then went on to explain just who Paul was. Sally lived the opposite way from school to Pedro and Freddy so had not been with them the previous night when they had seen Paul go up the hill to his grandfather's house. "In that case I won't say anything," replied Sally, "but I will ask my dad where he is working Pedro and tell you the next time I see you."

Just then Miss Richards came out to call them into school. When they were all seated she explained that she had made a list of all the jobs that needed to be done and would be splitting them up into small groups so they could get everything done by 11:15. She went on to say that as Paul had not been there all the term, it was unfair to ask him to help with the cleaning but that she had asked him to carry the exam papers up to Mr. Bilk's house and let him know that they would be ready for him at 11:30. Mr. Bilk always liked to come and say a few words at the end of term. It was about the only time anyone could remember him being nice to anyone. She still did not tell the children that Paul was Mr. Bilk's grandson.

Miss Richards then split the children up into groups of four and gave each group their various jobs. There wasn't really a lot to do and the children found it quit fun doing them. All the class rooms that would not be open for the visitors to look round had to have their chairs stacked on top of the desks so that the proper cleaners would have an easier job when they came to give the school a really good clean during holidays. All the blackboards in all the rooms had to be cleaned and all old notices and pictures taken down. The main hall had to be swept and all the chairs stacked neatly at one end. Pedro's group was given the job of pulling the collapsible tables out from under the stage, making sure their legs worked all right and them making equally sure they were nice and clean. These tables would be used on the sports day to put the food on.

Sally and her three friends had what they thought was the best job. They had been sent into the drama room to sort out and fold up neatly all the various costumes that were used in the drama classes. Naturally they couldn't resist trying on a few costumes. Miss Richards looked in on the group, attracted by the girls' laughter at the way some of them looked. She didn't really mind what they were doing but just asked them to make sure that all the costumes were folded and put away nicely. "It's nearly eleven o'clock," she said, "so you haven't got much longer." With that, the girls stopped playing and finished folding all the dresses and other costumes and put them neatly in their correct boxes.

By quarter past eleven all the jobs had been done and everything had been cleared away. Miss Richards suggested that they all went outside and waited for Mr. Bilk to arrive. "Go round to the back of the school and wait there," she told the children. "That way you can all sit on the grass while we hear what Mr. Bilk has to say." The children did not need telling twice and all wandered around to the other side of the school where there was a large area of grass. They either sat or stood around in small groups discussing amongst themselves what they hoped to be doing during the holidays.

Jimmy told them that he would be away for about two weeks. He had a false left arm and had to go to see a specialist to get it adjusted. He had fallen over the previous week helping his father in the garden and it had knocked it a bit out of shape. "My hand keeps turning the wrong way." He explained. Jimmy had lost his arm when he was about six years old. It was before he and his family had moved to Marbleville. He had been knocked over by a runaway horse, which had sent him and a lot of other people crashing into some fencing. Jimmy's arm had been trapped between the metal parts of the fence and had to be cut off there and then because it could not be freed.

"Will you be back for the sports day?" asked Freddy, who was worried in case Jimmy would miss the football game.

"Oh yes" replied Jimmy. "Me, and my mum are going on Monday and as the hospital is close to where my aunty lives we are going to stay there while the hospital puts my arm back together. They may even make it a bit longer at the same time." He held both arms out together showing the rest of the children that his left arm was indeed about four inches shorter than his right arm. "It's been three years now since the last adjustment and I have grown quite a bit since then. They may even give me a complete new one because the last time they lengthened it they said it could not be adjusted much more." He looked at Pedro, "If they do give me a new one I'll see if

I can bring this one back for you so you can have a bit of extra help when you are in goal!"

"Thanks very much," laughed Pedro. "I sometimes feel I could do with a bit of help."

Just then Miss Richards came round the corner with Mr. Bilk and Paul. She asked everyone to sit down and listen to what Mr. Bilk had to say.

"Good morning everyone,' said Mr. Bilk once they were all settled. There were a few 'Good Mornings' in reply but as he was not a very popular person in the village and in their lives most of the children were a bit wary of him. Miss. Richards felt a bit embarrassed for the way the children had reacted and hoped that Mr. Bilk had not taken too much notice. If he had then she hoped he would put it down to the children being a bit in awe of him because of who he was. It appeared that that was the case as he continued, "I would like to say to each one of you 'Well Done' for the test results. I think they are the best this school has produced in a very long time, so again very well done indeed. You should all give yourselves a round of applause." At this the children relaxed a little and did indeed start to clap and in some cases a few cheers could be heard. After a few seconds Mr. Bilk held up his hands and the children quietened down again. "These results," he continued, "and the excellent attendance record you have all achieved this last year have certainly earned you the extra half day's holiday Miss. Richards requested. I was more than happy to contact the education authority on her behalf and I am happy to say they also agreed to the extra half-day." This brought more excited response and clapping. When it died down he went on, "I am looking forward very much to the sports day that is being arranged for half way through the holiday and I am more than happy to donate cups and medals for the winning teams or individuals. I hope it will be a day thoroughly enjoyed by all who come to either take part or watch. I am sure that everyone from here who takes part will give the school from town a good run for their money and show them who's best."

The children all cheered again at this last remark. As it died down Mr. Bilk said, "There are just a couple more things I have to tell you and then you are free to go. The first is that when you return after your holidays, you will see a nice big new board beside the main entrance. It will read, 'Marbleville Manor School' Owner Mr. C.M.Bilk, Headmistress Miss D.J. Richards." Again everyone clapped at this bit of information. Mr. Bilk waited for the clapping to subside then turned to a stunned and very surprised Miss. Richards and said, "Sorry to spring this on you like this but it is something I think you thoroughly deserve and I requested the local authority to allow me to do it and they readily agreed. Many congratulations."

With that he walked over and shook Miss. Richards by the hand, at the same time telling her quietly that there would also be a nice little increase in pay to go along with her new status. He turned back to the children and told them he had decided to give the school a proper name as opposed to just the Village school. He went on to explain that many, many years ago there had been a very large Manor House standing where the school now stood, part of which had in fact been used as the school. There was a terrible fire and most of it was destroyed. It never was rebuilt and over the years the ruins began to collapse. When it was decided to build a new school there seemed to be no better place than the old manor. A lot of the bricks that had been part of the old house had been used in the construction of the school. "Lastly" he said turning to Paul who had been standing beside him all this time, "I am sure by now that most of you will have met my grandson Paul. His father has gone away on business for a few months so I invited him to come and live with me. I hope you will make him welcome and become friends. Now off you all go home, have a wonderful holiday and I will see you all on sports day." With that he walked away and after shaking hands with Miss. Richards again left the school. Paul walked over to where Pedro and his friends were.

All the children got up and as they did so gave another cheer that their holiday had at last started. Miss. Richards had been a bit apprehensive and slightly worried as to what the children's reactions would be when they were told who Paul was. There were looks of shock and some of fear on others. The Bilk family especially the male side, had left a deep feeling of disquiet among the residents of Marbleville, and for some of the children the knowledge that there was now a Bilk of their own age amongst them would do little to boost their confidence.

Apart from the wives of the three mine owners over the years there had only been one female Bilk and she had been the sister of the present owner. Her disappearance many years ago had never been fully explained or investigated. Some of the children came up to her after Mr. Bilk had left and spoke to her about their feelings. Quite a few of their fathers and indeed a couple of their mothers had suffered a bit of mental abuse and bullying over the years they had worked at the mine and so were naturally concerned at the news about Paul.

"Will he be like his grandfather?"

"Will we have to do what he tells us?"

"How long is he here for?"

These questions and many more were asked of Miss. Richards. She on her part did her best to allay any fears they might have. "Don't worry," she said, "I am sure he is a perfectly nice young man who just wants to be friends with you all." Miss. Richards had not lived in the village very long so did not really know much of the history of the way the workers had been treated over the years.

"Perhaps he is completely different from his granddad," commented one child, "and will be O.K. with us."

"That's a very kind thing to say," commented the teacher, not really knowing who had spoken, "now off you go and enjoy your holidays and I will see you and your parents on sports day." She escorted the children to the main gate, and after seeing them safely on their way went round the school checking that everything had been left as it should be before locking up and setting off for home herself.

On her way home she wondered just what had gone on in the past that made everyone so wary and in some cases afraid of the mine owner. For her part, he had never been anything but courteous and polite to her, but then again she thought, she did not work directly for him, but was employed by the local education authority. It just so happened, that living in one of Mr. Bilk's cottages came as part of her salary. As she had no idea how long she would be there at the school it made perfect sense to continue with that arrangement. Certainly for her at this moment in time it worked out cheaper to take up the offer of 'tied' accommodation as part of her salary than to rent privately.

Continuing her way home, she wondered just who she could ask about what had gone on in the past. She didn't know many of the parents very well. The only family she had had any real dealings with had been Pedro's when she had visited them over the test mix-up. Perhaps she could ask them sometime, she thought. She thought that perhaps she could also ask Mrs. Trent who worked in the local Post Office as well. She had been born in the village and lived there all her life so perhaps she would be able answer a few questions. 'I will need to be very careful though' Miss. Richards thought to herself. Although the village people had seemed to welcome her, she was very aware that they had been a bit distant towards her at times. Maybe they were just naturally wary about strangers. After all it did seem to be a very close-knit community. There was nothing that she could really put her finger on but she had noticed more than once that as she entered the shop and there was a group of people already in there, then the conversation would dry up and all would go quiet for just a fraction of a second. She realised she would have to very careful the way she asked any questions.

When she arrived at her cottage she found a large bouquet of flowers had been left on the seat by the front door. Reading the card attached to it she discovered they were from Mr. Bilk thanking her once again for the excellent job she had done at school with the children since her arrival, and congratulating her once more on the very good test results. There was also an open invitation for her to have dinner with him sometime over the holiday period, at his house. The happiness she had initially felt upon receiving the flowers was now dampened somewhat by the invitation. Again, it was nothing she could actually put her finger on, just a funny feeling. She knew there was no reason she could give not to accept but she would think very carefully before she did.

Chapter Four

The Walk Home

Pedro had left the school with Freddy and Simon. He looked for his grandfather but could not see him anywhere. Paul called out to them and they stopped and waited until he caught up with them. "Didn't know you were Old Man Bilk's grandson," said Freddy, "That was a surprise to us all. How long are you staying with him?"

"For about a year I think," replied Paul. "My dad is going to be away about that long. My granddad says he wants to show me all about the workings of the mine if I am interested. I think it will be rather fun. Then if I want to I can work there all the time when I leave school. All through the holidays I am going to be helping him for two hours each day. Starting next week he is going to teach me about the different areas in the mine and the different levels. I am too young to go into the mine at the moment but in three months time I will be 14 and then I can go in and have a look. Granddad said he would put me to work helping some of the men who work down there, but only with those men who he thinks will be the better teachers. Perhaps I may get to work with your fathers. What area does your dad work in Pedro?"

"I don't really know," said Pedro. "He doesn't tell me as far as I can remember."

"What about your dad Freddy, where does he work?"

"Area two I think he worked the last time he mentioned it. I remember him saying it was nearer to the entrance to the mine so it was not quite so hot." In fact Freddy's father worked in one of the deepest parts in area seven but he wasn't going to tell Paul that. It wasn't really a lie because his father had indeed once told him he was working in area two. With Paul telling them about working with his grandfather on the different aspects of the mine and then coming out with questions straight away about where their fathers' worked Freddy had a feeling that Paul had been sent amongst then to seek out what information he could. He had no idea why. Surely Mr. Bilk himself should, more than anyone else, know just who was working and where. He hoped he was wrong but certainly Paul had been asking a lot of questions in the short time he had been in the village.

Just then they rounded a corner and they saw Pedro's grandfather coming towards them and he had a dog on a lead. It was Simon's dog and as they got closer the dog strained at his lead to get to Simon. Pedro's granddad let the lead go free and the dog headed straight for Simon. "Hello boys," said granddad, "Saw your mum in the shop Simon and I told her I was coming down to meet Pedro. She said you always walked home together so suggested I bring your dog to meet you."

"Hello Mut," said Simon as his dog leaped all over him.

"He certainly looks a lot better now," remarked Pedro's grandfather, "Why do you call him Mut?" "Because we are not quite sure what breed he is," answered Simon. "When we first rescued him from the dogs' home we were told he was a bit of a mixture of two different terrier types so dad said that was a good name for him, MUT meaning Mixed Up Terrier." They all carried on walking home together, and Pedro explained to his grandfather that Paul had come to live with his grandfather for about a year while his own father was away on business. "I knew your grandfather when I first started work at the mine," said granddad, "in fact, my wife, Pedro's grandmother went to school with him, but I haven't seen him for many years. Knew your father too when he was a young lad." By now they had reached the bottom of the hill where Paul said goodbye to them all. "Maybe I will call round to see you in the next few days Pedro,' he said as he set off up the hill, "You live in the yellow painted cottage don't you?"

"That's right," said Pedro, "but I may be going out quite a lot with granddad." He said that hoping Paul would take the hint and maybe not call round but in his mind he knew Paul had every intention of calling on him. As they said goodbye to Paul and carried on along the road, the two boys let their feelings show.

"Hope he doesn't come round to my house," said Freddy.

"Or mine," added Simon.

"Now boys, it's a bit unfair to say things like that when you hardly know the boy. I know why you say what you do but it might just be that Paul is completely different from his father and grandfather. At least you ought to give him a chance."

Pedro's grandfather always looked to see the best in people and he had said what he did hoping to put the other boys' minds at ease. Freddy was the next to leave them. He said goodbye to the rest and made his way home up a long track, which led to a farm. Freddy's father was the dairyman on the farm. "Bye Freddy," said granddad, "Maybe you will be able to out with us one day when we go off for a walk. Simon's mother already said it was O.K. for him to come. I asked her when I saw her in the shop this morning."

"Thanks a lot Sir," said Freddy, "I will ask my dad and let you know" Simon was thrilled that his mother had said he would be allowed to go out with Pedro and his grandfather. "Will I be able to bring Mut as well?" he asked. "Certainly," replied granddad, "it will give him some good exercise and help to get his leg back in shape." As they continued on their way Pedro and Simon told granddad all about what Mr. Bilk had said that morning and that he was going to give the school a proper name. "Makes sense, seeing as how the old Manor House use to be there," replied granddad, "I remember seeing pictures of it when I first came to Marbleville but it was all burnt down by then." They told him too about Miss. Richards being made

Headmistress. Granddad said that that also made a lot of sense as how she was such a good teacher and how she had managed to teach them all this past year so they all past the tests.

By now they had got to where Simon had to leave them to go to his house. "Come round in the morning if you feel like it," said Pedro.

"O.K. thanks."

Pedro and granddad carried on to their own house. As they went granddad could see that there was something troubling Pedro and asked him what it was. "It's just this Paul thing gramps," he answered. "Ever since he came, things have seemed a bit different somehow. We can't talk about anything without him butting in and asking questions. It's not questions about what we were saying either. It's always things about the mine such as 'what marbles have you found, what areas do your fathers work, can I see your marbles sometime.' None of the rest of us bothered about things like that. I know all my friends were interested what marbles I had found but once I had shown them they were quite happy. We all agreed that it was just pure luck that dad happened to be working in an area that had some lovely marbles, but we also said that one day, things might change and it would be someone else's father who would be finding good rocks and marbles."

Grandfather agreed that it was certainly very strange the way Paul was asking lots of questions. "Best not tell him too much if that is how you feel about him," said granddad. "Do the other children think the same?"

"Yes they do," said Pedro, and then went on to say that some of the children had agreed between themselves that they would not say anything to Paul about the marbles that Pedro had been finding. As far as they was concerned they were just different to any marbles that had been discovered so far, each one secretly hoping that it would be their turn soon.

"Well if that is how you feel amongst yourselves then you must do what you think is right. Just give him a chance is all I am asking," said granddad, "he may be just showing a genuine interest in things." What he didn't say out loud was that he had his doubts about the true way young Paul was behaving. He was all for not pre-judging people, but in his mind he could see Mr. Bilk being behind Paul's behaviour, and constant questioning of the children.

By now they had reached their cottage and Pedro went into the garden to find and say hello to his mum and granny. "Hello," said his mum, "Bet you're glad that school is over for a few weeks." She gave him a kiss and a hug, and then asked if he had seen his granddad. "Yes, mum he came to meet us with Simon's dog. He had seen Simon's mum in the shop and asked if he could bring him along. Hello granny," he said as he gave her a kiss, "how are you feeling?"

"I am feeling very well thank you Pedro. Had a good night's sleep and got up feeling really refreshed." Granddad then appeared round the corner of the house and said hello to his wife and daughter-in-law. "Lunch won't be long now," said mum, "Your dad said he would be home a bit earlier today because it is Friday, so then we can all eat together."

"Getting Friday afternoons off?" exclaimed granny, "Bilky must have been in the sun too long, coming up with things like that. Used to be at one time he kept everyone there until the very last minute." Her husband looked at her and said, "Maybe he has turned over a new leaf." But as he said it he didn't believe it for one minute. There must be another reason why Mr. Bilk was being so kind to all his workers, but at that precise moment in time he couldn't for the life of him think what it was. No doubt it would all become clearer sooner or later.

Pedro's father arrived home at that moment and after saying hello to his parents and Pedro, went into the house to get changed out of his work clothes and have a wash before lunch. Soon they were all sitting down to a nice salad lunch. The talk was about everything and nothing. Pedro repeated to his parents and his granny what he had told his granddad about what Mr. Bilk had said when he had visited them at school. "Still think he is up to something," said granny, "I've never known old Bilky to do anything for nothing. Maybe I am wrong, and I hope I am, but I wouldn't trust him as far as I could throw him. We will just have to wait and see."

Always in her mind was the way she had known Mr. Bilk to be years ago and that quite understandably clouded her judgement of him. What was always in the back of her mind also was what she had read over the years in the old lady's diary. She said no more and they all settled down to eat their lunch. Pedro was simply dying to ask his grandmother what she was going to tell them all about his marble collection but thought it was better to wait until she was ready.

"Which day were you thinking of taking the boys out for the day?" Pedro's mum asked granddad.

"I hadn't really thought about it, although Pedro and I already invited Simon and Freddy to call round in the morning if they wanted to, to go for a short walk." he replied. "I suppose one day next week would be a good time for a longer day out, shall we say Thursday? That way they can have a few days of their holiday and will also give us time to get the things together we will need. Would you like to stay overnight Pedro?"

"That would be really great Gramps, will we still be able to take Simon?

"I don't see why not but we will have to ask his parents."

"That will give you time to get the tents out and make sure they are O.K." said Pedro's father, "The blue one should be big enough for you and Simon and your granddad can have the green one. I will get the lamps out and make sure there is enough fuel in them for you."

"Thanks dad." said Pedro. He was so excited at the thought of going off for a whole night with his grandfather that for a short while all thoughts of marbles and what his grandmother was going tell him had gone out of his mind. He was completely lost in thought as to what they may see on their outing. He was brought out of his daydreaming by his mother, who was clearing the lunch dishes away.

"Pedro! Your grandmother said to go and fetch your marbles and she will tell us all about them. I am just clearing away these dishes and I'll make us all a cup of tea and then we can sit and hear what she has to say. Pedro went up to his room and collected his boxes of marbles, including the funny shaped ones.

When he returned to the garden he found that his mother had brought out the tea and a few biscuits as well for everyone.

"Lay your marbles on the table next to me Pedro," his grandmother said.

Pedro carefully emptied the boxes of marbles on to the table and started to sort them out according to their colours and sizes. His grandmother picked up the odd one with only two stripes and handed it to her daughter in law. "This is the one you noticed last night Mary," she said, "you thought it had three stripes but then you saw it only had two, remember? Keep it for now then it won't get mixed up with the others again." Pedro's mother took the marble and kept it in her hand.

CHAPTER FIVE

GRANNY'S STORY –
PART ONE

Once Pedro had laid all his marbles out his grandmother looked at them all very carefully. Every one watched as she slowly moved a few of them around. It was just like watching a magician with a pack of cards before asking someone to choose one.

"Are all your marbles like this Pedro?" she asked indicating the ones with four stripes.

"Yes, they are, or at least they were until the last few days when dad started bringing home some weird shaped rocks, but I haven't opened all those yet. Some of the different ones are here in this tin," answered Pedro, "but I haven't polished them yet."

"In that case," she continued, "I think you have some very special marbles indeed and it is no wonder old Bilky is keen to know where each child's father is working. I am sure he would love to get his hands on these."

"Why is that mum?" asked Tom

"I will tell you in a minute but I must make sure I am correct. There is just a little test I want to carry out." Everyone wondered just what sort of test she would do. She turned to her daughter in law and said, "Mary, if you could make a wish right this minute what would it be?"

Mary thought for a couple of minutes and then said, "Well I suppose seeing as how we have all had such a nice lunch and are now nice and comfortable here in the garden I think it would be that I didn't have to go in the kitchen and wash and clear away the dishes. I wish they would wash and put themselves away." Just as she had finished talking there was quite a clattering noise came from the house. "What on earth was that?" Pedro's mother exclaimed. "It sounds like the table has collapsed in there!" With that she leapt up from her chair and went running into the house to see what had fallen. Pedro's father started to get up as well to go and help his wife but his mother put her hand on his arm and told him to stay. "Everything will be O.K. Tom you wait and see."

They all sat silent for a while not really understanding what was happening. Eventually Pedro's mother emerged from the house looking a little pale and started walking back to down the garden. As she slowly walked towards the table, she kept turning round and looking back at the open kitchen door. Grandmother was the first to break the silence. "Everything alright in there was it Mary, everything put back where it should have been?"

"Yes it was, but I don't understand." She replied looking extremely puzzled as she sat down.

"Have you still got that marble I gave you?" asked grandmother.

"Yes I have," replied Mary and opened her hand to show them all, but the marble she had in her hand had no stripes at all. It was just a plain glass marble. "What on earth is going on?" she said as she looked at her mother in law. "The one I had before had two stripes in it, one red and one yellow, now there is nothing!"

"Calm down Mary, everything is perfectly alright. It is as I suspected when I saw all these marbles on the table," Grandmother looked up at the rest of the family and then at Pedro and said, "What you have here young man are WISHY MARBS, and they haven't been seen for over thirty years if not more. These marbles with the four stripes have the power to grant wishes to whoever has them about their person at the time. So for example, if you make a wish and the marble is in your pocket the wish might be granted. Each time a wish is granted a stripe disappears. Depending on the wish depends on how many stripes are used. The wish your mother just made used up two stripes, because it was quite a big job she wished for and so that meant both the stripes disappeared." They all looked at her in amazement at what she was telling them. She looked at her daughter in law and said, "Remember last evening Mary when your ankle hurt, you said 'you wished it would just get better' and later on I asked how it was and you said it was fine. Then you looked at the marble you had been holding and saw that it had only two stripes when you thought it had three? That was because you made a wish while you were still holding it. It wasn't a big wish so it only used up one stripe."

"But why did it only have three stripes in the first place," asked Pedro. "I only keep the marbles with four stripes in that box."

"You must have made a wish yourself without knowing," replied grandmother. "Try and remember when you had them and what you were doing the last time you had them altogether." Pedro tried to think when he had last had the box out. "I think it was when we were waiting for Miss. Richards to come to the house about the test," Pedro said to his parents. "I think I wished that she would hurry up and arrive at the house. The next thing I heard was the garden gate opening and her knocking on the door."

"That's when the one stripe was used then," said granny. "It wasn't a big wish so only used the one stripe."

Pedro sat and thought about what his grandmother had said and suddenly a thought jumped into his mind. He went on to tell her that early in the week he had taken a test at school and had got so many questions right that the teacher had thought he had been cheating. In fact she had come to the house and he had taken the test again with his mother and father there. He also told her that he remembered while he was doing the test that he wished he knew the answers to the last eight questions and that when he later got out his marbles to show the rest of the children, all he found were plain glass ones and how upset he had been.

"That was because you had used a stripe for every answer you needed to know," said his grandmother. "As I said earlier, you don't always have to be holding them for the magic to work, although if it is a very special wish you want then it is better to have them in your hand."

Another thought then came to Pedro. "That means the teacher was right and I did cheat," he said.

"No you didn't really Pedro," granny assured him, "You had no idea at the time what you had in your pocket and if I hadn't been here today to tell you then you would still not know. It's not as if you did know and had made use of the magic stripes. I think that the test results should be left as they are." Pedro looked across at his parents and they both agreed with grandmother and said that as he had had no idea at all what was going on, he had done just what any other person taking a test would do, and that was to wish they knew the correct answers. Pedro felt better after what his parents had said and asked his grandmother what else she could tell them about the marbles; where they came from, who had found out they were magic, and why was it only the ones with four stripes that were.

"There is so much to tell you about the mine and the marbles,' said granny, "But before I do I must ask you to promise me one thing Pedro, and that is you will never use the power in the marbles you have to do anyone any harm or cause anyone to be hurt or upset in any way, or to use the power to get you something personal that you would not normally be able to attain. You have to be very careful when you are in possession of these marbles that you don't just wish for silly things like I wish the bus would hurry up or I wish it would stop raining, although I suppose that one wouldn't be too bad, but you see what I am trying to say to you Pedro?"

"Yes I do granny," said Pedro and promised her and his granddad and parents that he would not make wishes for the sake of it. "What about if I wanted to wish for something nice to happen to someone?" asked Pedro.

"That would be alright up to a point, but not to wish for something to happen to someone that would not normally happen." replied his grandmother. "When I let your mother, make her wish, after lunch and she chose to have the washing up done for her that was just to demonstrate to you all what the marbles could do. Making a wish to get something done because you can't be bothered to do it would not be a good way to use the marbles. Now, let's look at what you have got and I will try and remember as much as I can about them."

Pedro had laid out the marbles in some sort of colour order as best as he could. The ones with four different coloured stripes he placed all together and then the ones with stripes all the same colour he put in a separate part of the table. Some marbles had four stripes but in different combinations of colours. There were some with three stripes the same colour and one stripe of a different colour and then some with two sets of different coloured stripes. Then there were the very small ones with thin coloured stripes all going the same way. When granny saw those she put them to one side saying they were not the normal wishing type marbles on their own but would explain about them later.

CHAPTER SIX

GRANNY'S STORY – PART TWO

"There has been a marble mine here in this area for as long as anyone can remember," said granny. "No one knows when it was started. I remember asking my grandmother about it but all she could tell me was that it had been there as long as she could remember as well. It had also been in the same family, the Bilks for all that time. Most of the families in the village over the years had worked at the mine one way or the other. There was no other work available in the area so it was the understood thing that when people were old enough to start work then that is where they would go. The men would be sent underground while the girls and ladies would be found jobs on the surface cracking open and sorting the marbles. In later years," granny went on. "The job of cracking open the rocks, was handed over to men who were too old to go down into the mine and the sorting was left to the ladies. They sorted them into their various colours and patterns and packed them into pretty boxes before they were sent to the shops in various towns.

One day, so the story goes, a few marbles were found different to any that had been found so far. No one thought much of them at the time. It just meant that they had to get a different box to put them in as they had more stripes than any they had found so far. The Mr. Bilk who was the owner at the time took no notice of them either apart from saying that he would put a higher price on them because they had more stripes. Not many of the new marbles were found at first and as there was no indication what part of the mine they had come from, and because no significance was placed on them then they were just treated as slightly better marbles.

About a month after the discovery of the four striped marbles while one of the girls was polishing one she happened to wish that it was lunch time as she was ready for a break. Another of the girls agreed and wished as well that the lunch break could be two hours instead of the normal one hour. All of a sudden there was a funny noise, the lights flickered and the two clocks at either end of the room made a whirring sound and their hands moved very quickly round to twelve o'clock. The bell, which rang at the end of the morning shift also sounded. Margaret the supervisor came out of her office and announced that it was time for the lunch break, and for today they didn't have to start back until two o'clock. The girls could not understand what was happening. Nothing like that had ever happened before, especially not being given more time for lunch, and what on earth had made the clock go like it had and the bell starting to ring. Whatever it was, they took advantage of it and enjoyed their extra-long lunch break. They all went back to work at two o'clock and finished at five o'clock as usual. None of them realised that there were not as many boxes filled and wrapped as there normally were at the end of the working day. The woman in charge bade them all goodnight as usual with nothing being said about the drop in production.

The following days the girls worked as normal and no one said anything about what had happened previously until one girl mentioned that she wished it was lunchtime and just like the other day wished they could have and extra-long lunch again. As soon as she said it the same thing happened as before: the clocks made a whirring sound, the lights flickered and the hands on the clock went round to midday. Again they were told by the supervisor it was time for lunch and for them not to come back until two o'clock.

The girls all went off and sat outside, had their sandwiches, and started discussing what was happening. One of the girls suggested in a joking manor that she thought it had something to do with the marbles they were sorting. She went on to say that the last time it had happened was on a day when they were sorting the marbles with four stripes. The others agreed with her but could not really see how it could be, but as no one could come up with a better suggestion they had to admit that that was probably the case. After a while another girl did remark that the marbles with four stripes in them did feel somehow sort of different in that they had a softer feel to them and cleaned up a lot better. The others again, for the want of any other explanation had to agree that that was probably the case. After a bit more discussion it was decided that the next time they were dealing with the 'four stripers' someone would wish for something and see what happened.

A few days later the opportunity came for them to try out what they had planned. It was not a very nice day with rain and clouds overhead. One of the girls wished that it would stop raining so they could go outside for their lunch. Within two minutes the rain had stopped and the sun was shining. That proves it the girls agreed, it was something to do with the 'four stripers'. What they hadn't noticed at the time was that the stripes were missing from the marble that was being handled when the wish was made. Because it was such a large wish then all the stripes had gone."

Granny leaned back in her chair and said, "All that talking has made me thirsty, any chance of a cup of tea Mary?"

"Certainly, shall I make one or wish one? Mary laughed.

"Better make one I think. Don't want to waste any of Pedro's marble wishes," replied granny, "he might be able to make better use of it one day."

While his mum was away making the tea, Pedro asked his grandmother a bit more about Mr. Bilk. "Why do you think Mr. Bilk is letting all the fathers bring home bits of rock granny? If he is just like you say he, is why is he giving marbles away?'

"Because," said his granny, "I think he wants to get his hands on the source of the 'Wishy Marbs". He doesn't know what part of the mine they are being found and by letting fathers take home a couple of pieces of rock each night he is no doubt hoping that if any of the 'Wishy Marbs' are found then the father of the child who received them would probably say something at the mine, like, 'My kid found a marble with four stripes in last night.' Although the father wouldn't know what they were Mr. Bilk would, and when he got to hear about it would immediately find out where that man had been working. I have no doubt at all," continued granny, "That old Bilky will have at least a couple of men working in the mine listening out for just such a comment, and then relying on them to report back to him what they had heard."

"You have probably hit the nail on the head," Pedro's dad said, "There are three new men who came to the mine about four weeks ago and if my memory serves me right, that was about the same time also that we were allowed to start bringing the rocks home. They are from a town a few miles away and we were told that they were just there to see that all safety procedures were being carried out. They don't do any mining though. They just wander around looking at things and making notes. They do go up the hill to Mr. Bilks house each evening at the end of the shift. Either that or Mr. Bilk is there to talk to them when we finish"

"That's what it will be then," exclaimed his mother, "I told you he never did anything for nothing, but if my guess is right, he is after more than the ones with four stripes in."

"Do you mean he is after these?" asked Pedro, pointing to the large ones with spots on them.

"No," replied granny, "He is after far more powerful ones than those." Just then his mum arrived with cups of tea for the adults and a glass of juice for him so he thought he had better wait until his granny had had her tea and then hope that she would continue what she was telling them. While they were having their drinks granny asked her son if any sort of triangular rocks had been found, but he said that as far as he knew no, nothing like that had been discovered.

"That's a relief then," replied granny but she said it in such a low voice almost as if she were talking to herself. Tom had not heard his mother because by then he was talking to his father but Pedro heard her, and when he looked across at her he could see she had a bit of a worried look on her face so he decided not to say anything.

"Well then," said granny when she had finished her tea, "Where were we?"

"You were telling us about the girls in the sorting shed finding out that they thought the marbles with four stripes in allowed them to make wishes." said Pedro.

"That's right," said his granny. "Well, they continued to make small wishes, just for little things like wishing the clock would get to five o'clock a bit quicker, or that certain items would be on the menu when they had lunches at work. Not really important things. It went on for quite a while before it was sort of discovered what happened to the marbles when a wish was made."

"How was it discovered?" asked Pedro's mum.

Granny looked at her daughter in law. "While they had been making wishes none of them had noticed the stripes disappearing from the marbles. That was because whoever was making the wish had just been sort of holding the marble and polishing it prior to placing it in the box. The marble was passed from the polishing cloth in one hand to the fine packing paper in the other hand so the marble was not really looked at when this was going on. By this time the girls had accepted and believed that the 'Four Stripers' as they were labelled on the boxes were indeed some sort of magic marbles with the power to grant wishes. In fact it was those girls that first called them 'Wishy Marbs', a name that was to stay with them forever. On days when they were sent the ordinary two and three stripes marbles to pack and they made wishes nothing at all happened. The other way they were discovered was far more serious. One day Nathan Bilk, who was the owner of the mine at the time and the grandfather of the present Mr. Bilk came storming into the room where the polishing, sorting and packing was carried out and yelled for the woman in charge to come out to him. All the girls stopped work at this outrage and watched as Margaret rushed out of her office and down to where Nathan Bilk was standing. She started to ask him what the problem was but before she could get the question out, Nathan threw down the four boxes he had been carrying and demanded to know just what was going on. She had no idea what he was talking about and told him so. Still shouting in a raised voice he explained to her that four of his best customers had returned boxes of marbles and demanded their money back because not all of the marbles had been of the special variety. Some had only three rather dull looking stripes in them, some only two and some with no stripes at all. He again demanded to know just what had been going on and where were the marbles that were supposed to be in the boxes. He accused all the girls of keeping the special ones for themselves and substituting them for different ones. Margaret assured him that that was not the case at all but at the same time could offer no explanation as to how the mix up could have occurred."

Granny looked at them all and said, "Of course, this Margaret knew nothing of what the girls had been getting up to. So when she told Nathan Bilk that she had no idea how the mix up had happened she was telling the truth. He however did not believe her, and accused her of organising the whole thing and told her to get her things and leave at once. While all this was going on Julia, one of the girls who had been the first one to make a wish when they had first started it all had a thought and, picking up a 'Four Striper' silently made a wish that the door behind Nathan Bilk would slam shut. As soon as she said that there was a loud bang and the door did indeed slam shut with such a force that it broke the glass. At the same time she looked down into her hand and saw one stripe slowly disappear from the marble she was holding. She said nothing but while everyone was calming down after the shock of the door banging shut she made another wish that Nathan Bilk would call

Margaret back and ask her to stay and apologise for being so hasty. Which is what happened. He said that perhaps he had been unfair and quick to judge then asked her to stay, but at the same time he was holding her personally responsible to see that in future no more mistakes would be made, and if they were and more boxes were returned then the cost would be taken out of her wages. She thanked him and promised that in future she would watch proceedings a lot closer. This seemed to pacify Nathan and turned to leave. As he did so Julia, who was still holding the marble, made another silent wish that he would trip over the step as he left. Again, that is just what happened and the other girls had a bit of a giggle at the sight of their boss laid out on the grass.

They all watched as Nathan got to his feet and went walking across the yard towards the mine's main building. As he did the girls saw him stop and speak to one of the maintenance men, and pointing towards the door that had just slammed shut. He was obviously telling him to repair the window. Julia then said to Margaret and the rest of the girls that she knew where the problem with the marbles had come from. She showed them the marble she had in her hand and they could all see it had only one coloured stripe. Handing the marble to the supervisor, she told her to make one simple wish. Margaret was not sure what to wish for but in the end looked down at her black shoes and wished they were red. Straight away they changed colour. Julie told her to open her hand and look at the marble. Margaret and all the rest of the girls could clearly see that the one stripe had gone. That's the point at which the marbles were first called 'Wishy Marbs'" said granny.

The family had all sat listening to what granny had been telling them about the marbles and again it was Mary who asked the question as to what happened next. Granny explained that Margaret and Julie decided that it was only fair they should tell Nathan Bilk the truth. They picked up a marble with four stripes and headed to the offices and asked to see Nathan. He let them into his office and asked what they wanted. Margaret explained to him what Julie had found out about the 'Four Stripers' and why it was that they had been packing boxes with marbles that did not always have four stripes. Nathan asked for a demonstration so Margaret gave him the marble she had brought with her and said for him to make a wish. Still a little upset with the girls and Margaret in particular he looked at her and wished that her hair was a different color. Margaret had black hair but as she stood there Julie and Nathan watched as it turned to a light brown colour. Margaret, although she couldn't see her hair, could tell by the look on the faces of the other two that she now had different coloured hair. Julie said for him to look at the marble and Nathan saw that it now had only three stripes. He then wished that one of the windows would open and straight away it did and he again saw the marble had lost a stripe. With that, he demanded that Margaret and Julie should go straight back to the sorting building and bring all the marbles with four stripes to his office and said he did not want them to send any more out. He had obviously decided to keep them for himself. As they walked back across to their place of work the two girls were suddenly drenched to the skin in a sudden down pour of rain. The sky had been a bright blue a minute earlier so it was quite obvious that Nathan was having a bit more fun at their expense with the marble he still had.

When they got back to the sorting room they told the other girls what had happened and said they had to collect all the 'Four Stripers' and take them to the office. When they had collected as many as they could find Margaret and Julie carried them across to the main building and went to Nathan Bilk's office to hand them over to him. He was looking a bit puzzled as they entered and had to admit that he had caused them to get wet because he had wished it to rain for a few minutes. What he couldn't understand was that there were now no stripes left in the marble when only three wishes had been made. It was suggested by Julie that perhaps something like wishing for it to rain required the use of two stripes. Nathan agreed that that is what it must have been although he couldn't see why. He sent the girls away with instructions that in future all 'Four Striper' marbles had to be brought to his office."

Granny again stopped talking and looked at her family. "That was the start of it all." she said. "After that Nathan, as well as having all the marbles with four stripes delivered to his office also set about finding out just what part of the mine they were being found. When he found out, he put a team of his own men in that area with instructions to them to collect the rocks themselves and to break them open and deliver the marbles directly to his office. They were to tell no one about what they were doing. Apparently this went on for a long time, but eventually they got fed up with the way Nathan treated them, and left. When this happened Nathan closed that part of the mine and stopped anyone working there. He gave the excuse that the area was unsafe. By now he had collected many of the four striped marbles so was quite content for the time being."

Granny had been talking for so long with everyone listening to all she had to say they had not realised just how the time had passed by.

"Let your grandmother have a rest now Pedro," said his father. His mother agreed and said she would go and make some sandwiches for tea. "And they won't be wishy ones either!" She said.

"I promise I will tell you more later Pedro," his granny said.

"Come on Pedro," said granddad, "Lets you and I go and finish opening some more of the rocks that still need to be done. You crack them open and I will polish them for you." Pedro and his grandfather went off to continue with opening the rocks.

"Do you know?" remarked his father, "I have never known Pedro sit so long and seem so interested in anything for a long time. It was as if he was taking in every word you were saying mum." His mother smiled and said she had noticed it too. She also said that she was not too sure if she should tell him a lot of what happened with the mine in case it should upset him. "Some not very nice things happened after it was discovered what the power of the marbles could do in the wrong hands," said his mother. "I think I will keep one particularly nasty episode away from him or else I think he would get too upset, but I will tell you and Mary later when he is in bed. In fact there are a couple of things not even your father knows about. I hope he will understand. In all our life together that is the only thing I have kept from him, apart from when you were a little bit naughty when you were young but that is the sort of thing mothers do."

"I am sure he will understand mum, and as for Pedro, just tell him what you think is best for the time being." said Tom.

His mother agreed then said to her son, "Tom, have you still got that box I asked you to keep for me all those years ago when you first moved into this house?'

"Yes I have," replied Tom, "it's under the bed in the room you and Dad are using. Pedro sits on it when he is playing in there with his trains. He often asks what it is and I tell him it is something you asked me to keep for you. He asks what is in there and I have to tell him that I honestly have no idea and anyway the 'box belongs to your granny and she has the key'".

His mother nodded slowly, "And is the grandfather clock I gave you still going O.K.?"

"Yes it is mum, although every now and then it goes real slow and the pendulum almost stops at times. No matter how I try to adjust it, I can't seem to make it tell the correct time for very long."

His mother gave a sly smile and said "I would like you to do two things for me before the others get back if you will please Tom"

"Of course, anything," replied Tom wondering what his mother had in mind.

"Go into the house," said his mother, "and bring out the box we were just talking about. On the way to get the box, open the casing door on the Grandfather Clock, look behind the pendulum and bring to me what you find there."

Her son went off to do as she had asked and she sat back in her chair and realised that at last it seemed as if it was time to reveal some of the secrets the old lady had entrusted her with all those years ago. She remembered that the old lady had told her that she would know when to tell some if not all the secrets. 'You will know just what to say and how much to say when the time comes.' the old lady had said, 'don't tell everything at once, just as much as is needed at the time.'

Tom reappeared carrying the box and set it on the table in front of his mother. He then produced a small brass key, which he had found stuck to the back of the pendulum of the clock. "Do you mean to tell me that that key has been there all these years, mother?"

"Yes it has, and I am just so very happy that you never thought of getting a clock maker in to see what was wrong with that clock. I think you will find it will keep good time again, now that little weight has been removed from the back of the pendulum." She smiled at him and told him that she was glad he had not been as inquisitive in his older years as he had been as a boy and not tried to open the box.

"If Pedro had had his way it would have been opened a long time ago mother. He was always asking me what was inside. I told him that I had no idea what was in there, but that one day we might know.

"That day may very well have arrived, Tom, but I don't think I can tell all the secrets that are in there, at least not yet. It won't be all pleasant Tom," his mother said looking a bit down crest, "but I will do my best to tell things as I remember them."

Tom assured his mother that he would respect whatever she had to tell them and said at the same time he was really intrigued as to what they all may hear later. Then added, "As for the clock, I think I would have used up a whole year's supply of those 'Wishy Marbs' the number of times I have walked past it, saw it was running slow again and wished it would tell the correct time.

CHAPTER SEVEN

SOME SECRETS FROM THE BOX

Once they had all had their sandwiches and everything had all been cleared away, they again gave all their attention to grandmother who was opening the lock on the box. "This box has not been opened for a great many years," she told them. "I was entrusted with some very important papers when I was very young by the grandmother of the present Mr. Bilk. I was asked to help to look after her by her husband Alfred who was the owner of the mine at the time. She was very insistent that I should not let the contents of what is in this box fall into the wrong hands. She trusted me and I am asking that you too, will respect her wishes, and keep whatever I tell you within the family, at least for the present. There may come a time at a later date when we shall have to involve other people but it will only be someone we all agree we can trust."

She looked around at her family and they all agreed to what she was asking of them. "Before I start, there is one thing I must say." Looking at her husband she continued, "In all the years we have known each other I have never lied to you, but when you asked me once what was in the box, I remember giving you a sort of off-hand reply about it just being something I wanted to keep safe. You never asked me again but I have always felt guilty that I couldn't tell you what was really in here. The same goes for you Tom when you moved into this house after you married Mary and I asked you to look after it for me. I never gave you a real explanation as to what the box contained. To both of you I offer my apologies."

Both Tom and his father assured her there was no need to apologise. Tom said it was nothing to do with him anyway, he had been asked to look after something for her and he had done so. His father on the other hand took hold of his wife's hand and said, "I have a little secret too Joan. Just after old Jessica died and I first started courting you I was up at the old Manor House doing a job for Alfred. He came round to see how I was getting along and started talking about the fact that we were walking out together. 'She's a good girl is that one' he said, 'My Jess thought the world of her.' Then he went on to say, 'Always chatting away they were. I reckon she gave your girl the family skeletons to look after.' Soon after that, Jim the carpenter told me you had asked him to make you a box to keep papers and things in. Told him you needed it to be lined so nothing would get damp. I didn't mind when you told me that just contained things you wanted to keep because of what old Alfred had told me."

"Well I never!" said his wife, "So you have known for all these years."

"Yes I have but had no idea what was in there. I'll let you into another secret too my dear.' This time he had a mischievous look in his eyes and he smiled as he said to her, "You once asked what the long brass box-like thing on my watch chain was and I said it was just a weight to keep my chain in place. Well, inside that brass weight is a key identical to the one you are holding. Jim the carpenter gave it to me after he had fitted the lock for you and given you your key. 'Best keep this somewhere safe,' he said, 'your young lady may lose the other one.' I had no idea at all where you kept the original and I still don't. I just made sure I never lost the one I had. The key is inside that little box and I had it packed in sawdust so it would not rattle around" His wife laughed at what they had all been told, then went on to explain where her key had been all these years."

"Seems you both had a couple of secrets, but at least they were nice ones," said Mary.

By now her mother in law had removed a few of the envelopes from the box. They could all see that they were numbered and she explained to them that she had numbered them as the old lady had given them to her. The ones she had been given in the nursing home after the old lady had passed away she put to one said saying that she thought they would contain even deeper secrets and didn't think the time was right to open them. Pedro looked at the seal on them and noticed that in the middle of the seal was a fancy letter B. His grandmother explained that the B was the Bilk family seal. She told him that when she was cleaning for the old lady it was one of her duties to make sure the letter B stamp was always kept free from dirt so that it would make a good seal when it was used. It was just like a large salt pot with a big B on the bottom. She went on to explain that old Jessica wrote a good many letters to various people and always sealed them with the fancy B.

She withdrew the contents of the first envelope and everyone could see it was a sort of plan. She opened it out and laid it on the table.

"I reckon that's a plan of the mine," said Tom, moving round to stand behind his mother to get a better look."

"It certainly seems like it Tom, but what about all these strange markings on it?"

Tom's father had now also moved round to stand behind his wife in order to get a better look at the plan. "It's not the plan of the mine as it is today," he said. "It looks more like it did when I worked there." He pointed to a sharp bend in one of the tunnels. "That's the tunnel where we lost Joshua. He went down there to fix some of the lanterns and refill them with oil. It took us two days to find him again. He had taken a few wrong turnings and couldn't find his way back again. His own lamp had run out of oil so he was left in complete darkness. While he was trying to find his way back he had stumbled and spilt the can of oil he was carrying to refill the lamps on the wall, so he didn't even have any more to fill his own lamp. No one really missed him because he was not supposed to be working that day. He had called into the office to ask for a couple of days off to go to his cousin's wedding in the next town. The foreman on duty at the time asked him if he would take a quick look at some of the lanterns and of course Joshua had said yes. We were all quite young in those days and eager to please for fear of losing our jobs. Joshua was only fifteen at the time and was really too young to go into various parts of the mine alone. At the end of the shift everyone went home, not knowing he was still down there. The foreman had not told anyone he had sent Josh down there and as he was not supposed to be there anyway, he was not on the checking off list. It was only when his mother got worried as to where he was and went up to the manor house to report that he had not arrived home that the alarm was raised. The foreman did not live in the village so it was old Alfred himself who had to deal with it."

"Was he alright John? His wife asked.

"Yes he was, but he never went down into the mine again. It really scared him. In fact he left a short while after that and joined the Navy."

Pedro, who had been studying the map from the other side of the table said, "Look, those funny signs and marks are the same as the stripes in the marbles we have all been getting. See there," he pointed to a mark on the map, "That mark has four little stripes, and there, a little way away are some marks with only three stripes. And there look!" by now getting really excited and putting his finger on a mark at the bottom corner of the map, "That is just the same as the little marbles you brought home the other day dad. The stripes are all close together and all run in the same direction and are very thin. I've got them here look." He proudly showed them the smaller marbles in a different box. "You have only brought me six of those so far dad."

By this time even Pedro's mother was getting all excited "Is that because you have been working in a different part of the mine Tom?

I know you said just the other day you needed your jacket because it was colder now where you were working."

"That's right," replied her husband, "I was asked to go down and work in area six. The foreman knew I had worked there before and so knew my way around. He asked me to take David along to get him used to the area.

"Did he bring any rocks out with him?" his mother asked.

"Yes but he doesn't have any children so he gave me his two rocks as we left the mine. That's how you got four rocks last night Pedro."

Pedro's grandmother had been studying the old map while all this conversation had been taking place and looking at her grandson said, "I think you have hit the nail on the head my boy. There definitely seems to be a connection with the marks on the map and the marbles that are being brought home by your father. Do you know if any of your friends have opened any different marbles?"

"Sally Sutton had some funny shaped ones," said Pedro. "They were a bit larger than normal sized ones and had a sort of dent in them. They also had four coloured spots in the dent. She said they were no good for rolling but she was going to keep them anyway because they were different from the ones everyone else had been finding."

"I think we are beginning to unravel the mystery here a little,' said granny. "Let's have another look at this plan of the mine."

They all looked at the map more closely this time. Again it was Pedro who spotted what they were looking for. Right in the top left corner of the map was a little picture showing a larger circle with a little bit cut out of it and four coloured dots next to it. He pointed it out to them all and said that looked just like the marbles Sally had shown them a few weeks ago. He had also spotted something, which he meant to ask his grandmother about but he forgot at the time. When he did remember he decided to keep it to himself for the time being. It felt good to him to have a secret.

"That's in area two," said his father. "Mr. Bilk sent a couple of men to work there about three weeks ago. He told us that it was one of the older parts of the mine that had been blocked off when there had been a landslide, many years ago. He wanted to see if it could be opened up again. One of the men, Jack who went there, came back after the first shift and said he would not go back there because he reckoned it was haunted on account his grandfather had told him that he had lost his brother in that part of the mine in the land slide and they never did get his body back out. He said he didn't want to go digging around in there and find his great Uncle's bones. Freddy Sutton, the other man sent in there only worked in that area for about five days before he too told the foreman he would not go back there. He said he heard strange sounds when he stopped working and sat there in the quiet eating his sandwiches during his break."

"Mr. Sutton is Sally's father," said Pedro. "That would explain why Sally never brought any more of those larger marbles to show us again. She told us that her dad had gone back to working where he had been before."

"This map certainly dates back to before the landslide," said granddad. He pointed again to the sharp bend in the tunnel where Joshua had got lost. "That part of the workings was completely blocked off after the accident and was no longer accessible."

"That would all tie in with the amount of time I have had this map then," said his wife. "I was given these papers by old Jessica long before the accident, just about the time we met John. I think that old Bilky is allowing the workers to take home the rocks to try to find out where the different marbles are located."

"He certainly has been moving men around to different parts of the mine Mum. I have worked in three different parts in the last two weeks. Funny though, he never asks any of us about the rocks we bring home."

"I reckon that's what he's got his grandson here for then," replied his mother. "He thinks that by getting him to ask questions to the children he'll get the answers he wants."

"Paul's certainly been doing a lot of that granny," said Pedro. "He even asked if he could come round here to see my collection because he had heard from some of the other children that I had some special ones. That was before we knew who he was. Now we have decided amongst ourselves we won't tell him anything."

"But you can't not show him your marbles if he comes round Pedro." his mother said. "After all he knows you have them and knows you have some with four stripes."

"Yes and you can be sure if they are the ones his grandfather has asked him to look out for he will try his best to get them from you," said his grandmother. "How many of the four striped ones do you have Pedro?"

"About twenty now I think, but I still have some rocks to break open."

"Right then," said grandmother, "I think I know a way to make sure he doesn't get any marbles with magic in them. Pass me four of your four striped marbles please Pedro." Pedro did as he was asked and gave his grandmother four marbles that had stripes all the same colour in them. "Now pass me another one please." Pedro again did as she asked. His grandmother held the four marbles in one hand and picked up the other one in her other hand. "I wish the magic in these marbles will not work for anyone but Pedro." As she said this she opened her hand with the single marble in and they could all see one stripe had gone. She gave one of the other marbles to her husband and asked him to make a simple wish.

"I wish the shed door would close." Nothing happened so the marble was passed to each of the adults in turn with the request that they make a simple wish. They all did and nothing happened. Pedro was then given the marble and asked to make a wish.

"I wish the shed door would close," he said repeating what his grandfather had said. As soon as he said it the shed door did indeed close with a bang.

"Well, that seems to be alright,' said his granny, "Now we had better put the stripe back into the marble." With that, she held the marble she had used to make the first wish and wished that the marble could have four stripes again. They all watched as the fourth stripe returned to the marble, and they all saw that the original marble had lost another stripe. She put the "Wishy Marb" back with the other three and set them down on the table. "Right Pedro," she said, "If Paul comes round asking to look at your marbles make sure you show him these four. You can't mistake them; they all have the same coloured stripes in them."

"I'll put them in the box with the ordinary marbles, the ones with only two or three stripes in them." said Pedro, "and I'll put all my other marbles in a bigger box and keep them in the shed and put the lock on the door."

While all this conversation had been going on, Pedro's mother had been studying the mine plan a bit closer and drew their attention to a faint name at the bottom of the plan. "Look here, there's a name in this corner." They all looked to where on the plan she was pointing and could just about see a name written there.

"Can you see what it says Pedro?" asked his father, "Your eyesight is probably a lot better than ours." Pedro moved around the table so he could take a better look.

"It looks like 'Samuel B" said Pedro.

"That would be Jessica's husband's grandfather," said granny, "old Bilky's great grandfather. Now we can get some idea how old this plan is. He must have drawn this plan so he could set the miners to work in different parts of the mine depending on which of the marbles he wanted. I think we will find out lots more, as we open the rest of the envelopes." She looked at her family and suggested that they put everything away and had a nice relaxing evening. "After all we have been talking about all this for a long time and I am feeling quite tired." Everyone agreed, and grandfather offered to help Pedro put away his collection and then suggested the two might go for a walk.

"Perhaps we could walk up to Freddy's house and asked his mum if he can come with us one day."

Pedro thought this was a great idea and so the two of them cleared away all the marbles and put them in the bigger box Pedro had brought from the shed. All the rocks that were still to be opened were wrapped in a piece of cloth and put in the shed also. Meanwhile, Pedro's father put the envelopes they had been looking at back into the wooden box and carried it into the house to his mother's bedroom.

Pedro and his grandfather went to say goodbye to the rest of the family saying they were going for a walk and would call in at the farm to see if it was O.K. for Freddy to come out with them one day. Pedro's mum asked them to wait a minute and went into the kitchen. When she returned she had a container with her. Handing it to Pedro she asked him if he could get her some milk as they were running a bit low.

"Don't need to pay for it," she said, "I gave Freddy's mother some potatoes from the garden the other day so she said she would let me have some milk in exchange."

"That sort of thing still goes on then does it?" said granny. "We used to do that many years ago."

"Yes it does," replied her daughter in law, "sometimes it's the only way we can get a few extras we need."

Chapter Eight

Day Out With Granddad

The following morning Pedro was up bright and early, eager to go off for the day with his grandfather. They had called at the farm the evening before and arranged to call for Freddy about 9 o'clock. They had also seen Simon's father and said if it was alright with him then they would be round for Simon as well. Sally had mentioned to Pedro the day before that she would be going out with her mother so it would be just granddad and the three boys going off for the day.

Pedro was still eating his breakfast when Freddy knocked on the door. He said he hoped he wasn't too early but his dad was going over to one of the other fields so gave him a lift down on the tractor. "Don't worry," said Pedro's mum, "come in and have a cup of tea. There's some toast as well if you would like some." Freddy explained that he had already had his breakfast but would like a cup of tea.

Pedro's grandfather who had been outside in the garden came into the kitchen, said hello to Freddy then asked the boys where they would like to go on their walk. They both said they didn't really mind. "In that case, I think we will go over the hill behind Bilky's house. I haven't been there for years. We always seemed to go the other way when we go out don't we Pedro?"

Pedro agreed and said it would be good to go somewhere different. He reminded his granddad that they had always been warned off from going to that part of the village without a grown up with them but didn't know why. "That's because that part of the village was close to where the accident in the mine happened and no-one was too sure how safe the ground around that area might be. Although the accident was underground it affected a lot of the surface too. A couple of large trees were up rooted when it all happened. "In fact," granddad told the two boys, "there was a large farm building collapsed as well. It was a very long time before anyone ventured anywhere near the place." He went on to explain that it was a shame because in the winter that hill had been the best place for the children of the village to have fun with their sledges.

The boys and granddad went off for their day out. Granddad was careful not to let the boys go anywhere near the area where the collapses had happened. As they got to the top of the hill his attention was drawn to a part of the hill where the large farm building had been. It looked as if part of it had been removed. It was also the area where a lot of the rubbish rocks from the mine had been dumped. The pile of rubbish had over the years become so overgrown that it was hard for granddad to remember where it had been. Telling the boys to stay where they were he started down the hill to investigate what might have been going on. When he reached collapsed building he could see that quite a bit of work had been done. It looked as if someone had been digging in the area but at the same time had taken an awful lot of trouble to try to hide the fact The inside of the wrecked building had been supported on the inside so that from a distance no one would be able to see what had been going on.

As he investigated further, granddad came across a strange sight. Two sets of footprints in the soft soil led from nowhere to the outside of the building. He walked down to where the footprints started but they just seemed to immerge out of the soft hillside wall behind a large bush. He looked around a bit more but could not find any answer to what he had found. He was about to start back out of the building when he thought he heard a faint voice. He could not tell where it came from or what it had said, but it made the hairs on the back of his neck stand on end. He looked around a bit more but the sound was not repeated. He put it down to the fact that maybe a part of the mine still being worked was close to that area. He made a mental note to ask his son about it when he got home. He went back up the hill to rejoin the boys but said nothing to them about what had happened. When they asked him what he had found he just told them that it looked as if there had been a bit of work to try to make the fallen building safe. The boys appeared to be satisfied with his explanation and asked him no more about it.

They carried on their walk and indeed hadn't realised how far they had walked until they discovered they had come back to the village from the opposite direction from which they had started. They saw Freddy's dad working in a field and when he saw them, he offered them a lift back home on the trailer he was taking back to the farm. When they got to the farm, Freddy thanked Pedro's grandfather for a very nice day saying he had really enjoyed it. Granddad, Pedro and Simon said goodbye and made their way home as well. Making sure that Simon got home safely Pedro and his grandfather then walked back to his house, where they were met by his mother who said she was beginning to worry as they had been gone for so long. "Sorry about that, I suppose we just lost track of the time." said granddad.

"Never mind, you're both here now. Get yourselves a cold drink supper won't be long. I expect you are really hungry after your day out."

Pedro went off to get a drink as his mother had suggested but granddad went to look for his son to discuss with him what he had discovered on the far side of the hill. He really couldn't understand what it was he had heard and needed to try to put his mind at rest. In fact it had bothered him a lot since it had happened. He had a very strange and disturbing feeling that he had half recognised the voice but he just couldn't think who it might have been. He hadn't worked at the mine for years and so apart from his son and family, had had no contact with anyone connected with it. It was in the back of his mind that it was a voice from way back in his past, but who it was he just couldn't recall.

Chapter Nine

Memories from Granny's Childhood

Once tea was over and Pedro's mum had cleared everything away the family just sat out in the garden relaxing and enjoying the peace and quiet. Pedro was keen for his grandmother to continue with her tales of the mine but didn't want to appear to be too anxious. They just chatted in general and his grandmother asked if they had enjoyed their walk. Both Pedro and granddad said they had, and granddad went on to explain that it appeared that some work had been done on the old "Winter Shed" as the big building had been known years ago.

"Why was it called that?" asked Pedro and his mother at the same time.

"From what I can remember my grandmother telling me, it was the place the whole village moved to during very bad winters," replied granny. "It came about because when the real bad snows came in the winter the main road out of the village would be blocked for about four months at a time. There was no way to get food etc. into the village and as the snow was too thick for wood for the home fires to be collected it was thought best that everyone moved in to the "Winter Shed" so they could all be safe together." She went on to

91

tell them that the large building was divided into separate spaces for each family. There was a main dormitory for the older children to sleep in and in fact she said that the children quite liked it, and treated it as a bit of an adventure.

"What about the men who worked in the mine Mum,"

Granny turned to her son and explained that as far as she could remember what her grandmother had told her, there was a back entrance to the mine close to the Winter Shed and the men would enter the mine workings through that. "Mind you," said his mother, "I remember my grandmother telling me that it was so cold in the mines that the men could not do a full shift, so some worked in the morning and some in the evenings. They also had to cut down to two or three days a week because they had to be careful about not using too much oil in the lamps as they would not be able to get any more until after the road was open again."

"Bet that didn't please whoever ran the mine then." said her husband.

"No it didn't John. Plus at that time both sides of the Bilk family owned the mine jointly, and when the winters came and the main road to the village was blocked, the other side of the family who lived in a different village about six miles away had no idea what the Male Bilks were up to and quite frequently there were family arguments about how much work had been done in the mine during the bad season."

"Why were they called the Male Bilks?" asked Tom.

"One half of the mine belonged to the male side of the family and the other half to the female side. The females were three sisters, and were the daughters of the original owner. They were known locally as the "Bilk Maids." They lived on a large dairy farm which had originally been owned jointly by the collective Bilk families but over the years the male side of the family showed little or no interest in the farm so they were bought out by Farmer Bilk who continued to run it as a family concern with his wife and daughters. He still kept his interest in the mine which had been in the Bilk family for generations, and insisted that a manager appointed by him, should be allowed a job in the mine so he could keep an eye on what was going on. This man eventually went missing in what was later called the "Great Disappearance." None of the sisters ever married so when their parents eventually passed away, each sister inherited one third each of their parents half of the mine. They were quite happy to let the male Bilks actually run the mine but kept a close eye on what was going on. Of course they only had the word of the male partners as to how things really were so it was quite easy for them to be kept in the dark about a few things. This situation led to many family feuds and as the sisters had no husbands to help them out they nearly always lost any argument."

"What did you mean when you said the great disappearance?" asked Mary.

"From what my grandmother could remember from things told to her by her mother, strange things started happening and people started to either leave the village or just seemed to be no longer there," said her mother- in-law. "The cows on the dairy farm started to get very ill and stopped producing milk and things went from bad to worse on the farm it's self. It appeared that the three sisters just gave up and moved away and the farm fell into ruin. Another story is that the last sister to survive past on her share of the mine to a male member of the family. All that is certain is that the sisters were not around anymore. No one could actually remember them going and as there was no one to run the farm, the whole place was just left as it was. No records were ever really kept so a lot of what I was told as a young girl was hearsay. People thought up all sorts of things to explain what had happened including witch craft and that sort of thing but nothing was ever proved."

Pedro's grandmother sat back in her chair and relaxed after her little story telling. She looked across at Pedro who had fallen asleep with his head on his arms on the table. "Looks like someone we know is tired out," she said.

Pedro's father nudged him awake and suggested that it was time for him to go to bed after the long day he had had with his grandfather. Pedro said good night to everyone and his mother took him into the house to get him ready for bed.

"Probably got a bit bored with what I was saying," commented Granny.

"Maybe he did," replied her husband, "but now he has gone there is something I wanted to tell you and Tom about this afternoon"

He went on to tell them what he had discovered on his walk with the boys and what he had seen at the site of what he now knew was the old Winter Shed. "The two sets of footprints intrigued me," he said, "and the fact they seemed to appear from a bush by the hillside. Plus I could see no evidence that they went back again, they just went one way. And, there are certainly signs that some work has been done on and around the old shed."

He looked at his son and wife and said that he had not mentioned anything to the boys for fear of scaring them and that was why he had waited until Pedro was out of the way. He then asked his son if there were any men working in a part of the mine where they had been that afternoon and told him about the strange feeling he had that he had heard a voice. Although he couldn't make out what was said he was certain it was a voice from his past but just could not put a finger on it.

"Not as far as I know dad," Tom said. "That part where you were is the farthest from where the main workings are and is in fact the oldest part of the mine. The part that was involved in the great fall and collapse all those years ago."

"Well, certainly something strange is happening over there," said his father, "perhaps you and I can walk over there one day when Pedro is not here and see what we can find out."

"Next Tuesday would be a good day for that," said his wife, "Mary and I had already decided to take Pedro into town on the bus to get him his new school uniform ready for the new term."

"That's what we will do then," said Pedro's father, "I have two weeks off work now so that will be ideal. In the meantime we won't mention any of this to Pedro you know how curious he can be. We'll just wait until we know anything for certain."

Pedro's mother came back into the garden just then carrying a tray with two cups of tea and two bottles of beer. "Pedro went straight off to sleep as soon as his head hit the pillow," she said, "so I thought we could all finish off the evening with a relaxing drink.'

The rest of the family agreed and as they sat there drinking, filled her in with what they had been discussing in her absence. She thought it was a very good idea to keep things quiet where Pedro was concerned until they knew more of what was going on. "Sounds a bit creepy to me," was all she said.

During the relaxing chat, Tom's father commented that he had noticed on the bus ride to their home that the old cottages at the other end of the village were still not being lived in, and in fact some of them appeared to have been boarded up. His son told him that some of the people who still lived around that part of the village had talked about someone or something trying to get in some of the cottages.

"Animals do you think?" asked his mother.

"Don't think so mother, the damage was more than an animal would be able to do." replied her son. "The damage was repaired and the homes boarded up, and all the remaining unoccupied cottages had also been made safe from intruders. In fact, when people go out now they lock their doors for fear of intruders, a thing they never did before"

"It could be that some of our questions will be answered in those envelopes and packages I have," said granny "From what you have been saying John, it certainly seems as if there is a mystery to solve. If it gets too much involved I think it might be best if I look at some of the information first before we all have a general look like we have been doing. We don't want Pedro getting upset about what we might find out."

The others agreed but also insisted that as far as possible Pedro would continue to be part of it all. "After all," said his father, " it was all down to him opening the rocks with the "Wishy Marbs" in that started all this off."

CHAPTER TEN

DISCOVERIES AT THE WINTER SHED

The next two days were spent just doing general family type things. On the Sunday Pedro and his Granddad went along to visit Jimmy to wish him well on his visit to the hospital. He told them he was leaving on the early bus the next morning and would be away for about 10 days if all went well. In the afternoon the whole family went for a nice long walk so by the time they had eaten their evening meal everyone was quite tired and ready for a good night's sleep. For once thoughts of the marbles and what secrets they held seemed to have been forgotten by Pedro. He was thrilled just to have his grandparents staying with them and the days never seemed to be long enough for all they wanted to do.

On Monday Pedro's mother and grandmother spent a bit of time in the garden and his father spent most of the day sorting out the tents and other things that would be needed for when Pedro and granddad went camping.

Pedro and his grandfather opened up and sorted out the rest of the rocks that were left to be opened. They had by now quite a collection of various types, some of which his grandfather said he had never seen before.

Tuesday morning saw the whole family up bright and early. Pedro and his mother and grandmother were hoping to catch the early bus into the town to get as much shopping done as they could before it was time to come home. He was looking forward to getting his new school uniform. Now that he was getting older and going up to the higher classes he was required to wear a proper uniform whereas before he wore ordinary clothes.

Once they had seen them on their way, his father and grandfather locked the house and headed off towards the "Winter Shed' area to have a good look round. They carried a lantern each because although it was daylight, granddad had a strange feeling they might need them. They also had a stout walking stick each so they could use them to beat back any undergrowth they may have to pass through.

Upon arrival at the site Granddad led his son to the place where he had heard the noises and more important the voice.

"Certainly looks like something has been going on here," Pedro's father said as he looked around the area. "See here, there are what appear to be footprints, but they are very small just like a child's. I wonder if any of the village children have been playing here."

"I doubt it," replied his father, "most of the villagers keep far away from this place because of the mysteries of what went on in the past."

Both of them continued to look around, each going in a different direction. After a short time, Tom heard his father shouting something but could not be certain what he was saying. He hurried over to where his father was to see what had happened.

"What happened, Dad?" He could see his father was quite disturbed about something and was sitting down holding his head in his hands. His father just pointed at an area over to his right where, when Tom looked, could only see a large bush seemingly moving in the breeze.

"They went through there, they went through there!" his father said.

"Who did Dad?"

"The children, the children!" his father replied, pointing to the big bush. "They just seemed to move the bush to one side and disappear behind it."

Tom went over to the bush to investigate, but even though he looked all around, could find nothing to indicate that anything had taken place.

He walked back to where his father was still sitting and sat down beside him.

"How are you feeling dad, and can you tell me what you saw?"

His father, when he looked at his son, was as white as a sheet and clearly still visible shaken by what he had witnessed.

"Take it easy dad," Tom said,

It was several minutes before his father could begin to relay to his son what he had seen,

"I came over that little ridge over there," his father said, pointing to the direction he had chosen to investigate, "when I spotted a couple of children walking towards me. As I shouted to them they looked up, saw me and ran straight towards that bush over there and as I watched it just seemed to move to one side and the children vanished behind it."

"Stay there and take it easy dad" Tom said, "and I'll go and have a look around."

He walked off in the direction his father had indicated and soon came upon the bush he thought his father had been talking about. It was the only one of any size in the area. It was quite a large bush and seemed to be growing out of the side of the hillside. He searched all around but could not see any signs of anything untoward. He was about to return to his father when he saw something bright lying on the ground reflecting in the sun. Picking it up, he saw that it was some kind of medallion with a piece of chain attached to it. He walked back to where his father was sitting to show him what he had found.

When his father saw what his son had found, he got his second shock of the day.

"That," he said pointing to the design on the medallion, "is the old Bilk family seal mark. I remember it from when I first started work at the mines. It was stamped on all the original machinery. It was not machinery as we know it today and mostly it was made from wood, but at least it took some of the backbreaking work out of the miners' day. As old parts broke down, any that had that mark on them had to be replaced with new parts, but why it should be on a medallion I have no idea."

Father and son sat there for a little while longer until the older man felt able continue. They walked back over to where the children had been spotted to have a better look around, but after about half an hour could find nothing to explain what grandfather had seen.

They then decide to look inside the ruins of the old Winter Shed. As his father had explained to the family, Tom could clearly see evidence that some sort of work had been carried out, but nothing they could actually put their finger on. The ground over the far end of the shed was all disturbed but again no evidence of what had been accomplished or attempted presented itself.

It was as they were standing quietly looking around that they heard a very faint sound coming from behind the woodwork of the shed.

"Hear that?" said granddad clutching his son's arm.

"Yes I did," replied his son, at the same time indicating for them to remain silent by putting his fingers to his lips.

Both men stood perfectly still straining to hear any sounds that might be heard. After about five minutes they heard a very faint voice seeming to ask for help. Granddad moved as close to the spot as he could. He then tapped lightly on the shed side to encourage who ever or whatever it was to repeat the sound.

"Can you help me please!? Any other body there?"

Tom looked at his father to indicate that he had heard the sound and again saw the older man sit down heavily and looking just as pale as he had when he had spotted the children earlier, but this time was visibly shaking.

"What's the matter dad, are you alright?" His father just waved his hand as if to say he would be O.K. in a couple of minutes. Again Tom waited until his father was ready to speak. When he did start to explain to his son what the matter was his voice had a definite tremble to it.

"Remember the other night son when I was telling you about what I had heard when I was here with the boys and the voice I heard seemed to remind me of someone from my past. Well that voice I am now certain belongs to a friend I was an apprentice with when I first started work here. It is not only the voice, but also what was said that convinces me who it is. There was one thing he always said which amused us all. He always said ", Any other body there, or any other body coming, instead of just anyone else there or anyone else coming as you and I would."

"Can you remember who it was?"

"Yes I can, it belongs to my best friend back in those days. His name was Joshua Temple. He was about the same age as me. We went to school together and started work together. I started to train as an electrician and Joshua went on to train as a carpenter as had his father before him. He got lost in the mine soon after he started. It scared him a bit and later left to join the navy. Your mother was friends with his sister, and at one time, they were inseparable. The whole family just up and left the village without saying a word to anyone. They left their cottage as if they were simply going out shopping or something like that and were never seen again. The incident just became another of the mysteries that seem to be associated with this place. One thing I can't explain though is, if that is Joshua behind that bit of the old shed, what on earth, is he doing there. He left as I told you to join the Navy." He went on to explain to his son that their old cottage was one of the ones he had seen boarded up and was asking Mary about.

They sat there for quite a while longer in order to give the older man time to recover and also to listen for any other sounds coming from behind the shed, but nothing was heard again.

When he felt able to continue, granddad got to his feet and suggested that they make their way back home. "Better not discuss this in front of Pedro, he would only want to come up here and look around for himself and we are not at all sure what might be going on. We'll talk about with the ladies once he is in bed."

His son agreed and both of them took a slow walk back to their home, just chatting in general about what they had seen and heard that day.

CHAPTER ELEVEN

THE MYSTERIES DEEPEN

The ladies were home by the time Tom and his father arrived there, but there was no sign of Pedro. When Tom asked where his son was he was told that they had met Simon and his mum in town and Simon's mum had invited Pedro to stay for the night. She said that Simon's father would bring him home in the morning.

"That's quite fortuitous," said Tom, and went on to quickly explain a rough outline of what had taken place with him and his father.

"Seems like we had better open a few more envelopes after supper." said his mother.

Having been told by his wife that supper would not be ready for about an hour and a half Tom suggested to his father that they take a stroll down through the village checking on just how many of the old houses and cottages had been abandoned and boarded up.

"Why don't you take your mother with you Tom, she will be more help filling in the details than I would be. She knew most of the people because she was born here."

Tom could see his father was still a little bit upset by what had occurred so quickly agreed with the suggestion. He would also be able to give his mother an account of what had happened.

There were a total of nine homes that had been left empty where the families had just seemed to decide to leave the village. None of those who left ever told anyone they were going and were never seen or heard of again. Out of the nine houses, four showed signs of someone or something having tried to gain entrance. These houses had been secured with boards and the windows also boarded up where they had been broken.

"The house with the blue and green door over there is where my best friend Rebecca Temple lived. We painted the door that colour one Saturday afternoon while her parents were out. We thought we would get into all kinds of trouble when they got back but they said it had been done very well and decided to keep it that way.

About two weeks after that I went into town with my grandmother and when we came back I called at the house to show Rebecca what I had bought but there was no one at home. I thought this was a bit strange because at the time her mother had been quite seriously ill. She had fallen down two weeks earlier and had broken her leg. Although it had been put in plaster the fall had badly shaken her up and she spent most days just lying on the settee.

The family was never seen again and eventually the village elder at the time contacted a relative from a distant town who came along and locked up the house. I never wanted to come to this part of the village again but had to pass it to get to the school, which at that time was held in the old Manor House. When I got here, I crossed to the other side of the road."

Tom listened to all his mother said about the cottages but didn't mention anything about what he and his father had experienced at the old Winter Shed. He thought it was best that she was told about it when they were all together later. She had clearly been very upset at the time when her best friend and her family had disappeared.

Once the evening meal had been completed, the family gathered around the table in the garden. Tom had collected the box from the spare room and laid the plan of the mine on the table. His mother looked through the envelopes and packets she had been given to see which ones she thought would help them.

"Before we start anything this evening Joan, there is something you should know, something which happened to Tom and myself this afternoon." Her husband leaned across the table to hold his wife's hand as he went on to tell his wife and his daughter-in-law, first about seeing the children disappearing behind the bush, and then about the voice which seemed to be calling for help.

"Two more bits of the mystery," Tom added, "is that dad is more than sure the voice we heard belonged to a schoolboy friend of his by what he said and there is this." He then held up the medallion attached to the bit of chain he had found close to where the children had disappeared.

This time it was his mother who turned quite white and put her hand to her mouth.

"What is it Joan?" her husband asked.

His wife just held out her hand for her son to put the medallion in her hand so she could have a closer look. While she looked at it, the rest of the family could see she was visible shook up.

"Take your time Mum," said Tom moving round the table to be beside his mother. When she could eventually speak she explained that the medallion they had found was one that they were all given at school. "It was given to us so that when we went into the town for lessons or sport at the big school, the teachers there could easily see which child belonged to which school. All those years ago there were not enough teachers for all the subjects to be taught so the older ones were taken to the town school. Back home," she continued, "I still have mine." She also went on to explain that a lot of the children scratched their names on the back. She looked at the one Tom had found but could find no evidence of a name anywhere.

"What do you think this all means?" asked Mary.

"What I think it means," replied her mother-in-law, "is that we may be on the verge of discovering something very sinister that happened many years ago, which may also explain why so many people disappeared all those years ago."

"And I wouldn't be surprised," added her husband, "if your old lady who gave you all these packages, knew or at least suspected, something of what had occurred in the past, and secretly collected as much information as she could, then waited for the right time and the right person to come along so she could pass it all over. And that person my dear was you. She must have thought a great deal of you and judged that you were just such a person to look after the secrets of the past."

"I agree with dad," Tom said, "and I think what we have to do now mum, is honour the trust put in you, and all of us do our very best to help you do the right thing, after studying all information you have there in that box."

"You are right of course Tom, but it really is a big responsibility." She started to sort the envelopes into their correct order. She looked at her husband and said, "One thing you haven't told me, is who you think the voice you heard belonged to."

"I am certain that it was the voice of Joshua Temple, the brother of your best friend Rebecca."

This fresh bit of information again seemed to upset his wife, who simply put her head in her hands wondering out loud what they had let themselves in for.

Tom was quite concerned about the effect this was all having on his mother and asked her if she was certain she wanted to continue. She assured him that she was and started to open one of the packets. "We'll just take it one step at a time," she said.

The first packet contained a list of all the people who had suddenly left their houses in the village. She looked down the list and sure enough saw the names of her friend Rebecca and her family. The paper gave no indication as to why these people just disappeared.

Another of the packages also contained sheets of paper with lists on them and also what appeared to be dates and diagrams but was in a language none of them could understand. At the bottom of one of the pages written in bold letters, which Joan recognised as the old lady's writing, it said LET THE CHILDREN HELP YOU.

"What on earth can that mean?" said Pedro's father.

"I think it means what it says," replied his mother, "children are the key to the whole mystery or at least part of it, and somehow by reading the papers, the old lady had managed to decipher part of what is written in that strange language." She continued to look very closely at the paper she was holding, and after a while exclaimed, "Well would you believe it!" The others looked to see what she had seen. "Look at that word there," she said pointing to some of the writing halfway down the page. "What does it look like to you?" Mary was the first to say anything. "If I didn't know better I would say it is a funny way of spelling Pedro."

"I agree, that's what made me speak out," said her mother-in-law. The two men, after studying the word for a while longer agreed.

"And look at that word there," said an excited Mary, pointing to a word at the bottom of the page, "what do you think that looks like?"

This time it was her husband who was the first to speak. "Sally, I think it is meant to say Sally"

"Correct," agreed his mother. "What on earth have we stumbled on here?"

"Sally is the name of one of Pedro's friends isn't she Tom?"

"Yes she is dad. I wonder if we can find any other of Pedro's friends' names on these pages as it seems as if they are the ones involved in all this."

They all studied the paper with more interest, but none of them could see any words remotely resembling any other of Pedro's school friends.

They could find nothing else useful in any of the other packages they opened as they were all in the same strange language. At the bottom of one of the pages however, were two diagrams one showing four coloured dots and the other four coloured lines. The lines were green and the dots were red. They were roughly the size and shape of a marble.

"They look just like some of the marbles Pedro has found," said Tom.

Upon checking the pages they had previously looked at, they saw the same kind of diagrams. They had obviously failed to notice them once they saw pages with writing on they couldn't understand.

"I think we are going to have to let Pedro in on all this," said granddad, "he is the one with the marbles which certainly seem to be the key to the problem and it seems the solution." They all agreed with what he said and decided to tell Pedro everything when he returned home.

"It could very well be," added his wife, "that some of his friends would have to be involved to because they also appear to have special marbles."

With that settled, they cleared everything away and made preparations to have a final cup of tea before retiring for the night. Grandmother said nothing more to the others, but she had a very strange, unnerving feeling within herself, that the marbles were not the only "magic" connected with the mine and not all of it good either.

CHAPTER TWELVE

PAUL'S VISIT

Pedro arrived home the next morning just as they were having breakfast. He was all excited at having been able to stay at Simon's for the night. Simon's father was with him and Pedro's mother invited him in for a cup of tea. "Simon not with you?" asked Mary as she poured the tea. "No he has taken Mut to the vet to get him checked over," replied Simon's father.

Pedro by now had gone up to his bedroom to get changed and Mr. Bloom took the opportunity to speak to Pedro's parents and grandparents. "Something very strange happened in the village last night," he said. "It seems as if someone tried to get into one of the boarded up cottages. I don't know which one but I think it was the one with blue and green door." He looked across at Granny. "That's the one where your friend lived isn't it? I remember my mother telling me something about it. Anyway this morning as I was out with Mut for his early walk before the boys were up I noticed quite a few people gathered near the cottage. Old man Bilk was there and so was a young lad who I can only assume was his grandson, who I heard was staying with him for a while. They were both looking all over the place. I talked to some of the villagers who were gathered around and asked them what was going on. All they could tell me was that there had been some sort of commotion during the night but no one seemed to have seen anything. How old man Bilk got to hear about it I don't know."

He finished by telling them that he had not said anything to the boys, and that by the time he had walked Pedro home, all was very quiet. He said that the only person still hanging around was Bilky's grandson who shouted across to Pedro to not forget he would call round and see him one day.

Pedro came back downstairs just as Simon's dad was ready to leave. Pedro thanked him again for letting him stay and hoped that Mut would be O.K. at the Vet's. "I'm sure he will be, thanks for the tea Mary, see you all again soon."

Pedro's father got up and told Simon's dad he would walk with him to the gate. He really wanted to have a quick word about a couple of things out of Pedro's earshot.

Pedro sat down at the table and looked at his grandfather, "What shall we do today Grampy, go out for a walk again?"

"What I think you and I ought to do young man, is to finish off splitting the rocks you have not opened yet and polish and sort out whatever we find inside. To be honest, I had quite a day of it yesterday when I was out with your dad, so a day spent around here taking things easy would be great if that is alright with you Pedro."

Pedro was more than happy to agree. As long as he was with his grandfather he was as happy as he could be, especially as his grandfather was going to help him sort out his marbles.

"Just let me finish my cup of tea and we'll get started," granddad said.

"O.K., I'll go and get things ready, see you round at the shed." Pedro told him.

By the time granddad reached the shed, Pedro had got everything ready. The rocks that still had to be opened were all lined up ready. "Want to open or polish, Grampy?" Pedro asked. "I don't mind at all young man," replied his granddad.

"Let's do half each then," said Pedro.

"Right you are, you start opening and I'll do these you opened the other day but never had time to polish."

They both set about doing their allotted tasks, Pedro chipping, and granddad polishing and sorting the marbles into their boxes according the patterns they had.

By the middle of the morning all the remaining rocks had been opened and the marbles inside polished and sorted. Some he had opened had contained only two stripes, which were sort of wavy with the same color. Pedro didn't think they would be much good so put them to one side.

"You certainly have a good selection here Pedro," remarked granddad.

"Yes, and quite a few different ones too, granddad, I wonder if they are all "Wishy Marbs.""

"I think your grandmother will be the best person to tell you that, young man."

Pedro liked it when his grandfather called him that. It made him feel a lot older than he was.

They finished sorting out the marbles according to their patterns and marks just as they heard someone shout from round the other side of the house. Pedro looked out the shed window to see Paul walking towards them, accompanied by Pedro's mother, and it was she who had shouted his name.

Pedro looked round to where they had been sorting the marbles, panic beginning to rise in him, but he saw that his grandfather had quickly put all of the boxes away except one. This one box contained the two marbles that he had had in his pocket when he had taken the test so had no stripes at all. He also put the marbles with the wavy stripes in there as well.

Just then, the door opened and his mother entered with Paul.

"Hello Pedro," said Paul, "thought I would pop round to see how you are, and to look at the marbles everyone at school was talking about."

Pedro was not happy to see Paul, but it was not in his upbringing to be nasty to people so he simply greeted him as he would any other of his friends, and explained that he and his grandfather had just finished polishing and sorting his last lot of marbles, brought home by his father before the holidays.

Paul moved over to where Pedro had indicated the marbles were and started to have a good look at them. Meanwhile, his mother had gone back to the house. Grandfather was sitting at the end of the other end of the bench polishing some marbles and putting them on their box.

"Which are the special ones your friends were talking about?" asked Paul.

"You must mean the ones I have just finished polishing," said granddad, pointing at the box on the bench. As Paul moved over to have a closer look, Pedro gave his grandfather a worried look, but he in return just gave Pedro a wink and look indicating for him not to worry.

"How many of these do you have?" enquired Paul.

"I'm not sure to be honest. I have some more but they are locked away and my dad has the key."

"I think they there were about eight that I saw," butted in granddad, "but I am not too sure." That at least was the truth. He had only seen the eight "Wishy Marbs" Pedro had brought out the night when his wife had told them what they were.

"Do any of the other children have any like these?" asked Paul.

"Not that I know of Paul." This again was the truth as he himself was the only one with these patterned marbles.

Paul stayed a little while longer just looking at things in general and asking quite a few questions all it seemed connected with the marbles and who had found what. He also asked Pedro if he had ever been to the mine with his father and if he had which area was it he worked in. Pedro told him that until next year he was too young to go to the mine on the regular 'Miner and Child' day but was hoping to go next year.

Pedro's mother then re-appeared at the shed to inform Pedro and his granddad that lunch was ready. She asked Paul if he would like to stay and eat with them but he said no thanks, as he had to get back to help his own grandfather with few things. They all started back to the house but as they got round the corner heading to the front gate Paul made an excuse to nip back to the shed, saying he must have dropped his handkerchief inside. They waited for him to return, walked him the rest of the way to the gate, said goodbye and watched as he hurried up the lane towards his grandfather's house

As they entered the house for lunch, granddad said he was quite confident that when they returned to the shed in the afternoon, one or more marbles would be missing.

"Do you really think so?" asked Mary.

"I'm certain of it," replied her father-in-law, "just as I am certain he was sent here by old man Bilk to see what he could find out. He asked far too many questions to have just called round to see a friend as he tried to make out."

"Hope you didn't tell him too much," his wife, who had listened to the conversation said."

"No, we didn't Joan, we told him nothing but the truth to the questions he asked. Mind you, if he had asked any awkward ones we may have been a bit pushed to answer honestly, but as it was, he went away with honest answers to questions his grandfather had obviously primed him to ask."

Mary announced that lunch was ready and for them to come to the table. Pedro's dad asked him if would like to go to the village with him in the afternoon. He said he had promised to take some of the flowers grown in their garden to the village store. The lady there made them into bunches of posies which the children bought for their mothers' on their birthdays.

"You are coming as well grampy?"

"No Pedro, I'll stay here with your mum but I think your grandmother would like to take a walk."

It was quite clear that grandfather was still a bit tired from the previous day's excursion.

"Yes, I'll come with you both," said his grandmother, "it will be nice to look round the old place again. I will show you where I used to live when I was your age."

Pedro was first to finish his lunch just ahead of his grandfather, who when he had finished suggested to Pedro that they go into the shed to see how many if any, marbles had been taken by Paul.

Pedro's father, who had been unaware of the visit, asked what he meant. His father quickly gave him brief details of what had happened in the morning. From what he was told, he agreed with his father that Paul had been sent round by old man Bilk on a "snooping visit".

"You two go off and check on things then, and by the time you have done that I will have collected the flowers to take with us and we can go."

The two of them walked on round to the shed wondering just what they would find. They looked on the bench to where the boxes of marbles had been placed.

"Just as I thought," said granddad pointing to the boxes, "two of the four striped marbles are missing."

"So are the two of the ones I opened this morning, the ones with the wavy lines," added Pedro, "but look here grampy, there are three other ordinary marbles in the box and they are not mine."

"It certainly looks like he came here prepared and intended swapping some of your marbles. How he hoped to get away with it I don't know. We do know that the ones with the four stripes won't be any good to him," granddad said, "as for the other ones, we have no idea what they were or what if anything they did."

They put everything away and locked the shed door as they left, then went back to the house to tell the others what they had discovered.

"Better not let on that we know anything for the time being," said grandmother when she heard, "and let's just see what, if anything comes of it all."

The three of then set off for the village each carrying an armful of flowers from the garden. They met Simon on the way who said that the Vet told him that Mut was doing fine, and would no longer need to take the tablets he was being given following his operation.

When they arrived at the village store there seemed to be a commotion going on, with quite a few people crowded round the main door.

"Wonder what is going on there." said Pedro's dad.

"Don't get too close," advised his mother, "we don't want to get involved."

They made their way to the shop attempting to enter by the main door to deliver their flowers. They were prevented from going inside by the amount of people wanting to see what was happening. When they got close enough they could see the imposing figure of Mr. Bilk shouting, and waving his arms at the present owner of the shop. What it was all about was not immediately clear, but certainly he was unhappy about something. His grandson Paul was by his side looking very sorry himself and, from what they could see very wet also.

"What happened," granny asked the person next to her.

"Don't really know for sure," said the lady, "I was here to get my cakes for my daughter's birthday party when that young man, over there in the yellow jumper, demanded that he be served first because his grandfather owned the shop and the whole village."

Upon hearing this, Tom's mother told him and the lady, that the village shop, the village hall, plus the land the village hall was located on, had nothing at all to do with the Bilk family. "In fact," she said turning to her son, "the village hall, plus the land it stands on belongs to me and your father."

"I never knew that," said her son.

"Not many people do, as we have tried to keep it quiet over the years," replied his mother.

"We were planning on giving you and Mary all the details and the paperwork while we are here this time."

By this time Mr. Bilk and his grandson were pushing their way through the crowd of people. Paul still looking very wet and very unhappy, was being led quite roughly by his grandfather who had his hand round Paul's upper arm They didn't seem to notice anyone standing there but Mr. Bilk did appear to be telling his grandson not to go around the village as if he owned the place. "Most of the people here work for me and I need to keep their respect, which will not be achieved if you go throwing the family name around, demanding this that and the other You are supposed to be staying with me to help me, but this is not the way to go about it."

It was very clear that Mr. Bilk was really very annoyed by what his grandson had started, and in fact looked quite uncomfortable and embarrassed by the whole situation.

The crowd had now all gone about their business so Pedro and his family went into the shop to hand over the flowers. Mrs. Trent, who ran the store and was the post mistress, was busy clearing up the mess at one end of the shop. She stopped what she was doing when Pedro's father said hello.

"Nothing like a bit of excitement to brighten the day Julia," he said trying to make light of the situation.

"I could certainly do without that sort of excitement that is for sure Tom." She then noticed that Pedro and his grandmother for the first time. "Hello Pedro," she said, "and how nice to see you again Joan." She went over and gave her old school friend a welcome hug.

"What on earth happened here Joan?"

"Well," said her friend, "that young lad who I now know to be Mr. Bilk's grandson came in here asking for some chocolate and demanding to be served first saying, 'did I know who he was?' and pushing himself to the front of the queue. Mr. Watson who was also in the shop just said to him gently that he should wait his turn and tried to move him away from the counter, where upon the young lad started shouting again, telling us we would all be sorry when his grandfather heard about the way he had been treated. At this point we still had no idea who he was."

"So what made all this mess Julia?" asked Tom.

"That is the bit about all this I can't quite understand Tom. The young lad stood over there by the shelves with the flowers on, pointed at me and started saying something like, ' I' wish...I wish I wish those shelves above your head would all fall down on you!' and as he said that, the shelves above his own head fell on him, covering him with water and flowers."

Joan could see that Julia was still very upset by what had happened and went over to comfort her. "Have a sit down for a while and take it easy, we'll give you a hand to clear up the mess, and I am sure Tom will be able fix the shelves for you."

"Thank you very much, you are very kind, but it is Mr. Bilk I am worried about. His grandson did have a bit of a cut on his forehead."

"I wouldn't worry about all that Julia," said Tom, "from what he was saying to Paul as he led him away, he was furious at the behaviour of his grandson. I wouldn't be a bit surprised if he sent Paul in later to apologise to you."

"That would certainly be a first, a member of the Bilk family saying sorry to someone." Joan said.

By this time, Tom was having a good look at the shelves that had caused all the trouble, but could find no reason why they had collapsed. He had managed to put them back where they should be and could find nothing at all wrong with the fittings. He even tried to pull on them but they wouldn't move at all. "Why these shelves collapsed will remain a mystery I think," He said, "I can't see anything wrong with them at all. It also seems as if only one vase broke, so we can put all the rest back for you Julia."

Pedro, who had been cleaning up the mess as best he could, announced that he had finished. Both his grandmother and Julia said he had done a good job. Julia also told him to go and help himself to an ice cream if he wanted one.

Once Pedro had his ice cream, and making sure that Julia was O.K. they left the shop to continue their walk through the village. Julia did ask them that if they wouldn't mind, could they call in and ask her assistant to come in and help her out for the rest of the day. She told them where she lived and Tom said it would be no trouble at all. He also said they would call in on their way back through on their way home to see that all was well.

The three of them walked on into the village discussing in general what had happened at the shop. Grandmother said that she thought there was a lot more to what had happened than appeared on the surface. "It is quite obvious," she said, "that Paul had clearly thought he had got some "Wishy Marbs" in his possession with what he had taken from you Pedro. But, and it is a big but, how did he know that maybe some of the marbles had magic powers. Old man Bilk must have got some sort of idea from somewhere. If he has, then that also goes a long way to explaining why he has been letting the miners take bits of rock each day. He must also have told Paul what to look out for. It could also mean," she went on, "that perhaps there were more old papers relating to the old mine other than those I have in my possession."

They carried on walking through the main street of the village. Pedro's grandmother was stopped quite a few times by people who recognised her and wanted to say hello and ask how she was, and if John was in good health. They also called at the house where the shop assistant lived and gave the message that Julie had requested her to go to work for the afternoon if she could. They gave her a rough idea of what it was about but said that Julie would give her more details when she got to the shop.

They continued to walk through the village and very soon came to where all the cottages had been boarded up. Tom's mother was quite upset at what she saw, so he led Pedro ahead a little to leave his mother to her own thoughts. His mother eventually caught up with them, and they soon they came to a junction in the road with the Church on the corner. They turned left and walked up the street until they came to a two storied house with a well, kept garden.

"This is where I lived when I was about your age Pedro," said his grandmother, "in fact, that big tree over in the corner is where I could climb from my bedroom, down to the ground if I didn't feel like going down the stairs." Pedro liked the idea of that.

After a while they decided to head for home. They called at the shop as promised but everything seemed to be O.K.

When they arrived home Tom and his mother relayed to his wife and father what had happened at the village shop. Pedro meanwhile went round to the shed so make sure all was well. He had decided while walking back, that he would move all his marbles back up to his bedroom, as he did not for one minute trust Paul not to call round again whether anyone was home or not, to see what he could get hold of.

CHAPTER THIRTEEN

THE PAPERS REVEAL MORE SECRETS

Following the visit to the village, it was agreed by everyone that in future they would look at the papers from the old lady only in the confines of the house.

When the evening meal was over grandmother once again opened the box and got out some of the papers. She unfolded the one sheet they had been looking at the previous evening, the one where it told them to "Let The Children Help You".

Pedro's grandmother asked him to come round to her side of the table, so she could show him what they had been looking.

"See these diagrams here," she said to Pedro, "your father was telling us that you have some marbles with the same kind of markings on them." When he confirmed that he had, his grandmother asked him if he would go and get them for her.

While he was away getting the marbles she told them that she had had an idea.

"Here you are granny," said Pedro, and placed the marbles on the table.

Granny took the marbles from her grandson and placed them in the diagrams at the bottom of the page, putting each marble on the appropriate diagram according to their markings. For a few seconds nothing happened, and granny was just about to think that her idea was wrong when the sheet of paper folded itself up round the marbles, making them all jump. It shot up in the air making funny sounds and giving off strange lights. It seemed to hover over the table for a little while, then settled back down and opened up again. This time when it opened up, they were faced with what appeared to be a moving picture of some sort of collection of buildings. It was just as if they were looking down on their own village but from a great height. In fact it was John who was the first to partly recover and pointed to what seemed to be the village church but not the one they knew.

Pedro, who had been just as shocked by what had happened, had hidden behind his grandmother and slowly moved back round to see what the rest of them were looking at. For a very long time, nobody said a word. They had all been shocked by what had occurred, but again it was John who brought their attention to the fact that the writing on the paper had changed to their own language.

"Can anyone read what it says," he asked.

"I can," said Pedro, and leaned forward to get a closer look. "It says that this is where the first lost people can be found. And we have to move the marbles around to learn more." When the paper had settled down again the marbles had remained inside the round marks.

"You do it then Pedro, they are your marbles." said granddad, moving out of the way to allow Pedro to reach the marbles.

Pedro put his hand very carefully on the marble with the stripes and slowly turned it. As they all watched the whole "model" of the village seemed to enlarge itself and they could actually see what they thought were people moving around. He continued to turn the marble and as he did so everything continued to get bigger. As he turned it more, the village got so large that they actually seemed to be part of it. They all continued to be amazed by what was taking place each one too mesmerised to say anything. As they looked they could see people walking around. It was just as if they were all sitting round a wooded table in the middle of the village. There was no evidence on the faces of the people that they could see the onlookers. It was just as if they were invisible to them.

"See anyone you recognise?" asked granny in a whispered voice.

"None that I can see," answered granddad, also in a whisper.

Granny had another idea and said in a louder voice, "Hello can you hear me?"

They all watched, but none of the people they were looking at made any indication they had heard anything,

"They obviously can neither hear us nor see us." said Mary, "what on earth are we going to do?"

By now it seemed as if the village had taken over the whole of the room they were sitting in. Pedro still had the piece of paper in his hand with his hand on the marbles.

"Turn the marble back again Pedro," instructed his grandmother.

Pedro did as he was asked and everything slowly went back to normal with the paper again just lying on the table. He removed the marbles from the diagrams and for a long time everyone just sat not saying a word.

Mary broke the silence with, "I think we could all do with a cup of tea after all that," at the same time getting up and heading for the kitchen.

While Mary was making the tea none of the others scarcely said a word, but just sat there trying to make some sort of sense of what had happened.

"So what does anyone think about what we have just seen?" said Mary as she brought in the tea.

"I'm sure I really don't know," replied her father-in-law, "that was the most amazing thing I have ever been part of. It's no wonder your old lady didn't want anyone else to get possession of what she passed on to you Joan."

"I agree," replied his wife, "and it frightens me a bit when I think of what other things I may have to do." She went on to say that although what they had seen appeared to be their village it was not as they knew it today. The church for instance was a lot smaller than the one they knew. Plus the people we saw were not wearing clothes as we know."

"One thing I noticed," said Tom "is that we saw no signs of any children." His parents agreed with what he had said.

Pedro who had been sitting very quietly since things had returned to normal said in a very quiet voice, "I wonder what would have happened if I had turned the second marble? I only turned the one with the stripes."

"I'm sure I don't know," said his father, "we will obviously have to do it all again sometime to see what happens when you do turn the second marble."

"Your father is right Pedro," commented his grandmother, "and when we do we will be more prepared for what we know will happen initially. Did you manage to read anything else on the paper at all?" she asked him.

"No I didn't granny." He still had the paper in his hand and looked down at it. "But look here," he said to everyone, "the writing has stayed in our language so we should be able read what it says."

He put the paper back on to the table so they could all see what he was talking about.

"You read it Pedro," said granddad, "your eyesight is probably better than any of ours this time of the evening."

Pedro had a closer look at the writing on the paper and started to read what it said. He read for a while and then looked up and said, "It says that the village we saw is the one where all the people were moved to, by some person called Mantel Helter many, many, years ago. It says this Mantel Helter was very displeased with the people and used the magic obtained from the ground to punish them by moving them back in time. They could only be brought back when someone with the correct knowledge made contact with them."

"I've heard of that Mantel Helter person before somewhere," said his grandmother. "It must have been in some of the other paperwork I was reading left by the old lady. Not a very nice person from what I can remember. It was a woman as far as I can recall, who had strange magic powers and used them in a not very nice way."

"Does it say anything else interesting Pedro?" enquired his father.

"Not as far as I can make out dad, just seems to repeat again that the people will only be released from their punishment when someone with the correct information or knowledge arrives in their village."

"What a horrible person that Mantel Helter must have been," said granddad, "wouldn't be at all surprised if she was related to the Bilks!" He said this in fun knowing that there could be no connection with that person and the Bilks, although as he said, "Many a true word said in fun!"

"There is something else here," said Pedro who had continued to read the Paper, "It says that some of the people who had been sent to this place would never grow any older than they were the day the spell was cast."

"That could be the reason we never saw many children," his mother said, "how awful and what a horrible thing to happen to anyone."

"Do you think we can do anything to help granny?" asked Pedro.

"Maybe, but I think we should have a real hard think before we do something that may harm these people instead of helping them. Goodness knows how many years ago this all happened."

Granddad who had been sitting very quietly deep in thought said, "I wonder, just wonder if all the people in our village and who we knew, who went missing, were treated in the same sort of way. After all, every person or family who went missing just seemed to vanish into thin air leaving their homes, possessions and friends."

"You may have a point John," said his wife.

"And what about the children we saw at the "Winter Shed" area and the voice Tom and I heard," continued his father. He realised as he said that, that Pedro did not know about the children disappearing behind the bush or about the voice he had heard, so quickly told him what had happened the day he and Tom had gone for their walk.

"If we are compiling things that seem to be connected with all this, don't forget what it said on one of the sheets we were looking at." They all looked at granny as she said this and then she reminded them, "Let The Children help you," she said.

"There is one more important item to remember also mum," said Tom, "and that is the two names we thought we saw written down."

"You are right Tom." She said then looked across at Pedro and explained that they thought they had seen his and Sally's name in the documentation they had been reading.

"Wonder what that all means." Pedro said to no one in particular.

"That is something we will have to look at very closely son," said his father, "but I think we have seen enough for one night and it is getting way past your bedtime."

"Goodness so it is," said granny. She then looked at Pedro quite concerned and asked him if he thought he would be able to sleep.

"Yes I will be O.K. thanks granny."

Before they put everything away for the night granny said to them all that it was very important that they mentioned to no one at all what they had found out. "It seems as if I, and all of us as a family, have been entrusted with this special task to solve the mystery. It might be that we will have to involve other people in the village, especially your friends Pedro, but until that time we will just proceed as we have started, and try to solve some of the mysteries ourselves, before we have to approach other members of the village."

The rest of the family agreed entirely with what she said.

CHAPTER FOURTEEN

MAKING CONTACT

The next morning, Pedro's father suggested to the family, as they all sat down to breakfast that perhaps for the next two days they should suspend all their activities concerning the marbles and mine etc. and give all their minds a chance to take a bit of a breather. Pedro was a little disappointed but his granny made a promise to her grandson that on Friday evening they would all get together again and she would inform them all of anything new she had found out.

Granddad came to the rescue by suggesting that they go and see Simon's parents and ask if it was alright for him to go with Pedro and himself for the night out he had promised. Pedro thought this was a good idea and got really excited about it. They went to Simon's house to ask his parents who readily agreed. The three of them plus Mut set off in the early afternoon. All three of them plus Simon's dog had a really good time, and both the boys learnt an awful lot from what granddad showed them, and told them about things that went on in and around the countryside. The diversion worked and all thoughts of what had happened about his marbles and the mine went completely from his mind.

Grandma meanwhile had used the peace in the house to relax a little and sit by herself, looking through more of the papers. She explained to Tom and Mary that she felt it was her duty to study everything she felt relevant to what had happened. She told them that on Friday evening as promised, she would be in a position to reveal as much as she had managed to find out. Tom and Mary spent much of that time working in the garden and taking some of the produce to the village shop, leaving Joan completely on her own to study the documents.

Lunchtime Friday saw the return of the "Adventurers" as Pedro called themselves. He said he and Simon had a really great time and looked forward to when they could go again as granddad had said they would.

"Let's go and sort out all the equipment Pedro," suggested his father, "it will need to be cleaned and the tents will need to be hung over the washing line to air and then folded away properly."

The sorting out of the camping equipment took them all afternoon so by time it was all completed it was time for the evening meal.

When the meal was finished, grandma suggested that the table be completely cleared of everything, so she could spread out the papers, and notes she had made during her study of the contents of her envelopes.

With this completed, the family watched as she laid everything out. She also put on the table one of the funny shaped boxes that she had been given. No one had ever seen it before and wondered what it was. "All part of the mystery." was all she would say. She asked Pedro to come and sit next to her so he could help her when required. This set Pedro's mind wondering on just what he would be required to do and said as much to his grandmother. Again her answer was short and to the point, "Be patient, and you will see."

When everyone was settled she began to tell them what she had found out so far.

"Before I tell you what some of the papers have revealed," she said, "I will tell you what I think happened to young Paul in the shop the other day." She looked at Pedro and asked him just what was on the marbles Paul had taken from the shed. He told her that Paul had taken four with four stripes, and also two he had opened that morning which had wavy lines on them. Granddad butted in here and told her that the four he had taken were the four she had "fixed" by removing their magic and that he had put them on the bench while Paul was busy looking the other way.

"That confirms to me what I think happened. It seems as if the marbles with the wavy lines are called "Punishment Marbs" and when someone tries to use a wish to harm anyone, then they actually work on the person making the wish. So, when Paul wished that shelves would fall on Mrs. Trent, the wish worked against him and the shelves above his head collapsed on him instead."

"Bet that gave him a shock granny."

"I expect it did Pedro, but I doubt if he knew what caused it. He probably thinks it just happened.

It would be interesting to know how many of the stripes were used, but I doubt if we will ever find out. Hopefully, if old Bilky does have a bit of information about some of the marbles, and how he got that I don't know, I doubt also that he would know anything about the "Punishment Marbs."

Granny then drew everyone's attention back to the papers on the table. She told them that as far as she had been able to work out, the disappearances, which had happened many years before, had been done as a sort of punishment against either a single person or in some cases entire families. Why, she had not been able to find out yet, as some of the papers were in that strange language they could not understand. That could also explain, she went on, how the entire village vanished all those years ago from the Winter Shed.

"I think," she went on, "that my old lady unearthed some sort of records about things that had gone on in the past and spent the best part of her life trying to discover more, and at the same time trying to put things right. I also think that by giving me the things she did, she felt in some way that she was doing just that."

Granny then amazed them all by suggesting that her old lady had actually travelled back, using some sort of magic, to a time when some of these dreadful things took place.

"How could she do that do you think mum?"

She looked at her son and said she thought it would have been done, by using a box like the one she had put on the table. They all looked at it as she said that. It was the box that appeared to be in three sections but although they moved slightly could not be separated. They could see it had carvings of three flowers on the top, each with a hole in the middle of the petals. The edges of the holes were each marked with a different colour.

"What do you think the box does Joan?" asked her husband.

"I don't know exactly John, but I don't think we should try anything until we are absolutely certain we know what we are doing." She really emphasised her statement and they all agreed.

"There is something I think we can do," she went on, "and that is, I think we should have another try at going back to that village we visited the other evening, and if possible try some sort of communication. We know what to expect now so we won't be caught out or surprised."

Everyone thought it was a good idea and Pedro surprised everyone by coming up with another one.

"Why don't leave some sort of a note if we can," he said.

"That is a brilliant idea Pedro," granddad said, "but as they could not see us when we were there last time, how could we leave something for them to see?"

"I don't know granddad it was just an idea I had." said Pedro.

"I think that is a very good idea," granny said, "let's write a small message and attempt to leave it somewhere if we can."

"What shall we put on it?"

"Just something like "Hello we would like to help you"," I think said granny, "in fact if we did manage to leave one we could watch to see if anyone noticed it and picked it up."

"Just one more thing before we go on our travels," granny said, "Once we are there, I am going to ask Pedro to slowly turn the second marble to see what happens."

The whole family then got themselves ready and granny laid out the paper with the two circles on the bottom as she had before. She asked Pedro if he was ready and when he said he was asked him to put the two marbles inside the circles. He did this and just as on the previous time the paper shot up in the air with the same sort of sounds and bright lights. When it settled back on the table they could again see a plan of the village. Pedro looked at his granny who gave a nod and he started to turn the striped marble very slowly. As before the "village" enlarged itself until once again it seemed as if they were part of it. Although they were still at their own table it was just as if they were sitting at a table in the middle of the village. There were people walking around as before but they appeared not to notice their visitors. As they just sat there, it appeared as if one couple actually walked through them. It seemed so lifelike that granddad actually moved to one side because they were heading directly at him.

"Turn the other marble Pedro"

Pedro, with his other hand slowly turned the spotted marble. Nothing seemed to happen but then they could all hear the people talking. The more he turned it the louder the voices became. It was acting just like a volume control.

"Can you hear me?" tried granny in a quiet voice, but as they watched there was no indication that anyone had heard anything. She tried it again this time much louder and they saw that at least one person, a rather older man, seemed to look up into the air as if trying to locate whatever it was he thought he had heard. The old man appeared slightly different from the rest of the people. He was also dressed more like the clothes the family was wearing. He seemed to have a bit of a limp. As he walked they could see that his left leg appeared to be much thinner than his right leg, and that was the one causing the limp.

"We are here to help you," said granny. This time the old man appeared to look in the direction he thought the voice was coming from.

The man looked in their general direction and said something, but as with the notes on the papers they had been reading, it was in a language they could not understand.

"Try putting the note down Pedro," said his father.

Pedro placed the note very close to where the man was standing, but he didn't see it.

They continued to watch for several more minutes but nothing changed so granny suggested to Pedro that he turned the marbles back again to return them back to their own room.

"Well that was very interesting," commented Mary, "It appears they can hear us, or at least that older man could, but can't see us."

"It certainly seems that way," agreed her mother-in-law. "We will have to study the papers a little bit more carefully to see if we can gain any other clues as to how we might make contact. In the meantime," she continued, "I have an idea to discuss with you all about how we might discover the mystery concerning the two children you saw at the old Winter Shed area John, and the voice you heard as well."

"Let me make us all a drink before we hear you thoughts," said Mary, "it will also give us a chance to relax a little after what we have just seen."

Joan thought that was a good idea and asked her son in the meantime if he would bring her the medallion he had found on his walk with his father.

When they were all settled back round the table with their drinks, granny outlined her idea.

"It appears," she said picking up the medallion Tom had given her, "that this old school identity disc may give us a clue as how we might contact some of the missing people. You say John that you saw two children running towards and then just disappearing behind a bush," Her husband nodded and said that was what he had seen.

"In that case, I wonder if this medallion somehow triggered the bush to move, so the children could escape behind it, and in their panic to get away from you John they dropped it."

"I think you are right about that my dear," her husband agreed, "but what about the voice I heard, do you have any ideas about that?"

"Yes I have," his wife said. "Over the past two days as you know, I have been studying those papers more closely, and I think I have come across a plan that may indicate a little more about the Winter Shed. Remember I told you that it was the custom all those years ago for the whole village to assemble for the winter in that one large building. I also told you in answer to a question you put to me Tom that the miners continued to go to work by entering the mine through an entrance close to the back of the building. The plan I have been looking at in one of the papers, showed some sort of plan of a very large building divided into various sections but as it was in that strange writing, I could not understand it."

She looked at her husband and said, "It also seemed to indicate a sort of passage leading from the back of the building, which could be where the entrance to the mine was located. I think somehow, someone, and this could be your old friend Joshua, John, has managed to make his way along that old entrance but could get no further because it was blocked by the wreckage of the old building. Probably on hearing your voices he took a chance and called out to you."

"I wonder why he didn't continue," said Tom.

"That I can't answer," replied his mother, "and that is why I think we should make some sort of effort to get in touch with whoever is behind both the bush and the building."

"So what is your idea granny?" asked Pedro.

"My idea," she said, looking at Pedro, "is for you three men to take a walk round to that area again one afternoon. When you get there, let your grandfather show you the bush where he saw the two children disappear. All of you walk carefully towards it, holding the medallion in your hand, and see if anything happens to the bush."

"What should we do if it does move, or something?" asked Pedro.

"That will be for your father and grandfather to decide, Pedro but I would strongly recommend that we do nothing rash at this point until we know what we are up against. The mystery has stayed hidden all these years so there is no need to rush at things. Whatever forces put the people where they are may still be there and if we do something which, although we would be doing it with the best of intentions, may just make things worse for them."

Her son promised his mother that they would do nothing, apart from approaching the bush as she had requested, but look around the area to see if they could find any other evidence of activity since they were last there.

"Thank you Tom, but of course it doesn't mean that if you hear a voice again you shouldn't try to set up a conversation with whoever is attempting to talk to you."

All the talk about the future re-visit to the sight had completely taken their minds away from what they had started the evening attempting. It was Pedro who brought the subject back to their attention by asking what the funny little box on the table was for.

His grandmother explained to them that she was sure that it was connected to what they had tried earlier in the evening, and that was to make contact with the people in the village. As they had failed to make any significant progress, then the time was not right to bring the box into operation.

The rest of the evening was spent deciding on when Pedro and his father and grandfather would go back to the site. His grandfather thought that they had better wait a couple of days. When he was asked why, he explained that after the episode in the village shop, he wouldn't be surprised if old man Bilk would be sniffing around.

"He obviously has a very rough idea in his mind that some of the marbles from the mine are different from the majority and because of the visit to see Pedro by his grandson, and what happened later, you can be sure that he will be keeping an eye on this family." said grandfather. "Now don't go getting all upset and worried about what I have just said," he continued, looking around at them all. "We just need to continue as normal, and act as any other family around here. Just make sure that anything to do with what we have discovered and especially your marbles Pedro are kept out of sight and locked away."

Grandmother completely agreed with what her husband had said, and also suggested that the next day she should fix a couple more of Pedro's marbles as she had before just in case "Bilky" did come round asking questions. She added that they must also bear in mind that it was quite possible that they would eventually need to involve one or more other families in the village, reminding them that they thought they had seen Pedro's friend Sally's name in the writings they had been studying.

CHAPTER FIFTEEN

THE RE-VISIT

Everything for the next few days carried on as normal as any other family household. Granny did as she had suggested and did indeed 'doctor' two more of Pedro's marbles so they no longer had any powers.

The half expected visit from any member of the Bilk family did not happen, and even on any of the family's trips into the village there was no sign that either Paul or his grandfather had been back since the episode in the village shop. The only person from the bilk household who had been seen was the housekeeper who had been in to do the normal shopping which she did every week. When asked by Mrs. Trent how Paul was, she was told quite abruptly that she had no idea what she was talking about.

Granny on being told this by her friend, commented that the housekeeper had more likely been told not to mention anything if asked. As she obviously valued her position in the Bilk household she did what she had been told.

It was more than a week before Grandmother thought it was safe enough for a re-visit to the site of the 'Winter Shed'. It was decided that the best day for it would be a Saturday, for the very reason that it was the day when she and Mary went into the village with any produce from the family garden. The male members of the family never accompanied them on this outing, so the trip would be seen as a normal Saturday visit by Mary and her mother-in-law.

There was a bus that passed by their house about ten thirty on Saturday mornings, so the ladies decided that because they had quite a bit of produce to carry they would use it to travel to the village.

Pedro and his grandfather and father, waved them on their way then prepared themselves for their walk to the 'Winter Shed'. Pedro had remembered to ask his grandmother for the medallion his father had found and it was safely in his jacket pocket.

It didn't take long to walk to where they needed to be. The first thing they had decided to look for was any evidence that anyone else had been there, or if there were any footprints around either the bush or the place where the voice had been heard.

As far as they could tell, nothing had disturbed the sandy ground other than they had noticed before. In fact there seemed to be less marks on the ground. Tom, discussing this with his father, agreed with him, thought it was likely that the ground had been cleared a little by the higher winds that had been blowing the past few days.

They both showed Pedro the large bush where the children had been seen, and asked him if he was ready to try out their little experiment.

He told them he was, and took the medallion from his pocket. His grandfather told him to just walk slowly towards the bush. He told Pedro that he and his father would be right behind him.

The three of them, with Pedro leading, walked towards the bush watching carefully to see if anything happened. When they were about three feet away they thought could detect a slight movement, which they hoped, was more than that caused by the slight breeze that was blowing but at the same time was probably wishful thinking.

"Hold the medallion out a little Pedro," whispered granddad.

Pedro did as he was asked and lifted his arm up a little and pointed the medallion directly in the direction they were walking.

Sure enough, as they got closer the bush did indeed move out from the bank it was growing against. They moved closer still and very soon they could definitely see some sort of small opening behind the thick foliage. Anyone going through there would have had to crouch down to enter the space.

Pedro looked round to his father and asked what they should do. He in turn looked at his own father who told them that he didn't think they ought to proceed any further, as they were not sure what they would find.

"Let's do what your mother suggested son and not do anything we can't be sure of."

His son agreed and suggested that they get as close as they could without actually entering the space, to see if they could detect any sound, but after moving almost but not quite behind the bush, they could see or a hear nothing at all. Grandfather put his hand gently on Pedro's shoulder and slowly eased him back from the bush. As he did so it slowly moved back, to where it was before.

The three of them walked away from the bush not saying a word for quite a while.

"Well, at least it wasn't my imagination after all,"joked granddad, "and it proves that indeed, there is something strange and mysterious about this area."

He moved over towards where he was certain he had heard the voice, picking up a stick on the way, saying he wanted try something else. Pedro and his father followed him and watched as he lifted the stick and the side of the shed where he thought he had first heard the voice. He gave a series of loud knocks, which he repeated three times in succession. Five loud knocks a slight wait five more and then another wait before five more. He explained to the other two that what he had just carried out was the old signal, which was used many years ago whenever a miner got lost or was maybe trapped by falling earth. It was used to let the lost or trapped miner know that help was on the way.

Pedro had just started to ask his grandfather if there was a reply signal when they all distinctly heard four sets of four loud knocks from behind where grandfather had knocked with his stick.

"Shush." Granddad said holding his finger to his lips, walking back to repeat his first signal with the stick. Almost immediately the reply signal was heard. Moving closer to the side of the shed and dropping his stick he asked who was there.

"Who are you?" asked a very faint voice, "can you help us?"

"This is John Vendell, who are you?"

"John! Is that really you? This is Joshua, remember me?"

"Joshua! My old friend! Of course I remember you. What are you doing there and how can we help?"

"Can you return early in the morning tomorrow, before your sunrise, we are not so closely watched then?"

That was all he heard before granddad turned to Pedro and his son.

"Did you hear all that?" he asked them. They told him that had heard most of it. Tom could see that his father was visibly upset by the short conversation and suggested that he sat down on the grassy bank and had a little rest.

Pedro walked back to where his grandfather had been and put his ear close to the side of the shed. He listened for a while and thought he could hear lots shouting slowly getting fainter. When he could no longer hear anything he went over to his father and grandfather to tell them what he had heard.

"There seemed to be an awful lot of yelling and shouting going on, and then it all went quiet." He told them.

"I wonder what he meant by before 'your' sunrise," Tom said, "and what did he mean when he said that they weren't so closely watched. It's almost as if they are in a prison."

"I'm sure I don't know son, but we will certainly have to return in the morning as he asked us to. I just hope there is some way we can help him and whoever else is trapped behind there."

Suddenly, Pedro, who had been sitting there beside his father grabbed his arm and in a whispered voice drew his attention to the bush they had been looking at before. As they all watched in silence the bush moved away from the hillside as it had done before. They continued to watch, and as they did so, they saw an arm appear from behind the opening. It was at ground level so whoever it belonged to must have been lying down. The hand of the arm slowly and deliberately dug a shallow hole in the ground just past the opening. It continued digging for a while and then withdrew into the opening. Within seconds it reappeared again, this time holding something, which it placed in the hole it had just made. It then covered it up again, smoothed the sand over, and withdrew behind the bush. The bush then moved back against the hillside.

"Shall I go and see what was buried there?" Pedro asked.

"Yes I think you should," answered his grandfather, "It is obvious who put whatever it there intended us to collect it."

"Leave the medallion here though Pedro." said his father. "We don't want to move the bush again."

Pedro walked over to the bush and slowly scraped away the sand until he could feel something under his fingers. He dug a little more then found what had been buried there. It was some kind of book. He pulled it right out, and replaced all the sand into the hole. As he stood up to return to his father and grandfather he heard a sound. He listened and was certain the voice, which he thought belonged to a girl said 'thank you'.

Pedro walked slowly backwards, with the book in his hand all the time looking at the bush. He bumped into his father who had been watching and had come to see why Pedro was walking backwards. He asked him what had happened and Pedro told him about the voice thanking him.

They both walked back to where granddad was still sitting and sat down beside him and told him what had happened. Pedro realised he still had the book in his hand and gave it to his father.

"This is what was buried there, dad." He said. "It looks like just like the books we have at school."

His father took the book from him, and after studying it for a while looked at his own father and asked him what the surname was of his friend he had just been communicating with. His father told him it was Temple, and asked him why he wanted to know. Tom said nothing but just held the book he was holding so his father could read the name on the cover. The name, although the writing was a bit faded clearly said Rebecca Temple. His father just sat there staring at the book his son was showing him.

"Isn't that the name of mum's best friend when she was at school and the sister of Joshua?"

"Yes it was, is," replied his father who was now, Tom could see getting quite upset again.

"Come on dad let's get you home, I think this is all becoming a bit tiring for you."

John allowed his son to help him to his feet and all three of them started to slowly walk home. He needed to rest a couple more times before they eventually reached their house. As soon as they walked through the door, Joan could see there was something wrong with her husband. She asked him what the matter was but he walked straight past her with a dismissive wave of his hand and went and sat down very heavily in the large armchair by the fireplace.

"What on earth is wrong with your father Tom?"

Tom said nothing, just handed the rather dirty book they had found to his mother. This time it was she who turned quite pale in colour.

"Where did you find this Tom?"

Tom suggested to his mother that she too should sit down. When she was settled, he began to explain to her all that had occurred on their return visit to the 'Winter Shed' site.

"Something is definitely going on there Mum," and then told her everything, from the bush moving as Pedro held the medallion, to the way his father had knocked on the side of the shed, and then

Joshua answering him, and finally to them all seeing the bush move again and the hand burying the book she was now holding. He then told her that Joshua had asked then to return in the morning before 'your' sunrise and he would be able talk to them better.

"It sounded, from what this Joshua was telling dad, that they are being watched by someone, and early in the morning was O.K. but what he meant by 'your' sunrise I have no idea."

"How did Pedro take all this?" asked Mary.

"He was just great Mary, and behaved as if this sort of thing happens to him all the time." replied Tom.

"So what are your intentions now Tom?"

Tom told his mother that he intended to return to the site early in the morning, hopefully with his father but if his father felt like he was not up to it then he would go alone. He said that Joshua was obviously relying on them to go back, and was putting himself at some considerable risk to try to talk to them again, so it was only fair they should make the effort.

"I'm sure he will want to go Tom, Joshua was his best friend but what about Pedro?"

"Well mum, if he wants to come with us and everyone is in agreement, I think he should be allowed to. As we have said before, if it wasn't for him finding the marbles then we wouldn't doing all this. He has been in it right from the start."

"I'll go and ask him, I think he went up to his room when you all arrived back." Pedro's mum said.

Tom asked his father how he felt about going out again in the early morning. His father replied that he would be fine by then. He said he was still a bit shocked hearing his friend's voice after all these years.

"What time do you think we should leave?" Tom asked his father, "and what do you think Joshua meant about 'your' sunrise?"

"I am sure I don't know. As for the time to leave, I think we should be in position as early as possible, and as far as Pedro is concerned, then I think yes, he should be allowed to join us if he wants to. He has behaved very grown up about all this right from the start."

Pedro's mother came back into the room to say that Pedro would like to go back out there in the morning and was already talking about going to bed straight after tea. She also asked her husband and father-in-law if they would want to take any sandwiches with them. They both thought that would be a very nice idea.

Grandma who had been quietly inspecting the book her son had given her, said that as far as she could tell, everything written in the book appeared to date back to the time when she herself was at school, which as she freely admitted was 'many years ago'. The teacher's name on the cover was one she remembered as being a very kind lady called Miss. Tilk who had changed the first letter of her name so that people would not associate her with the infamous mine owner. Her name had in fact been Bilk but that had just been a coincidence and was no way connected to the mining family.

"She was a really lovely lady, and in was another person who mysteriously went missing the same time as a lot of others in the village."

"Is there anything else in the book to give us a clue as to what is going on mum?" Tom asked.

"Not really Tom, it is just a book we used at school at the time, and there doesn't even appear that anything new has been written in it since then." His mother replied.

She told them she would continue to study it during the evening and if she found anything interesting before they left for the site then she would tell them.

Chapter Sixteen

Dawn Visit

Pedro was awake very early the next morning. Although when he had gone to bed the night before he didn't think he would be able to sleep, because of the thought of the next day's adventure, he had in fact slept very well. Now he could hear voices downstairs and realised that everyone else was already up an about. He had a wash, got dressed and was just going downstairs when his mother called up to tell him that breakfast was ready. He had never been up before as far as he could remember when it was still dark.

After breakfast everyone sat round the table discussing what the visit was all about, and what they would do or say should they make contact again with Joshua.

Granny said that although she had studied the book very carefully, she could find nothing else that might help them. She told them that she had thought of writing a message on one of the pages and getting them to open the bush again and throw it in, but she said that perhaps if they did that then they could well cause trouble to whoever put it there in the first place. "It seems to me that the people behind the bush and shed certainly have something or someone they need to be weary of," she said, "so I think the best thing you men and Pedro can do today is to go along to the shed area and see what occurs. If contact is made try to get as much information as you can."

She turned to her husband and continued, "If you think it is safe and you have time, and it is your friend Joshua, then by all means tell him a little of what we have been finding out and ask him how we may help, if in deed we can." She finished by stressing to them again to be very wary, adding, "We have no idea what we are up against."

Granddad suggested that they had better be leaving, as they needed to be there well before dawn. He checked again with Pedro if he still wanted to go with them and Pedro assured them he did.

"Do you have the medallion Pedro?" granny asked, "It might be that you may need it"

Pedro told her that his father still had it from the time before when they were there and he had gone to collect the book and had not wanted to activate the bush by mistake. His father told him that he would keep it for the time being for the same reason.

With that settled the ladies wished their men folk good luck as they left for the site.

It took them a little longer to get there in the dark but they were in place in plenty of time. It was still quite dark although a little bit of light could be seen in the distance where dawn was slowly approaching.

Granddad suggested that they had better wait close to the side of the shed where they had spoken to his friend the afternoon before. They thought this was a good idea and settled down to wait. They had only been there about five minutes when they heard faint sounds coming from behind the wood. The tapping of the old rescue code could be clearly heard and granddad had no hesitation in sending the reply code back.

"Is that you out there, John? This is Joshua."

"Yes this is me," replied granddad, "how are you and what can we do for you?"

"Well, I hope you will be able to help us get out of here, old friend."

"We will do all we can, that's for sure, but we need to know how. How long can you stay here and talk?" asked granddad.

"Not much more than about half of one of your hours. We are not really looked over during the night time."

There was so much, granddad wanted to ask his friend but he thought a lot of what he wanted to say and ask could wait until another time. The important thing now was to see what they could do to help the people behind the shed.

"So how can we help you all Joshua? And how many of you are there back there?"

"There are many of us here in this village but a great many more in the other land."

Just tell us what you can my friend in the time you have. I have my son Tom here with me, and my grandson Pedro. We three plus my wife and daughter –in– law are the only ones who know about this place although the ladies have not been here."

Joshua went on to say that it would be a great help if someone could try to get through to them from the outside. "We have been trying for ages but we are watched so closely that we cannot always stay out there for more than about one of your hours. In fact the children are the ones who have been doing most of the work as they are not so easily missed on this side, but as they are only young and not very strong they haven't had much success."

He went on to tell them that they had discovered this old entrance to the mine many months ago and had slowly been digging away to try to get through. Because of the way they were closely watched it was only possible to work at night, and even then they had to do it all in the dark as they had no means of lighting on his side.

"We have not been able to work very often and when we do we can only work for so long or else we may be too tired the next day to do the work we are expected to do on our side. If that were to happen then it may be discovered that we had been doing something else instead of sleeping. So far they leave us more or less alone once we had been locked in our huts for the night. The only time they come round is if there is something they want doing during the night. If that happens then they usually tell us in advance and we are sent home early to get some rest."

Granddad told him that they would be more than willing to do what they could. "Does anyone watch things from this side?" he asked Joshua.

"Not as far as I know," his friend replied, then went on to explain that he was sure that the "watchers' had no idea that they had found a way out through the bush. "We found that out, completely by accident one day. As it is, it is only the children who can get out that way. One of them is my own daughter Rebecca. She's the one who left her schoolbook for you to find. She also dropped her old school medallion in the hope you would be able to open the bush from your side."

Granddad told Joshua that they had found the book and the medallion and had actually managed to get the bush to move, but not knowing what was on the other side had just had a look and closed it again. He then asked his friend if he wanted them to try to break all the way through the woodwork.

"Not all the way through, at least not until we have a definite plan for getting out of here. Just knowing that someone is on the other side will really keep our spirits up. What I will do John," he went on, "is to drive a short wooden stake through from this side, so when you reach your end of it then you can let me know and I will know you are only a little way from breaking through."

Joshua said he had better be going soon but would be able to get back there in two days at the same time.

"Is there anything we can get for you?" granddad asked.

"Not really, it is just wonderful to know you are out there and willing to help." He told them that he wasn't sure how many people on his side he could trust to tell things to, and granddad told him that it was the same for him.

"Would it help if we wrote you a note telling you what we had found out and left it by the bush the way the book had been left?"

"That would be great John. It is only Rebecca and her two friends who go out through the bush so it would be quite safe."

"That's what we will do then," said granddad. "We will leave the note inside the book and bury it in a small hole just like Rebecca did when she left it for us. We will bring it tomorrow so we can put it there in the daylight." Granddad told Joshua they would put the book there just after midday his time. He also said that they would not wait around when Rebecca collected it in case she got a bit nervous when she retrieved it.

Joshua then said he really did have to go as it was beginning to get light his side and he needed to get back to his hut before the doors were unlocked.

Granddad said goodbye and told him he would speak to him in two days' time.

By this time it was just about light their side and granddad suggested that they started to make their way back home. His son agreed but thought it wouldn't hurt to have a quick look at what it was they were supposed to do to break through to Joshua and his friends.

The area where they had been speaking to Joshua was a bit of the shed that appeared to have a few loose boards. They supposed that it was what the children had been trying to do, but not being very strong and only trying to do it with their bare hands, had not got very far.

"I think," said Tom, "If we move about three of these boards it will give us a space to work in, then when we have finished each time we can replace them and no one will know we have been here."

His father thought it was a good idea and also suggested that they find a place where they could hide their tools so they didn't have to carry them there each time.

Once again it was Pedro who came up with the idea of opening the bush and just slipping them inside the space.

"What a brilliant idea Pedro, we'll check if that is O.K. next time we speak to Joshua." said his father.

The three of them then slowly made their way back home to tell the ladies what had happened. On the way back granddad and Tom discussed whether or not now might be a good time to see if the ladies thought it was time to discuss involving anyone else in what they were doing. They thought that perhaps it was time and would put the suggestion to them when they got home.

"We certainly can't continue with everything ourselves," said granddad. "The question is who to ask, and certainly who we think we can trust to keep it secret." His son agreed and gave it some deep thought as they continued home.

They were very close to their house when they heard someone calling Pedro's name. Looking over to their right they saw Paul running towards them.

"Where did he come from?" muttered granddad, "bit early for him to be out isn't it?"

By this time Paul had caught up with them. He said hello and asked where they had been so early.

"Nothing like an early walk to give you a good appetite for breakfast young man." said granddad, "but I could ask the same of you, you are certainly out and about early as well."

Paul told them that his granddad had suggested to him that as it was a nice bright morning he might like to go for an early walk also. He told them that it would be good for him to get to know the area a bit more as he was now living there. He said his grandfather had asked him to go up to the farm to get some milk but he seemed to have taken the wrong direction and had not found the farm. That was when he had spotted the three of them.

"We'll show you where to go," said Pedro, "in fact I expect mum could do with some milk as well so I will go with you. Come with us to our house then I will show you a quick way for you to get back once you have the milk."

Paul thanked them and walked with them He asked them where they had been and granddad told him that they had been nowhere in particular. "Like I said just a nice walk to build up the appetite for breakfast."

By this time they had reached their house and Pedro went to find his mother first, to see if they did need any milk, and secondly to warn her and his grandmother that Paul was with them and not to say anything about where they had been.

"Yes we do need some milk Pedro, the container is in the kitchen," said his mother. She saw Paul then and asked him if he had a container for the milk. He told her he hadn't thought about it and certainly his grandfather had not said anything about one.

"Well we have a spare one if you would like to use it. I expect your grandfather just never thought of it."

Paul thanked her, took the container she offered him and then he and Pedro set off for the farm.

When the boys had gone, grandmother asked where they had met Paul. Her husband explained that he had caught up with them as they were walking home. In answer to her next question he said that no, he didn't think Paul has seen where they had been. He said that they were a good way from the site and over the other side of the hill from it, when Paul had spotted them.

His wife said that that was a relief but that they would have to be careful in future if he was going to be wandering around all the time. Her husband agreed and joked that they would soon have to employ lookouts!

CHAPTER SEVENTEEN

PUNISHMENTS

During the day the family carried on as normal. Pedro returned with the milk and told them that Paul had not really asked him anything else about where they had been so early in the morning. He said that to try and put him off a bit, he told him that it just so happened that he was awake at the same time as his father and grandfather and they just thought it was a good idea to go for an early walk.

"That seemed to satisfy him, but I still don't trust him," said Pedro. The adults agreed, and said that they must assume that anything that Paul did or said, was instigated by his grandfather.

"He did ask me when I was next going for milk and I told him that it would be the day after tomorrow."

Pedro looked at his father and said that he thought if he said that, and in fact he did go and Paul went with him, then he and his grandfather could go and contact Joshua again knowing that they were safe to do so.

"That was a good idea Pedro," said his father, thinking that in all that was happening, his son seemed to have suddenly grown up both as a person and in his way of thinking. He, of course had no idea that his own mother had been instrumental in the way his son was now acting and behaving.

Pedro went into the village with his mother in the afternoon while his grandfather had a bit of a rest because of the early start they had had that morning. His mother told Pedro that she wanted to call in the Post Office to see that Julia was alright after the incident a few days earlier. When they got to the shop they were told by the other assistant that Julia was in fact not at work that day. When Mary asked why not, she was told that the previous evening as she was locking up the shop, Julia had heard some noises out the back of the premises, and when she went to investigate, she saw two people leaving from the back entrance with what appeared to be some of the old boxes that were stored there. She had been unable to see clearly who it might have been but they were small people she was sure of that. The whole incident had really shaken here up and consequently did not feel like working the next day. The assistant Janet said that Julia had called in at her house on the way home and asked her if she would kindly look after the shop for her.

Mary asked if the incident had been reported to anyone but Janet said that as far as she knew, no it had not been reported. Apart from anything else Julia was not at all sure just what had been taken.

"I'll mention it to Tom when I get home and see what he thinks," Mary said, "and on our way home Pedro and I will call in to see how Julia is."

"Wonder what that was all about." said Pedro as they left the shop.

"I'm sure I don't know but we will tell you father and grandparents when we get home to see what they think."

They called in at Julia's as promised and she assured them that she was feeling a lot better, but was very worried about what had happened the previous evening. Mary tried to put her mind at rest saying that it seemed as if nothing much was taken but at the same time would ask Tom to see about making the back gate more secure. Julia said that she wished she could be more helpful about who it might have been, but apart from the fact that whoever it had been had been small in height she had no idea at all who it might have been.

Upon returning home, Mary related to her husband and parents –in- law what had happened at the Post Office. Tom told her that he would go to the shop the next day and see about making the back gate more secure.

"Funny things certainly seem to be happening," commented grandmother, and added that she wouldn't be at all surprised if everything that was happening was all connected in some mysterious way. She also suggested that they try to revisit the 'Paper Village' as they had started to call the place they were transported to when they opened the map. "And this time," she said, "I think we will just sit there and observe what might be going on and not try to make contact."

The others agreed and so after the evening meal, they once again cleared the table, and granny slowly unrolled the map. As on the previous occasions the map lifted its self into the air and settled back down on the table. This time when it had settled they appeared to be in a different part of the village. The church was no longer visible and they seemed to be looking at a rather large green area just like the village green in Marbleville. With a nod from his grandmother, Pedro placed the striped marble in the circle on the map and as on the other times he slowly turned it so that it seemed that either they got smaller or the village scene before them got bigger so that they were once again part of the scenery.

This time they appeared to be sitting at their table, which was situated at the top of a small slope overlooking a large group of people who were all sitting or standing around the green. They were just chatting to one another, but after a short while they all looked in one direction to a very large figure that had appeared to the left of where Pedro and his family were sitting and observing.

He was a very imposing looking man, dressed in a long green and black cloak that covered him from head to toe. It had a hood attached, but was this was hanging down his back. He was holding in his left hand some sort of rod or staff, which seemed to be carved the whole of its length. On top of the rod was a very nasty looking head or skull. He was accompanied by three equally, nasty looking men, also dressed in long cloaks but this time they were all black with red stripes on each arm. Each one carried some kind of nasty looking club in his hand.

As he stood there the 'observers' could sense a hush had come over the crowd. Certainly from what they could see the whole crowd seemed to be a little in awe of the man. They could also see that any children present immediately hid behind their parents.

"This is the first time we have seen any children," said granddad, "must be that something important is about to be said."

His wife agreed and suggested to Pedro that he put the 'volume' marble in its circle and to turn it so they may be able to hear what was being said.

They couldn't hear clearly what the man was saying but he was obviously very angry about something. As he spoke, every now and then he would point to a person in the crowd and one of his three assistants would push his way through the crowd and drag the person out to the front of the crowd. After a short while four people, two men and one woman and an older boy had been dragged before the crowd. As each one was grabbed, the people close to them had tried to stop them being taken, but had merely been pushed away and hit with a club.

Pedro's grandmother indicated to him to turn the marble a little more, and as he did so the man's voice came over to them quite clearly.

"These four here," he said, at the same time walking around them, "have been most displeasing to the "High Person" and for that they will be punished. "You two," and this time he prodded the two men with his staff which caused one of the men to fall over, "will be taken away for nine 'periods' of time and will be put to work in the punishments pits." As he said this, a gasp went up from the crowd. Quite clearly this was a particularly nasty form of punishment.

"You," he continued, poking the woman with his staff, "will be sent to the child farm for five 'periods'." The woman put her hand to her mouth as she was given her punishment, but refrained from saying anything less she provoked more anger from the man, who by now had turned his attention to the older boy and informed him that he would go away for eleven 'periods'.

As the four offenders were led away, the man turned back to the crowd and informed them that they were also to be punished for allowing the four people to carry out their misdoings without either trying to stop them, or reporting them to the 'High Person'. He told them that they would all be confined to their dwellings for one 'period' once their days work was done.

"Don't any of you try to disobey my orders by leaving your dwellings," he said and then pointed up to one of the trees at the edge of the green where they could all see four huge birds looking down at them. They had purple bodies but black wings and green beaks. One of their eyes was red the other was a bright yellow. They also had three feet. "They will be my eyes and ears and will report to me at once if any of you try to leave your dwellings. Now, go to your dwellings and remember that it is most unwise for you to displease the 'High Person'". As he finished saying that, and the crowd began to disperse to their dwellings, he waved his staff in the air in a circular motion and simply vanished before their eyes.

Within a few minutes the whole area was empty. Most of the people seemed to head to somewhere behind where Pedro and his family were sitting. Three couples, one of them with two little girls appeared to walk right through them.

Sensing it was the correct thing to do Pedro slowly turned the 'volume' marble and then the other marble, which brought them all back to their own living room. No one said a word for a very long time, each one sitting there deep in thought with what they had just witnessed.

It was granddad, who broke the silence by wondering aloud how long a 'period' was, and what the punishment pit was and what went on there. He then looked at them all and asked if anyone had noticed that they could understand all the man had been saying yet could not understand what the other people had been saying before, and how it had happened.

"That is something we will have to find out John," said his wife. "We really must find a way to help those poor people. I think I will spend tomorrow going through a few more of the papers I have to see if they can shed any light on what we are dealing with." She looked at the rest of the family and told them that it was now more than ever, time to consider letting a few more people they thought they could trust, into what was happening. "As it is getting rather late now, may I suggest that we retire for the night and have a really good think about this tomorrow?

Chapter Eighteen

Recruiting Trusted Friends

Over breakfast the following morning there was a general discussion as to who they knew that could be trusted to join them in their venture to help whoever was trapped behind the 'Winter Shed', and indeed, help them with the mysteries in general surrounding the paper work that grandmother had been reading.

"Well, I think we ought to see who else had family members disappear in strange circumstances, and approach them," said Tom. "Who used to live next door to your friend Rebecca mum?"

"One side was the Stubbs family and the other side was the Nobles. Both families had daughters who went missing at the same time as Elizabeth Bilk, the daughter of the old lady who gave me all the papers to look after."

"The Stubbs I know live by the church now," said Mary, "the family couldn't face continuing to live in the cottage after the girls went missing. Where the Nobles moved to I have no idea, although I have seen Jacob Noble once or twice when I have been in the village. He must be about your age now do you think mum," she asked her mother-in-law.

"I think he was about three years older than me. When he left school he moved away somewhere. I remember him saying he could not go on living in the same house his sister had disappeared from.

I don't think he ever really recovered from her going. If I remember correctly, his mother never really got over the incident and her health went from bad to worse and some say she just gave up, especially after Jacob left. Her husband was one of the men who perished in the mine when they had that terrible collapse."

"I could ask Julia next time I go to the shop," Mary said, she might know where he lives now."

"Good idea Mary. Now who is there still living in the Stubbs family, does anyone know?"

Tom said he thought that William was still around. He was Jennifer's father, although as Tom pointed out, he too was badly affected by what had happened and had grown old before his time. He said that he doubted if it would be wise or indeed kind to involve him at this stage. The others agreed with him.

"Didn't Jennifer have a brother?" asked his mother, "I seem to remember a boy was sometimes in the house when I called round to see her."

"I think you will find he was a cousin who came to live with them," replied her husband, "he came from the big town. His mother had died giving birth to his brother. The baby was sent to live with his father's sister and he came to live with his mother's sister. He was quite a bit older than Jennifer so only lived there until he went to the big school in town."

"He was certainly living there when Jennifer went missing," replied his wife, "I remember going with him when we were all doing the search."

"We might be able to get hold of him then, mum." Tom said. Mary said she would also ask Julia about him as well.

Grandfather asked, "What about that friend of Pedro's, the one who came for the night out with us? Simon wasn't it? We could ask his father, he seemed a sensible person from what I saw of him. I don't know if his family had any connections with the people who went missing but it wouldn't hurt to let him in on what is going on and see if he will help us."

"Good idea dad and I think I know Sally Sutton's father well enough to sound him out, if we all agree."

The rest of the family said that would be O.K. so it was decided that Tom and Mary would walk into the village that afternoon, Mary to have a word with Julia, and Tom to see if he could have a chat with Simon and Sally's fathers. Sally's father was also on holiday from the mine so should be at home, but they may have to call at the farm to see Simon's dad. Pedro asked if he could go with his mother and father and he was told of course he could. "After all," said his dad, "it's the parents of your friends we are going to see, although I don't think it would be wise stage this stage to tell them anything about what is going on. Maybe later."

Pedro agreed, so it was decided that they would leave soon after lunch. That way granddad would be able to have a rest and grandmother could have some time to herself to look over more of the papers on her own in peace.

As they were leaving the house to walk to the village they saw Paul walking towards them. He was coming from the direction of the area where the 'Winter Shed' was. He asked where they were going and they said they were just going to the village shop for some things. He told them that he had been for a walk round the back of the hill from where his grandfather lived, and thought he would call at their house to see if Pedro would be going to the farm the next day for milk and if so could he go with him.

"Certainly," said Pedro. "I'll be leaving my house about half past eight, so I can meet you at the bottom of your hill if you like."

Paul said that would be fine, and walked with them until they did in fact come to the turning up the hill to his grandfather's house.

"See you in the morning then Pedro." He said goodbye to Pedro and his parents and set off up the hill to his home.

"That could have been a bit awkward,' said Pedro's father, "I was half expecting him to ask if he could come to the village with us."

"So was I dad," replied Pedro.

They carried on to the village and were almost there when they saw Simon's dad approaching the gateway to one of the fields on his tractor.

"That's a bit of luck Tom," said Mary. "You stay and have a word with him and I will carry on to the shop. I will meet you and Pedro in a little while. I will wait for you by the crossroads near the children's playground. There is a bench there I can sit and enjoy the sun."

Pedro opened the gate for Simon's dad to drive the tractor out and while he went to close it, his father had a chat with him about what they had been discovering over the previous few days. Mr Bloom said he and his wife would be more than happy to help in any way they could. Pedro's father told him that he was also going to have a word with Sally's dad. Mr. Bloom thought that was a good idea. They all shared the same general dislike and mistrust of the Bilk family and would be more than happy to find out what was going on.

Pedro's dad said he would contact him again when he had seen sally's father. "One thing I have just thought of," he said to Simon's dad, "and that is we will have to be very careful about all meeting together. If old man Bilk sees us all together he may wonder what is going on." He went on to tell him about the way Billy's grandson had come to stay and had been snooping around.

"Is that the lad who wears the yellow jumper? I've seen him wandering around," said Simon's dad. "He asked me who I was and did I work in the mine or just on the farm. I thought it was a funny thing to ask but now I can understand why. I told him I had nothing to do with the mine, and that I was just a farm hand."

Pedro's father said that once he had spoken to Sally's dad then perhaps they could arrange a picnic with all three families. That would seem innocent enough and they could talk about things without anyone getting suspicious as to what was going on.

"Good idea. Just let me know where and when. I don't work Sundays so that might be a good time."

He got back on to his tractor and set off up the field to feed the sheep.

Pedro and his father carried on through the village to Sally's house. They knew roughly where it was but they didn't have to look too far. As they turned the corner by the church Pedro spotted Sally in one of the front gardens.

"Hello Sally," said Pedro," how are you?"

"Fine," she replied, "I was thinking of walking down to your house to see you tomorrow. My mum was wondering if you would like to come round one afternoon and stay for tea. We could go on a bit of a walk if you are not busy with your granddad."

Before Pedro could answer her, his father asked Sally if her father was at home. She told him he was down at the end of the garden and said to follow her and she would show him the way. When she got back to where Pedro was still waiting she asked him what the matter was.

"Your dad looked awfully serious; we are not in any trouble are we?"

"Certainly not!' replied Pedro, "I can't really say anything at the moment but I can tell you it is something to do with the mine, and the marbles we have been collecting. Please don't ask me to tell you any more. If all goes well then I think it won't be very long before you know everything."

Sally agreed not to ask him anything else but told him that he had really got her wondering.

"Come and see the latest rocks I have been opening," she said. "Dad brought them home on his last day at the mine. He had been working in a different area from before so they were different from the others he had brought home.

Pedro followed Sally round the side of the house to the back garden. They could see their fathers deep in conversation so kept away from them. Sally opened a large box where she kept her bits of rock and the marbles she had found so far. Pedro could see straight away the rocks sally had been talking about. As soon as he saw them he had a funny feeling that he knew or had heard something about their particular shape. They were triangular, not at all the shape of rocks they had normally opened. Then he remembered. His grandmother had asked his father if he had found any triangular shaped rocks and when he had told her no, he remembered her saying almost under her breath 'thank goodness for that'

'These must be the ones she was talking about' thought Pedro, and wondered how he could tell Sally that he didn't think she should open them, and to wait until he had been able to talk to his grandmother.

Just then Pedro and Sally's fathers came back up the garden from where they had been chatting. Sally's father was the first to speak.

Pedro's father has been telling me a few very interesting things Sally," he said. Both fathers had agreed that it was all right to tell her what they had been talking about. "It seems we have quite a bit of a puzzle on our hands. It is all connected with the marbles we have all been finding. I will explain everything to you and your mother while we are having tea. I have given Pedro's father our assurances that we, that is you, your mother and me will not repeat anything of what I have been told, and what I will tell you later. Do you agree?"

Sally said that she wouldn't say a word to anyone.

"Especially not to Paul should he come round to see what you have got Sally."

Again she agreed and said that she had already made her mind up that she would not tell him anything should he call.

As they were taking their leave and about to go to meet Pedro's mum, Pedro mentioned that Sally had showed him some triangular shaped rocks that her father had given her. He went on to remind his father that his grandmother had seemed quite concerned should any rocks of that shape be found. Sally's father asked his daughter to please fetch the rocks and he would give them to Pedro and his father to take home for his granny to see.

Sally returned with the pieces and gave them to Pedro. Wishing them goodbye and saying they would be in touch very soon, Pedro and his father left to meet his mother.

"Come round tomorrow if you like Sally. I am going to the farm for some milk early in the morning but I should be back by eleven."

Sally said she would see him in the morning, as she and her father went into the house.

Pedro and his dad walked on in to the village to me up with his mum. She was, as she had said, sitting on the bench by the children's playground. She told them that all appeared to be O.K. at the shop. Paul had been in there again to get a few things but had been accompanied by the housekeeper and so had behaved himself.

Her husband explained that he had seen Simon and Sally's fathers and they had both agreed to help in whatever way they could. He went on to tell her about Simon's father's suggestion about going on a seemingly innocent family picnic so as to not arouse any suspicions should any of the Bilk family be around. Mary thought that was a good idea and suggested that they try and arrange it for the following weekend. As she pointed out, they needed to get a plan together soon because the people they were trying to help would be expecting to hear from them soon. Tom agreed and said that he had been thinking that perhaps he and his father could take a walk round to the site again the following morning. He went on to explain that there would be very little chance of Paul being around because he had already arranged to meet up with Pedro to go to the farm with him.

They took a slow casual walk back to their home enjoying the peace and quiet of the place. Mary remarked that it seemed very odd that a place as calm and peaceful as their village seemed to be, could be surrounded by so much mystery and puzzlement. And all seemingly cause by just one family.

Chapter Nineteen

Another Map – Another Journey

When they arrived home they were nicely surprised to discover that granny had prepared a salad meal for them all. She told them that she had been studying the papers a little more and thought that she had some rather interesting things to tell them all later. Tom in turn explained to his mother and father, who had now joined them that he had been able to enlist the help of both Sally and Simon's parents, explaining that they thought it would be a good idea for all the families to go on a picnic on Sunday next.

"Good idea Tom," she replied.

After they had finished their meal and had cleared everything away, the rest of the family was all quite anxious to hear what granny had found out from the papers. She told them that even though it was a nice evening and it would be lovely to sit in the sunshine in the garden, she thought it best to stay indoors, as she had no idea if anything else would happen when she opened another of the maps.

"Don't need any prying eyes at this stage of the game," she said.

"Quite right there mum," said Tom and said he would nip out to make sure the latch was on the front gate explaining that at least they would hear if anyone came to the house. While he was doing that granny asked Mary to close the curtains, saying that it would not look at all out of place because they often closed them in the evening to keep out the glare of the sunset.

The family settled round the table, and as on the other occasions, granny laid out a plan for them all to see. Again as with the other plan they had looked at, it also contained some weird markings and diagrams, and also as before the writing was in a language they could not understand. Pedro noticed that there were the same two spaces for him to place the marbles, which seemed to have set everything off with the other plan, or diagram. He noticed as well that on this plan there was a larger round space marked out and he asked his grandmother about it.

"That space," she replied, "Is where this box should be placed I think," and picked up the larger of the boxes she had been given all those years ago. "If this map works the same as the other one, then I think we had better place to marble in the first small diagram just as before. That way, after it settles down again at least we should be able to understand what is written there."

Pedro placed his marble just as he had done on the previous occasions. Once again the whole paper lifted into the air, and as it settled back on to the table the wording on the map had changed into language they could understand. They were not, as on the other occasions looking down on to a village scene. In fact there was nothing to be seen at all, apart from the writing.

"Can anyone see what the writing says?" asked granddad. He was sitting at the far end of the table and from his position the map was upside down.

Pedro was the first to say anything, telling them all, that from what he could read they were to follow the strange black and pink flowers until they came to three gates in a wall. It didn't tell them which gate to go through or if indeed they should go through any of them. "But I can't see any flowers," he said to them all, "nothing but writing."

His grandmother told them that she thought it was time to put the box into the larger diagram, but before she did she asked Pedro to go and bring three of the smaller marbles he had found, the ones with the three coloured dots. "I will need a red one, a yellow one and a blue one please," she told her grandson.

Pedro soon returned with his marbles, which he handed to her. She had already placed the wooden box into the circle on the diagram. She looked at the box and saw there was a number one carved next to the yellow flower, indicating she told the family, that that was where she thought the first marble should be placed. She looked at them all and told them that as before they had no idea at all what would happen when she dropped the marble into the middle of the flower. She asked them if they were all agreed she should carry on and they all said to go ahead.

She slowly dropped the yellow marble into the hole. At first nothing happened, then after a short while the box started to move around the diagram. Granny still had her hand resting lightly on the top, of the box so, just allowed the box to continue its movements. It finally came to rest in a space at the top right part of the map away from any other markings they could see. She removed her hand slowly, and as she did so the top section of the box slowly started to open. When it was fully open, it revealed an almost identical set of carvings on the top of the next section but this time there were only two carvings, again each of a flower, and each with a hole in their center. By the side of the blue flower there was a number two. She looked up at the family to see their reaction as to what had occurred, and to ask if they thought she should drop another marble into flower number two.

Granddad said that as they had come this far, they might as well carry on. The rest of the family nodded in apprehensive agreement so granny asked Pedro to do the honours. He reached over and dropped the blue marble into the middle of the carved flower. This time there was an instant reaction, which took them all by surprise. As before with the first map, the diagram moved around and shook a little. The room they were in seemed to go completely dark and the table they were sitting round lifted into the air. They all kept tight hold of the edge of the table more out of surprise than anything else. Pedro's mother gave a frightened scream and reached over to grab hold of her husband's hand. After what seemed like an eternity, the table settled back down, and the room lightened again. As they all got accustomed to the light, they found themselves still sitting round their table but in a completely different room.

For a long time nobody said anything. They just sat there trying to understand what had just happened. It was Pedro's father who was the first to speak and seemed to ask just what they were all thinking. "Where on earth are we?" he said. He looked at his mother as he asked the question, but she was trying to read something that had appeared on the diagram. He then looked at his wife who he could see had gone quite pale with what they had just gone through. She saw his concerned look and assured him that she would be fine in a few minutes.

Pedro by now had moved over to the only window that seemed to be in the room and moving aside the curtain looked out. All he could see was a lot of trees. "We seem to be in some sort of forest," he said, "all I can see are trees. There is a small path leading from this place but I can't see where it goes to, it just disappears into the trees." He let the curtain drop back into place and returned to the table and the rest of the family.

"Can you read what this says Pedro?' His granny was pointing to some writing on the diagram so he moved around to her side to try to read the very small words. He looked very closely and told her that it said something to the effect that they were all safe inside the hut and to trust and listen to Ishe.

He had just finished saying that when a voice from somewhere else in the room said, "That's me, that's me; I knew you would come one day!" This prompted another startled sound from Pedro's mother. They all looked over to where they thought the voice had come, from but all they could see was a rather dishevelled looking old doll sitting on the only chair in the room.

Before anyone could say anything, the doll spoke again. "Don't be afraid, please don't be afraid, I was left here to help whoever arrived here, but I need to check some things to make sure I am talking to the correct people."

Ishe settled herself more comfortably in the chair and asked her first questions.

"Are one of you ladies called Joan?'

"Yes, that is my name," said granny.

"And do you have a husband named John?'

"Yes I do."

"And when you were quite young, did you work for and become friends with a lady called Jessica?"

"That is correct; I helped her for quite a few years until she had to go into a home."

"In that case," said Ishe, "you are the family I have been waiting for all these years, and I can now reveal to you secrets that were entrusted to me by Jessica."

The family relaxed a little and upon invitation from Ishe pulled their chairs nearer to the chair she was sitting in. She began by telling granny not to let go of the box she was holding, saying she was not quite sure what would happen, if it was just left on the table, with no one holding it. She said it didn't matter who was holding it, just as long as someone was. She also instructed whoever it was holding it not to close the two sections.

Ishe began her story by telling them that she had first belonged to Joan's great grandmother, and had then been passed down to her grandmother. When it was Joan's mother's turn to have her she had not appeared to be interested in dolls and so she had been given to Jessica. At that time, before Joan was born, her mother had worked at the Old Manor House as a kitchen maid so one Christmas she had thought it was a good idea to pass the doll onto young Jessica. "She was forever losing me," said Ishe, "and would wander all over the house saying, 'Where Ishe Where Ishe'. She had problems saying my correct name, which was Belinda, so when she couldn't find me that is what she said. Of course she really meant 'Where is she, Where is she?' but it always came out as Ishe and that is what she called me from then on. In fact everyone else started calling me that." She finished by saying she was nearly two hundred years old.

"How did you get to be here?" asked granddad.

Ishe appeared not to hear him but they could tell by the look on her face that she thought someone had said something.

"Did someone say something," she asked. "I'm so very sorry; I should have said right at the beginning, I can only hear Joan's voice, so she will have to ask any questions on your behalf. That was the way I was left. To only hear your voice." She smiled and looked at Joan and asked what had been asked. Granny told her that her husband had wondered how she had got here in this place.

"I was brought here many, many years ago by Jessica long before she had got too ill to do much. She had been looking into the secrets and goings on connected with those 'Wretched Round Glass Things' as she called the marbles being found in the mine. She had been reading some old papers she had found and had discovered that by doing what you have obviously done with the box and the marbles she found her way here. She also found out that when she went outside the door of this place she was invisible to anyone she saw. She came here lots of times, usually after she had read some more of the papers, and when her husband and son were away from the mine on some sort of business. On one occasion she brought me with her and sat me in this chair. I suppose I was some sort of comfort to her. She used to talk to me as she was reading various things and then one day she said quite casually that she supposed it was about time to return home. I replied just as casually 'yes I suppose it is'"

Ishe said that her replying had shocked them both.

"How on earth could you have spoken?" she asked looking at me.

I told her I had no idea at all, and even as I said that it seemed unbelievable that her old rag doll was holding a conversation with her.

'I must get back to my room,' was all she said as she picked me up and did what she had to do to get back home. When we got back to her house she was still quick shook up over what had happened. She put me on the settee, which is where I usually stayed and sat down to slowly get her mind back to the present. She looked across at me and asked me again how I had managed to speak to her, but although I could hear her mouth I could not answer her. She muttered something about she must have been mistaken and went off to make a cup of tea."

" I was trying my best to yell at her, that she was not mistaken but no words came from my mouth," continued Ishe "It also appears that all the times she was reading the maps and muttering to herself what she was reading, I was obviously taking it all in without realising it. It must have been something to do with the fact that she had been here a few times and then each time she returned she would always walk over to me, pick me up, give me a kiss and start to tell me all that had happened during her journey. She always still had that funny little box in her hand when she picked me up so I suppose there was some kind of magic attached to it and by holding me a bit of it came across."

Joan said to the others that she thought it was about time they were getting back home, as they must have been gone quite a while.

"Not as long as you think,' said Ishe, "you will see what I mean when you get there."

"Speaking of which, how do we get back?' she asked looking at Ishe.

"Just sit back where you were when you came, and slowly close the second section and then the first section. You will find that as you do so the marbles you inserted into the holes will pop up back out again ready for you to use next time."

Granny thanked her for all her help and asked Ishe if she would like to return with them.

"Not on this occasion thank you but one day I will. I am quite content here and will look forward eagerly to your next visit. There is one thing that may help you though and that is if there is a paper in your collection that has a heading 'The House in the Woods' then bring it with you. It will tell you a lot more than I can about this place." She finished by saying they would not be able to understand it in their own home. "The only place it can be read is here in this house."

The family thanked Ishe for all her help and told her that they would return again very soon. She smiled, thanked them for coming and sat and watched as granny slowly turned the middle part of the box back into its place. As she had said, the marble popped up into granny's hand. Granny then slid the top section back over the middle section and once the marble had re-appeared and she had it in her hand, the room went dark, and with a few strange noises the next thing they knew they were back sitting round the table in their own living room.

Nobody said anything for a very long time and it was Pedro's mum who broke the silence by asking if what had happened had actually happened.

"It certainly did Mary you can be sure of that," replied her mother-in-law.

"What do we do now granny?' asked Pedro who seemed not to have been affected by the experience one little bit.

" What we do Pedro.' she said looking at her grandson but speaking to them all, "is sit down and discuss the whole thing. It seems to me that we have two very different parts of the same mystery. There is the part we have just seen and there is the part connected with the Winter Shed. It will help us greatly if we can discover just how closely they are linked if at all."

"I also think my dear that we should keep quiet about tonight's little adventure when we meet our friends." John looked at his wife and said that it was not as if they were deceiving them, they were meeting with them to tell them about the activities at the Winter Shed.

Granny agreed with her husband and so did Tom saying that there may come a time when they would require some help with this new episode but until they could be sure what it was all about then they should keep it to themselves. She said that the next day she would look through the papers and find the particular one Ishe had mentioned.

CHAPTER TWENTY

THE PICNIC MEETING

On the following Sunday, as planned, Pedro and his family met up with Sally and her mum and dad, who introduced themselves as Helen and Peter and headed off in to the village for their picnic. Sally told them that Simon and his mother and father would join them later. Simon's father had a bit more ploughing to do so they would be a little late. When they arrived in the village, they could see that other families had had the same idea about having a day out. There were quite a few families sitting around while the children ran around enjoying themselves. Pedro's father knew most of the men as they were all mine workers like him and were also on holiday. While the ladies started laying out the picnic things, Pedro's father walked over to some of the families and introduced his father to them. His father knew quite a few of the families but only by name as he had left the village many years before. He was able to tell a lot of the people his son introduced him to that of course he had known their fathers and uncles as they had been at the mine when he was there.

When they returned to their own family area the saw that Simon and his family had arrived. Simon's father William introduced himself and his wife Angie to Pedro's grandfather, who he had never met. It was still a little too early to eat so they all sat around just chatting about things in general. Granny wanted to make certain that none of the other families there could over hear what they were going to talk about, but like themselves, families had formed themselves into little groups and were busy just chatting to one another. The children from all the families were all playing together and Pedro, Sally and Simon went off to join them leaving the adults to talk among themselves.

Granny started by telling the others all she had told Tom and his wife about how some of the marbles being found contained magic powers. She told them that they had been discovered many, many years before and that the owners of the mine through the years had used the powers to their own ends. "There was nothing they would not do to gain control of all the 'Whishy Marbs'", she said to them. She then went on to tell them about how she had worked for the late Jessica Bilk, who had in turn entrusted her with some of the secrets she herself had managed to find out over the years, and that everything appeared to be connected with the disappearances over the years of certain people in the village, which of course she assumed they knew about. They replied that they did know and in fact Sally's mother told her that her own aunty had gone missing. She had been in the village visiting them and had gone to call on one of her old school friends and had never returned. When they went to look for her, the house she had visited was completely empty as if all the occupants had just up and left.

As with other people who had disappeared, no trace of them was ever found. "What was her name?" asked granny.

"Beatrice," replied Helen. "She was my mother's elder sister. She moved away from the village when she got married and occasionally came to visit. It was on one such visit that she went to see her friend and that was the last we saw of her."

"I do seem to recall," said granny, "that at the time my friend Rebecca disappeared, there was talk of another lady going missing but no body at the time seemed to know her name, just that she had been visiting someone. We searched and searched but no trace was ever found of any of the missing people. Did your aunt's go missing as well?"

"No, when my aunt arrived at her friend's house she was out, so as far as we know she went to call on another old acquaintance. That was the last anyone can recall noticing her. We can only assume that the person she went to call on also vanished but as we have no idea who it was, we have no trace of her."

For the next hour or so granny told them as much as she could about the marbles and what they could do. She also told them about the findings at the old winter shed and that her husband and son were going back one morning soon to see what else they could find out, and if they could help them in any way. Both Simon and Sally's fathers said they would be willing to help in any way they could but Simon's dad did point out that he was quite busy on the farm at the moment and until all the ploughing was complete then he wouldn't be able to promise too much of his time.

Granddad thanked him and said that if they required help then they would certainly call on the two men. "The one thing we have to look out for though, is that we can't be seen going to the old Winter Shed too often and certainly not in any great numbers. We have been very lucky so far, in that the only person who has seen us anywhere near the place is Paul, Bilky's grandson. We managed to convince him we were just out for an early morning stroll before breakfast. We think he believed us as he had no reason not to but at the same time we do need to be careful."

The two men agreed and were quite happy to leave things in the hands of Pedro's dad and granddad, but emphasised again that should their help be required they only had to ask.

"There is one strange thing we read in one of the papers I have been entrusted with," said granny, "and that is there was a sort of statement written there saying, 'let the children solve the mysteries". She went on to explain that it had been written by the old lady she used to work for, so she could only assume that in her own investigations of the goings on, then old Jessica had found something out, and had come to some conclusion that only the children could solve it.

"I am sure the children would love to be able to help solve the mysteries," said Helen, "to them it will seem like a wonderful adventure, but we must be very certain in ourselves as responsible parents that the situation is safe for them to proceed."

"You are right there Helen," granny agreed, "with a bit of luck, the next visit Tom and John pay to the 'Winter Shed' site will give us much more information than we know at present." She looked at Helen and said that in the meantime it would be very helpful if she could remember, or find out any more information on her aunt's visit and disappearance, it would be extremely helpful. Helen said that she was going to visit an old uncle in the next few days and would see what he could remember. He was her aunt's brother and had been quite a lot younger than her and was supposed to have joined her in her visit but was not very well on the day so stayed at home. She said that he never really did get over her disappearance. She promised to get as much information as she could without upsetting him too much. Granny thanked her and said that would all be very helpful.

By now the children were on their way back so the adults set about getting the picnic food ready. They decided to move over to one of the big trees where they would be in a bit of shelter from the heat of the sun. They talked about things in general as they enjoyed their picnic. One topic of conversation was the upcoming sports day. Pedro said he had been picked for the boys' football team and Sally told them she had also been chosen for the girls' hockey team. Simon said that although he had not been picked for any of the sporting events he had been asked to help get the spots field ready. His father had been told by the farmer he worked for, that he had promised the school to send him over with his tractor and grass cutting machine so Simon was going to help out in that way.

After the picnic was over, they all just sat around relaxing. Grandfather lay back with his hands behind his head and closed his eyes for a bit of a nap. The ladies cleared away the remains of the food and gathered the plates and cups together ready to take home. The children and their parents got a bat and ball out and along with a few of the other parents and children had a bit of a game of cricket.

Granny just sat back and relaxed, leaning against the trunk of the tree where they had moved to have their picnic. After a short while granddad opened his eyes and looked up into the branches of the tree. He had been awoken by a noise above his head. He couldn't really believe what he was looking at and shielded his eyes with his hand to make sure. When he was certain about what he had really seen, he slowly nudged his wife's foot to get her attention. When she looked at him. He indicated to her with a frown and an upward movement of his eyes for her to look into the tree above her head. Sensing it was something to do with what they had been through she lay down on the grass as her husband was doing and closed her eyes. After a few moments she slowly opened them and looked up into the branches. There she saw exactly what her husband had seen. A very large blackbird with strange looking eyes, two different coloured wings and most of all THREE FEET!! She kept very calm, sat up again and said to her husband that she thought it was about time they got everyone together as it was beginning to get a little chilly, and headed for home. She shook her head slightly as she looked at her husband as if to indicate not to mention anything about what they had just seen.

The rest of the people also seemed to have had the same idea and had finished playing cricket. Everyone wished everyone else good night and the groups of families moved off in the various directions to their homes. Simon and Sally's parents walked with Pedro and his family as far as their turning and upon leaving told them that they had had a really nice time and that they would be in touch again soon. Pedro told Sally that she was more than welcome to call round any time she liked. She said she would like that very much. He offered the same invitation to Simon when it was time for him and his family to go turn off the road to their house.

On the way home, both granny and her husband had been keeping a wary eye out to see if they could spot the blackbirds following them but neither saw any sign of them. In the circumstances granddad thought it was unnecessary to warn either of the sets of parents not to talk on the way to their homes about anything they had discussed earlier. To do so would have meant him explaining about the other side of their investigations, and as it was something they had agreed not to do at the present time, he was relieved not to have to do so.

Once Pedro and his family were safely inside their own house and had settled down for an evening cup of tea and chat, granny and granddad told him and his parents what they had seen up in the tree while the others were playing cricket.

"Are you sure they were the same birds?" Tom asked his mother.

"I know they were Tom, there was no mistaking those feet!"

"In that case, we had better be wary about what we say where ever we are. Luckily there are not many trees round here, so as long as we keep clear of anywhere they can land and listen to what we are talking about we will be ok."

"I have had another of my ideas Dad," Pedro said in reply to his father's statement, "and that is, if ever we do spot one or more of those birds, then we just talk about anything but marbles and the Bilk family, or anything at all to do with the mine. That way they will soon get fed up with hanging around."

Granddad told Pedro that it was a good plan, but said to all the family that he was most concerned as to how the birds had got out of the village where they had seen them when they had been on one of their 'paper travels' as he called them. "There is quite obviously a connection between everything we have seen and heard so far. And I wonder if it was just by chance they were perched in the tree where we were sitting."

"It must have been dad," said Tom, "apart from anything else it was the only tree around that area, and also we did not make ourselves known to anyone on any of our visits. But I do agree with you, that it is a great mystery as to how they are in our time as it were and yet can get back to where we saw them."

His mother agreed and said that in the future they must be very careful how they go about things. She added that perhaps they had better pay a visit to ISHY again soon to see if they could learn anything else that would help them in their quest. "I will also have another look at some of the papers again to see if they can shed any light on what we are up against."

Mary asked her if it was her intention to invite either Sally or Simon's parents on any of the visits.

Her mother in law admitted that in the end they would have to do so but at the present time she thought it would be best to keep it just between themselves. "After all, we don't really know too much ourselves so I would hate to put someone else in any kind of danger without having more knowledge of what we are able to do or not do. There is also the fact to be considered that we don't know how many people can go on one of the journeys. It could very well be that the magic will only work for a certain amount of people at any one time. If that turns out to be the case, then someone may well have to stay behind." She finished by saying that they would cross that bridge when they came to it. "In the meantime," she said holding back a yawn, "I have had a very long day and am ready for a good night's sleep."

The rest of the family agreed and made preparations to retire for the night.

CHAPTER TWENTY-ONE

GRANDDAD CHATS WITH JOSHUA, AND PEDRO TALKS TO PAUL

Pedro's father and grandfather were up bright and early the next morning, long before sunrise. They wanted to make sure they had plenty of time to chat with Joshua if indeed they could make contact with him. They had with them a spade and a long metal rod which granddad had filed to a nice sharp point at one end. He was going to use this rod to try to break through some of the earth behind the old shed. They didn't want to take too many tools with them at this point because of having to hide them in a safe place away from prying eyes when they left.

It was still quite dark when they arrived and granddad went straight over to the spot where they had last made contact with Joshua and immediately gave the signal as before. Straight away he heard the replying signal. Putting his ear close to the wall he called out Joshua's name.

"Is that you John?" he heard his friend ask.

"Yes it is," he replied, "how are you and are you free to talk?"

The voice of his friend was quite muffled as before, but considering it was coming through quite a few feet of earth it was not too bad.

Joshua informed him that he was quite well and that as far as he knew he had not been detected on his way to the mine. He told him that he had brought a trusted friend with him who was going to give him a hand to knock the piece of wood into the bank on his side so the John would have some idea when he was nearly through his side. He explained that it was about eighteen inches long and that he would drive it into the wall his side to a depth of about eighteen as well. Joshua they said they would first drive a piece of tubing through from his side, which would make communicating a lot easier. He had, he told granddad been slowly driving it through from his side ever since they had first made contact.

"I have managed to get it through most of the way, and I think it will not be long before it is all the way. There is a stopper in the end that will come through to you. All you will have to do is remove it and tidy up the tubing where it has pushed through the earth. When it is through, we should be able to chat a lot easier instead of hearing a muffled voice as we do at present."

Granddad told him that he and Tom would go for a little walk away from the area while Joshua completed the task. "That way, should anyone come by this way they won't see anything. They will just think we are out for an early morning stroll."

Joshua said that was fine and that he didn't think it would take very long to push the tube right through.

Tom and his father walked away from the site and headed in the general direction back to their home, so that should they meet anyone then it would seem clear that they had indeed been for a walk and were on their way back. They hadn't gone far when they heard someone coming towards them. As they got a bit further down the path they met Pedro.

"What are you doing here?" asked his father.

"I came to bring you the medallion dad, you left it on the kitchen table and I thought you might need it if you were going to hide the tools behind the bush."

"Thank you very much son. Do you want to stay with us now you are here? What time are you meeting Paul to go to the farm?"

"Not until about nine thirty."

"We should be home long before then," said granddad, "so you might just as well stay. We have made contact with Joshua again and we are just keeping away from the site while he finishes pushing a communication tube through so we can talk to him better. In fact he has probably finished by now so we can head back there."

When they arrived back at the site they saw that the end of the tube was just starting to appear through the wall of earth. Granddad went over to it and proceeded to clean the end and remove the stopper Joshua had placed there. When it was clean, he put his mouth near the opening and asked his friend if he could hear him. Joshua replied that he could hear him just fine. He told granddad that as they had been quite a while pushing the tubing through and had been away from home for about two of their hours, he couldn't really stay too much longer or else he would be missed. Granddad said he understood the situation but did he have time to tell them how they could help.

"You are being a big help by at least giving us all some hope we may at last get away from this place." replied Joshua. "I have told a couple of families I know I can trust about the contact I have made. They are more than willing to help, but are fully aware of the risks they put other people in by agreeing to assist us. I assured them I would do nothing to endanger them or their family and friends."

Joshua went on to say that he thought the least number of people who knew about things the better at this stage. "I am not too sure who I can trust. I suspect a few of the men on this side are just a little too friendly with the 'management' here. It always seems to be the same group of men who seem to casually ask questions. It is the same on the women's side. Whenever the ladies get together, the wives or girlfriends of these same men ask the same sort of questions."

"We have done the same here Joshua. We had a meeting with two families we know we can trust, and we will keep everything between just them and us for the time being." Granddad then asked his friend what he would like them to do to help."

"If you could start trying to break through from your side that would be great," said Joshua. "If you start to make your hole about six feet to the right of where this tube is, then we will do the same six feet from the left of the tube this side. We will have to do this as quietly as possible and for this reason I have made you a very simple drill. It is made of wood and is roughly twelve inches in diameter. I have not managed in the time to make a handle to operate it but I have made the end square so you should have no trouble in fixing something to the end."

"That will be no problem at all my friend, I can soon make a key to fit."

When granddad told him that they had brought a couple of tools with them and planned on leaving them behind the moving bush, Joshua said that he would get the children to leave the drill there for them the next time they came.

"Much as we would love to get you all out as soon as possible, I don't think it would be very wise to come here too often. I think if we made it about every third or fourth day that should be O.K. we don't want to attract any attention to ourselves." Joshua agreed and said they would try for the same sort of rota but it all depended on his and his friends' work pattern as to when they could get away.

Tom asked his father to quickly mention to his friend that perhaps it might be a good idea, if it was safe to do so, that perhaps they could communicate by letter or notes and get the children to leave them just inside the bush. He said it would be much safer to leave them inside the space behind the bush so no one would see the disturbed earth should they happen to walk that way.

Joshua thought this was an excellent idea and would make sure there was a note for them the next time they came. He said it was time he and his friend made their way back to their homes. He thanked John and Tom for all their help and told him that the drill would be there for them in two days' time, explaining that they had to move it under cover of darkness and only when it was perfectly safe to do so. Granddad said they were more than happy to help and would start on their side of the hole in three days' time. "We will put the couple of tools we brought with us behind the bush before we leave here."

"That will be fine, and I will make sure the children know and not wonder what they are. I will contact you again very soon and thank you all once again."

Granddad could hear through the tube, the sound of his friend putting the stopper in the tube, and did the same with his end. He then pushed some earth in and around the hole where the tube had come through and then placed a couple of pieces of wood over the area.

When he had finished he said to his son and grandson that he thought they had better start to make their way home again. He asked Pedro to go over to the bush with the medallion and open it just far enough so they could put their tools into the hole behind. When Pedro had done that they made sure there were no footprints in the earth surrounding the bush and left the area to make their way home for breakfast.

On the way home they discussed what had happened with Joshua and wondered just what they could do to get the people out from where they were trapped.

"Whatever it is we do dad," said Tom, "it will all have to happen at one time. We can't have half the people on this side and the rest left back there. It sounds as if it would not be a very nice place to be, and not very nice people to be left with." His father agreed, adding that it would have to be planned very carefully so as not to endanger anyone. He then said that perhaps there might be a few back there who for one reason or another very rarely went out and so were not seen very much in public. If that were the case then maybe those people could be got out first without anyone noticing.

"Good idea dad, that is the kind of thing we can ask when we leave the notes for Joshua."

Pedro then said that he would get one of the boxes he had been using for his marbles and that could be used as a sort of 'Post Box' to place behind the bush with the notes in. His father and grandfather both said that was a good idea.

"I have just thought of another thing." said granddad, and went on to say that now they were going to communicate with Joshua through the note system, there would be no need to go to the site in the early hours. "We can go along anytime we want to, do a bit of work and then when we are ready to speak to Joshua again leave him a note arranging a time and day to be there."

"That will certainly make things easier," said Tom. "It will also help to prevent Joshua and his friends from getting caught trying to sneak off to meet us. They will be able to do their digging at a time it is safe for them."

By this time they had reached their home and all admitted that the smell of breakfast cooking as they got to the kitchen door made them realise just how hungry they were.

The ladies welcomed them back telling them to wash their hands and come to the table. As they sat down to eat, granddad went over to one of the windows to open it to let the smell of the cooking out and to let some fresh air in. He glanced into the garden and sitting on the handle of the garden spade he had left there the previous evening, he saw one of those strange blackbirds with three feet. He quickly moved to the table and as he sat down he said quietly to the rest of the family, "Three footed bird sitting on the garden spade! Don't say a word about what we have been doing today. Just talk about things in general." The others looked a bit alarmed at this information, but realised they had to do just what granddad had said.

The family continued with their breakfast as any normal family would. When they had finished Pedro's mother asked him what time he was meeting Paul to go to the farm for the milk. He told that he was supposed to meet him at the bottom of the hill to his house about nine-thirty. "In that case, I think I will come with you both if that is O.K. I need to get some eggs from the farm as well as the milk."

"That will be fine mum," replied Pedro.

"What are the rest of you going to do?" she asked turning to her husband and parents.

"Well, as far as dad and I are concerned, we have some work to be getting on with in the shed. Apart from anything else, it could do with a really good clean out. I don't know the last time I did that."

"In that case," said granny, "if you, Mary are going with Pedro, and you two men are disappearing into the shed, I think I will settle down and do a bit more reading. I seem to have got to quite an interesting bit. Now off you all go, I will clear up here and then settle down and have a nice quiet morning reading. Go on, Shoo the lot of you!!" She gestured with her arms for them to leave the house. John and Tom both knew from experience that when she had made up her mind about something, nothing would shift it so it was just best to do what she said.

They all left the room, Pedro and his mum to get ready to go to the farm, and Tom and his dad to go out to the shed.

On his way past the window, granddad had a quick look out the window but there was no sight of the "Bird Spy" as he had begun to think of him in his mind.

Granny cleared up the breakfast things and once Pedro and his mother had left the house she closed the door and the window, went to collect the envelopes she had been studying and settled down to see what other information she could get from them. She had it in her mind that they had better pay a return visit to Ishe quite soon to see what else they could find out from her. She was also very aware that any future visits would have to be timed very carefully if they were not to be spied upon by their inquisitive bird friends. She thought she had come up with an idea how to go about this and would put it to the family when they all got together again. Her and Mary still had yet to hear of how the men folk had got on at the site that morning.

Tom and his father set about doing the tasks they had in mind in the shed. Tom did as he intended and started to give the place a good clear out. His father meanwhile had found a piece of wood just about the size he needed and started to fashion it into a long handle. He made a small hole about half way along. This was going to be the key or lever for turning the screw bit Joshua was going to leave for him. As he did not know the size of the end of it, he just left it with the hole for the moment.

Each man in turn kept going out of the shed as if to get something, but it was really to see if there was any sign of the bird. It seemed as if it was happy with things for the time being because they never saw it again all the time they were working there.

Pedro and his mum had just arrived at the bottom of the hill leading down from the Bilk house when they saw Paul approaching them. They all wished each other good morning and set of for the farm.

"How is you grandfather today Paul?" asked Mary. She wasn't all that interested really but felt she had to say something.

"Not very good I'm afraid," replied Paul, "it appears that he has been up most of the night. I didn't hear him at all because my room is at the back of the house in the old wing. The housekeeper has asked me to ask you Mrs. Vendell, if you would very kindly ask the doctor to call round and see him. She says she has no idea at all where the doctor lives. She has never had any cause before to contact him."

Pedro's mother told him she would certainly call at the doctor's for him. "I will do it before I come up to the farm. Is there any particular time for him to be there Paul?"

"Any time to suite him will be fine, thank you Mrs. Vendell. My grandfather is not going anywhere and it is the day when the house keeper stays all day so she will be there to let him in."

They carried on towards the farm. When they arrived at the path leading up to it Pedro's mother told the boys to go on up and get the milk and she would go on to the doctors house. "Tell the farmer Pedro, that I would like a dozen eggs and a block of butter, and I will collect them in about an hour. I want to call in the shop after I have been to the Doctor's."

"O.K. mum," said her son as he and Paul headed off to the farm. "Wonder what the matter is with your granddad," he said as they walked along the path.

"I don't know, but the house keeper said he was making horrible groaning noises when she arrived about seven this morning. She said she asked him what the matter was, but he just shouted at her to go away and mind her own business."

"Not a very nice thing to say to someone who was only trying to help."

Paul agreed but said that for the last few days, his grandfather had been in a very bad temper and even he had been afraid to say much to him.

"What have you been doing with yourself then?" asked Pedro.

"Just messing around really. I was looking at a lot of stuff to do with the mine but I didn't really understand most of it. A lot of the papers and diagrams seem to be in some sort of funny language. There are a lot of pencil marks and things written on them but none of them made any sense to me. A lot were also tied up with either red or blue tape or ribbon. I dare not open them in case I couldn't tie them up properly again."

"Was there anything else there which might help you to sort things out?" Pedro was hoping that Paul might give something away which might tie in with what his granny had been finding out.

"Not really, but on a couple of the map type diagrams there were funny round rings with dots or stripes in them. They had pencil crosses on them as if they had been crossed out."

"Perhaps you granddad will tell you what they are one day," said Pedro.

"Maybe, but I daren't tell him I have been looking at those diagrams, they were tucked away at the back of his desk. I only took a chance to look at them because he was in his room or like yesterday when he went on the train to see someone."

The pair had just about arrived at the farm when Paul said he remembered something else about the map type papers he had been looking at. He told Pedro that on one of them there were a few extra pencil drawings. He couldn't quite make out what they were but on one of them there were definitely a couple of drawings that looked like big birds. "They were really weird looking things, and it looked like they had three feet but that could just be where whoever had drawn them had made a mistake and not rubbed one of the feet out."

When he heard this, Pedro could hardly contain himself and couldn't wait to tell his family.

They collected the milk from the farmer and also decided to take the eggs and butter as well. The farmer put them in a box for Pedro so it was easy to carry. Paul offered to carry Pedro's milk until they got to the bottom of the hill. Pedro said that by the time they reached the bottom his mum should just about be there after her visit to the shop and the Doctor's house.

"We can sit and wait for her anyway," said Paul, "I am in no rush to get back home, especially if granddad is still in his bad mood."

As they walked back down to the road, Pedro began to wonder to himself if perhaps he and his friends had been a bit too hasty to take a dislike to Paul, but then again, he told himself, he had been asking all those awkward questions. He decided to say nothing for the time being but would mention it to his family when they were next all together.

They arrived at the road and sat down under the big tree so they could at least put the eggs, milk and butter on the ground round the shaded side away from the sun.

Neither boy mentioned anything about what they had been talking about before, but went on to discuss the coming sports day at Pedro's school. As it turned out, it was just as well they were only discussing the sports day because if either of them had looked up into the branches of the tree. They would have seen one of the weird black birds!

"Will you be coming to the sports day?" Pedro asked his friend.

"I expect so, granddad said he wanted me to go with him. Of course I can't really take part in anything as I am not yet properly at the school."

"I don't see why not, you are a part of the school, it's just you haven't started yet. You did attend for the last three days of last term and helped out with a few things." Pedro was really trying to cheer Paul up a bit. He had taken an unexpected liking to him and felt sorry for him having to live with his grumpy old granddad.

Just then Pedro's mother arrived from the village and was quite relieved to see the boys had brought the eggs and butter down for her. "I didn't really feel like walking up to the farm," she said. "What did the farmer say about paying?" she asked her son. Pedro told her that he hadn't said anything but just gave them the eggs and butter in a box and that was that. Paul then realised that he still had the money for his milk in his pocket. Both of the boys had completely forgotten about paying for anything!

"Never mind, I'll get your dad to nip up there either tomorrow or the next day."

"Shall I give you the money for our milk as well Mrs. Vendell?'

"Yes that would be lovely Paul. That way we can pay for everything at the same time."

They all started walking back home and Pedro's mother told Paul that the Doctor would call to see Mr. Bilk about three o'clock that afternoon.

"Thank you very much," said Paul, "let's hope granddad is in a better mood by then." He then went on to tell Pedro's mother how bad tempered his granddad had been for the last few days. "It has been really not very nice living there."

Pedro's mum was very tempted to invite him down to their house but decided against it knowing how he had been in the past.

When they reached the turning leading to Paul's house he said goodbye and headed up the hill.

Pedro and his mother continued along the road to their house and as they went he said to her that he was beginning to feel a bit sorry for Paul, and was also feeling a bit guilty about the way he had treated him and what he had thought about him. His mother reassured him that he shouldn't feel guilty, but to look upon him in a different way in future. 'We will just have to wait and see how things turn out,' she told her son.

Arriving back at their cottage they discovered that Granny had made them all some nice fresh sandwiches and cold drinks and suggested that Pedro went round to the shed to fetch his father and grandfather. "We can sit outside and enjoy them, it's lovely and sunny and there is a bit of a breeze so we won't be too hot."

Pedro ran round to the shed and soon returned with his father and granddad. They all sat down at the table in the middle of the garden where Mary and her mother-in-law had brought the sandwiches and drinks. As he sat down, granddad had a quick glance round the garden to see if he could see any sign of the birds. "I can't see anything," he whispered to the family, "but to be on the safe side let's not talk about anything to do with marbles or the mine."

Mary told them all about Mr. Bilk not being very well and that he had asked Paul to ask her to call in to the doctors to request a home visit. Paul had no idea what was wrong with his grandfather, but did say that he had been in a terrible mood for a few days.

Paul told me," said Pedro, "that it really was not very nice living there at the moment. I feel sorry for him having to be there for the next year or so."

"Maybe the doctor can sort out what is wrong with him and he will soon get better." Mary always did like to see the good side of people.

"Perhaps," replied granny, "but he will only have himself to blame if no one wants to help him, not the way he has been to folk in the past."

Eager to change the subject of old Bilky's illness John asked his wife if she had managed to get much reading done while she had been on her own.

"Yes I did," she replied, "and the plot was just as I thought it might turn out to be." She was acutely aware of not saying anything specific about what she had been reading just in case 'strange ears' were listening, but could see by the looks on the faces of her family that they understood what she meant.

"What about you dad, did you and Grampy manage to get done what you wanted?"

"Yes we did, the shed has never looked so clean and tidy." His dad said he would take Pedro round there later to see what he had done. "Granddad also made you a special cupboard to put all your things in, so you won't have to just leave everything on the bench."

Pedro thanked his granddad and then asked what everyone was going to do that afternoon.

Granddad said he was going to do a bit of gardening, his wife said she was going to do a bit more reading until it was time to help Mary get the evening meal ready. Mum told them she had some tidying up to do in the house where she had not been able to do it that morning because of going into the village.

"That just leave you and me Pedro," said her husband, "what shall we do?"

Before Pedro had a chance to answer, his wife explained about the fact that none of the things they had brought from the farm had been paid for, so perhaps he and Pedro would like to take a stroll back to the farm and pay the farmer.

"Sounds like a good idea to me, what do you say son?"

"Sounds like a good idea to me too dad." Pedro was also thinking it would be a good chance for him to tell him a bit of what Paul had been saying.

Mary gave the money to her husband and also explained that the extra was money Paul had given her to pay for his milk. "For some reason the farmer neglected to ask the boys for the money when they were there."

As they were leaving, granddad called after them and making an upward gesture with his eyes suggested that perhaps they could do a spot of bird watching on their walk. His son understood just what his father meant and said they would keep a good look out for any unusual species.

CHAPTER TWENTY-TWO

NAGGY'S STORY

B y early evening the whole family was back together again sitting around the table enjoying the meal Mary and Joan had prepared. Talking was kept to a minimum apart from general chat about what had occurred that day,

On completion of the meal and after everything had been cleared away and dishes washed etc. it was beginning to get a bit dark outside granny suggested that they close the window and curtains. Granddad said he would take a last casual look round the garden before they settled in for the night. When he returned, he told them that he could see no signs of anyone or anything out there. He had made sure that any gardening tools had been put back into the shed and that the shed had been locked.

With this information, granny felt it was quite safe to sit and talk about what the men had managed to accomplish that morning, what she had read in the papers she had been studying and about a couple of ideas that had been running around her head.

Her husband told her and Mary what had happened at the site and how Joshua had made him a tool to help him get through the wall of earth. Granny thought the idea of communicating with notes was a very good idea. She said she would make a list of questions she would like to ask.

Mary then suggested that Pedro should tell them about the conversation he had had with Paul that morning. Pedro told them all he could remember, especially about what Paul had said concerning the papers he had been looking at. He explained that Paul had seen strange markings similar to the ones the family had been seeing on their maps and papers. He then went on to tell them about the pictures of the birds and the fact they seem to have three feet!

Granny said that could explain why Bilky was so anxious to get hold of any marbles. "He's got a copy of the paperwork but no means of doing anything with it," she said "We had better make doubly sure that he doesn't get his hands on any marbles or anything else. Also we had better try to solve things as quickly as we can and help those poor people before he does anything rash or nasty. You know what he is like."

The family agreed and asked granny what she had managed to find out and what ideas she has come up with.

She started by telling them that she thought that a return visit to Ishe was most important. "It appears," she said, "that there is someone back there who has some connection with the situation and could be of help to us, but I have no idea who it is. All that plus what Pedro said that Paul was telling him means that Old Bilky appears to be sniffing around things but without any Marbles he can't get anywhere."

"It sounds as if we need to go sooner rather than later mum,"

"Yes I think you are right son."

"Can we go tonight then?"

"I don't see why not if everyone is in agreement."

The rest of the family said they were quite happy to go so granny said she would fetch the correct map and in the meantime asked Pedro to go and fetch the two marbles they would need for the journey.

She would also bring the three sectioned, round box and the marbles to operate it. Granddad told them he would just take a quick look around the garden 'just to make sure.'

When granddad returned he locked the door and said he could see nothing untoward in the garden. By this time the map had been spread out on the table and they all took their places as before. Granny placed the round box in the space on the map and dropped the yellow marble into the hole. As before, it started to move around until it stopped in the same place as before in the top right hand corner. The top section of the box slowly opened to reveal once more the hole in the centre. With a nod from his grandmother, Pedro dropped the blue marble into the whole. This time the family were ready for the action and even Pedro's mum sat there quite content knowing that they would come to no harm.

Again they found themselves sitting around their table in the same room as before. Just as they all got accustomed to the light they heard Ishe's voice welcoming them back. "I knew you would come back," she said. They all said hello to her. It seemed to them to be the most natural thing in the world to be talking to a stuffed rag doll.

Ishe started by asking is she had brought the piece of paper she had requested. Granny told her that she had and unfolded it. As Ishe had said it was now in their language. Ishe explained that it was in a funny language to prevent anyone who should not be reading it from doing so.

"It explains a lot about this house, where it is, how to get out and how to return safely." said Ishe. "You are perfectly safe as long as you take the box around with you. No one can see you but you must follow certain rules or you will be detected. The ones you need to be very wary of are the big black birds. They seem to act as spies for the man known as the High Person. He is the one everyone is afraid of. Where he came from no one really knows. He seems to have been there forever. The back birds also change themselves into ordinary men and often leave this place and go to another settlement but I don't know where that is. How they get there I do not know. I think old Jessica was on the verge of finding out when she started being taken ill and so could no longer come here so often."

Ishe told them that before she was placed in the nursing home Jessica made one final journey here, brought her with her and placed her in the chair. "She had given me the option of staying in this house or going back to her house. I chose to stay here. She said I would be perfectly safe there and she knew the secrets would be safe with me and that one day I would get visitors who would be attempting to do what she had been doing, and that was to discover what had gone on in the past and try to put things right." She looked at granny and said that that was how she knew her name.

Ishe looked at Pedro and asked him if he would mind going over to the chest of draws at the end of the room and getting the piece of paper he would find there. When he retrieved it, Ishe asked him to read what was written there.

Pedro studied it for quite a while then looking up at his family started to read.

"Wear something Green, you will not be seen.

Wear something Red; they can hear all that is said.

Wear something Blue, they can talk with you."

"That is a warning about the birds," Ishe told them. "You don't have to wear all green, just as long as you have something green on. It seems to protect you from their sight. It is quite alright to talk if you see them near as long as you are not wearing anything red, or anyone you are talking to is wearing red. I don't know if the same things apply when they turn into men, nor do I know if there is any way to recognise them when they do change into men, so you can be weary of them."

"Perhaps there may be some information about them in some of the papers I have yet to read," said granny.

"Maybe Joshua will know something," commented granddad and granny had to explain to Ishe about what they had been finding out nearer their house at the site of the old winter shed. Ishe told them that she had once spent winter there many, many years ago. "I think it was when I belonged to your grandmother," she said to Joan, "long before the disappearances."

"There is someone else here I would like you all to meet," Ishe told them. "I thought he might have been here by now, he is not usually this late. I do hope nothing has happened to him."

The moment she said that there was a noise, which came from the other room in the house. After a couple of minutes the door to that room opened and in walked the old man they had seen in the village when they had gone on a journey using the other map. He was quite small, probably about the same height as Pedro. He had white hair and a white beard, which he kept plaited under his chin and tied with a green ribbon. He walked with a bit of a limp. That was because his right leg was just a wooden stump below his knee with a sort of shoe fixed to it.

"This is Naggy," said Ishe, "he has been here a lot longer than I have. I was hoping he would call whilst you were here this time. He can tell you lots more about what is going on here than I can. He can also hear all of you, unlike me who can only hear Joan,"

Naggy, came right into the room and shook hands with all the family and said that he was delighted to meet them at long last after hearing so much about them from Ishe. He settled himself onto a chair, which he brought and placed next to the chair Ishe was in.

"How can I help you all?"

Granny said there was so much they would like to know but wondered if they had enough time on this visit to hear all he could tell them.

"You don't need to worry about that," said Ishe. "Did you notice that when you returned to your house the last time that hardly any time had passed at all?"

Granny told her that no, she had not noticed.

"It's just as if time stands still while you are here. That is why Jessica could come here so often. She could visit, do what she had to do and then return with no one being any the wiser."

"In that case, I suppose it is best if I explain first what we have been finding out about the "Wishy Marb," some residents from years ago who vanished without a trace and with whom we have made contact, and our visits to another part of what must be this place, by using the papers and maps Jessica gave me all those years ago." It was only granny who could tell the story because it was only Granny who Ishe could hear.

When she had finally finished telling all they knew so far, Ishe and Naggy both seemed to be very excited about what thy had been told.

"This could mean that the nightmares could very soon be over," said Naggy. It was his turn now to explain to the visitors where they were and what had been happening for many, many years. He suggested that before he started his tale, they should all have a drink. He asked each member of the family in turn what they would like. When they had given him their choices he clapped his hands a few times and pointed to the table behind them. They looked around at the table and there were all of the drinks that they had requested. No one asked him how he managed to do that. It was as if by now they had come to accept any sort of magic that happened in that place.

Naggy started by telling them that he first came to the village many, many years ago. He didn't know exactly how many years because the 'High Person' had used some kind of magic to alter the length of days, weeks and years. This was to get more work out of everyone. He said he had gone to visit his brother who he had not heard from in a very long time. When he arrived at the village it had been completely empty. It was just as if everyone there had decided to leave at the same time. "Sounds a bit like what Jessica had told me had happened to the old Marbleville residents years later," He said he could find no one in the village at all. He went home telling himself he would return at a later date when he had more time to try to sort out what had occurred. He would try and get a couple of friends to come with him as well. In the event he could only persuade one person to go back there with him. This was because at around that time, very many strange things had been occurring in and around the ancient mines. Granddad asked him what kind of kind of things and Naggy told him. "Men going missing in the mines for days on end and strange rock collapses in perfectly safe parts of the mine. People asked questions of course but no proper answers are given. There was an awful lot of punishment handed out around that time as well for seemingly minor offences."

He went on to say that when a miner disappeared, if he had any child over the age of eight, then that child would be required to go to work in his place.

"I did return with my friend Niggy and we both started to search the houses to see what we could find. He started at one end of the village and I started at the other end. After about an hour of searching we could find nothing to give us a clue as to where the population of the village had gone. We decided that we would look in the one place we had so far not been to and that was the church. Niggy said he would look around the main body of the church and I said that I would go down and look in the room under the church. This was a sort of cellar where apparently members of the village committee met to discuss what they could do about the unfair goings on in the village and the mine. It must have been like a secret society."

Naggy went on to say that while he was down there he heard his friend shout out his name and it sounded like he was shouting for help. By the time he had returned to the main part of the church, there was no sign of his friend at all. "While I was looking around I heard a sound back down the cellar where I had just been. I returned to the cellar but could find no trace of anyone. However, I did notice a door in one of the far corners, which I had not noticed before, so I decided to investigate. I couldn't open the door but did notice there was a key hanging on a hook beside the door. I used the key, unlocked the door and went cautiously through to the other side. As I passed through the door it closed behind me and I heard the key being turned in the lock. I was now trapped so had no option but to carry on."

He then told them he went down what seemed to be a very long passageway, at the end of which was another door made of branches and twigs. He pushed the door aside and found himself in the middle of a very dense wooden area. He could see no one else around.

"I was completely alone. When I turned round to go back through the door it had disappeared completely. It was as if it had never been there. Now there was no way back."

"What did you do Naggy?" Asked Pedro

"There was not a lot I could do. I was in a strange place with no hope of getting back to where I had come from so all I could think of was to go on to see if I could find out where I was. I walked for what seemed like hours. I sat down on the ground to rest for a while then started walking again not knowing where I was going or who I might meet. I walked a little further then I kicked something in the grass. I bent down to pick it up and it was a funny round box." He pointed to the one granny had used to get to Ishe's home.

"It was a lot like the one you have on the map on the table Joan, except mine only had two sections. As I stood looking at it a house appeared right before me."

He said he kept hold of the box as he walked towards the house. He slowly walked all the way round but could find no way of getting in. There appeared to be spaces where windows might have been but no actual windows as far as he could make out. Just then as he rounded a corner of the house a door opened. He could swear there was not a door there before.

"I entered the house and just as before, as I walked through the door it closed behind me. I was standing in complete darkness. I still had the funny shaped box in my hand and as I stood there it began to shake in my hands. After a while the room I was in got slowly lighter. It was quite a small room with just a table and chair in it. There were now two windows but I could not see out. It was funny really," he told them "because when I walked around the house outside, I saw no windows at all." After a while he heard a loud noise coming from the door at the far end of the room. "After my experience with doors that day I was a bit reluctant to open it, but I thought as I had come this far another door couldn't hurt me could it?"

"I opened the door very slowly and very carefully, making sure I did not go all of the way through and also making sure I did not let go of the door. The room seemed to get brighter the wider I opened the door. In the room alongside the far wall, was a bed. In the bed I could make out the shape of someone lying there. Whoever it was in the bed told me not to be afraid and to come right into the room," said Naggy. "I moved further into the room and walked over towards the bed. In the bed was a frail looking man with a long red beard, a lot longer than mine. His beard was plaited into three parts each one was tied with a green ribbon."

"The man told me not to be afraid. He said he had been waiting for this moment for a very long time and that now he could disappear in peace knowing that the person he had been told about many years before was here to take over from him."

Naggy said that the man in the bed had told him that his name was Balbus and that he had occupied this house for many, many years. He said he had been sent there to try to find where all the people of the old village of Marbleville, had been vanishing to. 'No one can see this house, as long as you have that box you are holding.' he told me. "I hadn't realised I was still holding the box," said Naggy. "I asked him how he knew I would come and he said he just knew. It was written in the 'pages.'

What pages he never did say.

Balbus told Naggy that he would now be in charge of bringing justice to the people of the village. He said the village did not have a name. The 'High Person' would not allow anyone to give it a name.

"I asked him what led me to his house and he told me that I must have been destined to arrive through the 'invisible passage.' He said this was a passage that started somewhere in the village through which the 'Enforcers' went when they were looking for more workers for the farms and fields."

"He told me that once they passed through this passage they could not be seen so could wonder around the village without being noticed by anyone. If they saw a worker that they thought would suit their cause they simply walked up to him, touched him on the shoulder. At that point the worker too would become invisible and would be led away and brought here. He also said that because I had come through the same passage then I was invisible to everyone as well. There was another passage leading back to the village but where it started or finished he had no idea. The only one he had used had been in the cellar of the old mission house, which he understood was now a proper church."

"Which is how I got here all those years ago. No one can see me, but they have an idea I am around."

"Balbus explained that he had found the funny shaped box which I was still holding one day when he was walking around in Marbleville. He told me he had no idea at all what it was, but it seemed to be urging him to walk towards the mission house. He said it was as if it was taking over his every movement. He told me had done just as I had done and gone down into a cellar-like room, opened the same door as I had and from the moment he emerged through the door, the box seemed to take over where he walked until he found himself at the house I had been led to."

Naggy said that Balbus told him that it was as if he was meant to be there to take on the work of the previous person who had lived there. Balbus said there were lots of writing on various bit of paper and on the walls of the house, so he just tried to follow what was written there.

"One thing that Balbus told me was that I should never go out of the house without taking the box with me. I would never find the house again should I go out without it. "As you go through door," he told me, " the box will get smaller so you can put it in your pocket. When you are ready to return, take it out of your pocket and it will lead you back here." He said I was not to worry about being seen. As long as I wore something green I would be invisible to the villagers.

"I asked him how he was sure that I would be coming and he told me he had received a 'mind message' that someone was coming to take over his responsibilities and that is why he opened the door one last time and left the box where it could be found.

Naggy said he spent a very long time talking to Balbus as he passed on so many of the things he had learnt over the years.

"It was he who told me about the big Black Birds. They belonged to a not very pleasant lady who came to visit the High Person. She came to visit here quite regularly from another time and brought the birds with her. They did all she told them to do. It seemed as if she was determined to find out the long lost secret of the mines so she could have absolute power over the people in her time. He told me that each time she visited, then the High Person would disappear for a few days with whatever she had brought for him, leaving her in complete control over everyone. This was a time the people feared the most and tried to stay in their homes whenever she was there. Of course the men had to leave their homes to work in the fields, but the woman folk mostly managed to stay out of the way."

"After about three of my hours as I knew them then, Balbus asked me if I would kindly fetch him a glass of water from the other room. I did this, but when I returned to the room, the bed was empty and all that was left were two pieces of paper with a few directions as to where to go when I left the house. There was also a thick book on the table, which appeared to be moving around and vibrating. As I got closer to the table, the book moved slowly across the table towards me and stopped."

The family has all sat spellbound as Naggy told this tale. Eventually it was Pedro who broke the silence again with a question the rest of the family were thinking and that was how he had found Ishe's house.

"One day I decided to venture a bit further away from my house and in the opposite direction to the one I usually took. After a short while the box in my pocket began to vibrate. Thinking I must have somehow walked in a circle and had arrived back at my house, I took it out of my pocket and let it lead me where it wanted to and eventually I ended up here. I had no idea it was not my house until I walked inside. From the outside the two houses are identical. The only way I realised it was not my house was because of the room I had entered had different furniture to mine."

"That was when I nearly made him jump out of his skin!" said Ishe.

"She certainly did and it took me a long time to realiise that the voice was coming from the old chair in the corner of the room and that I was listening to a doll!"

Naggy told them that once he had got over the shock he and Ishe got on really well. "She told me an awful lot about what the place was, who lives in the village, who the 'High Person' was and how badly the people were treated by him."

"One day," said Ishe, "Naggy suggested that I should go with him when he next went to the village. He said that as long as he put something green on me, no one would see me." Ishe turned to granny and said that Jessica had discovered the secret of wearing green to remain undetected and had spent a large part of her visits knitting long green scarves.

"She must have known you would eventually find this place Joan and wanted to leave things ready for you.

The family all looked over to where Ishe had indicated and Pedro, being Pedro went over to have a better look. He opened the lid of a box and looked inside. "There are lots and lots of scarves in here," he told the family. "There is even a little jacket."

"That is what Jessica knitted for me to wear when she took me with her," said Ishe.

"How many times did Jessica go into the village?" asked Granny.

"Many times, but towards the time she was beginning to not feel too well, hardly at all. That is also about the time she told me about you Joan and told me that if she had done her job properly, you and her family would be the next visitors to arrive at this house."

Every one sat in silence for a very long time, each one thinking about what they had been told on their visit, both by Naggy and Ishe. Eventually, Pedro went over to his grandmother and whispered something in her ear. When she heard what he had to say, she smiled and looking at Ishe told her that Pedro had brought with him one his 'Wishy Marbs' and would she like to use it to make a wish that she could hear everyone and not just her voice. Granny said that under the circumstances she thought that would be a case of using a wish for a good thing.

"That would be very kind of you Pedro," replied Ishe, forgetting for an instant that he could not hear her. She realised what she had said and turning to Granny told her that she would like that very much if Pedro was sure he wanted to use one of his wishes for that purpose. Granny told her that he must have had that suggestion in his mind all the time if he had gone to the bother of bringing a 'Wishy Marb' with him.

"I think he should make the wish, don't you Ishe?" Ishe nodded and Granny turned to Pedro and told him to go ahead with his wish. "You can either say it out loud or just to yourself," she told him.

Pedro took out his 'Wishy Marb' and holding it for them all to see said in a loud clear voice "I wish that Ishe could hear and speak to all of us." As he said the words they all looked down at the marble Pedro was holding. They saw that very slowly one of the stripes disappeared. Ishe clapped her hands together and told him she could hear him very clearly.

Once she had said that, the whole family in turn looked at her and said hello to her and told her he how pleased they were that now they could also talk to her as well.

When they had all said their hellos and settled down again, Mary looked at her mother in law and suggested that as they had granted a wish for Ishe, could they perhaps do the same for Naggy?

Granny though that was an excellent idea and turning to Naggy asked him if there was anything he would like to wish for. Naggy looked all embarrassed and told her that there was nothing he really needed but thanked Mary for her kind thought. Once again it was Pedro who perhaps said what they were all thinking.

"What about a new foot Naggy?" there are three stripes left on this marble so I am sure they will be enough."

The rest of the family spoke out in agreement with what Pedro had said. Granddad looked at Naggy and told him that he thought there was no more deserving person that he could think of to have a wish granted than him.

"You seem to have done an awful lot for Ishe and Jessica and also by inference for us as well so I say go ahead and done be shy."

Naggy looked around at the rest of the family and they all smiled at him and told him they agreed with what Granddad had said. "That would be very kind of you if you are sure," he said.

Pedro already had the marble in his hand. He walked over to Naggy, placed it in his hand and said that it would be nice if he could make the wish himself.

Naggy looked around the room at everyone and in turn they all nodded for him to go ahead. In a very quiet voice he wished that his missing led and foot would return. Not daring to look down at his foot, he stared instead at the marble in his hand. Slowly but surely one of the striped disappeared. The rest of the family had been looking at his false leg. Just as with Ishe's wish, Naggy saw a stripe in the marble disappear. At the same time the family saw a leg and a foot replace the stump that Naggy had been using for many years. Naggy looked down at his new foot and leg then looked up at the family and Ishe who by now were all smiling and clapping for him. He thanked them all over and over again and told them it was one of the best days of his life.

"Perhaps we can make it even better," said Granny.

"You only have one shoe so I am sure the rest of the family won't mind if you use another stripe to get a decent pair of shoes or sandals."

Before he could say anything Pedro quickly took the marble from Naggy and made the wish for him. Within seconds a new pair of sandals appeared on Naggy's feet. The family smiled and clapped again as Naggy walked around the room getting used to his new foot and sandals.

Granny turned to Ishe and asked her if there was anything else she would like to use the final stripe in the marble for, but Ishe said that there was nothing at the moment that she could think of.

"In that case we will keep it and bring it next time, so if by then you have thought of something then you can use the last wish."

Ishe thanked her very much. Naggy said that he thought it was about time he started for home. Although he knew he could not be seen, he said he still preferred not to be out after dark.

Granny also said she thought it was about time they were thinking about going. She told Ishe and Naggy that they had really enjoyed their visit and thanked them for all they had told them.

Ishe told her that it had been a pleasure to have helped and said that perhaps when they came the next time, she and Naggy could help even more.

Naggy wished them all goodbye and went into the other room from where he had emerged upon his arrival.

The family sat around the table again, said goodbye to Ishe, and at a nod from granny, Pedro turned the section of the box that would start them on their return home. Within seconds only it seemed, they were back in their own home. This time as they arrived back, the map folded itself up and slid slowly under the box Granny was holding. They all gazed in amazement at this. Pedro's father said that perhaps it was a sign that they were being trusted with what they were finding out.

His mother agreed with him and said they had better make sure they did not betray the trust. "It could be that a lot of people are going to be dependent on what we can do for them."

"Have you seen the time Joan?" Granddad said. "Look at the clock; we have only been gone about half an hour. It was just as Naggy and Ishe told us." They all looked at the clock and saw that he was right.

"In that case," said Mary "we have plenty of time for a cup of tea and a bite to eat."

"While you are doing that I will have a quick look round the garden, coming Pedro?"

"O.K. gramps." The two of them left the house and slowly walked around to the shed. Granddad said nothing to Pedro so as not to alarm him, but he wanted to make sure there were no uninvited guests around. When he was sure they were on their own he asked Pedro if he had enjoyed the visit they had just been on. Pedro told him that he had but he was more interested in the 'Winter Shed' site.

"I must admit I do in some ways, but I think that is because there is a chance I will see my old friend again."

"Do you think granny's friends are there as well?" asked Pedro

"I certainly do, from what Joshua has been telling me," he sighed and said, "all of a sudden we seem to have the responsibility of helping an awful lot of people. I only hope we can manage to do things right."

Having seen nothing untoward in the garden, granddad suggested that they went back to the house for that cup of tea Pedro's mum said was going to make.

CHAPTER TWENTY-THREE

SPORTS DAY CANCELLED AND MUM AND GRANNY MAKE A VISIT

The following day, Pedro's Mum reminded him that the sports day was fast approaching and did he think he should go to the school to see if there was anything that he needed to do to give them a hand.

"I was thinking about that myself mum. Paul was saying he wanted to go there as well. I am meeting him again this afternoon to get some more milk from the farm so I will ask him then."

"That's good Pedro," said his father, "and then your granddad and I can have a walk over to the winter shed site and take the key for the drill Joshua had made. Knowing that Paul is with you will make it easier for us. At least we will know he won't be bumping into us asking what we're doing."

"O.K. dad, I will make sure we are gone for the whole afternoon so that you have plenty of time."

"Why don't you go with the boys Mary," said granny. "That way I can sit in peace and read some more of the papers and look in the last of the envelopes."

"That's fine by me if Pedro doesn't mind."

"Course not, mum! Plus if you are with us it will stop Paul from asking awkward questions. I'll just go and get the milk containers."

When he was gone, Joan took the opportunity to remind her husband and son to wear something green. "Just in case," she said, "and don't forget to take that little box Pedro gave you with the questions inside to put wherever you told Joshua you would put it."

Tom and his dad set off soon after that saying they would see everyone later. Pedro and his mum left to meet Paula and once again granny settled down to read some more of the papers. She closed the curtains 'again' and she said to herself, 'just in case.'

Paul was just about at the bottom of the hill from his house when Pedro and his mum arrived there. The first thing Mary asked him was how his grandfather was feeling. He told her that he was not really that much better, but said that hadn't stopped him yelling and shouting all the time. He said that two men had come to see him and he could hear then talking about the mine.

"They told grandfather that he really shouldn't have given the miners two weeks holiday. They said the men should be back there, searching for the 'Dishy Warbs' or at least that's what it sounded like. It is hard to understand what he says sometimes when he shouts so much. Goodness knows what 'Dishy Warbs' are or where. I think they must be something that he may have lost when he went into the mine one day."

Pedro and his mother asked Paul if there was anything she could do to help him with, but he just thanked her and told her the house keeper was doing fine at the moment. "Besides," he said, "I don't think that grandfather would like anyone else in the house. I am surprised she stays the way he yells at her."

"Well if he does he only has to ask,"

"Thank you, Mrs Vendell, I will tell him,"

They decided it would be best if they went along to the school first. Once they had found out if anything needed to be done for the sports day, the boys could go to the farm over the hill behind the school. Pedro's mum could call into the post office and then meet them as they came down the lane from the farm on her way home.

When they arrived at the school, there were lots of people there all looking very upset and angry. They could see Miss. Richards in the middle of them all trying to calm things down. Pedro saw Sally and Simon with their parents and walked over to them to see what was going on. As they approached them Sally looked up and seeing Paul with Pedro asked what he was doing there. She seemed quite upset that he was with Pedro. Before Pedro had the chance to say anything her mother told her to stay calm and to wait until they could find out the truth as to what had happened.

"What has happened Sally?" Pedro asked

"Someone has stopped our sports day, that's what's happened!" replied Sally very close to tears.

"All the equipment has been stolen and the sports ground has been ruined. Come and see for yourself!"

Pedro could not believe what he was looking at. The whole of the field had been ripped up, the goal posts had been broken in half and the hut where everyone met and sat to watch the games and sporting events had been pulled down and lay in bits all over the ground.

"But who would do such a thing?" said Pedro

Clearly, still very upset by it all, Sally who was normally a very pleasant girl suggested that maybe Paul knew something about it all.

Miss Richards who had followed them to the playing field and heard Sally's outburst, told her that she thought it was very unkind of her to suggest that Paul either knew, or had anything to do with what had happened and she said she thought that an apology was in order. By this time Paul had arrived at the scene along with Pedro's mum, Sally's parents and some of the other parents. They all gathered around Miss. Richards to discuss what to do next.

Paul walked over to join Pedro and Sally who looked him straight in the eye and asked him if he knew anything about what had happened there, Paul told them that no, he hadn't. "In that case, I am sorry I thought so," said Sally, but Pedro could see by the look on her face that she still thought it was possible that at least a lot of what had been done had something to do with the Bilk family.

"So what do we do now?" asked one of the parents.

"I don't honestly know," Miss. Richards said. "Clearly we can't have our sports day here now and I know we can't use the playing field at the school in town because they are using the time of the holidays to have it all re-grassed ready for the new term."

"Perhaps we can all get together one day and have a big picnic on the village green," someone suggested, "I am sure between us we can get enough food together to have a nice time. The children can play a few games and enjoy themselves and the parents can have a nice relaxing day chatting to one another."

"That is probably about the best we can hope for at this stage," said Mrs. Richards. "Is there anyone here who would organise such a day?"

"Yes my wife and I will," volunteered one of the fathers. We will go round to the families and find out what they are willing to contribute and organise the day from there."

Miss. Richards thanked them and the parents there gave a round of applause. Already offers of help could be heard among those parents. "But," she reminded them, "We still need to find out who was responsible for all this damage."

"Bet we will never know," said Sally's father, "it's just the sort of mysterious thing that used to happen years ago around here. Ask any of the older folk and they will tell you many tales of strange goings on with no explanation as to how they happened."

Miss. Richards said that she would have to go at once and tell Mr. Bilk what had happened because after all he owned the school.

"Excuse me Miss," said Paul "but at the moment my grandfather is quite ill, so perhaps we should wait a while before we tell him,"

"In that case, perhaps now would not be the best time, but he will have to be told eventually." Miss Richards replied. "Perhaps you could kindly let me know when your grandfather is well enough for me to visit him"

Paul said that he would and with nothing more that could be done, everyone started to leave. The parent, who had said he would organise things, promised he would be round to see everyone in the next few days to see how they would be able to help out.

Pedro had managed to get close to Sally to ask if she would like to come round to his house the next day. He made sure that Paul was not within hearing distance when he asked her. Sally said that would be very nice and went to ask her parents. They were talking to Pedro's mother and said yes that would be fine. They said that they were planning to go into town on the early bus so they would bring her to Pedro's house about eight thirty if that's was O.K. Pedro's mother said yes that would be fine and then Pedro told them he would walk to the bus stop and meet Sally. It was on the way to the shop so he could get the paper for his granddad at the same time.

By now Paul had joined them, so they all walked together until they reached Sally's house. They all bid each other goodbye and Pedro and his mum and Paul continued down the road. As they reached the turning for the farm they realised that they had forgotten completely about the milk. All the goings on at the school had made it go right out of their minds.

"You carry on home mum, Paul and I will go for the milk."

"Alright, if you are sure Pedro, I need to get home to start getting the lunch ready. Good bye Paul, I hope your grandfather feels a bit better soon."

"Goodbye Mrs. Vendell, I am sure he will."

The boys walked up the hill to the farm to get the milk. As they returned back to the road they just chatted about nothing in particular. Pedro was glad about that, as he really didn't feel like any more of Paul's probing questions. Paul asked Pedro what he would be doing the next few days. Pedro said he would be going out with his granddad but he wasn't sure where or when. This was the truth, as nothing had been decided about when they would go back to the 'Winter Shed' site.

At the bottom of the hill leading the Bilk house, they said goodbye to each other with Paul saying that maybe Pedro would like to come up to his house one day. Pedro replied that, that would be nice but secretly he didn't really want to. From all he had heard about the old man Bilky he thought he would be a bit afraid to go there.

When he arrived back home, he found that his father and grandfather had returned and were being told what had happened at the school by his mother.

"Who on earth would do such a thing?" said his grandfather

"I doubt if he could do something like that, but I bet it is in some way connected to the Bilk family."

His wife agreed, but added that they would never be able to find out.

Tom asked his mother if she had found out anything interesting in the papers she had been reading.

"Yes I have and I think there is a way to help the people in Naggy's village. If I have read things right, it will take a bit of doing but I am sure with Naggy and Ishe's help we can. I will tell you all after lunch. We can sit in the garden as I tell you. There are no trees there, so we will not be overheard if you see what I mean."

Over lunch the two men told the rest of the family that they had visited the other site and had encountered no one on the way there or back. They had used the medallion to open the bush and had put the box with the questions granny had written inside the passageway behind it. Granddad said he had left a note of his own to Joshua thanking him for the drill he had made for him. He had seen it behind the bush and had taken the size of the end of it so now he could finish making the key to turn it. He added that Tom and he had decided that they would work on making the hole during the night when they were less likely to be spotted. He had said this to

Joshua in the note he had left. As long as they took all precautions they should be able to complete the task quite quickly. "The good thing is," he told them "the wall where we have to try to get through is behind part of the old shed wall so we will be out of sight as well. We will just have to make sure we leave no evidence as to what we are doing. That means disposing of any soil that is displaced by the drill."

"I have decided to take out my old painting bits and pieces I used years ago, so if anyone stumbles across us once it is light, we can make out we are there to catch the sunrise and paint it."

His mother told Tom she thought it was a good idea.

Everyone was eager to hear what granny had read in the papers she had been studying while they had been out, so they quickly helped to clear away the lunch things and they settled round the table in the garden.

Granny had brought with her a few of the envelopes and also the box similar to the one they used on their 'journeys' but not so big.

Once they were all settled and granddad had made sure there were no 'prying eyes' they gave granny their full attention.

She started by telling them that she had opened one of the smaller packages the old lady had given her. In it were instructions as to what to do with the little box she had. " It can only be used in the 'Land Of The Lost,' as the old lady had called it in her notes but, used the right way will help those who have been affected by the bad magic. It can also be used to reverse any bad magic and punish those responsible for the misery they have caused people." She looked up at the family and said that they had to be very careful at this point that they did not allow the people in that place to use that part of the system just to get revenge for what had been done to them in the past,

"I can understand that will be what some of the people might want to happen, but we must try our very best to make sure it does not. I am sure that with Naggy and Ishe's help we will be able to accomplish that."

Granny then asked Pedro which of his friends had found some funny shaped marbles.

"Sally, she had some with small dents in them and the dents had different coloured spots. Why granny? "

She didn't answer him straight away, but did ask him to confirm that he had some quite small marbles with coloured spots on them instead of stripes. When he told her he did, she said, "In that case Pedro, you and Sally, if I have read these papers correctly, have the means of communicating with the people in 'The Land Of Lost."

"What do you mean granny?"

She looked at Pedro and told him that many, many years ago people and in some cases whole families just seemed to disappear from the old village but no one knew where they had gone to. Of course, back in those days it was most unusual for people to leave the village they were born in. They had no means of transport and the only other people they saw would be the occasional traveller who passed through. Consequently they had no means of finding out where the missing villagers had gone. There was no law and order, as we know it today. The village would be looked after by one person who was known as the High Person and everyone had to do what he or she demanded. Punishment was swift for anyone the High Person felt deserved it. The punished person would quite often be sent away to work and in most cases never seen again. If the High Person thought the offender had committed a really bad offence, then his or her whole family would be taken away.

"From what I can make out, reading old Jessica's notes, someone, had at some time found out where the people were being taken and tried to visit there. The first person that tried never returned but had left notes about what they were going to do so that a long time later another person attempted to do what the first person had tried. And I think," she said looking at the family, "that person may well have been Balbus, the man Naggy found lying in the bed in that house he discovered when he himself took the strange journey."

"Do you really think so granny?" Pedro asked

"From what I have read in the papers and from notes made by Jessica herself, then yes I do. All the dates and times seem to add up. The only thing that is not quite clear, is how long had passed between the people going missing and Balbus arriving on the scene."

"But how can the marbles Sally and I have help with talking to the people?"

"I think Naggy and Ishe will have to provide the answer to that mystery Pedro, but again from what I have been able to find out from the papers, those marbles were used way back in time by a kind and magical lady who was in direct apposition to the Mantel Helter person we heard about. Whether she was around at the same time as her or came on the scene later I have no idea. The notes in the papers were not all in order so perhaps they are not related to the same time span. Over the years she tried her hardest to help the people of the village where families were disappearing, but Mantel Helter's powers were greater and in the end she was defeated. Before she too disappeared, she managed to use her powers sufficiently to adapt some of the marbles being found at the time to enable who ever held them to communicate with another person who had a marble containing stripes by placing the two together. What this means is that if we take either yours or Sally's marbles with us on a visit, we need to find someone who has the opposite part of the puzzle. She also cast a friendly spell over that certain part of the mine to ensure that those kinds of marbles would still be found in the near future."

"Do we know the name of this magical lady mum?"

"No we don't Tom, but I am hoping that either Naggy or Ishe will know."

"That Mantel Helter person sounds as if she was a really nasty person," said Mary

"Yes I think she was," replied her mother in law, "but you also have to remember that back in those days, with no outside communication

217

for the villagers, then someone like her could have absolute control over everyone. Where she came from I have no idea. With her power and I venture to say with unlimited access to the 'Wishy Marbs' of her day, she could do just what she wanted, when she wanted. All she had to do was select a few not very nice people to act for her and her domination over everyone was complete."

"What's your plan now, Joan?"

Granny looked at her husband and said that she thought that perhaps she and Mary could make a quick return visit to Ishe's house so she could ask her a few questions she had and also give her and Naggy a rough idea of what was in her mind regarding helping people. "That is if you don't mind Mary."

Mary told her that she didn't mind one little bit and asked when they were meant to be going.

"I think as soon as possible. The sooner we can help sort out those poor people's problems the better."

"Why don't you go this evening mum? Dad and Pedro and I can potter around here and no one will be the wiser.

His mother thought that was a very good idea and suggested to Mary that they went inside to get ready for the journey.

"If we go from the front room, that will leave the kitchen free for the men to use. We don't know what would happen if they entered the same room we had travelled from."

Pedro and his dad and granddad wished them a safe journey as the ladies went into the house, then the three of them went round the house to the shed. As they got nearer to the shed Pedro looked up and saw something that made his heart skip a beat. He nudged his grandfather and told him to look on the roof of the shed. Pedro's father also heard what Pedro had said and looked to where Pedro and his father indicated. Sitting on top of the shed were two of the three legged, blackbirds.

"Good job we are all wearing green," said granddad. "We had better not go into the shed. If we do and we make any kind of noise, they will know that someone is in there and try to see who it is and investigate."

"I wonder how long they have been there," said Pedro, thinking about how they had all been sitting around the table earlier. "I know they can't see us because we are wearing green, but what about the things granny had on the table?"

His grandfather said that he didn't think that the birds had been there then and anyway they had all been sitting in the middle of the garden with nowhere for the birds to perch."

"What do we do now?" said Tom.

"I think we should go into the house, make ourselves a nice cup of tea and come back into the garden and sit where we were before. While we are in the house we can take off anything green we are wearing and just come back out with our tea. That way, if the birds are still around, will spot us and see we are doing nothing out of the ordinary."

"Good idea dad, and while I make the tea, why don't you leave a little note for mum and Mary so if they return while we are still out here they too can take off their bits of green, and will also know not to say anything about how they got on when they talk to us."

Pedro walked back into the garden and sat down at the table from where he could just about see the shed. The two birds were still sitting there and now looked in his direction. As his granddad and dad came back out with the tea, he had one of his great ideas. When they were all settled he told his father in a low voice that the birds were still sitting there and could now see them. His father asked him to keep a crafty eye on them and let him and granddad know if they flew away.

"Did you leave a note for mum and granny?" he asked his grandfather.

"Yes I did and I told them to be very careful what they said if they came out."

Pedro then told them of the idea he had had, and to add to the note, that should they arrive back while and we are still in the garden, then for granny or his mum to look out of granny's bedroom window to see if the birds were still there. If they were, then to quietly walk out of the front door, rattle the gate as if they were just returning from a walk, and then come round the house to the garden.

"You can't see the gate from the shed, and the birds may wonder where granny and mum are as they are usually here with us."

Granddad thought that was a good idea and getting up from the table said in a voice loud enough for the birds to hear that he had forgotten the sugar and would go and fetch some. He winked at Pedro and Pedro knew he was going to add his suggestion to the note he had left.

When he returned with the sugar, he said to them both that he hadn't realised at the time but the birds couldn't hear what they were saying because none of them were wearing anything red.

"Never thought of that granddad, still doesn't hurt to be safe rather than sorry."

They sat around talking about nothing in particular. Pedro did bring up the subject of the damage at the school, and that now they would not be able to have the sports day he was so looking forward to. As he spoke, he kept a careful eye on the shed but the birds continued to just sit and stare. At one point he thought he saw three of them, but put it down to the fact that the sun was beginning to set and was in his eyes.

After what seemed like only minutes, they heard the front gate open and a couple of minutes later his mum and grandmother came walking round the side of the house. At the same time, they heard the sound of the late evening bus going down the road, so it would appear to the birds that they had indeed been out somewhere.

As they sat down, Joan suddenly remembering that time spent on a visit was as if no time at all had passed in real life, quickly said they had only gone a short way towards the village but as it was getting quite chilly they caught the bus back. Tom asked if they would like a cup of tea. Telling him that would be very nice, his mother said to her husband in a low voice that it was a good job they had seen his note.

"That was Pedro's idea." he told her and then asked in an equally low voice if they had managed to get answers to their questions. She indicated with a nod of her head that yes she had.

Tom brought out the tea for his mother and wife and they all sat round and continue to enjoy the fading sunset. After a while Pedro's mother suggested that perhaps they should think about going back inside, as it was getting rather cold now. As they returned to the house Pedro glanced at the shed but there was no sign of the birds.

CHAPTER TWENTY-FOUR

GRANNY AND MUM'S REPORT AND A SECOND VISIT FROM PAUL

"We're going out into the garden now Pedro, don't forget to put the green scarf on before you come out."

"O.K. mum, I'll be there in a minute."

The family had decided to wait until the following morning before they listened to what granny and mum had to tell about their visit the previous evening. As they settled at the table in the garden and waited for Pedro to join them, granddad had a quick look round to see if they had any winged visitors, but all seemed clear. As well everyone wearing something green, Pedro's mum had put a green cloth on the table.

Pedro joined them and sat next to his granddad, eager to hear about the visit.

Granny started by telling them that they had been lucky, as when they arrived at Ishe's house, Naggy was also there. He had called round to tell her that he thought he had found a way to talk to someone who, in his opinion, could be trusted with the information they had gathered. "He told us that because he couldn't be seen he had been able to walk around freely and listen to what people had been saying about things in general and about the situation they all found themselves in. It appears that quite a few of the families were beginning to form a kind of action to try to deal with their plight. The only thing is, they need to be very careful, because although they know they can trust each other, they are very unsure as to who else may wish to genuinely join them." She told them that Naggy had said that in the past people had tried to do this kind of thing, but had always been found out and of course it had resulted in their disappearance.

"Why does he think the time is right now?" Tom asked his mother.

"Because, apparently, when he was walking round the place one day, he came upon three families all sitting together on the grass, and he overheard one of the men say that he thought it was now or never to have a go at overturning things. The man told his friends that he thought the best time would be just after the next period started."

"It seems from what Naggy heard," granny said, "that at the start of each period the 'High Person' goes away for a few days. Where he goes no one knows, but the man thought that time would be their best chance they would have. Either then or when the big birds went off somewhere. Again, as with the 'High person' they had no idea where they went, but quite often they were done for a few days."

"Well we all know where at least two of them were yesterday," said Pedro, and explained to his mum and granny that two of the birds had settles on the shed just as they had gone into the house to go on their journey. "That is why granddad left you the note."

Joan asked her daughter-in-law if she would like to continue with the tale, so Pedro's mum told them that Naggy thought he had stumbled on some ancient way of talking to certain people but only if that person had a certain shaped stone with coloured dots on it. He said he had overheard another of the group telling her friends that she had this funny shaped stone which had a bit of a hole on one side with four red dots. Her great aunt had passed it on to her many years before and had told her that if ever she came across someone with a stone to match it, then it would mean that person would have arrived in the village from far away and could possibly hold the secret to helping them out of their dire situation. She said her aunt had given no indication as to what she had to do with the stone, but she had kept it in a safe place ever since hoping that one day it would come in useful. Apparently, none of the rest of the group had any idea as to what to do with it either.

"That is where they had a problem," Mary said. "The group of friends had no idea at all who they could trust to ask for advice on the matter. We told Naggy that perhaps we had the solution to their problem and explained that we were in possession of the same kind of stones, or marbles as we called the."

Granny took over the story again and told them that as far as she had been able to make out from Jessica's notes, if someone from this side went over to the other side with a matching marble then they would be able to see and talk to that person who had the stone.

"As you know, we are invisible to the people back there just as long as we are carrying that little box we take with us. Before we go back again, Naggy is going to see if he can find out who this lady is that has the stone and try in some way to let her know that he has friends, meaning us, who would be more than willing to help them."

Granny went on to say that the next time he went onto the village he would take Ishe with him to see if she could remember anything from the times when Jessica used to take her.

"We also emphasised to Naggy," Mary said, "that we would only be willing to help them as long there were no thoughts of nasty, cruel revenge against the 'High Person' or anyone else that had mistreated them along the way. We told him that that it was quite understandable that the people would naturally think along those lines but that was not the way to sort things out, or to have our help."

"I asked him, should he be able to contact the group, to tell them that a suitable punishment which had to be agreed by everyone and was acceptable to us, would be fine and indeed we would be willing to help them along those lines, but definitely no revenge type punishment. The manner of the punishment must be such that the

"High Person' and his assistants were made to see the error of their ways."

"When are you planning on going back there mum?" asked Tom.

"We thought that perhaps the day after tomorrow. That should give Naggy and Ishe plenty of time to try to sort a few things out."

"That will also give dad, me and Pedro time to go over to the 'Winter Shed' site to see how things are progressing there. There may also be a reply to some of your questions we put behind the bush," he told his mother.

"Oh! I almost forgot," exclaimed Joan. "Ishe told us that during her visits, Jessica had managed to make contact with a very old lady who everyone referred to as the 'keeper of the secrets'. It seems as if she had been the source of a lot of the information Jessica had written in her notes. Naggy said he would try to find out where she lived, if indeed she was still alive. It appears she was one villager the 'High person' was very wary of. He never called on her or bothered her, but he made sure that his helpers kept a close eye on her and reported any visits she made to anyone. The person she had visited was also very closely watched for a few days. I will have a look this afternoon, through some more of the papers to see if I can find any reference to this 'keeper of the secrets' lady"

As they all sat there relaxing, and thinking about all they had heard from the two ladies, the sound of the front gate being hastily opened brought them back to the present. Granddad was the first on his feet and started round the house to see who had arrived. He almost knocked over a very upset crying Paul. Granddad put his arms round the boy's shoulders and led him round to where the family were sitting.

"What on earth is the matter Paul?" asked Pedro's mum.

"It's my grandfather! It's my grandfather!"

"Why what has happened to him, is he worse?"

"I don't know what's happened to him Mrs. Vendell. I went in to see him this morning but he was not in his room. I couldn't find him anywhere in the house, so I went out into the garden. As I walked round to the orchard at the back of the house, I saw him shouting up at one of the apple trees! I didn't dare go any closer so just stood there watching. Then I saw two big funny looking blackbirds in one of the trees and it looked and sounded as if granddad was arguing with them." Paul looked at Pedro's mum and said. "Why would you argue with birds?"

Granddad, who still had his arm on Paul's quietly asked him, "What did you do then son?"

"I just stood there staring Sir. I didn't know what to do. I daren't let grandfather see me. I couldn't believe what I was seeing. The birds were answering him back which made grandfather even angrier. They appeared to be giving him orders. Grandfather was yelling back at them saying he needed more time, more time. Then the birds flew away and as they flew over my head I could swear they had three feet! But who has ever heard of birds with three feet. By this time I was crying a little, so maybe I was seeing things through my tears."

Mary, who had gone into the house during this time, returned with drinks for them all, tea for the adults and cold drinks for the boys. She had heard most of what Paul had been saying.

"What happened then Paul?"

"Something else I couldn't understand. My grandfather went into the house then came out again but this time he was carrying some paper and sticks. He made a small bonfire, and when it was burning nicely, he took off his blue jacket, threw it on the fire and said something about not taking any orders from them again."

The family passed looks between one another unseen by Paul, each one remembering the rhymes they had read at Ishe's house concerning colours and the birds.

"Would you like us to come back to the house with you and check on your grandfather?"

It was Pedro's grandfather who had asked the question, but Paul told him he really didn't want to go back there at all, that he was frightened about what he had seen and what his grandfather would say.

"In that case, would you like to stay here with Pedro and his mum and dad while I and my husband go to see how he is?"

Paul looked at Pedro's granny and said he would like that very much.

They could all see how very upset Paul still was, so Pedro's mother told him to just sit and relax and when he felt better then they could all go for a nice walk while Pedro's Granny and granddad went to see his grandfather.

"After all, Pedro's grandmother went to school with your grandfather, so at least they know each other."

CHAPTER TWENTY-FIVE

RESCUING 'BILKY'

Pedro's grandparents set off to see what had happened at the Bilk home, but before they left, Joan had suggested to her husband that perhaps they would be wise to wear something green.

"You never know what we may come across."

As they were about to turn up the hill to the house, they saw someone practically running down towards them. It was a middle-aged lady and she appeared to be in quite a state.

"I don't know who you are, but you would be very wise not to go up there to that mad house! I will certainly never set foot in there again; I've had enough of his bad tempers and weird visitors. Not to mention him talking to birds all the time. Not only talking, but arguing with them."

Joan put out her arms to stop the lady as she met them and asked her to tell them what she was so upset about. Joan told her that she went to school with Mr. Bilk and that Paul had come to her son's house that morning saying that his grandfather had been acting a bit strange and that he had left the house because he was afraid of his temper and didn't wish to stay there anymore, and she and her husband were doing to the house to see old Balky to find out what was going on.

By now the lady had calmed down a little and granddad suggested that she took a seat on the trunk of a fallen tree to get her breath back so she could tell them properly what the matter was.

She told them that her name was Harriet Jakes and she was the house keeper up at the Bilk house and had been for over ten years, but in all the time she had worked there, nothing had happened during those years as strange as was taking place there now.

"I sometimes think the old man has gone completely mad." she said. "He seems to spend most of his time locked in his room. I can never get in there to clean. All I can hear is him arguing with someone, and yet I know he has had no visitors. I would have had to let them in if they had come to the door."

"What kind of things did he appear to be saying?" asked Joan.

"It was hard to understand sometimes. He would be saying things like 'I need more time' or one day he said, 'I know I shouldn't have sent the men on holiday,' and 'No, I can't get them all back to work yet. You will just have to tell her to be patient.' I had no idea at all who he was talking to. As I have told you, no one had come calling while I was up and about. I suppose it may have been possible they arrived before I got up, but they would have had to have arrived very early as I get up at half past five each morning. Mr. Bilk is very strict about things and he always wants his breakfast by six thirty."

Joan asked her if there had been any other strange things going on.

"There was one thing that puzzled me one day last week. I had heard him go back in to his room after he had eaten his breakfast, and a few minutes later could hear him talking to someone again. Now I know there was no one in the room because I had been in there giving it a clean while he was in the kitchen having his breakfast.

Anyway, soon after that I went out into the garden to pull some carrots to put in the stew he had asked me to make for him that evening. I could hear his raised voice, and looked over to where his room was. The window was open and it seemed as if he was arguing with two big black birds that were stood on the window sill. Funny looking birds they were as well, with different coloured wings and I could swear it looked as if they had three feet! I just stood there, half of me wanting to run, and the other half of me rooted to the spot too scared to move. That is when I heard the old man say again what he had said the previous time. 'Tell her I am doing the best I can!' With that, the birds flew away and the old man slammed the window shut so hard one of the panes of glass fell out."

"How did he seem to be with young Paul?" granddad asked.

"He was fine when he first arrived, but over the last week or so, it seemed as if the lad could do nothing right in his eyes. He gave him a big pile of papers to read one day and told him to study them one at a time. He said that if he was going to be any good to him in the future he would need to know all there was about the mine. At first Paul did as he was asked and read the papers, but as the days passed, I could tell that he was getting bored with it. Mr. Bilk would call him into his room now and then and ask him questions about what he had been reading. I don't think he was very pleased with the answers Paul gave him, and one day yelled at him that he was just as bad as his father. Paul came out almost in tears that day."

"So what happened then?"

"It was rather strange really. The next morning Mr. Bilk called Paul into his room and they were in there for quite a while just talking. I could hear their voices but couldn't hear what was being said as they were talking just normally, no yelling or anything like that. The next thing was, they both came out of the room and Mr. Bilk told me that Paul was going on an errand for him. He said he was going to see a boy called Pedro. I had no idea who Pedro was; I just assumed it was someone he had met at school. As he was leaving Mr. Bilk gave Paul a little bag and asked him if he was sure he knew what he had to do. Paul said yes and went on his way."

"That must have been the day he came to visit us," said Joan, and explained to Harriet that they were Pedro's grandparents and were here for a few weeks holiday. "Anything else happen at all?"

"Well, the next day was my day off and I left that evening to visit my friend in the village. We had arranged to go into the town on the early bus so I had arranged to spend the night at her house. I often did that if we were going out early. As it turned out, my friend didn't feel too well the next day so we decided to just go into the village and call at the shop for a couple of things. Just as we arrived there, we saw Mr. Bilk come rushing out of the shop and it looked as if he was pulling young Paul out by one ear! He was shouting at him about how he had only asked him to do one thing and he couldn't even get that right, and what use was he going to be in the future if he couldn't even do one simple thing."

Harriet said her and her friend decided not to go into the shop then but wait until later as they could see there were quite a few people in there already. "When we called in later there was the assistant serving. We asked her what had happened but she said she really didn't know, just that she had been asked to work that afternoon."

Joan then asked her what the situation was like up at the house after that.

"Not too bad. Of course Paul and his grandfather had no idea I had witnessed what had taken place at the shop so had no reason to mention it to me. I decided to try to help the lad by getting him out of the house and suggested to Mr. Bilk that perhaps Paul could go to the farm to collect some milk. "'I suppose so. He can't mess that little job up surely.' was all he said, so after that I tried to get him out the house to do bits of jobs for me as often as I could."

"What happened to make you leave this morning?"

Harriet said that she got up as usual and started to do her normal duties. The Doctor had been the previous day to see Mr. Bilk because he had not been feeling too well, and had left instructions as to what he was to have to eat for his breakfast.

"I prepared the food just the way the Doctor had told me, and then placed it on the kitchen table ready for when Mr. Bilk came down. I had my back to him when he came into the room. I heard him sit down and said my usual cheery good morning.

The next thing I know is he started shouting at me and asking where his usual breakfast was. Before I had a chance to explain to him about what the doctor had said, I felt something hit the back of my head. I put my hand up to my head and it felt all wet and sticky. He had thrown his breakfast at me. I turned around just in time to see him pick up the plate and throw that as well. I managed to move out of the way and the plate hit the wall.

At the same time young Paul came into the kitchen. He saw what was going on and turned round and ran out of the house and into the garden. Mr. Bilk got up from the table, and as he did so tipped it over in his temper, and then he too went out of the back door into the garden. I put the table back up on its legs, and made some effort to start to tidy things up. I happened to glance out of the kitchen window and saw that once again Mr. Bilk was arguing with those birds.

This time when they flew away, he came into the house, picked up some paper and matches and went out into the garden again. As he rushed out the door he turned and looked at me and told me he would deal with me later. I decided there and then I would not stay any longer in that house. I went up to my room and locked the door thinking that I would stay there until he had calmed down a little then I would leave. The window in my room overlooked the garden and as I stood there I saw Mr. Bilk take off his blue jacket and throw it on the fire he had started."

Harriet then said that a short time later she saw Paul running from the garden and out of the front gate and down the hill.

"I waited in my room for quite a while before I dared to leave it. When I finally thought it was safe I started to make my way down the stairs. I pulled off my overalls just popping all the buttons in my haste to get it off. I threw it on the stairs as I made my way down. Just as I got to the bottom he came in through the back door and saw me. I managed to get out of the front door and started running as fast as I was able. I could hear him yelling at me but had no idea what he was saying and had no intention of stopping to find out. That is when I saw you two good people walking along the road."

By this time Harriet was really shaking and started crying hysterically. Joan put an arm round her shoulder to comfort her and tried to calm her down. She told her that Paul had arrived at her son's house in quite a state.

"He told us what had happened as far as he knew. He was determined he was not going back to the house again. He is back there now with Pedro and his parents. I suggested that he stayed there whilst my husband and I came to see what was going on in Bilky's house. I went to school with him so he knows me. I also know what a nasty temper he has. He was just the same at school. I think it must run in the male side of the Bilks. The only one who was not as bad as the rest was Jessica's husband, who was this Mr. Bilks father."

Granddad told Harriot she was more than welcome to come back to the house with them but she said she had no intention of ever stepping inside that house again as long as 'he' was there. She told him that she felt a lot better now and would take a slow walk into the village to her friend's house.

"Is there anything we can get you from the house?' Joan asked.

"Well I did rush out without my handbag, so if you could try to get that for me I would be very grateful. It is in my room which is at the top of the stairs over the kitchen. It is a dark brown one."

"I will make sure I go and look for it so don't worry."

After making sure again that Harriot was O.K. to continue to her friend's house, Joan and John made their way up the hill to the Bilk house, wondering between themselves just what had been going on there and just what they would discover upon their arrival.

What met them when they got there was a scene of total destruction. Chairs had been thrown everywhere. Cupboards had been pulled away from the walls and were lying on the floor. Drawers were also lying on the floor with their contents scattered everywhere. They followed the sound of Mr. Bilk's voice as he shouted and screamed at someone in the main room off to the right of the entrance hall.

"I told you not to come back here and I will not wear that jacket again no matter how much she threatens me!" they heard him yell.

John and Joan looked into the room where Old Bilky was doing all the shouting. He had his back to them so did not see them. What they could see were three of the strange blackbirds, two standing on the open window sill and one actually perched on one of the chairs that had not been upturned, and it was to this bird that he was addressing his yelling. Lying on the chair was a blue jacket. Realising they could not be seen by the birds, the couple stood very quiet and still. Eventually, one of the birds from the window sill flew over to Mr. Bilk, sat on an upturned chair and said in a very menacing voice, "You will do exactly as you are told or else you know what will happen to you. 'She' doesn't take very kindly to being betrayed and let down. It will be all the worse for you if she feels it is necessary to pay you a personal visit!"

With that he flew closer to the old man, gave him a nasty peck on the top of his head, which instantly started to bleed, then he and the other two birds flew out of the window, with a warning they would be back in the morning, and saying they hoped by then he would have made the right choice.

Mr Bilk collapsed on the floor holding his head and Joan and John decided that was a good time to make their presence known.

"What on earth is going on here, Bilky?" That was the name Joan had called him at school and it was more of a demand than a question.

'Bilky was still lying on the floor holding his head, but turned to look up at her as she spoke. "Joan Meaker!" he said using her maiden name he remembered from his school days, "what are you doing here?" then almost immediately went on the defensive and added, "I might have known you had something to do with all that has been happening to me!"

"I have nothing at all to do with whatever has been happening to you Bilky, nor have I any idea what has been going on, but I would guess knowing you of old, you have not been treating people in a very nice way and now you are paying the price of your nasty ways, am I right?"

She could see by the look on the old man's face that she had touched a raw nerve. "But, having said that I am willing to help you make amends and sort a few things out if that is what you would like."

She went further into the room and made out she had just noticed the cut on his head. "What on earth have you done to your head? You had better let me take a look at it. This cut looks quite deep."

She told him to sit up and at the same time asked her husband if he could go into the kitchen and get a bowl of water and a clean cloth. He did as she asked him them noticed her husband for the first time. "Vendell, you as well! I might have known."

John took no notice of him but went into the kitchen to get what his wife had asked. When he returned Bilky was in less of a defiant mood and talking to his wife quite calmly and answering any questions she was asking him.

"What about your housekeeper, is she not around?" asked Joan.

"Haven't had one for ages," was his reply.

"Don't you start lying to me Bilky or else I won't help you. I'll just leave you to the birds and fate."

Bilky looked up at her in surprise and asked her how she knew about the birds.

"I know lots of things, but you won't get one ounce of help from me or my family if you persist in lying to us."

She went on to tell him that they had met his housekeeper at the bottom of the hill and that she seemed to be absolutely terrified of him and the way he had been treating her, and of what was going on at the house.

"Oh, and by the way, just to complete today's little episode, we also had your grandson Paul turn up at our house with a similar tale and also saying he did not want to return to you or this house while you were behaving the way you are doing."

At this bit of information, Bilky appeared to just slump down further against the chair he had been leaning against.

"What do you want me do to, what can I do?"

The way Bilky looked up at her, Joan could almost feel sorry for him, but had to remind herself that he could be quite manipulative when he wanted to be, and would say anything if he thought he could benefit from it. She looked back down at him, and putting on what she thought was a stern voice told him that he would have to tell then all that had been going on over the years, and why 'She', whoever 'She' was had such a hold over him.

Hearing that Joan knew about the birds had come as a shock to him, but now she had mentioned knowing about the 'She' person as well really had taken him aback. He realised that he may well have to tell her the truth or else he would not get any help from her at all.

"Well, are you ready for us to help you?" The question brought Bilky out of the world his mind had disappeared into.

"I suppose I have no alternative do I?"

"No you don't. You have treated a lot of quite innocent folk very badly, so you have got a lot of making up to do. I and my family know an awful lot of what has been going on over the years, much more than you can possibly imagine, so if you try to cover up anything just because you think it will work in your favor, then you had better think again."

At this point, Joan looked him straight in the eye and told him that as he was very well aware, she had known him since they were children at school, and that all his evil, scheming ways were known to her, so unless he was prepared to be totally honest with her then she would, she reminded him again, leave him to whatever fate had in store for him.

"If you really want to put things right and do the right thing for everyone then we will do our very best to help you. I must warn you though; you will have to be prepared to take some consequences of your past actions."

Bilky could see that Joan meant every word she said, so he thought to himself that perhaps this may be a way out of all his past troubles, and could break the spell of many, many years. He had been influenced over the years by a legacy, which had influenced many of the mine owners in the past. The only one to have tried to go against it had been his father, and he had been punished by the very people he Cedric had been controlled by all these years. He looked up at Joan and her husband and told them that he really would like their help if they were willing to give it. Joan told him that yes, they were very willing, but he on his part must agree to be perfectly honest with them.

"The first thing you have to do is get rid of that blue jacket," She didn't let on that she already knew what had happened to the jacket. " Without that the birds will have no vocal control over you. The second thing is make sure you are always wearing something green. Take our word for it, by doing those two things you will be taking the first steps to becoming a decent man for the first time in your life." Joan was determined she would continue to lean quite heavily on Bilky until she was quite sure he had started to mend his ways and she felt he was sincere in wanting to become a changed person.

"The jacket has already been destroyed" said Bilky. He looked at Joan and said, "Can I ask just one thing before we go any further? It's not for me but for my grandson."

Joan nodded so he asked them if Paul could stay with them for a few days just until things had started to calm down a bit. Joan thought to herself that it would be a good idea for Paul to be away from his grandfather's influence for a while so she agreed she would ask her daughter-in-law when she got home, but could see no real objection.

"What do I have to do now Joan?"

"The first thing we have to do is get all this mess cleared up. What on earth happened in here?" Again it was more of a statement than a question.

"Then we will all have to sit down and have a good long talk. We need to know just exactly what has been going on here for the past few years, and just how much influence these people have over you."

Although Joan was trying to get Bilky to open up to them, she had no intention at this point in telling him anything they had found out. She wanted to be really sure he was telling them the truth and that he could be trusted completely in his effort to change. Knowing him of old as she did, it would take a lot of convincing on his part for her to become more relaxed with him. Still she would give him the benefit of the doubt until he proved otherwise.

The three of them set about trying to tidy up the mess Bilky in his temper had created. Things that were smashed beyond repair were thrown outside to be burned later. As she was putting things into a cupboard under the stairs Joan came across a pile of blue jackets similar to the one she had seen on the chair when Bilky was arguing with the three birds.

"What are all these jackets in here?" she shouted into the living room. Bilky came to see what she was talking about and explained that they had been brought to the house by two men who had instructed him to wear one when the birds appeared. He told Joan he realised that without wearing one he could not be heard by the birds but if he didn't wear one when they arrived they made his life a real misery so it was better to do as they said. He said he had tried a few times to not put one on but the birds always wore him down in the end. Joan told him that she would see to it that they were destroyed.

"How did they make your life a misery?" asked John.

Turning his back on the pair he pulled his shirt out of his trousers, lifted it up so the two of them could see the nasty scars and cuts on his back.

"This is what they would do," he told them. "Each time was worse than the previous. I tried to escape from them when I knew it was time for them to pay me a visit by walking into the village but they would just fly on ahead of me and when I was in a quiet part of the road would attack me. They always made sure no one else was around. There seemed to be no where I could get away from them."

"I think you should certainly go and see the doctor about the cuts on your back," said Joan, "a couple of them look really nasty."

"I did go one time about six weeks ago, but when I went in to see the doctor and lifted up my shirt to show him, there was no sign of anything. It was just as if they had never been there. I had to make out to the doctor that I had banged my back and thought that perhaps I might had cut it, but he just said there was nothing to see. I left feeling very foolish and also very puzzled as to what had happened to the cuts. As I reached the gate to leave the doctors garden, a movement above my head caused me to look up and there I saw two of the birds staring down at me. One of them flew down and sat on my shoulder and said right into my ear 'do not try anything like that again.'"

He told them that he was almost certain that the birds had somehow managed to make the cuts disappear as he went into the doctor's. "I think as well, that they have something on their beaks when they peck me, because when I put my hand to the spot where I have been pecked, it comes away covered in a sort of slime which doesn't come off even when I try to wash it off."

Joan could see by his face that Bilky was beginning to look very concerned about what he may have let himself be lead into all these years. She made a decision, which she hoped would be the right one. Looking him straight in the eyes, she asked him once again if he was sincere in wanting to change and to put things right. When he told her he was, she explained that she and her family had discovered an awful lot about the mine and the magic connected to it, and how it had been used in the past and not always to the good.

"I am going to take you at your word Cedric," she said, using his name for the first time in years, "and will reveal to you some of what we have discovered. I won't tell you everything at this point, not until I am convinced about your sincerity, I am sure you understand that." Bilky nodded in agreement realising that he had no option but to do so.

Joan then said they would take him back to their son's house with them where they would make him comfortable and try to treat his wounds.

"I will explain to everyone there that you have agreed to help us and for them to at least give you a chance to prove yourself. But!" she added, determined to keep the upper hand, "if I suspect you are not co-operating with us, then I can assure you I have the power to make your life much more miserable than those birds ever did. Now then have you anything green you can wear?"

Following directions Joan went upstairs and in one of the wardrobes found a very old green coat, which she recognised as one that belonged to Jessica, Bilky's mother many years previous. Returning to the two men she instructed Bilky to put the coat over his shoulders. "Don't worry," she told him, "we aren't likely to meet anyone who knows you, but you must wear it so the birds cannot see you." Bilky gave her a questioning look and Joan explained that it was one of the many things they would eventually disclose to him.

"There is just one thing you need to tell us though, and that is, how would you recognise those men if we saw them?"

Bilky told her that they always wore strangely shaped hats pulled down well over their faces, and they always kept their hands in the pockets of the long coats they wore. He said that the coats were black and had two different coloured cuffs on the sleeves just like the wings on the birds, He had never seen them anywhere else but in his garden, although they had visited him in the mine a couple of times when he went there.

Having made sure the house was locked up and all windows closed, the trio made their way down the hill. They saw no sign of either the birds or the men on their journey to their house. Joan thought it would be a good idea if she went on ahead to warn the family of what was happening, if for no other reason that to assure Paul that his grandfather was arriving. Bilky and John thought that was a good idea and slowed down a little to allow her to arrive ahead of them.

CHAPTER TWENTY-SIX

BILKY'S STORY – PART ONE

Paul gave his grandfather a peculiar look when he saw him, but his grandfather was quick to reassure him that it was O.K. and he need not be afraid.

"Your grandfather has agreed to help us in our quest to put right a lot of wrongs that have been going on for a good many years," Joan told Paul.

When they were all seated she said that it might be a good idea if they all sat out in the garden later and they could hear what Bilky had to tell them. She said she certainly had a lot of questions to ask him.

"And he has promised me he will tell us all he knows." she told them. "In return I, or I should say we, will tell him some of what we have been able to work out from the information left to me."

She had no intention at this point of telling him that most of their information had come from letters and papers given to her by his mother.

Pedro's mother suggested that perhaps the men folk should take Mr. Bilk outside to show him the garden whilst she and granny made them all some lunch.

She suggested also that he should keep his green coat on just incase they had any "flying visitors."

Paul, still wary of his grandfather, made sure he stayed a little away from him when they all went out. Pedro's granddad suggested that the boys might like to set up the table and chairs in the middle of the garden ready for when they all came out in the afternoon. In the meantime, he and his son showed Bilky round the garden, explaining that most of the work was done by Mary, Pedro's mother.

A little while later Mary called them to tell them lunch was ready. During the meal Joan suggested again that she thought it might be a good idea if perhaps, when they all went into the garden, Bilky should continue to wear the green coat. "That way, if the birds do appear, all they will see is our family just sitting around enjoying a nice afternoon in the sun. Pedro can take a some drawing paper and pencils or something out with him and he and Paul can be doing something together at the table."

She said that Bilky could just sit there in a chair and they could talk to him and he to them.

"All the birds will see if they do arrive is an empty chair. We won't look at you all the time as we are talking Bilky, but will look in your general direction from time to time."

"Perhaps we ought to laugh once in a while as well," suggested Mary, "that way it will really look as if we are just having a family chat in the garden."

The others thought this was a good idea. They continued with their lunch although Mr. Bilk said he really didn't feel like eating anything. He said he was still not feeling too good from the illness he had felt two or three days ago.

On completion of lunch granny suggested to the two boys that they should go with her into the garden to make sure the table and chairs were in place. Once outside she told them that she wanted to have a word with Paul and asked Pedro if he wouldn't mind going to get her one of his marbles from the shed whilst she did so. Pedro did as she asked and when he returned she sat the boys down and explained to Paul what was going to happen in the afternoon. She also explained about the marble Pedro have brought her and about its power.

"This particular marble will only work its magic for Pedro or myself," she explained, more to make sure that if Paul had any ideas about helping himself to it then it would put him off.

"Just to prove it, let him hold the marble Pedro. Now try to make a simple wish," she said when Paul had it in his hand. "Speak nice and clear so we can hear what you are wishing for."

"I wish that spade standing over there would fall over."

They looked at the spade but nothing happened.

"Now you hold the marble and wish for the same thing Pedro," granny said.

"I wish that spade standing over there would fall over," said Pedro.

No sooner had he said it than the spade slowly toppled over and lay on the soil.

"Let me look after the marble for the time being," said granny, and Pedro handed it back to her.

She continued by showing Paul that there were now only three stripes left in the marble. Next she looked directly at him and told him that he would hear things that afternoon that she was really hoping he would give his word to her and not repeat to anyone.

"It's only right and fair you should be included in everything now that you have become involved with your grandfather. You may also hear some disturbing and upsetting things once your grandfather starts to tell his side of things, but, I would ask you to please not judge him too harshly until he has told us everything. I have a strong feeling that he has been influenced by certain people for a very long time, as I am sure, have many members of your family in the past."

Paul promised her that he would not say a word to anyone at all, and would do his best not to feel any more worse of his grandfather once he had told his side of the story. Granny thanked him and reminded him again that his grandfather had been under some very great pressure for most of his adult life, and certainly following his taking over of the running of the mine, and was obviously now at the end of being able to cope with it all.

By now the family were coming out into the garden. Pedro quickly dashed into the house to get a couple of drawing books and pencils for himself and Paul.

Once they were all settled, granny explained to them all that she had spoken with Paul that some things he might hear would be a bit upsetting but that he had promised to face up to them in an adult manner.

She then turned in the general direction of Mr. Bilk, but at the same time not looking directly at him, and gave him a very rough idea of what she and the family had discovered over the past week or so.

"Some really terrible things have taken place over the past I don't know how many years, and an awful lot of people have been hurt and upset by them. Unfortunately Cedric," and this time looked more in his direction, "You have been a big part in what has happened."

Mr. Bilk looked visibly upset by this last statement, so granny went on to say that although he had been involved in what had occurred, she couldn't fully blame him as he had quite obviously been under the influence of other forces. He nodded his head in agreement at this, and told her he had felt compelled to do as he was asked at the beginning, but then they had started ordering him to do various things and it was at this point that he could not stop himself from doing as they told him.

The rest of the afternoon was taken up with granny telling Mr. Bilk a lot, but not all, of what they had found out so far. When she came to the part about maybe finding the people who had disappeared from the village in their lifetime, she deliberately left out that they were very close to releasing them from their ordeal.

She was still not completely convinced she could trust him with all they knew, and had it in the back of her mind that once he was back in his own house, the birds would somehow be able to make him reveal all he had been told.

She did tell him however that maybe, just maybe, they had located his long lost sister Elizabeth. His eyes lit up at this bit of information and he muttered something about the fact, that one act had been the one thing that had bothered him all his life.

This time granny did look directly at him, "What act was that, Cedric?"

His face changed again as he explained to her that it was one time when he was home from school after a bought of illness. He couldn't remember where his mother had been, but he did know his father had gone into the town with the latest batch of marbles to deliver to the toy shop.

" I heard a noise coming from my father's study and went in to see what it was. There I found two strange looking men searching through my father cupboards and drawers. They stopped what they were doing as I entered the room. Then one of the men came over to me and looked straight into my eyes. I tried to turn away but my head wouldn't move. He asked me if I knew where the 'Magic Ones' were. I told him I had no idea what he was talking about. He said he didn't believe me and that he would be back later in the day and I had until then to find what they wanted, or else something terrible would happen to the village and it would be all my fault.

"What did you do Cedric?"

"I looked all round the room but could find nothing I thought the man could have been referring to. I was very seldom allowed into father's room, only when he called me there and I was terrified at the thought he would find out I had been there that day."

"So, what happened Cedric?" granny repeated. Everyone present could see she was very upset and determined to get an answer from him.

He on his part felt very uneasy at her questioning and squirmed around in his chair. "I tried to tidy up the room as best as I could but was not too sure where everything went. By late in the afternoon, father had still not returned. Mother was back but was busy in the kitchen preparing the evening meal."

"CEDRIC!" granny said in a menacing tone, fearing he was trying to avoid telling her the truth.

"I went to my room and a little while later I heard a tapping noise on my window. I looked up and saw a big strange black bird there out side on the windowsill. I went over to the window and I heard him as clear as I can hear you telling me to open the window. I did as he said. I was too shocked at hearing a bird talk that I did it without thinking. He asked me again if I had found what they wanted and when I told him I had not, he said that what was going to happen in the village would be all my fault, and that I would have to live with that thought for the rest of my life. He then gave me a nasty peck on the back of my hand and as he left he said I would remember nothing of their visit until much later in life."

Mr. Bilk looked first at granny and then at the rest of the family, and with a look on his face that almost made them feel sorry for him told them that two days later came the news that almost all the people living in the older part of the village had just vanished.

"They had gone completely," he said. "My sister Elizabeth who was visiting her friend was also among those who disappeared. My father brought all the men who were working in the mine that day out to form search parties, but even though everyone searched for many days no trace whatsoever was ever found and the whole thing remained a mystery. Soon after that I was sent away and never did return to the old house."

"When did you remember all this Mr. Bilk?" asked Pedro's father.

"When I eventually took over the running of the mine. It came to me as I was sitting on my own in the garden one afternoon. Just as I started to remember everything about the strange birds visit I heard a noise up in one of the trees, and there were two of the birds. I had forgotten all about their visit when I was a young lad all those years before just like they said at the time that I would."

"Did they say anything Sir? asked Pedro.

Mr. Bilk just sat there as if in a daze and said that they asked him if he remembered their previous conversation many years ago and what had happened to the villagers. When he told them he did remember, they reminded him that all that was his fault and that now he was in charge of things they could expect further visits from them, and that they expected to by fully obeyed.

"That was the start of it all Joan," he said looking directly at her, "and it is something I have had no control over. The one bit of good that I can remember doing is making things so bad for my son James that he decided to leave home and live with one of his aunties on my wife's side of the family. I felt I had to do it that way, because if I just suggested he leave he might wonder why and refuse to go. By doing it the way I did, it was his choice. It really hurt me to behave that way but it was the only way I could think of to get him away from the influences that had started to take over my life. I was really very glad when he told me he had no desire at all to have anything to do with the mine."

"Do you feel like carrying on Cedric or would you like a rest?" Joan was worried that all the remembering would get too much for him.

"No, I'm fine for now. I want to tell you as much as I can now I have started. Is there anything you would like to ask me?"

"What sort of hold did the birds or the people they represented have over you?" This time it was John who asked the question.

"It all started when my father passed away and they came to visit me. They told me that he had been very uncooperative in his dealings with them and had displeased 'Her' very much. I found out that the 'Her' they were talking about was one of the daughters of someone from years ago who was called Mantel Helter. As far as I could find out there were two daughters. One of them refused to follow in the footsteps of her mother and was punished, but the other one turned out to be just as nasty and vindictive as her mother had been."

"What was it they were after Cedric?"

"They wanted me to keep them supplied with what they called the 'Wishy Marbs'. I told them I had no idea what they were talking about.

They didn't believe me and put some sort of curse on me. Every few days I felt really ill but could not say just what it was. As with the beak bites I have told you about, if I went to the doctor, then as soon as I got in to see him I felt fine. This went on for months with them constantly making visits to me demanding a supply of 'Wishy Marbs'. In the end I finally convinced them I had no idea what they were talking about.

The next time the birds paid me a visit they dropped a marble on my desk. It looked nothing special to me and I told them so. 'Hold it in your hand and make a wish' one instructed me. I didn't for one minute believe what they were saying but made a silent wish anyway."

"What did you wish for grandfather?" Paul asked.

"I looked at the bird who was perched on the back of one of the chairs and wished he would fall off!"

"And did he?"

"Yes he did. He wasn't very happy when he flew back up to the chair again and started to yell at me, but the other one told him to be quiet and said that it was they who had told me to make a wish.

The one who was doing all the talking told me to open my hand and take a look at the marble. I did and saw that the one stripe that had been there had gone.

'That was a 'Wishy Marb'' he told me. He then went on to say there were many more in the mine and it was my job to find them and give them all to them when they came calling. I told them I had no idea where they were located and for that I got another peck on the arm, saying they didn't believe me. They told me that my father must have had a supply of them somewhere and I was to look for them. 'He wouldn't always do what he was ordered and so he paid the price,' he told me."

Mr. Bilk looked at them all and said that he felt he had no choice but to do what they told him.

"I searched my father's office but could find no trace of any so called 'Wishy Marbs.'"

He said the birds paid him another visit a couple of days later to ask if he had done what he had been ordered. "When I told them I had been unable to find what they wanted, one of them dropped another marble on the floor saying that they had been told to give it to him and to use it wisely if he wanted to keep healthy."

"What do you suppose he meant by that?" asked Joan.

"I am sure he meant me to use the one stripe that was on there to find out where my father had kept his collection of 'Wishy Marbs' if in fact there was a collection. I searched all over the house, upstairs and downstairs, in the garden and any place I thought there might have been a hiding place but could find no trace what so ever of anything looking remotely like something marbles would be stored in. The one thing that keeps going through my mind, is that my father never did live in that house. We lived in the old Manor House, which as you know burned down after I had left and mother and father had passed away. The house I live in now was bought by one of my uncles with the inheritance money I received following my father's death. I think it did have some connection with owners of the mine many, many years ago, but it had stood empty for most of the time I can remember it. In the end I had to use the marble and the one wish, which I assumed was left on it. I stood in the middle of the living room and wished that I could find the 'Wishy Marbs'. Why I chose that particular room I have no idea, just that I was in there at the time I suppose."

"Anyway, nothing happened for a long time, and then I heard a faint rumble coming from under the floor boards in the corner. As I stood there watching, the large couch that was there started to move and lift a little. This went on for quite a while.

Each time it lifted the couch moved slightly until it was quite a way away from the wall. It eventually stopped moving. By now there was enough space between it and the wall for me to look behind. When I did I saw a small trapdoor set into the floor. It had a large round ring attached to it. I moved around the couch and lifted the trap door with the ring. There were a few steps leading down into a cellar. It was very dark down there so I decided to fetch a lamp so I could investigate further. I was just about to leave the room to get the lamp when I saw one of the birds flying towards the window. I quickly pushed the couch back into place before the bird could see what had happened."

Mr. Bilk looked so upset and stressed by this time, that Joan almost felt sorry for him, but she also reminded herself that so far he was one of the villains of the story. She told him in a kindly way to continue with what he was telling them but only if he felt up to it. He said that he was glad to at last have a chance to get everything out into the open. Joan had no choice but to believe him and asked him to continue.

"There was only one bird that day and in answer to his question as to whether I had found any marbles yet, I told him I had not. This was in fact the truth as all I had found was a trap door leading to a cellar. The bird said that I had just two days to find them or else 'She' would be paying me a visit and it would not be a very pleasant time for me. He said she very rarely came out of her 'High Place' unless it was of extreme importance.

The fact that 'She' had told the bird to tell me to expect a visit meant that she must have been getting very desperate for some of the marbles. Apparently he was also worried for himself because if 'She' deemed a visit necessary then it would be clear to herself that he had not been successful in his part of the operation and would be severely punished. He begged me for both our sakes to have a further look before he returned in three days time. He told me this was an unofficial visit to sort of warn me as well as plead on his behalf for me to help him.

'My brother who is usually with me is not as lenient.' he said, 'and loves to do all that 'She' instructs us to do. I hate all this threatening and punishment but have to pretend to go along with it for my own good.' I asked him how I would be able to tell the difference when they both returned and he said that he would be the one who would stand on the table. I told him to come back in the allotted three days and I hoped I would have better news for him."

At this point Bilky looked up and said that he felt he could do with a bit of a break, so Joan suggested that she and her daughter-in-law went into the house and made everyone some drinks. Turning to Bilky she told him that it would be better if he went inside with them and had his drink in the kitchen.

"That way if the birds do make an appearance they won't see seven glasses on the table when there are only six of us visible."

While the ladies were away in the house granddad said he would take a walk round the garden to see if he could spot any unwanted guests perched anywhere.

Chapter Twenty-Seven

Bilky's Story – Part Two

Paul had been quite quiet during his grandfather's tale and Pedro's father asked him if he was O.K.

"Yes thank you sir, but I am a bit worried what my grandfather will do next, and also what else he will tell us when he gets back."

"How has he been acting since you have come to live with him?"

"He was not too bad at first, but slowly over the days he has seemed a lot more bad tempered. It was like I could never do anything right for him. Some days he was very pleasant and promising to teach me all about the mine and how to operate some of the machinery, then the very next day or sometimes even the same day he would go in to one of his moods for no reason at all."

"Had anything happened that you can recall which made him suddenly go that way?"

"It always seemed to be after I had heard him talking to someone in his office, although I could not remember anyone arriving. I suppose it was possible the housekeeper had let someone in."

He sat deep in thought for a while and then said, "After what my grandfather has been telling us today it is quite possible he was talking the those birds. He did appear to be shouting at something up in the trees this morning before he started that fire and burned his jacket. I didn't stop to see. As soon as he went into the house I ran straight down here."

Pedro looked at Paul and asked him if it was his grandfather who had sent him to the house a couple of days ago and to take some marbles from the shed.

Paul said that he had and he was now very sorry he had done it.

"It was as if I had no control over what I was doing Pedro. I knew I was doing it but couldn't stop myself. I really am very sorry. My father always brought me up to be honest and to treat people with respect and then as soon as I get here my grandfather is asking me to do the very things I know to be not very nice."

Pedro told him not to worry about it anymore. "Now we know what made you do it we can maybe help sort things out."

"Thanks very much." Paul said, but Pedro's father could see there seemed to be something still worrying him and asked him what it was."

"It's just that I am a bit frightened to go back to the house with grandfather."

"I'm sure my mum wouldn't mind if you slept on the floor in my room for tonight. I'll ask her later on if you like."

Granddad arrived back at the table to say he had seen one large bird in the tree close to the shed but it had been so high up that he had no idea if it was one of 'theirs' or not. He had not been able to see how many feet it had.

The ladies appeared then with drinks for them all. Paul's grandfather looked a little better but still did not have much colour to his face. He was walking rather slower than earlier they noticed.

When they were all settled back in their seats again granny told them that Cedric had asked Pedro's mother if Paul could stay with them for a few days.

"He thinks the birds or the men form of them may pay him a visit and he doesn't want him there if they do."

She looked at Pedro and suggested that the two boys might like to go off around the garden and maybe in to the shed for a while explaining that it was not quite natural for two lively boys to be just sitting around with adults chatting when there were things they could be doing.

"That will look more natural if that bird your granddad saw in the tree is here to spy on us."

Her husband had called into the house and had mentioned to her and Mary what he had seen.

"Just watch what you say," she reminded them both pointing out that Paul was wearing a shirt with a lot of red in the pattern.

Promising they would the boys made their way round the house to the shed.

Joan looked at her husband and son and told them they she had sent the boys away for a good reason.

"While Cedric was in the house having his drink he told us that some of the things he still had to tell us were not very nice and he would rather the boys didn't hear them."

As they settled back into their chairs, Joan told Cedric that as there was a possibility that they had at least one feathered visitor in the garden, they would turn their chairs slightly more away from him to make it seem there was only the four of them sitting there. She invited Cedric to start whenever he felt like it.

"To get back to where I was earlier, I waited until I was sure the bird had gone away then closed the curtains to make doubly sure no one could see into the room. I fetched a lamp from the kitchen and went across to the couch and pulled it completely away from the corner. The trap door was quite easy to lift. Looking down into the hole I could see some steps leading down so I slowly climbed down.

There were about fifteen steps so you can imagine how deep the hole was. When I arrived at the bottom I held the lamp aloft and slowly turned around looking where I was. About halfway round I got my first shock. There were several small alcoves each with a door at the end of them. Each had a curtain made of some kind of sacking material covering the entrance.

I moved the sacking of one of the alcoves and saw the remains of a body propped up against the wall. They were just bones but still had some clothes on them. A shirt and trousers and boots such as the kind worn by the workers many years ago. My first reaction was to leave and climb back out of the hole, but I reminded myself I was there to find out where the 'Whishy Marbs' were.

I took a closer look at the remains then had the fright of my life. Around the neck was a large distinctive handkerchief the kind worn by the workers back then which they would pull up over their noses and mouths if the area they were assigned to was too dusty. It wasn't the presence of the handkerchief, which startled me but pattern or what was left of it. I recognised it at once as one belonging to one of my old school friends. His name was Dickie Loft, and the handkerchief round his neck was one that had been given to him by his grandfather when he came home one time on leave from the navy.

It was originally dark blue with yellow anchors on it. I have one exactly the same. Dickie and me were inseparable back in my early school days before I was sent away and he gave me one as well."

Looking across at Joan he said that she must have remembered him as well. Joan said that she did and could also remember him being up at the house doing odd jobs for Cedric's father round about the same time she herself was looking after his mother. She said she was quite shocked to hear just now what had happened to him.

"I thought he had just decided to move away."

"No," Cedric said, "he started in the mine with his father just as soon as he was old enough. Before that my father took him under his wing as he had been my best friend and I think he sort of treated him as a replacement for me when I was sent away following the disappearance of Elizabeth."

"How do you think he ended up where he did?" wondered Pedro's father.

"All I can think of is that he got into the cellar from one of the passages from the mine. I didn't know what to do with his body and so I left it where it was. I had a good look round the cellar and discovered that all of the doors opened towards me into the cellar. There were no handles of any kind on the doors but the wood was so badly rotted I was able to poke my hand through and pull then open. I wedged the doors open with bits of rock and walked a way down the passages.

The passages were quite steep so I assumed they were leading down to the mine workings. On that first visit I didn't go very far as my lamp didn't have much oil in it and I didn't want to be caught in the dark. One thing I did notice as I returned to the cellar, was that on one post of each door frame was a hole about the size of a marble. I could just make out the faint markings in them. Some had two coloured dots, some three, and some had coloured stripes. The post of the frame where I had found poor Dickie still had a marble in the recess. I can only assume that the doors could only be opened from the other side. Poor Dickie must have used the marble to open the door, not wedged it open and the door had closed behind him. I suppose he just sat there until he died of starvation. Even if he did find the steps and tried to climb up and open the trap door, there must have been something heavy on it to prevent it opening."

"What an awful way to die," said Mary, "what did you do with him?"

"I left him where he was, but the next day I returned with a lamp filled with oil, to give me plenty of time to do what I had to do. I had noticed the day before when I was looking in the passages that there were a lot of loose rocks and stones. I had taken a shovel with me so I dug a shallow hole as best as I could and laid poor Dickie to rest. I covered him with a blanket I had brought with me, and then covered the blanket with loose rocks and stones. I said a small prayer for him and left him in peace. As I came back out through the door

I removed the marble from the recess and closed the door firmly behind me"

"Did you go back down there again Cedric?"

"Yes Joan, I had to. The 'Wishy Marb' had led me there in the first place so I assumed that what the birds wanted had to be down there."

"And did you find what they wanted?"

"Yes I did but it took me all the three days I had told the birds I needed. It was the fourth tunnel I searched. It went down very steep for a very long way. When I got to the bottom there were lots of loose rocks lying around so I picked a couple of them up and hit them against each other. They eventually broke open and inside each one was a marble with four stripes in it. I wasn't sure if they were what the birds wanted or not so I decided to try a wish to see for certain. I held the marble and wished I could find four more the same.

As soon as I had said that, I heard a sort of rattling sound from behind me and four little identical rocks came rolling towards me. I opened them the same way I had the other two and again inside each was a four striped marble. I did the same again until I had used all the stripes in the first marble. By now I had twenty, four striped marbles. Thinking they would be enough to satisfy the birds, I left the tunnel and climbed back in to the room. I closed the trap door, replaced the carpet and then pushed the couch back in place."

"Did the birds come back?" asked John.

"The very next day just as I finished my breakfast, I was in the room I used as an office, and had just finished counting the men as they arrived at work, when I heard a pecking sound from the window on the other side of the room. I opened the window and the two birds flew in. One flew in and stood on the table. I could swear that as he did so he gave me a sort of nod of his head as if to tell me he was the one I had been talking to the last time.

The other one flew in and perched himself on the back of my chair. He asked me straight away if I had done as I had been asked.

I told him I had and went and picked up a bag I had placed the marbles in. I had decided to only give them ten marbles hoping that would satisfy them. He asked me to put the marbles on the desk so he could have a look at them. He moved then around a bit with his beak then satisfied with what he saw, told me 'She' would be very pleased with them but assured me that they would be back for more.

He then asked me if I had another bag so they could carry five each. Once I had done as he asked they each picked up a bag and flew out the window saying they would be back in a week or two for more of the same."

John, who had been sitting looking very thoughtful during Cedric's story, asked him if the birds were always black. Mr. Bilk told him yes they were.

"How long did this go on for Cedric?"

"Years and years Joan. They came back about every four weeks, sometimes sooner but never longer. The friendly bird came back a few times on his own and we had some quite long chats. I asked him what 'She' wanted the marbles for and he told me that they were keeping her alive and in power. When I asked him what he meant by that, he said she was over one hundred and sixty of our years. It seems she had discovered, or had been told the power of the marbles many years ago probably by her mother Mantel Helter. She herself had been using the marbles to keep herself alive as well. Eventually, the marbles ceased to have enough power to help her and she eventually passed away."

Mr. Bilk went on to tell them that in order to keep up the supply of "Wishies" as he called them, he had to dig further and deeper into the passageway. He told them he got so out of breath the longer he was down there breathing all the dust that he could only manage about two hours per day.

"Even when I came out of the cellar it took me nearly an hour to be able to breath normally again. In the end I could no longer keep up the demands of the birds and told them about my breathing. The next time they came, the one who always did all the talking and demanding flew onto my shoulder and gave me a sharp peck on my neck. He said that he had given me a health boost and that it would last for a few months.

'You will be able to breathe better and so will be able to continue with your task' he said to me. Certainly within a few minutes I did begin to feel better and breathe more easily.

"Did you continue to look for the rocks?"

"I had to, I had no choice. Eventually I could not dig any further into the first tunnel so I started to investigate one of the other passageways. The digging was a lot easier but I could find none of the rocks containing the marbles they wanted. In fact of all the rocks I did find and broke open, only two had a marble with any stripes and they only had two."

The listening adults could see that by now Mr. Bilk was looking very tired and Joan asked him if he wanted to stop for the day and take a rest, but he told them that now he had started he wanted to get it all out in the open. He did say that he would like a drink so Mary offered to go into the house with him. She said she would get fresh ones for the rest as well.

While they were gone Joan asked her son and husband what they thought of what they had been told so far.

"I think he was under terrible pressure to do all that was asked of him," said Tom.

"I think so too," said her husband, "but from what he was saying, it seems as if the whole line of Bilks have been treated the same way. It would be interesting to know just how far back it started."

"I agree," said his wife, "but I think we will find that his father, the Mr. Bilk who's wife I looked after, tried to break the system and was somehow punished. We will have to be very careful how we ask the questions from now on."

"Telling us all what has happened over the years has clearly had a bad effect on Bilky."

She could see Mary returning with the drinks followed by Mr. Bilk so added quickly, "Tonight I will have a search through some of the papers I have not properly looked at to see if they throw any more light on what went on all those years ago."

When they were all settled she asked Mr. Bilk again if felt able to continue and he assured her he wanted to go on, but asked her to remind him where he had got up to. She told him he had started to tell them about trying to find marbles in one of the other passageways.

"Of course, of course," he said. "Well I had no luck at all finding anything in the other tunnels, not even anything looking at all like they had anything inside them. I had used all the 'Wishy Marbs' I dared use in trying to help me find more of the same. When I did make a wish all it did was jump out of my hand and roll down the passage to the far end where I had managed to dig. It was then I had the idea to let the workers take home two rocks at the end of their shift and give them to their children. It was my hope that if they found anything of interest, then the children would tell their friends at school and their fathers who would then hopefully talk about them at work and in that way I could discover which part of the mine any 'Wishy Marbs' were being found.

I even put two men into the mine, supposedly to act as inspectors, but they were there really to listen if anything was discussed and report back to me. Sadly it seems no special marbles were found. That is when the birds, or at least the nasty one, started getting more threatening towards me. In fact some days they would not leave me alone. They seemed to be constantly in and around my home."

By now Mr. Bilk was sitting with his head in his hands and they had a hard job hearing what he was saying.

"When I told them I could no longer find what they wanted they said that 'She' would be very angry with him. They indicated that her health was also suffering. They also told me I would not be receiving any more health pecks to help me to breathe. On the next visit one of the birds dropped a piece of paper on the table. When I looked at it, I could see it contained a few drawings of different shaped and different coloured marbles. I was told that if I could find any of those then 'She' would be more than pleased with me. At this point I lost my temper and told them I had had enough of it all and for them not to bother me again. They flew away saying they would be back in the morning and hoped by then I would have changed my mind and come up with a plan to help both 'Her' and myself."

He told them that he had kept two of the 'Wishy Marbs' in case of emergencies, although I don't know when I could have used them. "I used one once to wish the birds would stop visiting me but it didn't work as the very next day they were back."

Mr. Bilk looked really very tired by this time but when Joan asked him once more if he wanted to stop for the night, he told her no.

"I hardly slept at all that night. I was worried what would happen to me, and was thinking of ways I could do as they would demand on their return. Just as dawn was approaching I came up with the idea of having Paul to stay with me. If I could get him to my home before the end of the term then perhaps he could get information from any of the children about any marbles there fathers had found. As luck would have it, fate lent me a hand. That afternoon my son James arrived at the house unexpectedly and asked if Paul could stay with me for a few months as he had been offered a job away from home and it would be in a place where he could not take his son. I told him that of course Paul was welcome to stay with me as long as he wanted to."

Bilky went on to say that it was as if his wishes had been granted and that he would be able to carry out what had been demanded of him. He said he told Paul in a roundabout way to see if he could discover who, if any, of the children at the school had found any special marbles in the rocks their fathers had brought home from the mine.

"All he could find out was that some of the children at school had mentioned a boy called Pedro, and that they thought he had some marbles which were different to any they had found."

"It was then that I had the idea to have him visit Pedro here and get some of his marbles. I couldn't just ask him to come down here and take some, because he would have wanted to know why, so the next time the birds paid me a visit I told them of my plan asked them if they could help me out by giving me something to give to Paul so he wouldn't really know what he was doing."

" One of the birds flew away at once and within a very short time returned with a small packet containing some red powder. He said that if I put it into Paul's tea in the morning and then told him what I wanted him to do he would do just as I asked."

John, who had been sitting looking very thoughtful during Cedric's story, asked him if the birds were always black. Mr. Bilk told him yes they were.

Mr. Bilk looked up at the family and said in a dejected voice that what happened then they now knew, and that they were now more of less up to date with all that had gone on in his life and at the mine.

"Can I just ask more question Mr. Bilk?"

Mr. Bilk looked up at Tom and told him of course he could.

"How is it that you did not know where the special marbles were to be found? You told us that when you were in the passageways you felt as if you were close to the mine workings. Could you not work out from the plan of the mine the general direction the passageways were heading from the house and put men to work there?"

"I had that very idea in my mind but if you remember, a few years ago, there had been a nasty fall in the mine and it seemed as if that had happened in the area the passageways were heading, so you see it was impossible to get at the rocks there. I had used up more of the marbles with the wishes in than I should have. When I asked a wish to find more marbles the one I was using just jumped out of my hand and rolled towards where I had been digging, but that was a solid wall I could not get through. That is when I came up with the idea of letting you all take two rocks home with you."

"I see, thank you sir," said Tom.

Mary then suggested they call it a day and all go into the house and have some tea. Mr. Bilk said he would rather be getting home but Joan said she wouldn't hear of it and told him that she and John would walk him home after he had eaten with them. "I don't suppose for one minute you have any proper food in the house."

Mr. Bilk knew it was no good arguing with her and admitted that a decent meal would be very welcome.

Granddad arrived at that minute with the boys. He had been round to the shed to collect them when the others went into the house.

Paul's grandfather told him that Pedro's family had very kindly said he could stay with them for a few nights, until he felt a bit better in himself. Pedro's grandmother told Paul she and her husband would walk his grandfather home to make sure he arrived there safe and would bring back anything he needed for his few days stay.

Chapter Twenty-Eight

The Bird's Visit

After breakfast the following morning Pedro's mum asked him if he and Paul would go to the farm and get some milk. They didn't really need any just yet but she thought it would be best to try to keep them occupied and try to keep Paul's mind at least, off what they had all been told the previous day by his grandfather.

As she walked back into the kitchen after seeing the boys off, she heard her mother-in-law talking to her father-in-law. She was telling him that there was something about some of the things Bilky had told them that didn't quite fit but she couldn't put her finger on it.

"I know what you mean, I feel the same. I spent a long time, awake last night going through all we had been told but just couldn't work out what it was. All I know is it is something connected with what he told us and what we have witnessed when we have been on our visits."

"Do you think it is something to do with the birds?" asked Mary, "because I have been thinking along the same lines."

"Yes I think it is Mary, but just like John, I can't work out the connection."

They sat there for a few minutes then Mary almost jumped for joy, "I think I have it! It is the birds. The ones we have saw on our visits were purple with different coloured wings, but the birds that visited and harassed Mr. Bilk were all black."

"I think you are right Mary." She looked at her husband, "is that the connection you were trying to make John?"

"It must be. I know it was strongly connected to the birds."

The three of them sat around discussing the mystery when Tom walked into the room. He looked quite pale and Mary asked him what the matter was. He looked straight at his mother and told her there was someone outside who wanted a word with her. She could see by the look on his face that it was serious so she got up and went to go outside. As she passed her son, he handed her a blue headscarf and said, "You had better wear this." He walked with her to the door and then told her, "You will find him standing on the bench in the shed."

"What was all that about Tom?" asked his father.

Tom sat down in the chair vacated by his mother. "I was in the garden round by the shed when I heard this rather strange voice trying to attract my attention. I looked around but could see no one. Then I heard the voice again and it was then I saw one of those birds standing on the pile of seed boxes by the side of the shed. "He asked me if this was where Joan lived. I was so taken aback by his actually talking to me I answered him without thinking, and told him yes Joan is living here. He then said could he please have a word with her and that it was very important.

Again I was still in a bit of shock at him talking to me, I just came in the house and told mum. On the way to get mum, I wondered how the bird could have spoken to me and then I realised I had this blue jumper on. It's an old one I always use for gardening and put it on this morning without thinking. I saw your blue headscarf hanging in the hall Mary and picked it up and handed it to mum."

"Wonder what he wants with your mum Tom," said Mary

"We'll soon find out, she's coming back in the house," Tom's father said, and pointed to the window where they could see Joan coming round to the door.

Tom got up as his mother came into the room to let her have her chair back but she waved her hand indicating for him to stay where he was.

"We have a bit of a situation on our hands," she told them. "As if we don't have enough to do, we now have old Bilky feeling quite poorly."

Looking at her son, she told him that the bird he had been talking to and who asked to see her was the good bird. He said he would like to take the opportunity to talk to all of us and tell us what has been going on and a bit about old Bilky. "We don't need to wear anything blue. Apparently he can hear us quite well, a secret he has kept from his elder brother all these years. As the boys are away at the farm, I thought it might be a good time to listen to him."

The rest of the family agreed so Joan went out to call him in. When she returned the bird was sitting on her shoulder. Tom got up and pulled out a kitchen chair so he could perch on the back.

"This is Kirkum," she said introducing him to the family. The bird hopped from her shoulder and settled on the chair Tom had pulled out for him. He then flew to the arm of each chair the others were sitting in and held up the middle foot to shake hands with each of them, saying hello, and telling them he was very pleased to meet them. They were all so astonished at what was happening, they shook his claw without thinking about it. He flew back to the dining chair and turned to face them all.

"Before I start," he said, "may I suggest Tom, that you remove the blue jumper you are wearing, and likewise too Mary if you could take that red ribbon from your hair." He went on to explain that although he needed nothing to help him see or hear them, it was not the case where his brother was concerned.

"He requires someone to be wearing blue to be able to converse with them, and red to hear what they are saying without him talking to them. Likewise, if you are wearing green he can neither hear or see you."

He said there was just one more thing he needed to say and that was, if while he was talking to them, he sensed his brother was around then not to be startled if he suddenly flew behind Johns chair which was in the corner.

"He has no idea I am here, but I will keep on talking to you from behind the chair if you wish. I can sense when he is around but he cannot do the same where I am concerned. I will explain all the differences between us as I talk to you. Please feel free to stop me and ask me any questions."

He settled himself more comfortably on the back of the chair and started talking to them.

"As you now know my name is Kirkum. I once belonged to a very nice lady called Mariem who was one of the daughters of a not very nice lady called Mantel Helter. She has, or I should say had, a sister called Tangler. That sister is now the one we call 'She', and insists on none of us ever using her real name, not that there are many who know her real name. Their mother Mantel was, as I have said, a not very nice lady. She had many magical powers and used them to her own ends, much to the discomfort of anyone who dared to displease her for whatever reason. She eventually became very ill and no amount of her magical powers could help her and she eventually died. She knew the end was close and chose to go for a walk into the woods and never returned. Mariem was with her when she just stood up, said she was leaving this life, that from now on her elder sister Tangler would assume all her powers and for Mariem to do all her sister bade her. "

"With those final words she walked off, forbidding Mariem to follow her. Mariem did not tell her sister until the following day. Tangler got very annoyed with her sister and realising she now had her mother's powers turned poor old Mariem into a statue and placed her in the middle of the village green. Such was the powers of Tangler she cast a spell over the whole village so that they would think nothing of seeing a statue on the village green. They would act as if it had always been there. The next few days Tangler turned her attention to changing many other things about the place. She lengthened the days so that the men would have to work a lot longer. She continued with the spell her mother had put on the people, and that was, some would never get any older than the day they were removed from Marbleville and brought to what she called Villmarb. That was the name her mother had given to the place she ruled. Her mother had literally taken whole families from their homes and put them into houses where she could keep a close eye on them.

"Did she have a reason for this?" asked Tom.

"Yes she did. She wanted as many mine workers as she could get to find for her the source of her powers, and that meant finding certain shaped rocks she knew contained the marbles with the wishes in. These were not the ones you have been finding Tom. These marbles contained only three stripes, but the stripes were crisscrossed over the surface of the marble. She could make one marble last for about ten or twelve wishes depending how strong her wish was at the time. As she made a wish, only part of one stripe disappeared. What it was she wished for I do not know. All I can tell you is that when she wanted to make a wish to continue her powers, she would go off into the woods and would not be seen for about four days."

"And did the miners manage to find her the marbles?" Joan asked.

"Yes, but after a few years they were getting very scarce. She felt that the workers were deliberately not finding what she wanted, and was afraid her power over the people would soon be lost. She threatened them with all kinds of punishment, but that made no difference, the marbles were simply no longer there to be found. It was then she decided to try to get hold of some of the four striped marbles. I suppose she thought that at least they would be better than nothing."

Kirkum looked at the family. "That is when Tangler started to send my brother and me to visit Cedric. She knew from stories her mother had told her and her sister over the years that she had been forcing the mine owners to keep her supplied with the four striped marbles. It seems as if Mantel Helter did not require such strong magic to keep her going. As the magic was passed down a generation then more was required which is why Tangler needed the other marbles. The one owner who put up a lot of resistance was Cedric's father. He stubbornly refused to do as he was asked, and for this he was constantly being punished. I can't tell you how he was punished because I do not have that information. I was not under the influence of Tangler at that time, but I am almost certain that his wife's early fall into bad health was part of the punishment, just as I am certain that the burning down of his old house was also arranged by Tangler. It could also be, that Tangler had been made aware of Jessica's visit to the old settlement."

"How could she know about that?" Again it was Joan who asked the question.

"The old settlement is lorded over by a man even more nasty than either Mantel Helter, or her daughter Tangler. He is a very distant relation to Mantel and has many more powers than she would ever have. If he has a name no one knows what it is. He is known only as the High Person. It was he who removed the entire original village of Marbleville about one hundred and fifty years ago. He transported them to a place of his own choosing. He had no interest at all in the mine, which was very small back in those days. It seems he just wanted his own kingdom. He put the men to work in the fields growing crops to feed him and his hierarchy allowing the men to have what he did not require, to feed their own families. He made up his own rules and regulations and was very strict on anyone who disobeyed them, but of course you have seen that for yourself on one of your visits there."

"How do you know about that?" This time it was John asking the question.

"I was standing in the tree the time you paid a visit. I was one of the birds the High person pointed to when he told the villagers we would be keeping an eye on them."

Again John asked the question, "But how do you travel between the two places?"

"That is all down to an agreement the High Person has with Tangler. In return for him supplying her with certain powders and potions she requires to keep herself going, he is allowed to call us to attend on him when he has village meetings. We never know when we will be required. We just get transported to his village. When we have served our purpose, he gives us the stuff to bring back to Tangler and we find ourselves back here again. I could quite easily disappear anytime now if he has need of us. As you yourselves have found out, when you visit there, it is as if no time at all has passed while you have been gone. You are back here almost before you have left."

"Can I ask a question of you please Kirkum?" He looked at Mary and said of course she could.

"It's more of a personal one really. Why do you have different coloured wings when you are in that other place, but here you have black ones? And why do you have three feet?"

"I wondered when one of you would ask about those things. When Mantel Helter was alive she gave each daughter a parrot. I was given to Mariem. She treated me very well and taught me to speak and took me with her where ever she went. Of course it was my brother Luffler, who was given to Tanglen. Right from the start she began training him to do her bidding. She took great delight in being not very nice to people and over a period of time he became just like her."

"You remember I told you about the time when Mantel had decided she had had enough of her life and walked into the woods? Well, in the period of her disappearing, and Mariem going to tell Tangler about their mother, Mariem took me into her room, closed the door and said she was going to put a spell on me, one which Tanglen could not undo. She was convinced that with their mother out of the way, Tangler being the eldest would try to cut back some of her powers. She put her hand on my head and I felt a surge of something pass through my whole body. I can't to this day say what it was, but I did discover later that whereas Luffler required people to be wearing blue or red in order to see and talk to them, I did not require such things. That, plus even when you wear green, I can still see you. My brother has no idea I am not under the same spell as he is."

He went on to tell them that when Tanglen took over from her mother, she did three things. "One was to turn her 'Goody Goody' sister as she called her, into a statue just as I told you. The next thing was, she turned my brother and me into huge blackbirds, telling us that from now on we were to do her bidding. The last thing she did was she gave us three feet, saying that no other birds would want to mix with us looking like that. Plus if we had three feet we would be able to carry more of anything she asked us to collect."

He looked at Mary and told her that they had different coloured wings when they were in that other place because the High Person thought we would look more menacing to the villagers that way. Here, so long as no one really noticed their feet, then they could pass as just ordinary black birds even though they were a bit larger than the rest.

"And why were there sometimes three of you when you visited old Bilky?" asked granddad.

"That was just another bird she had been trying to train to do her bidding, but he wasn't very good. When we had to visit Mr. Bilk he came along because he found him very easy to intimidate."

The family sat in silence for a while taking in all Kirkum had told them. He broke the silence by saying he had better get back to his brother because they were due to pay Cedric a visit later that day. He thanked them for their time and said he would be more than happy to answer any other questions they had on a future visit.

Joan thanked him on behalf of the family and told him that they certainly did have more questions for him but only when he was ready.

Mary in the meantime had opened one of the large windows for him. He thanked them all again as he flew out of the window saying he would be in touch again very soon. Within seconds he was back and told them that he was almost certain his brother would not come calling, but just in case he got curious and tried to put a few things together in his head, then they would know it was he Kirkum who paid them a return visit because he would carry a small stone in his middle claw. He also told them that should they need to speak with him at any time they were to lean the garden spade against the wall under an open window. When he saw that it would be a sign for him and he would come as quickly as he could when his brother was not with him.

The family began to discuss all that Kirkum had been telling them. It was granny who had been putting two and two together, some of the things she had heard.

"It was as I thought," she said. "When I was reading the papers left by old Jessie, I read them in the order they were given me, but after listening to Kirkum, some of the pages were obviously in the wrong order."

She explained what she meant by telling them they had thought the kind lady with the magic was someone who was around after 'Mantel Helter', but from what they had heard she was quite obviously a sister to Tangler.

"I suppose old Jessica wrote things down as she remembered them and it was quite possible that as she got older, her memory was beginning to go a little and so she could not keep things in the right order in her mind."

The family agreed and said that seemed to be what must have happened. At that minute they were all given a complete shock by the arrival of Kirkum who flew back through the still open window, and perched on the back of the chair he had used before.

"Don't worry it is me, I just didn't stop to pick up a stone before I flew back into the room." He looked directly at Joan and said that he thought there might be something wrong with Mr. Bilk.

"I flew over the house when I left here and saw him lying in the garden. I landed beside him and gave him a couple of gentle pecks on the shoulder, but could detect no movement whatsoever. I put my head very close to his mouth and he is breathing, but it sounds very funny, sometimes quickly and then sometimes a lot slower.'

When Kirkum had finished telling them about Cedric, Joan said that she must go to the house at once. She asked Kirkum if he wouldn't mind going back there ahead of her and sort of hang around till she arrived.

"After all, no one lives near there so you won't be spotted and I doubt if the housekeeper will have gone there today."

Kirkum said he would fly back there at once and wait for her.

As the bird flew out of the window to return to the Bilk house, John told his wife he would go and get his jacket, to accompany her.

"And I think my dear, on this occasion it would be perfectly in order for you to use a wish to get us there as quickly as possible."

His wife agreed and went to get one of the marbles, saying what a good idea that was because if they left and started walking, there was a chance they would meet up with the boys returning from the farm. She asked her husband to come into their room with her saying they would leave from there.

No sooner had they closed the door, than Mary heard the boys coming through the front gate.

"That was a close one Tom."

"Indeed it was," he replied.

The boys came into the house by the back door leaving the milk on the kitchen table. They both seemed quite happy with themselves. Paul excused himself saying he wanted to change his shirt, and headed for the stairs to go up to the bedroom he was sharing with Pedro. Pedro asked his mother where his grandparents were, and she explained to him that they had gone up to Mr. Bilk's house to see how he was. She didn't go into any details, just that they had gone to check on him.

Paul came back downstairs at that moment so both boys went out into the garden. Tom told his wife he would go out there, and try to keep them occupied till lunch. "The shed still need a bit more clearing out so they can help me with that."

Chapter Twenty-Nine

A Sad Day

John and Joan 'arrived' in Mr. Bilk's garden and immediately saw he was still lying on the ground. Kirkum was still there and told them Mr. Bilk had not moved at all since he had returned. An anxious Joan asked if he was still breathing. Kirkum told her he was but still in the same funny way as when he had first found him.

"We had better get him into the house, John."

"You are right my dear, lets hope we can manage to lift him alright."

"I think that once more just on this occasion we can do that easily."

Her husband saw that she had taken a marble out of her pocket and was silently wording something. The next thing he knew, they were in Bilky's bedroom, with Bilky himself lying in bed. Kirkum it seemed had also been included in the transfer and was perched on the foot of the bed.

Bilky's condition had not changed at all with his breathing still causing concern. Joan suggested that it was time to get the doctor up to have a look at him. John told her he would walk down to his office and ask him to come up. Joan thanked her husband and said she would stay at the house with Bilky and keep an eye on him.

After John had left, Kirkum too said he had better be leaving. He explained to her that he was almost certain that today was a day 'She' would send them to visit Mr. Bilk. He suggested that Joan found something green to wear, because then his brother would be unable to detect her presence.

"Just as long as you don't move anything while we are here he will have no idea you are in the house."

Left alone in the house, Joan, having made sure Cedric was still breathing, even if a bit funny still, began to take a closer look at her surroundings. She felt a bit like a snooper, but told herself that it was all in the cause of trying to sort out Bilky's life. She could see that two of the other rooms upstairs, had been occupied, one by the housekeeper and the other by Paul. She spent a little time tidying up Paul's room. It was evident that he had not returned to it the previous morning after witnessing the scene between his grandfather and the birds. She herself had only spent a few minutes in there the evening before when she had collected some clothes for his stay at their home.

Downstairs there were two main rooms, a kitchen and a small room, which was evidently the room Bilky used as an office, and was the most untidy room in the house, so it was quite clear to Joan that it was one room the housekeeper had not been allowed to enter. There were bits of paper and open books lying all over the place with no resemblance of any kind of order. Joan started to tidy up the papers and pick up some of the open books and to put them neatly on the desk. As she was sorting out some of the papers, she noticed that some of the maps and information on the ones she was looking at were very similar to the papers she herself had been reading, the ones given her by old Jessica. The difference between the papers she had, and the ones she was now looking at was the handwriting. Those she was reading now were definitely, not written by old Jessica. It became obvious to her that somehow Bilky had been able to discover a few of the secrets of the mine himself from somewhere. Maybe he had unearthed some long lost paperwork at the mine itself, and was desperately trying to use any information contained in them to please the birds whenever 'She' sent them to visit him.

She carried on reading some more of the papers scattered on the desk. There were also a few notes, and comparing the writing with that on the papers they had seemingly been made by Bilky, although at first glance she could not make head or tale of them.

She was interrupted in her reading by a noise, which seemed to come from upstairs. This was followed by another sound coming from just outside in the hallway. Then she heard an unfamiliar voice.

"Dad, Paul, are you there?"

Joan got up from the desk and made her way to the entrance hall where she met a man about forty years of age, looking very agitated, and dressed in a long thick coat, wooly hat and thick leather gloves, not at all the clothes required for the time of the year or the warm weather they were having.

"Who are you, and where is my father and son?"

"Hello I am Joan and I am looking after Mr. Bilk for the time being. I take it you are his son James."

The man shook her offered hand and told her that yes, he was Mr. Bilk's son, and asked her what had been going on, and how on earth had he got here. Seeing the state of James, and the way he was dressed Joan immediately suspected that some kind of magic had happened to bring him here.

She asked him if he would like to see his father, explaining to him that he had been found collapsed in the garden earlier that morning, and that she and her husband had managed to get him into bed, which is where he still was.

"My husband has gone into the village to ask the doctor to call round and see him when he has finished with his morning patients."

James discarded his hat coat and gloves, and followed Joan up the stairs to his father's bedroom. There they found Cedric halfway out of his bed. Beside him was an upturned bedside cabinet with one of the drawers open. In his hand he was clutching two marbles, one was clear and the other one had two stripes in it. James rushed to his father's side and helped him back into bed, asking him what had happened to him. His father put his arm around his son's neck and pulled him down so he could whisper in his ear. After a few minutes he relaxed back on to the pillow gave a small sigh, closed his eyes, and lay perfectly still. James stood up and Joan saw his shoulders droop and then he sat down heavily in the chair next to the bed. He put his head into his hands and started to weep very quietly. Joan went over to the window and opened it to let in some air intending to leave James to grieve on his own for as long as he wanted to. It was obvious to Joan that Cedric had passed away. As she looked out of the window she saw three black birds sitting in one of the trees at the bottom of the garden. They had obviously been sent on a visit. Joan looked around the room, spotted a green dressing gown and went over to James and asked him to please put the dressing gown on and come with her.

"I will explain everything later, but please do not be startled by anything that happens in the next few minutes, and please on no account say anything or make a noise of any kind."

James, still in shock at his father's passing did just as Joan requested. She then led him to the door of the bedroom and onto the landing. At that moment they heard a sound coming from the room and turned to see two of the birds fly into the room. Joan sensed that James was alarmed by this and put a friendly hand on his arm and put her finger to her lips indicating for him to keep absolutely quiet. As the two birds flew towards the bed, one perching on the back of the bedside chair, the other standing at the foot of the bed, the third bird flew in through the window and stood on the upturned cabinet. He looked across towards Joan and slowly, unseen by the other birds, lifted one of his feet. There in the middle claw was a small pebble letting Joan know he was Kirkum. Joan half lifted her free hand in recognition.

The three birds then started talking between themselves but it was in a language Joan could not understand. Kirkum, sensing that

Joan would like to hear what was being said asked his brother what they should do now, in her language. "Well he is clearly no use to us now," answered his brother, having seen for himself that Cedric had passed away, "and 'She' won't be very pleased at the news either."

"I agree," said Kirkum, "plus the fact that as far as we know, there is no one else to take over the running of the mine, she will have to find other ways of keeping her health going."

"What about the father of the family where the grandson is staying?" asked Luffler, "Doesn't he work there? Perhaps we can persuade him to do what the old man here was doing."

Joan shuddered inside as she heard this, but Kirkum quickly put her mind at ease by telling his brother that apart from working at the mine, the man of that house knew nothing about the power of the marbles.

To Joan's relief Kirkum's brother agreed with him and said they would just have to go and tell 'Her' what had happened and let 'Her' sort things out.

The arrival at the house of John accompanied by the doctor stopped any further conversation between the birds and they started to leave. Kirkum watched the other two fly out of the window before he himself started to leave. As he did so he told Joan not to worry, he would sort things out for them and would pay them a visit later in the day at her son's house. Joan thanked him, and went over to shut the window as he left and close the curtains.

James was still standing there as if in shock at what he had just witnessed. Joan went over to him and helping him out of the dressing gown told him gently to try not to think about what he had just seen, she would explain everything in detail later. "Oh and by the way, Paul is safe and well at my son's house."

The doctor, who by now had arrived in the bedroom, was kneeling down beside the bed and double- checking for any sign of life in his patient. Finding none, he stood up and formally stated that Mr. Cedric Michael Bilk, had indeed passed away.

Joan then introduced James to the doctor and her husband and explained that he had arrived just a few minutes before his father's demise. James told the doctor that his father had whispered something in his ear that he didn't quite understand, and had then laid back on his pillow, closed his eyes as if he was going to sleep, and had just stopped breathing.

"That was indeed a peaceful way for him to depart given all the troubles he has been having of late," said the doctor, but did not elaborate as to what the troubles might have been.

"I will report your father's death to the correct authorities," he said to James. Shaking James's hand and offering him his sincere condolences, the doctor left the bedroom saying he would fill out, and leave the death certificate on the table in the hall as he left. Joan thanked him very much for coming so quickly and John then escorted him down the stairs.

Joan asked James if he would like to spend a little time alone with his father.

"Yes I would like that please. Although we were not all that close and didn't have a lot in common, there are a few things I would like to say to him in private. Things that I should have said when he was alive, but never the less need to be said now so I can have peace with myself."

Joan left him with his father telling him she understood, and to come down when he was ready.

Downstairs the doctor was filling in the final details of the death certificate. He signed it and then took his leave saying how sorry he was to have lost such a person as Mr. Bilk.

"He was deep down a very nicer person despite what some people thought and said about him."

John was looking at the clothing thrown on the chair in the hall and asked his wife where it had come from. She told him that James had arrived wearing it, and explained that when they went up to the bedroom, Cedric had two marbles in his hand, one with no stripes and one with two.

"It is my guess that he used the wishes in the marbles to get James here, from where ever he had been. It must have been quite a long way away because it seemed to have used up six wishes. We won't know where James was until we speak to him."

Joan went on to tell her husband about the entry of the birds and how Kirkum had made himself known to her.

"James just stood there in complete shock, not believing what he was witnessing."

John suggested they go into the kitchen and make a cup of tea for them all. Joan agreed and said that they would need to have a long talk with James when he felt up to it to tell him all that had been going on and how his father had been involved.

"I think when all the dust has settles we will find that 'She' whoever 'She' is has been bullying Cedric for years into doing her bidding. It will be interesting to see what happens now that her source and supply of the marbles has come to an end."

"Maybe," said her husband, "lots of things will come to an end and hopefully all for the better. Don't forget my dear that we still have the task at the winter shed to sort out. Tom and I are due to go there tomorrow, to make contact with Joshua."

"Gosh, I had forgotten all about that with all that has been going on. The last two days have seemed to go by in a blur."

"And also," John reminded his wife, "We, or at least you and Mary, have to make a return visit to Ishe's house."

"We were planning on going there this evening until all this happened. Now of course we will have to take into consideration James's wishes, and what he wants to do about things."

James came down the stairs at that moment, looking a little better than when he first arrived.

"Everything alright James?" asked John.

"Yes thank you. I feel a lot happier with myself now I have that off my chest. It was something I needed to do, and even though I knew he couldn't hear me I feel a lot better for having said it."

"Sit down and have some tea James and we can try to fill you in with what has been going on here, and no doubt you have lots of questions to ask us."

James thanked Joan and said that yes indeed he did have lots of questions, the most obvious being what did the big black birds have to do with anything and how come they could speak in their language.

Joan told him that perhaps the best thing was for him to come back to their house, where he could see Paul and then they could sit in comfort and tell him in on all they knew.

"That would be very nice Joan and thank you, but I must also arrange things for my father."

As he said that, they heard a noise coming from upstairs.

"What could that have been?" said James.

"I think James, that the small problem of arranging things for your father has just been taken care of. Let's go up and have a look."

The three of them went upstairs and John opened the door to Cedric's room. As they all went in, they could see that the room was completely tidy, the bed was made and Cedric was no longer there.

"Where has he gone?" said James looking all around.

"I have a strange feeling that Kirkum, one of the black birds has taken care of things for your father."

As James continued to look in disbelieve, Joan explained that Kirkum was a good bird, and had tried to treat his father with kindness, but had found it difficult because of the attitude of his elder brother.

"Cast your mind back to when the birds were leaving. One of them flew close by us and said to leave everything to him, and he would sort things out. I now think this is what he meant. He has taken your father and laid him to rest in a peaceful place. He will no doubt tell us all about it when he next pays us a visit."

James just stood there rooted to the spot. Joan gently took him by the arm and led him from the room, telling him that once it had all been explained to him he would understand better what was going on.

Downstairs James saw his clothes lying on the chair where he had put them. "Getting here is a complete mystery to me. One minute I was stepping into the cold room where we keep our food samples and the next I was standing outside this front door."

"Your father must have used the last bit of energy in his mind and body to wish that you would come to see him before he passed away." Joan could see that James was still totally confused and assured him again that by the end of the day all would be clear to him.

"Is there anything you need from here before we leave?" John asked James when they had finished their tea.

"Nothing I can think of, thank you John. All I want to do is get away from this house for a while."

CHAPTER THIRTY

JAMES AND PAUL
LEARN ALL THE SECRETS

The walk back down the hill and back to Pedro's house was a very somber one. John and Joan did their best to keep the conversation on a light footing but the memory of what they had all recently witnessed was uppermost in all their minds.

James was anxious to know what it was that the family had to tell him, but Joan convinced him that it would be a lot better for him if he could contain his inquisitiveness until they could sit down and tell him in a relaxed atmosphere. James had to be content with that and filled in the rest of the journey by asking general questions of them both about their life since they had last met.

"I can't honestly remember when it was I last saw either of you."

He told Joan that he vaguely remembered his father many years ago talking about someone who he went to school with, and who had helped his grandmother Jessica in her last few years.

"I don't suppose he said anything very complimentary about me James. I'm afraid your father and I didn't always see eye to eye with one another. I think it was because I used to stand up to him when he got one of his 'not very nice' moods on him. I learned very early on though to try to keep out of his way when those days arrived."

"I know what you mean Joan. I too used to stay in my room or play out in the garden at those times as well. Of course as I grew older, I had different interests to keep me occupied so it was easier to stay out of his way. I just could never understand why he flew in to such nasty tempers now and then."

Joan told him that she was confident that once he had heard what she had to tell him, he would understand a lot more about his father's life and the reason he behaved the way he did.

By now they had reached Pedro's home. John invited James to come round to the back garden with him whilst Joan went into the house to let Mary and Tom know they were back.

As they rounded the corner, they saw Pedro and Paul playing football at the bottom of the garden. Paul, as soon as he saw his father, dropped the ball he was holding and rushed up to him with a delighted shriek. His father gave him a big hug and said how glad he was to see him safe and well. John introduced Pedro to James and then suggested to his grandson that he should come into the house with him whilst Paul and his father had a little time to themselves. James gave John a knowing look as if to say thank you, and putting his arm on Paul's shoulder, walked with him back round the house, to the front garden. Telling him about his grandfather's passing was not going to be easy but it had to be done.

On the way into the house granddad told Pedro about Mr. Bilk dying, saying that Paul may not be very happy for a couple of days so to be very patient with him.

In the kitchen Tom was suggesting that perhaps it would be a good idea if he and his father, and Pedro if he wanted, to pay a visit to the 'Winter Shed' site. "That would leave you ladies in peace to speak with James and Paul. I don't suppose from what you have been telling us mum, that there will be any visits from our feathered friends for a while.'

"Thank you Tom, that would be a good idea. I intend to tell James, and Paul if his father wishes him to know, absolutely everything we know so far, about both places and about our visits. After all, when you think about it, he is more connected with all that is going on than any of us."

Mary said she would get a little light lunch ready for them all. John, who had seen James and Paul approaching the front of the house, went to the door to welcome them both. He introduced James to his son and daughter-in-law and then invited him to sit down and have a drink. He looked at James who gave him another knowing look and a little nod of his head, to assure him that he had told Paul the sad news and he seemed O.K. about it at the moment. Paul and Pedro disappeared upstairs to the bedroom having collected a cold drink each from Pedro's mum.

"He seemed to have taken the news very well," James told them, "but then again, he didn't know his grandfather all that well. I think the longest time he had spent with him has been the last couple of weeks."

After lunch, Pedro and his father and grandfather prepared to leave for their visit to the 'Winter Shed' site. Pedro, not fully understanding what his granny had planned for the afternoon asked if Paul could go with them.

"I think that would be a good idea really," replied his granny. "It might get a bit boring for him just sitting there listening to me tell his father everything. You can tell him all you know about the place you are going to this afternoon, Pedro. I don't think for one moment you will be bothered by a visit from the birds, just as I doubt if we will, sitting in the garden, but he had better ask his father first."

Pedro returned with Paul saying he had his father's permission to go with them. That settled, they said cheerio to the ladies and Paul's father and started out for the site. Granddad had been round to the shed to collect the wooden key he had made to fit the drill Joshua had made. Pedro had also remembered to pick up the medallion for moving the bush. As they walked Pedro's grandfather explained a little of what they were doing to Paul, telling him that no-one else apart from themselves knew anything. They needed to keep it secret for a little while longer until they were sure they could help the people behind the old shed. He also wanted to try to get it into Paul's mind that he must also keep secret what he would see that afternoon, although with the sad passing of his grandfather, there was really no-one he could tell anything to.

Although not expecting any visits from the birds, they kept a good look out as they approached the site. When they arrived at the site, they could see that it had remained exactly as they had left it a few days ago. There were some small footprints leading from the bush to where the shed was, and back again but that was all. Tom went over to where the prints had stopped at the shed and saw behind a loose wooded slat there was a note pushed between the wood and the sand. He retrieved it and showed it to his father, who opened it to discover it was a note from Joshua. He read it through a couple of times.

"He says they are making good progress with the drilling on their side," he told them, "and in about two days time they will have finished the large part of the hole and will push a very thin piece of wood all the way through to our side to indicate where we should start our drilling. He says that behind the bush we will find the box we left the last time we were here with the answers to the questions they were asked. He says there is also a note for a Joan Meaker, but is not sure who that is." He looked at Pedro and explained that was his Granny's name before they were married. "Would you like to go and retrieve the box Pedro?"

Pedro walked towards the bush holding the medallion in front of him. As before, when he was a few feet away, the bush started to slowly move away from the bank. It stopped when there was a space just large enough for Pedro to look in, see the box and reach in for it. "Do you want me to bring your drill thing out as well granddad?"

"Not today, thank you. I think it will be better to wait until Joshua has managed to poke that thin stick through so I know exactly where to start my side of the hole."

Pedro collected the box and moved slowly backwards from the bush, which slowly moved back into place.

All this time, Paul had stood there amazed at what he was seeing. He asked Pedro if he could have a go at opening the bush, but grandfather answered saying that although he couldn't do it today, they would let him do it the next time it had to be opened, explaining that they were unsure just how many times the medallion would work. This seemed to satisfy Paul, who went on to ask what was in the box Pedro was holding.

"We put some questions into the box the last time we were here, because we wanted to know more about the people behind there so we can help them, and they have answered us. I will take the box back to my grandmother so she can read what has been said."

"Why don't we have a bit better look around while we are here," suggested Pedro's father, as much to stop any more potentially awkward questions from Paul as much as anything else. "We have plenty of time today. You boys go that way and dad and I will go round this way," indicating to the boys the direction for them to go, "but if you see anything you are not sure of leave it alone and come and find us. Promise?"

Pedro promised his father then he and Paul headed off towards the far end of the old shed ruins. The two elder men started off in the opposite direction.

They found nothing of any interest, and after about twenty minutes started to make their way back round from where they had started. The boys were waiting when they arrived and Pedro told them that he and Paul had found a strange hole with a little door attached to it. "Not much bigger than this," he said holding his hands slightly apart trying to describe the size. "Come on, we'll show you."

He and Paul headed off in the direction they had gone before, with John and Tom following close behind.

"There it is gramps," said Pedro pointing to what looked like a small trap door in the side of the bank just where the remains of the wooden shed ended. "What do you think it is?"

Granddad studied it for a while then told them he thought they had discovered just how the birds managed to travel from the 'other side' to 'our' side. He reached up and tried to open the little door but it wouldn't move at all. "Must be locked on the other side, so at least we know where they are."

"Well done for finding it son."

Pedro looked at his father and said it was Paul who had spotted it first.

"Well then, well done to you Paul."

"Would they be the birds that grandfather was always arguing with sir?"

"The very same."

"So why don't we just block that door so they can't get out again."

"Because Paul, that would give the game away and they would know that we have found out certain things, and we don't want that to happen just yet."

"I understand sir," replied Paul.

Granddad could see that Paul was a bit upset at not being able to do anything about the birds there and then. "What we can do," he said, "is that whenever we come here, you two boys can come round here and see if that little door is open or closed. If it is open then we will know the birds are on this side so we would have to be careful what we did but, if the door was closed then we could put something there to stop it being opened and we could do what we wanted in peace. The birds would maybe think it was jammed and not make any attempt to get out."

"If indeed that is how the birds are moving from the place back there to our side of things, then we have been very lucky we have not been caught out so far," commented Pedro's father.

His father agreed with him. He then suggested that perhaps it was time to take a casual walk back to the house saying that by the time they arrived home, the ladies would have finished telling Paul's father most of what he needed to know. "On the way past the bush, we had better make sure that nothing else has been left for us. We should also try to brush away our footprints from the area. No sense in giving the game away."

"I think I saw a loose branch with some leaves still on it at the edge of the clearing, just about the place you sat and had a rest that day dad."

Pedro and Paul found the branch in question and began wiping away all their footprints. His grandfather wondered aloud if perhaps who ever came out from behind the bush when they were not there, also used the branch to remove any evidence of their presence. "After all, we never seem to see much to indicate to us anyone has been there."

Pedro collected the little box and they all started back towards home.

The ladies, and James were still in the garden when the four of them arrived back home. Joan told her husband that James had been told everything they had discovered so far.

"I even told him about Kirkum, and how he would try and help us. I think he is still in a state of shock as to just how much his father had been involved, and has promised us that he will do all in his power to help put right any wrongs the people have suffered because of the name of Bilk." She then asked if they had had a successful visit, but before either her husband or son had a chance to answer, Pedro and Paul at the same time told her they had found out how the birds 'got out' as they put it.

"It was Paul who saw the hole first granny. I was looking in a different part and he called me over to see what he had found. When we showed dad and gramps, gramps thought it must be the way the birds used when they came to this part."

Her husband went on to explain to his wife, and James and Mary just what the opening looked like.

"I think they lock it somehow when they go back through because I tried to move it but it wouldn't budge at all. As Tom pointed out, it is very lucky we have not been spotted the other times we have been there."

Pedro then remembered he had the small box his granny had asked him to leave behind the bush and handed it over to her. She opened it with very excited fingers and picked up the paper she had put the questions on. The exercise book had been returned as well. They all sat there quietly while she read the paper trying to read anything in her expression as to what had been sent to her.

After what seemed like for ever, she looked up at them all and said, "You are never going to believe what I have just read."

"Go on granny!! Please tell us."

"I have a list here," she said holding up the paper, "of all the people who are behind that shed thing. There are many names I do not recognise, but there are an awful lot I do. My friend Rebecca is there, as is Jennifer Stubbs. James, you have an aunty back there. Her name is Elizabeth and she was your father's younger sister."

She carried on reading while the family quietly discussed what they had been just been told.

"From what I can make out, the people back there have remained exactly the same age as when they were taken. Which means," she said looking at James, "your aunt Elizabeth is not much older than your son!"

She opened the book and as she did so, a piece of paper fell from its pages. Picking it up she saw it was a note for her husband and handed it to him. Now it was his turn to sit and read. Eventually he looked up and told them it was a note from Joshua.

"It seems that he was on a visit to his family from the navy when they were all taken. As he says, he was 'in the wrong place at the wrong time'. He also says that they have set up a small committee consisting of a group of friends who they know can be trusted. They are not too sure who, amongst the people back there are, or are not, friendly with both themselves and the enemy. It appears they have established a safe house where they meet regularly when it is the time 'She' goes missing for a few days. He also suggests that we send a couple of children through the passage behind the bush. He says they will be perfectly safe. They have a mixture they put in a drink, which makes them invisible when they go outside. They have been using this method for many years to get messages to other people in the village. He says could we send at least one girl so the other girls there will have someone to talk to and see how they are dressing these days!"

He read some more then told them that the reason Joshua suggested children going through, is because the passageway is quite small, plus because of the invisibility aspect.

"He says to send any questions you would like him or the other adults to answer and they will do their best to reply."

They all sat very quietly for a while thinking about what they had just learned. It was granny who broke the silence.

"Well at least we seem to be getting somewhere with that side of things. Of course we must do as your friend asks John and let Pedro and Paul now he is here, and Sally through behind the bush. We had better contact Sally's parents tomorrow and tell them what is happening and ask if they will allow Sally to go with the boys. Does Joshua make any mention of when they can go John?"

John, who had continued to read the note told his wife Joshua had written that two children would wait behind the bush for the next three nights to welcome who ever we send and lead them to the safe house. He says that the passageway behind the bush leads directly into that house.

"From what he says, the night time is the best time as they are not closely watched then. He says who ever we send will be perfectly safe and that we should wait for their return the evening after they go through the bush."

"In that case, we should definitely go to see Sally's parents as soon as possible. We have no idea when the reply to my questions was placed there."

Mary pointed out to her mother-in-law that it was only late afternoon now, so she could quite easily pop along there now and see them. "If she agrees, then there is no reason why I couldn't bring Sally back with me and they could possibly go this evening."

"Good idea Mary. Maybe the boys might like to go with you."

Within ten minutes, Mary, Pedro and Paul left the house to see Sally's parents.

When they had gone, Joan suggested to her husband that if it was not too late when he and Tom returned from taking the children, it might be a good chance to visit Ishe again, taking James with them and introducing him to Ishe and Naggy if he was there.

Her husband agreed and told her Tom and he would leave with the children just as soon as it got dark. "Not that I think we will have any visitors, they don't appear to come out after dark but its best to be on the safe side.

Joan suddenly realised they had not asked James if he would allow Paul to go with Pedro and Sally.

"Of course, of course he must go. Anyway, I don't think we would be able to stop him do you?"

Within an hour Mary and the boys were back, together with a very excited Sally, so preparations were started for their visit through the bush. Mary explained to Joan that Sally's parents were more than happy for her to go with the two boys. Joan noticed that Sally was carrying a small bag and asked what was in it. Mary told her that when she explained to Sally's mother about the reason a request was made for a girl to make the visit, Sally immediately went to her room and came down with a few things she had outgrown and asked if she could take them to the girls behind the bush. Joan said that was very kind of her and perhaps they could do the same with some of the things Pedro no longer required.

Chapter Thirty-One

Two Separate Visits

John and Tom set off with the three children when they judged it was dark enough to be safe but not so dark that they would not be able fin their way. The three children were excited at what they were going to do and see. Pedro's father warned them all to be very careful and to respect the feelings of the people they would meet. "After all, you will be their guests, and they have invited you along so they can get to know you and try to see how we can help them, so be sure to try to remember all they ask you and say to you."

Pedro, Paul and Sally promised him they would not let themselves down. He turned to Pedro and gave him an envelope saying that his granny had asked that he give it to Joshua. "They are just a few more questions she would like answered. Also she has given him a rough outline of what else we have found out about the other place. "She has a special message for you to give to Joshua if you can speak to him alone. Your grandmother has mentioned in her note to Joshua about the birds. Tell Joshua, if one of the birds approaches him look to see if he is holding a pebble or stone in one of his middle claws. If he is then that will be Kirkum and he is willing to help all he can. Tell Joshua he can trust him completely."

Pedro said he would do what his father had asked. "Only tell Joshua if you can speak to him alone Pedro," his father emphasised.

"We don't want everyone trying to speak to the birds. Also as Joshua told us in his note to you grandfather, they are not completely sure yet who they can really trust."

"Don't worry dad, I will only tell him if I can get him on his own."

By now they had reached the site. Grandfather asked Pedro if he had the medallion. Pedro took it out of his pocket and handed it to his grandfather. They all approached the bush with granddad leading. As they got closer, the bush slowly started to move just as it had on other occasions. When it stopped a young girl crawled to the entrance, and said in a quiet whisper.

"Hello, I am Rebecca, I have been sent to meet you and take you to our house."

Grandfather knelt down to speak to her and told her that his name was John and that he was an old friend of her father's. He then introduced her to Pedro, Paul, and Sally. "They will be coming with you. I will leave them to introduce themselves to you properly when they get to your house."

He stood up out of the way of the entrance and indicated for the children to go with Rebecca. Just before Rebecca closed the bush, granddad reminded them Tom and he would return for them on the following evening. The children gave a quick wave and they were gone. The bush moved back into place, so the two men went to look for the little branch to wipe away any evidence they had been there.

It was a quiet walk back to the house, each man thinking, and hoping privately that the children would be O.K.

Everything was ready for the second visit of the night when they arrived home. They assured the ladies and James that the children had gone through the bush without so much as a backward glance.

"Biggest adventure of their young lives so far," commented Tom.

Joan had cleared the dinning table and had laid the folded map in the centre. She also had two wooden boxes, one she had used on other occasions and the smaller one she had not taken with her so far.

"Can you do the honours with the marbles?" she asked her son.

Tom took his seat beside his mother while his wife closed the curtains. Once every was settled Joan turned to James and told him not to afraid of what would happen in the next few minutes. "We are going to visit the other place we have called 'The Paper Village. The map will maybe rise above the table, there may be a strange noise and a few lights will flash but nothing at all to be alarmed about."

Asking if they were all ready, she asked Tom to place the first marble in its mark. As he did so, and just as Joan had told James, the map lifted, lights flashed and there was a strange noise. The room went dark and before they knew it they were in Ishe's house. The room got lighter again and there was Ishe sitting in her usual place in the old chair. She clapped her hands with delight at their arrival saying she was hoping that they would come back soon, and telling them she had some really good news for them.

Joan, as if it was the most natural thing in the world to do, went over, picked Ishe up and gave her a cuddle. She held her on her arm as she introduced her to James. "This is James, Mr. Bilk's son. James this is Ishe." James said a very cautious hello and even extended his hand to shake Ishe's hand. To his amazement she took hold of his hand and returned the action. Joan, seeing a look of embarrassment on his face at talking to, and shaking hands with a doll, put his mind at rest explaining that Ishe once belonged to his mother when she was a young girl. "Without her we wouldn't be where we are now in sorting things out."

Joan placed Ishe back in her chair and asked her if she was expecting Naggy any time soon.

"Someone mention my name?"

Naggy had quietly entered the room without anyone noticing. Joan, after Tom, John and Mary had said their hellos, carried out her second introduction of the visit. "Naggy this is James, Mr. Bilks son."

Naggy saved Joan the second part of the introduction by walking round the table to James and shaking his hand said, "Hello I'm Naggy, the messenger boy round here." James could see by the twinkle in his eyes that he was only joking.

"Take no notice of him James, he does a very good job for us. He can walk around the village out there without being seen," Ishe explained to James.

"Before we do or discuss anything this evening," said Joan, "we have to tell you two, that James's father, Mr. Bilk Senior sadly passed away this morning."

Both Ishe and Naggy said how sorry they were to hear that sad news with Naggy again going over to James and shaking his hand.

"Thank you both very much, you are very kind, but from what I have been able to learn about dad, he had not been well for quite a while. I had not seen him too often in the last few years. In truth we were not the best of friends. I think he was upset with me because I refused to take any interest in the mine, so in his eyes there would be no one to take over running of it when he was no longer able to. Now it seems as if I will have no choice but to at least try to sort something out." He went on to tell them that he would obviously rely heavily on other people to advise him what to do. "But that is in the future, don't let me spoil this visit telling you all my future worries."

"Don't you worry about anything James, I think when the time comes you will find people will be more than willing and may I say happy to give you a hand," Joan assured him.

In an effort to lighten the mood a little, John asked Ishe what the good news was she mentioned when they arrived.

"Well, seeing as Naggy is here now I think he ought to be the one to tell you. After all it was he who managed to get a few things sorted out. Off you go Naggy."

Naggy started off by telling them that he had managed to actually speak to two of the residents of a big house on the edge of the village.

"It was really strange how it happened. I was walking around as I normally do seeing if I could pick up any information that might help us in our, and your cause when one of those big black birds I told you about started to walk along on top of the wall I was going past. He kept up with me then all of a sudden started talking to me." 'You're Naggy aren't you?' he said." I replied that I was, as if it was the most natural thing in the world to be holding a conversation with a bird! He then said his name was Kirkum and not to be afraid of him. He told me he had spoken to you and your family Joan and was going to help you also. He said that if I went back to the village and waited by the pond in the middle of the green, he would send two gentlemen down to talk to me. 'They want to make things change for the better just as you do,' he told me. I asked him how they would be able to see me. In fact how was it he could see me. He explained that he had a few powers his brother, one of the other birds, didn't know he had. He said he had already spoken with the two men he would send down to talk with me."

Naggy told the family that he wandered off to the village green and waited by the pond just as Kirkum had told him. "Eventually, two men came down the road leading from the big house. As they approached the pond, I started to walk towards them to introduce myself, but they seemed totally unaware of my presence. I said hello but they continued to chat to each other. I was just beginning to think that something had gone wrong when Kirkum came flying towards us, and perched on the back of the bench. 'Good afternoon gentlemen' he said 'May I introduce you to Naggy?' As he said that, the two men turned round, saw me and came forward to shake my offered hand. 'Sorry for the wait' said Kirkum, but I had to make sure my brother was not around. Please feel free to talk to each other. I won't be far away but if I sense any kind of danger, or of you being spotted, I will make you disappear again Naggy.'"

"The men introduced themselves as David and Arthur," continued Naggy. "They told me that there were a few of the villagers that were eager to try to bring some sort of peaceful existence to their lives.

They said they were really fed up and miserable the way they had been forced to live for many years now. Each time they thought they had found a way of changing things, their plans seemed to have been discovered and relayed to the 'High Person' who took great delight in punishing the ones he thought were responsible. One day, as they were sitting under a tree discussing how they could beat the 'High Person' without any more villagers being punished, Kirkum flew down and started talking to them. He told them there were people who were in a position to help them in their mission to bring about lasting changes to their miserable life style. They asked who they were but Kirkum said he could not reveal who they were without their permission. Kirkum assured the two men that their secret was perfectly safe with him and he would be in touch when he had made further contacts. Apparently he told them that they would know it was him who approached them because he would carry a small stone in his middle claw."

"That is exactly what he said to us," said Joan.

"I told David and Arthur a little about you and your family Joan, but not too much. I did tell them that you all came from another time but that you were able to travel between the two places quite easily.

The said that they would keep all I had told them strictly between themselves for the time being because they needed to make doubly sure about anyone before they recruited anyone else. Arthur said he had a couple of plans he would try out on some people to test their loyalty. I told them I would be in touch very soon. At this point Kirkum flew down to say that a few families were approaching the village green so they would have to break up the meeting. He told David and Arthur he would be in touch very soon. Before he left he gave me this little bit of wood." He opened his hand to reveal a small round piece of polished wood. "He said when another meeting was arranged, I was to hold the wood in my left hand. When David and Arthur arrived at whatever meeting spot Kirkum would choose, I simply had to squeeze this little bit of wood, say hello to them both and I would become visible to them so we could talk."

"Kirkum certainly seems to be doing all he can to help us," said Mary, "when do you think your next meeting will be Naggy?"

"I don't know. Kirkum just told me to do as I have been doing, and that is to wander around the village each day. He will be able to see me although no one else can, and when he has arranged something he will fly close by me and tell me."

"So what do we do now?' asked Tom. "It seems as if a lot is coming together all at the same time."

"What we do now," said Ishe, who had been listening quietly in her chair, "is to tell you all a couple more secrets left by Jessica. Naggy, can you please open the top drawer in that little cabinet under the window and bring me the packet you should find there."

Naggy walked over to the window and retrieved the little packet and handed it to Ishe. Ishe, looking towards James and holding up the packet said, "This packet was placed in that drawer many years ago by your grandmother Jessica, on what turned out to be her last visit to here. A lot of what is in here concerns you and your earlier life. Some of the information will come as a surprise maybe even a shock, but it is something I was entrusted to pass on to you upon the sad passing of your father. Now, I can ask Joan to read it to you here, or you can take it away with you and read it when you are back in your own time."

"Does the information contained in that packet involve Joan and her Family?"

"Yes it does."

"In that case, I am more than happy to hear it with people who I have come to regard as friends."

Ishe asked Naggy to pass the packet over to Joan. As he did so she told Joan that she should find two envelopes inside, one with James's name on and one with her own. "I think it is best if you read the letter to James first."

Joan opened the packet and removed the two envelopes. The one for herself she placed on the table. The other one she opened, and saw that it was indeed written by Jessica. She looked at James and told him she would read it straight through just as it was written. Then he could ask any questions he may have when she had finished. James agreed with that so Joan laid the pages on the table ready to start reading.

"Just a minute please if you don't mind," said Mary. She walked over to Ishe's chair, picked her up and carried her back to her own seat round the table and sat her on her knee. Ishe smiled and said thank you to her. As Mary was doing this, Naggy clapped his hands, and, just as before drinks appeared in front of everyone.

When everyone was settled and ready Joan commenced reading.

CHAPTER THIRTY-TWO

LETTER TO JAMES

"Dear James, if you are reading this letter, or it is being read to you, then it will mean that my son Cedric, your father has passed away. I can only assume that if you are in Ishe's home you have been brought here, by a very good friend, and companion of mine for many years, Joan Meaker. (I am hoping that she married that nice young man of hers John Vendell.)

Your father, as a young man showed only a slight interest in the running of the marble mine, which had been in the Bilk family for more years than we had records for. Alfred, my husband and your grandfather I think secretly hoped that your father would have nothing to do with it at all. I didn't know the real reason myself at the time, but I do know he was often upset, by people who visited him at various times. On those occasions he would, very sharply, ask, or tell me in a quite stern voice to 'leave us alone please!' What he discussed with those people I have no idea, but once they had gone he would stay in his office for the rest of that day, only emerging when it was late evening. He would apologise for the way he had spoken to me then make some excuse to visit the mine to check that all was well.

The following day, it was just as if nothing had happened. This was the pattern of our lives for quite a few years. Over those years, he changed from the wonderful man I married into someone I could barely recognise at times. I seemed to live a completely separate life to him. I put it all down to the visits he continued to get from those strange people.

It was during this time that your sister Elizabeth disappeared. She was visiting her friend Jennifer Stubbs for the day when news came that she, Jennifer and a few other people had completely vanished.

All the people in the village searched for the rest of that day and all the next, but not a trace of them was ever found. Of course, I was extremely upset by the loss of my daughter, and for many weeks afterwards would speak to no one or allow any one up to the house. It was about this time that your father engaged a young lady by the name of Joan Meaker to help me around the house and keep me company. She worked in one of the offices at the mine so a couple of days, sometimes more each week she spent with me. I came over the time she was helping me, to completely trust her. I suppose it was true to say that I came to love her as I did my daughter who vanished. She was roughly the same age as Elizabeth and I suppose I thought of her as a replacement for her. I never gave her any hint of this, as I did not want to offend her in any way.

To get back to your grandfather: During the time he was having visits from the nasty men, as I had started to think of them as, I spent a lot of time on my own. I began to look at some of the mine records and other papers he had left lying around. I had more of a feeling than anything that strange things were happening at the mine, and I was determined to try and discover what they were. One day I discovered a very old piece of paper detailing where certain marbles could be found in the mine. It seemed that these marbles were very special and contained a sort of magic, but what that magic was, the paper didn't say.

Each day after that, whenever your grandfather left the house to go to the mine or even into the town to take a new supply of marbles to the local toy shop, I would go into his office to see what else I could discover. I had a very strange feeling that the reason for my husband behaving and acting like he had been doing, would be found in that mass of paperwork.

One day, I found a box containing three marbles, all with four stripes. I had no idea they were any different from any of the others, apart from the fact they seemed a lot brighter. I still had that one marble in my hand as I continued to look around the office. I remember thinking that I wished I could find out what was going on at the mine, and why the visits of the nasty men had such an effect on Alfred. I felt a funny tingle sensation in my hand. I opened it to discover that the marble I was holding was completely clear with no stripes at all. As I stood there looking at it I heard your grandfather coming through the front door, so I quickly made my way from the office to my sitting room still holding the marble.

Your grandfather never made any comment about one of his marbles going missing. Perhaps he hadn't looked in the box.

The next day he again had a visit from the nasty men. They all went straight into his office and closed the door. I was sitting in my chair reading a book. As I looked at the pages a picture appeared where the printing had been. It was a picture of your grandfather, and the two men in his office. I could hear and see all that was going on. They were shouting at him that he must try harder or else 'she' would be very displeased with him. 'And you know what would happen then,' they yelled at him. He told them over and over again he had no idea where the special marbles were they wanted. They told him they would be back in a few days and would expect a delivery then. They then said to him that he was not a bit as co-operative as his father Nathan had been, although he had got a bit stubborn towards the end. They then opened the door to leave and as they did so my book went back to normal.

It then occurred to me that I had perhaps found a few of these special marbles and by holding one as I made that wish about wanting to know what was going on the wish had been granted. It dawned on me, that is what the nasty men wanted and it was obvious they wanted them for not very nice reasons. I decided there and then to try to put a stop to all that was happening to my husband. I went back into his office and retrieved the other three marbles. Perhaps your grandfather didn't even know they were there. After all, I had found the box under a whole load of papers.

Sitting thinking about it all later, I had this strange feeling that all the things that had been going on in the village that could not be explained were all to do with the marbles and the nasty men. I made a decision to do something about it. I waited until later in the evening when I knew the mine would be closed for the day. I stood by an open window in the sitting room and holding two of the marbles in my hand, wished that the part of the mine where they could be found would collapse and bury them forever. At the time I had no thought as to how it would affect anyone or anything. All I wanted was to put an end to the misery that seemed to be engulfing everyone. As I stood there, I again felt the tingle in my hand. I opened it and saw that all the stripes from both marbles had gone completely. At the same time, I heard a terrible rumble and the whole ground seemed to shake. It went on for quite a while then everything went very quiet. Not even the evening birds were singing.

Your grandfather came into the room saying he must go to the mine, and that it sounded like there had been a fall.

About two days later when it was felt safe for people to enter the mine again, it was discovered that one part of the mine had indeed collapsed and it would be impossible for a very long time for anyone to work in that part again.

Two more things to tell you James and then I will finish this long letter. Firstly, I later went on to find out many more things about the mine, and the Bilk family in general, a lot of which were not very nice. The more I found out the less happy I was to be associated with the name. I don't wish I had not met your grandfather, I just wish he hadn't been a Bilk and had got involved in all the nastiness that seemed to go hand in hand with being a mine owner. All I found out, I wrote down on paper and handed them bit by bit to Joan, together with a couple of magic boxes I discovered along the way. These boxes, when used correctly will put an end to all the misery of the past. I sincerely hope that you James will play a large part in helping Joan to do just that.

Secondly, and this is most important to you James.

There is no easy way to tell you, but the man you have known all your life as your father, is not actually your father. Let me explain. Your natural parents were a very nice couple living at the far end of the village. Your father worked in the mine just like most of the other men. Your mother, I am sorry to say was not a very well lady. She was constantly under the care of the doctor. I don't think they ever did really discover what her illness was. When you were old enough to be taken from your mother, you were brought to Cedric's house each morning while your father went to work. Cedric's wife Amelia, who herself was unable to have children was happy to look after you. One day your natural mother became very seriously ill and despite all the efforts of the doctor, passed away after a few days. Your father never got over his loss. He continued to bring you to Amelia each day, but one day after he had handed you over to her, he left as if going to work but never arrived for his shift. No one ever saw him ever again, nor did he ever make contact with any of the villagers. No relatives came forward to claim you, so Cedric and Amelia just kept you as their own and brought you up. The elders of the village at the time raised no objections. They could see that you were being well cared for, so as far as they were concerned it was one less thing for them to worry about. Your adopted mother Amelia unfortunately died when you were about six years old, and that is when Cedric sent you away to live with various aunties.

Of course I was not around when all this happened. All that I am telling you I managed to discover by using some of the marbles to see into the future. Everything about how I did it and what else I saw is all explained in the separate letter to Joan.

The one thing I did want to make sure I explained to you myself, is that because you were adopted by Cedric, you will not be subjected to the terrible curses and mishaps which seemed to dominate the male side of the Bilks, for I don't k now how many years. I know you will inherit the mine because I have seen the documentation. What you will NOT inherit is the constant pestering Cedric, his father and his father before him had to endure. The curse of the male Bilks ended with the passing of the man you knew as your father.

In closing, I would ask that you do not judge Cedric too harshly. Most of what he did, he was not directly responsible for, and I am sure in his final days he was trying to make some effort to make amends for his bad past.

Have a good life with Paul, and your new friends. Run the mine, as it should be run and treat the workers, as they deserve to be treated. I may pop in to see you sometime but will not make a nuisance of myself.

Goodbye for the time being,
Your loving grandmother,
Jessica.

Joan read the last of the letter with tears in her eyes, and when she looked up at the rest of the family and friends, they too had been silently weeping. Even Ishe looked as if her face was a bit damp.

John was the first to say anything telling James how sorry he was to hear about Cedric not being his natural father. This was echoed by all of them.

"Thank you, thank you all very much, it is most kind of you all. I had no idea about my father, as I will continue to think of him, but it does explain a lot of what went on in my past life." He looked at Joan and asked her if she remembered the moment just before his father had passed away. "He pulled my head down to his face and whispered something which I could not understand at the time. After hearing what Jessica has just told me in her letter, I think I know what he said. I think he said something like 'You don't have to do it, you don't have to do it.' He must have been referring to what

Jessica meant, in that as I am not a natural Bilk the ancient curse or whatever it was, cannot affect me or my son."

"I think you are right James, and that now with our help to begin with, you and Paul can make a new life for yourselves in Marbleville if that is what you would like."

James told Joan that is exactly what he would like to do, and would be more than grateful for any help she and the rest of the family would be willing to give in the early days. "There is just one thing I think I would like, and that is until Paul is a good deal older and can understand things more, I would like him to continue to think of Cedric as his grandfather."

Joan agreed with him and said she thought that was a very good idea.

After a little while, Naggy asked John if there had been any progress with solving things at their end. John told him yes there had been, and went on to explain that at that very moment Pedro, Paul and a school friend of Pedro's a girl called Sally had gone behind the moving bush to meet some of the families trapped in the other world. "I don't think it will be very much longer before we will be able to get them out. I think it will very much depend on when that woman they call 'She' goes on one of her visits to wherever it is she disappears to."

Ishe agreed and told him that he was quite certain that when she left their place, she turned up at this place. "When that happens, she brings something for the High Person who himself goes away for two or three days." Naggy thought that would be the best chance they would have to make their move. "I will suggest that to David and Arthur and Kirkum the next time we have a meeting. Also by that time, David and Arthur may have been able to recruit a few more loyal people."

Assuring him that they would keep in very close contact with him, Joan suggested that perhaps it was time they returned to their own home.

Ishe thanked them all once again for coming and told Joan to make sure she read her letter from Jessica. "It will certainly explain a lot of what you have been wondering about."

Mary carried Ishe back to her chair, then they all said goodbye to her and Naggy and took their places back round the table for their trip home.

"Wait a minute!" said Naggy and took something out of his pocket. It was a little round stone. Giving it to Joan he told her that when she was reading the letter from Jessica, to be sure to have the smallest box she had been given on the table. Somewhere in the letter you will be asked to place that little round stone into the hole in the centre of the box. Also, if you have one, place a mirror upright on a chair somewhere in the room. Of course if you have an upright free standing mirror that will be even better."

Joan told him that she would do as he had asked, and with a final goodbye, opened the map, laid it on the table and put the marble in the correct space, gave it a slight turn and they were immediately transported back to their own living room.

Nobody said anything for a long time after they had returned. It was James who was the first to speak, thanking them for taking him along with them, and taking him into their confidence. "It certainly seems as if I have a lot to do."

"One thing is for certain, there will be no need to rush things," said Tom. "Just take and do things nice and easy."

Chapter Thirty-Three

Letter To Joan

Mary asked if anyone was hungry, but was told that all that after all had happened had taken any thoughts of food had gone out of their heads, although a nice drink would be welcome.

"Would you like me to read my letter this evening?" asked Joan.

"I don't see why not," replied her son, "we don't have the children to worry about and if you look at the clock, it is true what we have been told. It has hardly been any time at all since we left to visit Ishe.

"I'll just go and fetch the long mirror stranding in the hall."

"And I will go and get the little box Naggy was talking about," said his mother.

Tom returned with the mirror and stood it at the end of the table where they could all see it, wondering aloud what they needed it for.

Mary returned with the drinks and after a few minutes Joan asked if everyone was ready for her to start her letter. When they said they were, she took it out of the envelope, laid it on the table and started to read it out loud.

"Dear Joan, if you are reading this then so far everything I hoped for has gone to plan. Unfortunately it also means that sadly Cedric is no longer with you. You will also have discovered by now that he was not James's birth father. Of course, I never knew James in real life. All I know about him I have learned by the use of the marbles.

All the time the strange men were making visits to dear Alfred, I spent more and more time in his office hoping to discover what was going on and why the visitors were so insistent that my husband did as they told him. I found a large box of the four striped marbles hidden behind a large cupboard at the far end of the office. There were about thirty marbles, altogether. I had a feeling that poor old Alfred had no idea they were there. If he had, I am sure he would have handed them over to the strange men, in the hope they would stop visiting him.

I decided to take them to the sitting room over looking the garden. It was the one room if you remember from the days you came to help me that I told you I really felt at ease. Alfred very rarely came into that room so it was quite easy for me to find a place to keep them.

As I was sitting there one day thinking things over, I had the idea that maybe I could discover some things with the use of the marbles. I recalled the time I had observed what was going on in Alfred's office by making a wish and that the images appeared in a book I was holding, and wondered if it would work a second time.

I waited for a day Alfred had gone to the town with some mined marbles, and decided to put my wish to the test. I selected a larger book this time. I had no idea how many wishes I would need so picked up three marbles. Holding them in one hand, I opened the book, and laying it on my knee made a wish that I could see into the future and find out what would happen when Alfred and I were no longer around. After what seemed like an awful long time, the book I was holding started to shake and move around, so much in fact that it fell off my knee and landed on the floor by my feet. When I recovered from that little shock, I looked down at the book and could see Cedric in the garden of a house I didn't at first recognise, and he appeared to be arguing with something up in one of the trees. I watched for a long time. Eventually after much more shouting from

Cedric, a very large bird flew out of the tree, landed on his shoulder, gave him a peck on the neck then flew away. Cedric put his hand to where he had been pecked and yelled after the bird something about not coming back. He then collapsed onto the ground and sat there for what seemed like ages. Soon after, a young lady came into the garden shouting his name. She had a small child with her. She asked him if he was O.K. 'Course I am!' he said to her in a rather rough way. 'Just leave me alone!' It was quite obvious she was used to Cedric speaking to her in that manner. She took the child by the hand and said, 'come on James, daddy is a bit upset, let's go back into the house and have some tea.'

It was obviously after Cedric and his wife had adopted James. I had no idea what his wife's name was. At that point in fact I had no idea he was married. You may remember Joan that following the disappearance of our daughter Elizabeth, Alfred and I decided to send Cedric away to live with relatives. I suppose we were afraid the same kind of thing would happen to him. I very rarely saw him after that. He would be brought on a quick visit now and again by whichever aunt was taking care of him at the time but showed little or no interest in staying. That is why you were such a comfort to me in those days."

Joan took a rest from reading the letter and looked up at the family. "It must have been very heartbreaking for her and Alfred to decide to send Cedric away. From what she is saying in this letter she hardly saw him after that apart from a few fleeting visits. It makes you wonder just what thoughts were put into his mind during the time he was being taken care of by so called aunties."

"It does indeed," commented James. "I think who ever he was living with at that time and what they said to him over the years, had a lasting effect on him and the way he acted and behaved in his adult life."

"He didn't really stand much of a chance did he?' said Tom. "Brought up by folk intent on poisoning his mind about things, and also being born with the nasty Bilk attitude, although that side of things seemed, for the most part, to have not been in Alfred so much. I know he was controlled to a certain extent by the visits of the weird men, but I think overall he was trying to fight their influence over him. Perhaps that was the real reason Cedric was sent away."

"You may be right there Tom," said his mother. She picked up the letter, settled back in her chair and continued reading

"A little while after the young lady and James had gone into the house, the pictures in the pages of the book started to fade and very soon the book jumped back onto my knee. It was almost as if my lesson for that particular day had ended. I looked at the marbles in my hand and saw I had used three of the stripes in one of the marbles.

I went over to my writing table and wrote down all I could remember of what I had seen. I made a lot more visits to the future in the next few months, each time writing down what I had found out. I eventually went back to a time I witnessed Cedric getting married to the young lady I had seen on my first visit. Her name was Amelia. She unfortunately died of a mystery illness when James was about six years old.

I was very quickly running out of marbles with stripes in them. I had on a few occasions wished I had more of them. It worked a few times and I got about three every time I made the wish, but eventually it no longer worked and I was left with only four with stripes in them.

It was about this time I discovered one of the maps I passed on to you, Joan. I also found the two little boxes at the same time. I did just as you did with the map and found myself in the house where you were sent. Over a few visits I learned a bit about what had been happening over the years. I found the little piece of paper telling me what colour to wear if I went outside the house. I also found instructions about carrying one of the boxes with me if I did venture outside.

On my return from one such trip I was talking to myself, or at least thought I was when Ishe started talking back to me. She had always just been left in a chair in my sitting room. It seemed as if the magic I had been working with had brought her to life. Something in my mind told me I had to take her to the house I had been visiting, so on one of my next visits I did just that. From that time onwards, whenever I went on one of my journeys, I carried Ishe with me. We went outside the house many times, wandering around the village and learning the things I wrote on those papers I passed on to you.

There came a time that I got to be quite weak and decided that perhaps I had better stop my visits. I asked Ishe what she wanted to do and she told me she wanted to stay in the house. She knew I had been writing every thing down and passing the papers over to you. Between us we used what little magic we could get from the remaining marbles to put our plan into operation. That was for Ishe to wait patiently in the house for your visit. We knew that eventually you would open the packets with the papers in and start to work things out for yourself what you had to do."

Joan placed the letter on the table and relaxed a little. She was about to ask her family and James what they all thought about what they had heard when the letter started to move around and jump up and down on the table. Putting her hand on the letter to steady it, something seemed as if it was guiding her hand to the bottom part of the page. When her hand stopped, she looked at the paper and saw, in very tiny writing she had difficulty in reading two words, - 'Tap here.' Looking up at the family for encouragement she tapped very gently with her finger. For a while nothing happened, then they were all startled to see the mirror Tom had brought into the room start to shake a little and give off lots of bright lights. This carried on for a few moments then settled back down. The lights began to fade and there looking out of the mirror at them was Jessica.

Just as in the past when something new had occurred, no one said a word; they just sat and stared. Of course Joan was the only person in the room who had ever seen Jessica so she recognised her at once, but it was the old lady who spoke first.

"Hello to you all. It is so wonderful to be here to meet you."

Again, no one said anything. They just sat and stared, a little bit afraid if the truth was known, not knowing what to expect next.

It was as if Jessica could sense their feelings. "Please don't be afraid, nothing nasty is going to happen to you. Joan, would you like to introduce me to your family?"

Joan did as she was requested and introduced the family one by one. When she came to James, he himself said, "Hello, I am James your grandson. I am so sorry we never got to meet before."

"Hello James, I too am very sorry we never met in my lifetime." Turning to Joan, Jessica asked her if she had the stone Naggy had given her.

"Yes I do," and opened her hand to show her the stone.

"Would you please now put it into the hole in the middle of the little wooden box you have on the table, and please, none of you be afraid of what you will see."

Joan did as Jessica had requested. Once more the mirror started to shake around a little and this time a very bright light came from the centre, a light so bright they had to shield their eyes with their hands. The bright light slowly faded and when they removed their hands from their eyes, there stood Jessica in the room with them. As if the most natural thing in the world had just occurred, John went and fetched a chair for the old lady to sit down. At the same time, still recovering from shock, James went over to his grandmother and gave her a hug. Before sitting down and with the room still in complete silence Jessica went round to everyone and gave then a hug. She left the biggest one for Joan. Speaking for the first time, she told her how wonderful it was to see her again after all this time. Joan took her by the hand and led her to the chair her husband had brought for her.

It was Mary, practical as ever who asked Jessica if she would like something to drink.

"Thank you for the kind thought Mary, but I am unable to have neither food nor drink. I am not exactly a ghost because you can feel me and talk to me but my body will not take any food or drink. I am a 'Living Vision'. I am only able to appear to whoever has the stone to put into the box." She looked round at them all and told them how she had waited for this moment for many, many years. "I knew it would happen one day, but had to be patient for that day to arrive. I sincerely hoped that it would be you Joan, and your family who discovered the secrets in the papers I had given you. I was dreading the thought that, for some unlucky reason they may have after all fallen into the wrong hands."

She went on to explain that she had no idea what so ever who she would see when the mirror opened the room to her. All she knew was that when someone tapped the paper where it said 'tap here' she would appear to that person or persons who had been reading the letter.

Tom was the first to say anything. "What do we do now?' he asked no one in particular.

Looking round at them all Jessica said. "What I would like you to do, if you will, is tell me all that you have discovered about the village. It will be very interesting for me to know if you have managed to learn a lot more than I was able to do on my visits."

Between them Joan, John, Tom and Mary, relayed to the old lady and of course James who knew very little, all they had been able to discover and achieve. They finished by telling them where the children had gone and that they were hoping that when they returned, they would be able to put a plan into operation to free the people trapped behind the 'Winter Shed'.

"I was right!" said Jessica when she heard about the children. "I had a feeling from something I heard on one of my many visits to the other place that children would be able to play a big part in sorting everything out. When you release me from here and I go back to my resting place I will read again notes I made at the time as to how they can help. When I next visit you I will tell you what I have discovered. As far as my memory can recall, it was something I heard one of the black birds say when he was perched one day on the shoulder of the statue in the middle of the green. I had often seen him there when I paid visits to the place. He only seemed to talk to the statue when he was there on his own. If there were two or more perched there then he said nothing."

Joan quickly explained that one of the birds, Kirkum, had made friends with them and was also trying to help them any way he could. "I suspect that the statue he perches on is his young mistress who used to own him. He told us she was turned into a statue by her older not very nice sister Tanglen, who we think is the 'She' who sent the birds to visit Cedric. She seems able to go between both settlements as she pleases."

"That would explain a lot of things," said Jessica. Turning to Joan she said that it was time for her to return to her resting place. "I can only stay out of my comfort place for so long them must go back to rest and relax. But don't worry I will be back very soon, hopefully with some ideas to help you all. When you are ready for me to visit, just lay out the letter on the table and as before press the paper where it tells you to, and have the mirror in the same place. Now if you would be so kind Joan, would you please shake the little box upside down so the stone falls out. That will put be back inside the mirror. Once I am there please simply fold up the letter and that will send me on my way. It has been wonderful to meet you all and I look forward to my return."

She nodded to Joan who picked up the box, turned it upside down, and gave it a little shake so the stone fell out onto the table. Immediately, Jessica floated from the chair she had been sitting on, to the mirror. She lifted her hand to wave them goodbye as Joan folded the letter. This time there were no flashing lights; just a slowly fading glow as Jessica disappeared from their view.

Chapter Thirty-Four

The Return Of The Children

The next morning over breakfast the family and James discussed the previous evening's meeting with Jessica. James had accepted Mary's offer to stay the night and had used Pedro's room. All that had happened had been a lot to take in and understand. By now the rest of the family had come to accept whatever small 'magic' or 'unexplained' things took place. They assured James that so far nothing bad had taken place and that he had no need to worry.

"Perhaps you would like to come with us this evening when we go for the children," Tom suggested to James.

"Thank you, that would be very nice," replied James.

Tom's father suggested that they should leave for the 'Winter Shed' site late afternoon, explaining that they needed to make sure the birds were not "on our side". "Once we establish that they are not in our side, we can block the exit so they cannot come out and see the children returning."

Mary prepared an early lunch for them all and the three men left the house mid afternoon. Her father-in-law had explained that he wanted to get to the site well in advance of the time the children would come from the bush. He said he would feel a lot happier about things once he had had a good look round to satisfied himself that they would not be spied on.

"We need to make sure that the exit the birds use is not open. If it is, then we know they are our side of things. If that is the case, then we will have to conceal ourselves somewhere so we can watch for their return and lock the entrance after they have gone through."

On the way to the site Tom and his father told James all about the site and how they had come to make contact with people behind the old shed.

When they arrived at the area they had a good look round but could see no evidence that anyone had been there. There were no footprints around the bush and everything appeared to be as they had left it the previous evening. Tom went to inspect the bird exit and came back to report that it was closed. He told his father that he had locked it the way they had discussed.

"Better make sure we remember to unblock it before we leave."

All they could do now was wait for the return of the children. While they did so, John and Tom showed James where Joshua was making the hole and explained to him that they would eventually make it large enough for the people to pass through.

"How many will be coming through?" asked James.

"We are not sure. We may know more when the children return. What we have to remember is that everyone back there stayed the same age as when they disappeared. Your father's sister Elizabeth disappeared when she was very young and that is how she has remained. If you remember, my mother told you that you have an aunt who is not much older than Paul

James sat there thinking about what Tom had just told him. All this was so new to him, he was finding it a bit difficult to take it all in; talking birds, grandmother coming out of a mirror, 'trips' via a map on a table. He wondered what life for him would have been like if he had lived with his father all this time.

He was brought out of his thinking by a shout from John telling him and Tom that the bush was moving. He and Tom hurried over and arrived just as Pedro was crawling out of the hole behind the bush. Her had a huge smile on his face and ran straight over to his father who gave him a big hug. Sally was the next to appear and she too looked very happy. Of course there was no one of her family to meet her, so Pedro's grandfather went forward and helped her to her feet. Paul appeared next and his smile was equal to that of Pedro's. He rushed straight over to his father and said how happy he was to see him.

As they all stood saying hello to each other there attention was drawn back to the bush. Crawling from behind it were two young girls. Pedro and Sally went over to them and taking their hands brought them towards the others.

"This is Elizabeth," said Paul.

"And this is Rebecca," said Sally.

Pedro's grandfather stepped forward and introduced himself to both girls then introduced them to Pedro's father and Paul's father, saying to Elizabeth that James was in fact her nephew!!

Pedro explained to the three elder men that Joshua had asked if it would be all right for the girls to return with them. He said he thought it would help if the girls could tell them all in person just what was happening back in their life. Pedro's grandfather thought it was a brilliant idea and welcomed them again. Pedro, on hearing this, nipped back to the bush and spoke to someone in there saying it was O.K. for the girls to stay. With that, the bush moved back into its original position. Sally meanwhile was explaining that Joshua had hoped all along that the girls would be able to join them on their return visit and had arranged for them to misbehave themselves. That way they would be punished. She said that girls were not punished too severely, just made to stay indoors for whatever period of time 'She' decided. On this occasion they had been ordered to stay in for three weeks, which meant no one would expect to see them for quite a while.

Pedro's father suggested that perhaps it was time to tidy the area up and head for home. He also suggested that it might be best for Elizabeth and Rebecca to wear a green scarf each just in case the birds made an appearance. He didn't know why, but something had prompted him to bring two or three scarves with him. He asked James if he and Paul would like to go and remove the wooden wedge from the little trap door the birds used, so they could use it again if they desired. While they were doing that, Pedro and his grandfather used the branch to remove all traces of their footprints from the bush area. That done, and James and Paul having returned from dealing with the birds hatch, the party set off for home, first making sure Elizabeth and Rebecca had put on the green scarves.

"Someone is going to get a big surprise, that's for sure!" said Pedro's grandfather, trying to imagine the look on his wife's face when she came face to face with her best friend from many years ago.

The journey was uneventful with no sign of any visits from the sky. Pedro's father wondered if perhaps it would be a good idea if Pedro went on ahead and prepared his grandmother to expect a very pleasant surprise. His father thought that would be the decent thing to do, so Pedro and Paul ran on to the house to inform his granny and mum about the two extra visitors arriving shortly.

When Pedro told his granny, she had one of those 'I had better sit down moments' and asked her grandson to tell her again more slowly this time what he had just said. Pedro repeated his story at the same time feeling it necessary to hold his grandmother's hand as he did so. He had just finished when he heard the back door opening and the voice of his father greeting his wife. Pedro went into the kitchen where his father suggested that it would be nice if he and Sally took the two girls in to see his grandmother.

Pedro took Rebecca's hand and Sally did the same with Elizabeth. They all went into the front room where granny was sitting. There were tears all round as she greeted her long lost friend and 'Bilky's' sister. Of course Rebecca was just as granny remembered her, but it was a lot different for Rebecca, saying hello to a friend now old enough to be her grandmother who, at the time of her disappearance, had been the same age.

Joan then greeted Elizabeth with the same loving hug she had given Rebecca. Sally and Pedro brought two chairs for the two girls and placed them by granny, then left the room so the three friends could talk in peace.

Back in the kitchen, the adults were discussing where the two girls should sleep, and also how long they would be staying. Pedro told his parents that the girls had been punished for a period of three weeks, back in their time, which meant they would not be missed for that amount of time. He told them that Joshua had said someone would wait behind the bush every third night as from tonight ready to greet the girls whenever they wished to return.

"Rebecca has a letter for you from her father granddad, and also a note for granny. Maybe she has given it to her by now."

"Thank you Pedro, I will look forward to reading it," said granddad, "meanwhile we still have the problem of where the girls are going to stay."

"I have an idea," James said. " How about if I take the boys back to my father's house at least for tonight. Then the girls can stay here. I am sure there is no danger in that place now."

Pedro's grandfather thought that was a good idea as long as James was sure he felt O.K. returning there.

"Why don't I go as well," suggested Pedro's father, "in fact why don't all us men go there for tonight. That way the three girls and the ladies will be able to have a relaxing evening all together. We gave no definite time to Sally's parents when she would be returning, so she can stay here as well and we can take her home tomorrow."

Mary thought that was a good idea but insisted that she make them all a meal before they left and also get some food together to take with them.

They had just finished eating when granny came through from the other room with Rebecca and Elizabeth. It was evident from the looks on all their faces that it had been a bit of an emotional meeting. In fact it seemed as if granny was still a bit tearful. The two girls were introduced properly to Pedro's mother who fussed around getting them drinks. Tom explained to his mother what had been decided for the night; that he, his father, James and the two boys would go to Mr. Bilks house leaving the girls with her and Mary to get to know each other better. "We will take Sally home in the morning."

His mother thought that was a good idea. She then passed a folded piece of paper to her husband explaining it was a letter from Joshua. "I have one also from Rebecca's mother. It explains a lot of what had been going on back in their little world."

A little while later the three men and the two boys bid the ladies good night and started out for what was now James's home, telling them they would be back sometime in the morning.

"Probably be O.K. now but as a precaution just make sure all the windows are locked and the curtains closed," commented Tom as he said goodnight."

CHAPTER THIRTY-FIVE

REBECCA'S AND ELIZABETH'S STORIES

Next morning the 'Ladies' were all up bright and early, despite having spent the previous evening talking and getting to know one another again. It had been a very emotional evening for all of them; Joan because she was meeting her long lost childhood friends again, and Mary because she had been carried away with the talk and chatter of bygone days.

Rebecca had told them that she was with her mother and sister having their evening meal after school, when one minute they were sitting at their table and the next they were in a strange place. They found themselves sitting at a very different table in a strange house. Before they had time to get over the shock of what had happened there was a knock on the door and a very rough voice was telling them to 'Come outside now!!'

"We were too shocked and frightened not to obey the command," Rebecca had told them. She said that as they left the house, two men wearing long black and purple cloaks pushed them along telling them to hurry on to the green saying that 'She ' does not like to be kept waiting. Rebecca said that when they got to the village green there were lots of other families there, some from Marbleville who they recognised but there were many people they had never seen before.

Rebecca had continued, "After a while one of the two men told us all to be quiet because 'She' was approaching and was going to speak to us all. He said there was to be no talking while 'She' was talking."

"What did she have to say?" Mary had asked.

"We were told that we had been brought to this place because the people of Marbleville had displeased the "High person". In what way were never really sure, but it had something to do with the workers in the mine not working hard enough to get what was required from the mine. 'She' said that there the days had been made a lot longer so the miners would have to work many more hours a day. The nights had at the same time been made shorter. 'She' told the men present that when the working day was done there would be no time for anything else but having their evening meal and going to bed, ready for the next days work. She said a lot of other things but I can't remember what they were. We were then told to go back to our cottages, because that is what they were, and make them as comfortable as we could, telling us we would be there for a very long time. The men were to report back at the village green at first sunrise."

Rebecca went on to say that as her and her mother and sister started to make their way back to try and find the cottage they had left, she saw Elizabeth standing alone at the edge of the crowd. "I started to make my way towards her but as I did so one of the men went over to her and asked what her name was."

Elizabeth spoke for the first time saying that when she told them that her name was Elizabeth Bilk one of the men said that she was the one they had been told to look out for and that she was to go along with them.

"I was very frightened but the man had his hand on my shoulder and was pushing me over to where the woman who had been talking to us was still standing. She told me that life would be a lot easier for me if I was able to tell them some of the Bilk family secrets regarding the running of the mine. I told them that I had no idea whatsoever about anything to do with the mines. 'She' didn't believe me, saying that I must have heard something of what my father discussed with people that came to see him. I insisted again that I knew nothing. After a while she told the men to take me to the supervisor's house at the far end of the village. I was told that was where I would live and work. I would not be going to school with the rest of the children but would be looked after and taught by a lady called Agnetty."

Between them Rebecca and Elizabeth explained what life had been like in that place. The men went to work very early. They had a break about the middle of the day when they all went to a large building for their lunch. Lunches were prepared by some of the ladies of the village. About half the ladies worked making the food while the other half were put to work in the fields. This arrangement continued for about six weeks when the two groups of ladies would change; the field workers doing the lunches and the lunch ladies going out into the fields. Children, boys and girls were also divided into two groups, one group going to school and the other group helping around the village doing any work the men in charge decided needed to be done. As with the ladies, the two groups were changed round every so often. Elizabeth told them that after what seemed like a year she was moved from the big house and sent to live with a family in one of the cottages. She thought it was because 'She' had finally accepted that there was nothing to be gained from her despite the continuing questioning.

Mary asked the girls when they realised they were not getting any older. Elizabeth told her that it was explained to her while she was living in the big house that the 'High Person' had cast a spell on all who lived there that they would remain the same age as when they arrived, both adults and children alike. The 'High Person' gave his reason that by doing that everyone would stay a working age. Elizabeth butted in saying that at the same time as the age spell had been cast another spell ensured that no one would ever fall ill for any reason. That way they would all stay young enough to keep working.

"We had no idea at all how long we had been there until my father arrived," said Rebecca. "He had come home on leave from the Navy after being away for about two years. He said he had tried to get into our house but the door was locked. He asked around the village but no one wanted to tell him anything. As far as the people there were concerned Mum and my sister and I had left the village. Daddy broke the door of our house open and went inside. He found the place as we had left it when we were last there. The meal we were having at the time had been eaten by insects and mice, and anything else that had managed to get into the house. He said the place was very dusty and there were plants and small flowers growing up through the floorboards of the main room. He said he had been in there for only a few minutes when he heard the door slam shut. He walked over towards it but never got there. The next minute he was with us in our cottage."

Rebecca went on to explain that her father had arrived in the middle of the day so she and her sister were at school and her mother was working in the fields. "Luckily he never left the house so was not spotted by any of the men who wandered around the place checking on things. We had a really nice surprise when we arrived home from school, as did mummy when she got home from work later. We spent the evening trying to explain to daddy what had happened to us. It was then he told me that I still looked the same age as when he had left. We worked out that we had been brought to that place about three weeks after daddy had left home to go to sea."

"Has everybody stayed the same age?" asked Joan.

It was Elizabeth who answered, "Yes, but the never getting ill spell hasn't worked so well on the people who were already quite old when they were taken. Although they have stayed the same age, they are beginning to get a few things going wrong with them that older people get. One lady there says she is suffering from the same problems she remembers her own grandmother having when she was very old."

"How long before your father was discovered Rebecca?" Mary wanted to know.

"About five days. We thought it might be a good idea to not tell anyone about daddy. That way he would not have to go and work in the mines and perhaps use his time trying to find out a bit of what was going on in the place. In all the time we had been there we still had not been allowed out much so had not a clue as to what was happening. He went out after dark keeping in the shadows as much as he could. One evening one of those men was doing his rounds and spotted daddy as he walked back to the house. He was spotted because as he opened the door the light shone out. No one was ever allowed out after dark so the light gave him away. He was taken to the 'High Person' who immediately ordered him to start working in the mine the next day."

They had all sat very quiet for a while, the two older ladies and Sally, thinking about what they had been told by Rebecca, and Elizabeth. Joan could still not quite come to terms with the fact she was looking at her friend who looked no different from when she last saw her as her best school friend. It also suddenly came to her mind that it was quite possible that they may have another visit from Jessica via the mirror. What would happen when she came face to face with Elizabeth, her daughter she had lost all those years ago, and should she try and warn them both in some way to prepare them for the meeting? She decided she would ask John's advice. In the event, it was Mary who brought up the subject in a very different way by asking Elizabeth what she could remember about the day she was taken.

"Not a lot really," Elizabeth replied. "Daddy had gone to the mine and mummy was out in the garden. I was in a room I used as a playroom. I heard my name being called from the kitchen. Thinking it was mummy calling me, I entered the kitchen but she was not there. Instead there was a very large funny looking blackbird perched on one of the kitchen taps. He flew from the tap and landed on my head. Before I could do anything or shout for mummy he gave me a peck on my shoulder and the next thing I knew I was standing with a lot of other people, some I knew but most I didn't, in a strange place I had never seen before. I remember seeing Rebecca standing with her mother and sister but when I tried to go over to them I couldn't get my feet to move so had to stay where I was. After that things happened just as Rebecca and I have told you. The family I was sent to live with had no children so I was made to feel very welcome. They treated me very well and over the years I got to love them as much as I was able. The man Michael had been a worker at the mine for my father although he hadn't known him personally. His wife Eileen had helped in the nursery where the workers' children were placed each day so their parents could work in the mine."

The sound of the back door opening told them that the men and boys had returned. Everyone greeted each other warmly, the five children going out into the garden while the grown ups sat around the table in the kitchen. Tom explained that James wanted to stay at the house for a few hours to sort a few things out but would return later. John told his wife and Mary that he had read the letter from his friend Joshua. He told them that it looked as if a sort of plan had been started which when, and if, it came together would enable the people trapped behind the winter shed site to come out. "I think we will have to enlist the help of Kirkum, Naggi, Ishe and possibly Jessica as well if it is to succeed."

"Well, we know what we have to do if we want Kirkum to visit us," said Tom, reminding them about putting the garden spade under an open window.

"The first thing we have to do is get Sally back to her parents," said Joan, "they must be getting a bit anxious about her."

Her husband agreed, and asked them all in general what they thought about the idea of taking Rebecca and Elizabeth when they returned Sally home. "After all, it's not as if anyone will recognise them after all these years is it?"

"That might be a good idea, but first we must ask the girls and see what they think about it," said Joan. "I will go and ask them now. If they would like to go with us then we had better make sure they are wearing something green. We know Kirkum can see them, but it's no good advertising the fact they are here to his brother before we need to."

While she was gone, Tom suggested that perhaps he and Mary should go with the girls while his father stayed behind and told his mother just what was in Joshua's letter. At the same time he and Mary could then bring Sally's parents up to date with all that had been happening.

His father agreed saying he didn't really feel up to going into the village after walking down from James's house.

When Joan came back in she said that the girls would love to go with Sally. Tom told his mother about he and Mary taking Sally back and she thought it was a good idea. "There are a few things I need to discuss with your father anyway," explaining that Rebecca and Elizabeth had told them quite a lot about their life since their disappearance, things which might be useful to know when it came time to put whatever plan they made, into operation.

Mary called the children into the house to give them all a drink before they left. Joan then gave Rebecca and Elizabeth a green scarf to wear and she and John waved them all goodbye as they left for the village with Tom and Mary. She and John then settled themselves into the two comfortable chairs by the fireplace and prepared to tell each other what they had learned, she from the two girls and he from Joshua's letter.

CHAPTER THIRTY-SIX

TWO MORE VISITS

John thought it best if he gave Joshua's letter to his wife to read for herself. She settled down to read it while he started to work out in his mind just what they would need to do in order to help the people behind the 'Winter Shed' site.

It appeared from what the letter said that not all the people were anxious to return to their former homes. This appeared to be mainly the older ones. It seemed as if they were afraid that once they did return, they would suddenly advance rapidly in years. After all the time they had been kept at the same age, some of them would be very old indeed. That and the fact that the 'stay well' spell which had been put on them would suddenly wear off and not only would they be very much older, they would also be smitten down with all the ailments older people were subjected to.

Joshua stated in the letter that not all the people in the village had been spoken to as he still wasn't quite sure just who he could trust and who he couldn't.

The letter ended by Joshua saying that if any plan was to succeed, then it would have to be carried out at a time when 'She' went away on one of her visits to where ever she went. The problem was, they never knew when that would be. She would be there one day, than gone the next, and they would never be too sure either when she would return. He really hoped that John and his friends could help them out with that.

"I definitely think we need the help of Naggi and Ishe if any plan is to work," said Joan after finishing the letter."

"Plus Kirkum and to some extent Jessica as well," commented her husband.

"I think a return visit to Ishe's house as soon as possible is what we need to think about, but with the two girls here it may be a bit awkward."

"You have a point there, but perhaps you and Mary could go while Tom and myself took the children out for the day somewhere," said John.

"That's possible, and I could take Joshua's letter with me and read it to Naggi and get his thoughts on some kind of plan."

Joan told her husband that with the place to themselves for a while she would take the advantage of a bit of peace and quiet to get out a few more of the papers Jessica had given her and see if she could make any more sense of a few things.

"We still have no idea what the marbles in the triangular rocks are for, or will do. Or for that matter what part the children will play in all this. The papers we read told us to let the children solve the problem and Jessica hinted at it, but how many children and where must they go?"

John could see that his wife was already lost in her own little world regarding the papers and what they would tell her so he left her to it and went out into the garden. With all that they had been doing the past few days the garden had taken second place, so he set about doing a bit of weeding and tidying up. Whilst he was working, he too wondered just what part the children would play in solving the many riddles they seem to have got themselves caught up in.

James arrived after a short while and John took the opportunity to stop what he was doing and sit and have a chat. James said that he had been sorting out a few things in his father's house and had found some sort of diary his father must have kept.

"Not so much a diary, more a kind of record of visits from various people and the birds," he told John. "It seems they visited him a lot more often in the last two years and from what I can understand from his writing the demands made on him were getting more each time. He appears to have been punished a lot more frequently as well. He complains on many of the pages that his head and shoulders were hurting from the pecking one of the birds was giving him, and that despite many requests for help to reduce the pain, that help was not forthcoming. In fact it looks as if they were deliberately not helping him in order to get him to give them what 'She' kept demanding."

"Not very nice people at all," commented John. "Let us hope that very soon we can put an end to all this."

He went on to tell James about the contents of the letter the children had brought back for him from Joshua, and that it appeared that a visit back to Ishe's house was required very soon.

"I have suggested to Joan that perhaps we can take the children out of the way for a day while she and Mary seek the guidance of Naggi and Ishe. I certainly think that if we are going to have any success at all in releasing the people from behind the Winter Shed site, some sort of co-ordination and co-operation between both places is essential."

James agreed and told John that if he could help in any way he only had to ask.

"Perhaps another look round your father's house to see if you can unearth any more information about what has gone on in the past would help."

"I'll go back up there to sleep again tonight and have a really good look round tomorrow," James assured him.

The two men sat there chatting about things in general when Joan appeared with a tray of drinks for them all.

"Thought I heard your voice James," she said.

"Find out anything interesting in the papers my dear?' asked John.

"Yes I did but I don't think I had better say anything until I have had a word with Naggy. What I will say is, if I have correctly interpreted what Jessica has put in the papers, I think what we want to do will be easier than we thought."

"That is excellent news! Sure you can't tell us anything?"

Joan looked at her husband and told him no, she thought it best not to say anything until after her visit.

With that John had to be content. He knew from many years being married to her, that once his wife made up her mind about something then there was no changing it.

Joan went back into the house saying she would make a bit of lunch, leaving the two men to continue chatting and getting to know one another better. John told James as much as he knew about the goings on in the mine and about the village, saying it had not really been a happy place to live over the years.

"Sorry to have to say it James, but everyone lived in fear of your father at times. It was as if they could never do anything right for him, either in general or in the mines. Of course we now know that it was mostly to do with the way he was being treated and manipulated by outside powers, but with no close friends he had no one to turn to for help."

James agreed and told John that from some of the papers he had found so far in the house his father's one passion and something he held dear to his heart was the school.

"Yes I will have to agree with you there, James. He did all he could for the school and the children. It's just a great pity that with the reputation he had around the village, unfortunately the children did not really trust the Bilk name."

"Then that is something I will have to put right. It will take a lot of doing I am sure but with a lot of patience and help from friends I hope I can bring some respectability back to the family name."

John wished him well with his venture telling him that he could certainly rely on his family to do all they could to help.

They had just finished lunch when Tom and Mary returned home with Pedro and Paul, saying that Sally's parents had invited Rebecca and Elizabeth to stay with them until the next day. Tom said that he could see no reason why they shouldn't stay, so had happily agreed.

"Sally's mum will bring them back tomorrow afternoon," Mary said. "I think she was anxious to chat to the girls about people who had disappeared when she was very young who they may know."

Her mother-in-law said that it was fortunate the girls were staying with Sally for the night, explaining that she would like Mary to accompany her on a visit to Ishe's home.

"I have been reading some more of the papers left by Jessica and I think there may be an easy way to help both communities, but we need to talk to Naggy to see what he thinks."

"I am happy to go whenever you want to leave," Mary told her.

"Why don't you ladies go this afternoon? We men folk, and the boys can make ourselves scarce for a few hours."

James agreed with what John had said, adding that they could all go back to his house and see if they could find out any further information which would help to sort things out.

An hour or so later, the men and boys departed to go to the Bilk house while the ladies prepared themselves for their visit to Ishe's home.

On the way to James's home, the three men discussed various aspects of the situation they now found themselves in. Tom told his father and James that while he was at Sally's home, he had had a word with her father who told him that he thought he had found at least five other families who were willing to help them when the time came. The help they were offering was to get the empty cottages cleaned and fit for families to live in once more.

"What they proposed to do was clean and tidy all the old cottages so that if any of the original families decided to return then they would have somewhere to live." Tom went on to explain that if anyone should ask why they were doing what they were doing to the cottages, they would say that in their opinion it was a shame for the homes to be left to decay and so they had decided as a group to tidy them up. "Sally's father told me that they were still not sure just who in the village could be trusted, and told me that a few of the older families had more reasons to be grateful for their ties with the Bilk family from things that had gone on in the past. Now that Cedric had passed away, then those families might just be willing to join in what was going on but until they were sure of their allegiance then they needed to be kept at a distance."

"Of course," he added, "we don't know if all the people want to return. If we can make their circumstances better where they are, then they may be quite happy staying. When you think about it, a lot of them have lived there a lot longer than they ever lived here."

When they arrived at the Bilk residence, James suggested that the boys should look around the garden to see if they could find anything interesting while he and Tom and his father had a more detailed look inside the house.

Realising that none of them were wearing anything green Pedro's grandfather warned the two boys to be careful what they spoke about just in case the birds should appear.

"We know Kirkum is O.K. but he may have his brother with him," he said.

"O.K. we'll be careful granddad," said Pedro as he and Paul headed round to the back of the house and into the back garden.

"Where shall we look first?" Pedro asked his friend, to which Paul replied that his grandfather used to spend a lot of time in the orchard, especially where it seemed he stood yelling at the trees.

"Then let's go round there, although we now know he was talking and occasionally shouting at the birds that were in the trees."

The two boys wandered around the orchard and garden but could see nothing out of the ordinary, although there were places where holes had been dug and just left. They weren't very deep holes and there didn't seem to be any kind of pattern as to where they were dug. At the very bottom of the garden they found a much larger hole. It was also very deep, much deeper than either of the boys' height. There was a ladder lying on the ground beside the hole together with a couple of shovels. What did seem strange to the boys was that there was no pile of earth near the hole, so who ever had dug it must have scattered the earth over the rest of the garden. Three sides of the hole had already been lined and re-enforced with wood panels. A little way away from the hole they discovered under a large canvas sheet some more panels and what appeared to be a large door in a frame. The frame and door were roughly the same size as the hole.

"Looks like granddad was making himself a hidey-hole." said Paul.

"Probably to try and get away from those birds," replied Pedro.

They walked back towards the house up through the orchard at the other side of the house and this time they saw that some of the trees had ribbons tied round their trunks. Some had green ties and some had blue. There was one tree that was larger than the others and this one had both a green and a blue ribbon tied round it. Fastened to this tree also was a length of rope about six inches from the ground. The rope stretched from that tree to the one next to it. Along the length of the rope there were knots about two feet apart. Below each knot small holes had been dug into the earth, much like the holes they had found in the other garden. Nearer to the house they again discovered a canvas covering. Pulling it away the boys saw a square wooded cover with a handle at one side. They tried to lift it but it was too heavy for them.

"Better get our dads to help us lift that," said Pedro. Paul agreed but before they headed for the house they pulled the canvas back into place.

Just as they were heading for the house, both their fathers came into the garden.

"Found anything interesting boys?" he asked.

"Yes we have sir," replied Paul, and pointed to the canvas cover. Pedro, at the same time pulled the canvas away from the wooden cover. "But it was much too heavy for us to lift."

"Let's see what we can do then," said Paul's dad.

Between them the two men tried hard to lift the cover but could not move it at all. It was then that Pedro saw that it was nailed to a frame with large square nails. He had never seen any nails as big as that and said as much to his father, who told him that they were the kind of nails used in the mine when they were nailing supports together in the tunnels.

"Must be something special hidden under there son, we had better look around to see if we can find something to remove those nails."

"Perhaps we can push the garden fork between the cover and the frame and force it up," said Paul.

"Good idea," said his dad, "and then perhaps if we move it a little then we can push the spade under as well to lift the whole cover."

The two boys ran round to the other part of the garden to bring the fork and spade they had seen there. As they ran round the side of the house Pedro saw two birds sitting in one of the trees. Thinking quickly he whispered to Paul to carry on running round the house and to pretend they were just playing.

"Why?' asked Paul.

"Birds!! Just run back to our dads."

They ran round to where their fathers were waiting. Without saying a word Pedro quickly ran over to the wooden cover and pulled the canvas back into place. When his father looked at him as if to say what are you doing, Paul looked at his father and told him Pedro had seen birds in the trees round the other side of the house. They all walked away from the canvas cover and wandered down the garden. As they rounded the corner into the other part of the garden the two birds were still perched in one of the trees. They walked on without looking in their direction round to the front entrance to the house. One of the birds flew quite close to them as they got to the front door. Tom saw that he had a small stone clutched in his middle foot and realised it was Kirkum. Sensing the bird wanted to tell him something, he suggested that James took the boys into the house for a cool drink, saying he would sit on the step for a while. He could not remember if Paul knew about Kirkum being able to talk or not.

He sat there for a while just looking around the garden when Kirkum landed on the handrail of the steps. He still had the stone in his middle foot which he dropped as he arrived.

"I must say this quickly before my brother realises where I am and comes looking for me. Can you please tell your mother I will call and see her tomorrow morning if she would be so kind as to leave the window open for me. I have some good news for her and indeed for you all, which I am sure will help you all in your quest to bring peace to the two villages you are desperately trying to help. Tell her I think a solution may be very near."

With that, Kirkum flew away without a backward glance. Tom sat there for a few more minutes then went into the house to look for his father and relay to him what Kirkum had just told him.

He found his father with James and the boys having a drink in the kitchen. They were looking at a rough map laid on the kitchen table. His father explained to him that it seemed to be a rough layout of the garden and orchards outside. There were quite a lot of markings on it with crosses and ticks here and there. One part of the map had been torn off in the bottom left corner.

"I bet if we take this out into the garden, these crosses and ticks will relate to the little holes the boys found," he said.

"Can we take it outside and see granddad?"

He handed the map to Pedro and said, "Certainly. You and Paul go and see if you can make any sense of it all."

When the boys had left, Tom told his father and James what Kirkum had told him.

"Sounds like we may be close to resolving a few things," he said to his son. "Perhaps your mum and Mary may have also found out something by the time we get home."

The boys came back in the kitchen at this point to say that yes, they did think that the crosses and ticks on the map did line up with the holes that had been dug in the garden. Paul said that he thought that perhaps the ticks indicated that his grandfather had found something in the holes and the crosses told them he had not. "And, if you hold the map and look at the garden, right where the corner has been torn off is just where that wooden cover is. It could be that he didn't want anyone who looked at the map to know that place was there."

His father agreed with him. Paul went on to tell his and Pedro's father that he and Pedro had worked out that all the crosses and ticks were in line with the knots on the rope between the trees, and that if you looked at the map closely you could just make out smaller crosses under those made by his grandfather, so it was quite clear that he had used the map to know where to dig.

"I wonder who made the map in the first place," said James.

"Perhaps the same person who wrote this rough diary," said Pedro's grandfather walking into the kitchen. He had been looking around the other room when the boys had returned. He was carrying a very old school writing book. "The writing is not very clear and is quite faint but we may be able to learn something from it."

At this point Tom suggested that perhaps it was time for them to be heading home, saying that the ladies may have returned from their visit. His father agreed and said also that perhaps they should leave the lifting of the wooden cover until a later visit. "After all, we know what is under the cover but we don't know if the birds will return. We can bring suitable tools with us next time to open the wooden cover."

They all started down the hill back towards the village and home. The boys were racing on ahead, with the older men taking it easy wishing they were still young enough to have the energy the boys had.

As they came to a small tree near the bottom of the hill and just before they reached the road, Tom noticed one of the birds perched on a low branch. Before he had time to whisper to his father he saw that the bird had a small stone in his middle claw so he knew who it was. He dropped back a little from his father and James not sure whether they had noticed the bird. As he passed the tree Kirkum said that things had happened and that he would like to visit them early that evening if it was suitable. Tom told him that would be fine and that he would make sure the window was left open.

When they reached home, the ladies had indeed returned and had prepared a salad lunch for them all. They both appeared very excited so obviously the visit had been a success. Mary suggested that they had lunch in the garden and afterwards each party could tell the other of their morning.

While they were eating the boys told what they had found in the garden of the Bilk house and how there were lots of little holes dug all over the place and how the holes were just the same as marks found on an old map granddad had found in the house.

At the end of the lunch Pedro asked if he and Paul could be excused to go and play. His mother said in that case would the boys kindly go to the farm for some milk. This they readily agreed to as it meant they might have a chance to see Freddy or Simon on the way. Pedro's mother gave the boys a container each and asked them not to be too long and not to go all the way into the village. They gave her their word and set off to the farm.

On returning to the garden, she started to clear away the lunch plates to take in to wash them. Her mother in law laid a hand on her arm and said that on this one occasion maybe they could indulge themselves and use up one tiny wish. She gave Mary a marble that had just one stripe remaining and told her to have her wish. Mary smiled and silently wished that the table would be cleared and the plates etc. be washed and put away. With very little noise, all the plates, cutlery, dishes and drinking glasses lifted off the table and with a bit of a whooshing sound disappeared into the house via the kitchen door. They heard a few more noises coming from the house, and then the sound of cupboard doors closing before all was silent again. James, who had never witnessed that kind of thing before just sat there not quite believing what he had just seen.

"I think we deserved that," said Joan as she settled in her chair ready to tell the men about their visit to Ishe's house.

Before she and Mary began telling their news Tom related to his mother what Kirkum had told him.

"He said he had some good news for us about what we were doing mother."

"That just might tie in with what Mary and myself found out today," she replied.

She went on to tell the men that when they arrived at Ishe's house, Naggy had just arrived also. "He told us that as he had been walking around the village he had sensed an increasing tension among the villagers. So much so, that some of the more out spoken ones were openly talking about trying to do something about the High Person and his team of bullies as they called them. He said that one person who had been a bit more outspoken than the rest had been in the wrong place when he voiced his opinion. The next day he went for his morning walk as usual but his wife said he never returned. Naggy is convinced that his disappearance had something to do with the High person. Naggy also told us that he thinks a visit from Tanglen will be happening soon. The workers have been given extra tasks of cleaning up the big house in the same grounds as the house where the High Person lives, and that is usually a sign that she is about to visit."

"Did Naggy have anything else to say about the villagers?" Tom asked.

This time it was Mary who answered, telling him that a sort of committee had been formed and they were thinking of ways of carrying out what they had previously discussed as regards the High Person and what suitable punishment they could inflict on him. "Nothing too drastic and nothing to hurt him physically, just something to teach him a lesson and to let him see just how miserable he had made their lives."

"Another thing Naggy mentioned," said Joan, "was that he had had a long talk with David and Arthur about how the villagers might feel being able to return to their former life as it were. He said they had told him that as far as the ones they had spoken to were concerned, as long as they got some sort of peace in their lives then they would be more than happy to stay where they were for the time being. Most of them had been there for so long, they had nearly forgotten their previous life."

"Did they have any ideas as to what sort of punishment they had in mind for the High Person?' John asked his wife.

"No, I think they were hoping that we could help them with that when the time came."

"Better start thinking then," replied her husband.

"Nothing too drastic don't forget, and nothing that will cause them physical harm, although goodness me, it's what he deserves after the way he has treated the people over the years."

John assured his wife that he would try to think of something they would all approve of.

Joan then suggested that perhaps they had better go into the house, and prepare themselves for the visit from Kirkum.

CHAPTER THIRTY-SEVEN

MAKING MORE PLANS

Kirkum arrived about an hour after they had gone back into the house. He had a pebble in his middle claw so they knew it was he. Perching on the back of one of the dinning chairs he told them that he had some good news for them regarding the people they had been in contact with, especially a gentleman called Joshua.

"He told me all about how you were friends many years ago John," he said. "I introduced myself to him a few days ago when he was out walking. Like you my friends, he was shocked to hear a bird talking to him, but I convinced him in the end when I told him about a few things I knew about you good people and what you were trying to do for them back there."

"It would seem," Kirkum continued, "things back there in the village are just about ready to come to a head. His part of the hole in the wall is very nearly completed. He suggested however that they could do with a little help in trying to find out just who in the village is with them and who might still be on the side of Tanglen."

Did he say how we might help him?" asked Joan.

"He did indeed. He asked if it would be possible to send a few more children through the tunnel to his house. They could then walk around the village trying to find out what people were saying. As you know, any visitors coming through the bush are invisible to the people of the village once they leave Joshua's house. I would suggest however they wear something green so as not to be spotted by my brother and a couple of other birds he has recruited."

John told Kirkum that he was certain they would be able to get the children to help, but of course they would have to get the permission of their parents. Kirkum said he fully understood that.

"Did Joshua give you any idea when he wanted this to happen?' asked John.

"Not really but I think that in two days' time "She" is going on a visit to the High Person, so that would be a good time. I will call back when I have a definite day she is going."

"I think we could get things organised by then," Tom said, then asked Kirkum if he would be going with Tanglen when she visited the High Person.

"Not this time. My brother as I told you has recruited a few new pupils and is anxious for them to accompany him when he goes with 'her' so I will stay behind. That way I will also be around should Joshua and his friends need my help. You also need to tell them to be wary about any blackbirds they see. The ones my brother has recruited only have two legs. It is only him and me who have three from the curse Tanglen put on us when she changed us into blackbirds."

After Kirkum had flown away they all sat round the table discussing what he had told them. Tom noticed his mother was rather quiet and seemed deep in thought so asked her if there was anything on her mind.

"Two things really Tom. One is, with Joshua asking for the children to be sent to his house and it brings to reality the message written on one of the papers Jessica left me where it said, "Let The Children Help" remember?"

"Yes I do, it's strange how she should have written that. What's the other thing mum?"

"It is something that has been at the back of my mind ever since Pedro and his friends went behind the bush. Where do they go to when they enter the tunnel behind the bush? How do they get to Joshua's house? Not only that," she continued turning to her husband, "where is the village situated behind the old Winter Shed? All that is behind there as you look at it is a grass bank."

"I never gave that much thought," replied her husband. "But as far as the bush tunnel goes we can ask Pedro and Paul when they return."

Mary had been making a note of things they needed clearing up and asked if there was anything else they needed answers to.

"Well we do need to make a kind of plan as to what we will be able to do to help both sets of people," said Tom, "and give some serious thought about the kind of non-hurting punishment we can advise the people to pass on to the High Person and Tanglen."

"I think we will need to use some of the powers in the marbles for that part Tom, and we must not forget when we are doing all this that there is one other thing we have to do, and that is try to bring back to life poor old Mariem, Kirkum's mistress who was turned into a statue."

"That!" exclaimed John, who had been sitting very quietly thinking, "has given me an excellent idea about what punishment to hand out to the High Person and Tanglen." He looked at the others with a mischievous grin and said, "Why don't we try and turn Tanglen and the High Person into statues and replace them for Mariem on the village green?"

"Or" said his son before anyone had a chance to comment on what his father had suggested, "We could turn Tanglen into a statue and the High Person into a tree!"

"And" added Mary, joining in the fun, "we could turn Kirkum's brother Luffler into a small statue also and stick him on one of the branches!"

"I think we would have to get the approval of Kirkum to do that Mary," said Joan, "but certainly we could put forward the other suggestions to the people. And speaking of the people, we must make sure we set up a meeting as soon as we can with some representatives of the village to hear what they would like to do for their future."

"Can all these changes we are talking about making, the statues etc. be done with the normal Whishy Marbs or will we need something else?" Tom asked his mother.

"I am not too sure son; I think I will spend tomorrow looking over some more of the papers I haven't opened yet. There is one rather large envelope marked with the words, 'You Will Know When To Open This One' and with the Bilk family seal pressed on the flap. I have a feeling that is where we may find some important answers."

"Well in that case mother, we will leave you in peace tomorrow to do that while we all take the boys into the village for a walk around and call round to see the parents of Freddy, Jimmy, Simon and James and ask their permission to help us out. Of course we will have to tell them a lot more about things than we have so far but I am sure they will agree.'

"We can collect the girls from Sally's house as well," said Mary.

Joan asked James who she noticed had been sitting very quietly, if he had anything he wanted to ask or say.

"Not really Joan, you have all been part of this right from the start and I am happy just to assist in any way should you require it. One thing I have been thinking about, and that is I will have an awful lot to do to get the villagers' confidence back into the Bilk family name. My father, I am sorry to say, seems to have treated them very badly."

"What you say about Cedric is certainly true," said Joan, 'but I am more than confident that when we get things sorted out, as I hope we will, and we explain to everyone just how much pressure he was under and from whom, then I am sure the people will be one hundred percent behind you."

"Thank you very much, you are very kind," he said to Joan, then looking round at them all he thanked them for the way they had treated him saying that in the short time he had been there he felt like one of the family.

Pedro and Paul returned at this point and Mary went into the kitchen to put the milk away and to make some drinks for them all.

"See any of your friends Pedro?' she asked.

"We saw Simon, he was on the back of a tractor going into the fields as we got to the farm. I told him we might call round and see him one day."

Pedro and Paul carried the drinks into the other room and put them on the table. When they were settled round the table with the adults, granny asked Pedro if he would tell them all something.

"Of course granny."

"When you went behind the bush, how did you get to Joshua's house?"

Pedro said that they crawled along the ground for a little way until they reached a point where they could stand up. "Then Rebecca took a medallion from her pocket and pushed it into a hole in a sort of doorpost. A door appeared and opened and we walked through. We found ourselves in the middle of a wood. Rebecca walked over to the nearest tree and pulled another medallion out of the trunk. We heard a click and when we looked round the doorway had disappeared. The medallions she used were just like the one that had been left by the bush for us to find. The one she pushed into the doorpost she left there as we went through the door. She told us to follow her closely and very soon we came to a small shed type building. We entered the shed and Rebecca closed the door behind us. She then walked over to another door and opened it. We followed her through and found ourselves inside her house. Her mother and father were there to meet us. They made quite a fuss of us all and invited us to sit down and she would get us something to eat and drink. As I sat down, I looked towards where the door was we had entered by and that too had disappeared."

Paul then continued by telling them that while they were eating Joshua had left the house and when he returned he had two girls with him. "He introduced them both to us and told me that one of them was my aunt and the other one was Pedro's granny's best friend. He could see that we were confused and said it would all become clear later on, especially after we went back home, and that you Mrs. Vendell would be able to explain everything."

"On our return journey," said Pedro, "Rebecca pushed a medallion into the tree trunk, the door appeared, and we went through. She pulled the medallion from the door post on the other side, the door disappeared and we crawled back to the bush."

"It was dark when we first went behind the bush, but as it moved back into place the tunnel was brightly lit, but I couldn't see where the light was coming from," said Paul.

Pedro's granny thanked the two boys for helping to clear the mystery she had been wondering about.

"I expect there is a similar arrangement to get behind the back of the Winter Shed," said Pedro's grandfather.

"From what Joshua was saying gramps, I think he had to go down a tunnel from inside the mine workings. And even then he could only go down there when some of the guards had gone for their meals."

"Sounds to me as if he has found the old entrance to the mines the workers used when the Winter Shed was in operation all those years ago John."

"I think you may be right there." John replied to his wife, "and if that is the case then perhaps it may show up on one of those old plans we have of the mines."

"If it does then it could be very useful to Joshua and his friends. Perhaps we could send it to him with the children the next time they go through the bush."

Pedro looked at his father as he said this not knowing that Kirkum had paid a visit with a request from Joshua that perhaps the children could be of more help to them.

"Are we going back through the bush dad?" he asked.

"I think that maybe you are son, plus a few of your friends if their parents will let them. Joshua has asked if you can return with some more children to help him with a couple of things. Who do you think we should ask? I thought that perhaps Freddy, Simon, Jimmy and James. Plus of course, Sally".

"We need to check if Jimmy is back from the hospital yet. He went to get a new arm, remember?"

"Of course," said his dad. "We will go and see all the parents tomorrow and explain just what we would like your friends to do."

"When will we be going?"

"Probably the day after tomorrow. Kirkum will call back and tell us when the coast is clear."

The next morning the two boys plus Pedro's father and grandfather set of for the village to talk to the parents of Pedro's friends. James decided to go back up to his father's house to sort out a few more things and see if he could find anything else of interest. As they reached the bottom of the hill leading up to the house, James was about to say cheerio when Pedro's granddad saw he was wearing a blue jumper. He remembered the rhyme about the colours and suggested James removed his jumper and gave it to him to look after. "Wear something blue and they can talk to you," he said. As James took off the jumper Tom told him that if a bird did want to talk to him then to see if he was carrying a stone or pebble in his middle foot. Then he would know it was Kirkum.

They called round to see the parents of Simon first. As luck would have it Freddy's mum and dad were at the farm collecting some potatoes so they were able to talk to them all together. After Tom and his father had explained all that was going on and what they hoped would be achieved by what they were trying to do, they all readily agreed the boys could go. Tom thanked them and said he would get word to them when it would happen. He also said that if they would like to come to the house with the boys, then everyone could learn just what was happening. "We will be able to tell you and Sally and Jimmy's parents all together, while the children are away.

Next they went to Jimmy's house. He had indeed returned from the hospital and was eager to show Pedro and Paul his new arm. He showed them all the things it could do, but told them that at the moment he could only wear it for one day a week until he got used to it. Pedro's father had gone into the house to talk to Jimmy's parents. When he came out he told them that Jimmy's parents had said they would be happy for him to go with the rest of the children."

"Go where?" asked Jimmy.

"Better go inside and see your Dad, he'll tell you. Bye, see you soon," said Pedro's dad.

As they left Jimmy was running into the house to find out just where he was going.

When they arrived at Sally's house, granddad and the boys again waited outside whilst Pedro's dad went to see her parents. When he returned he told them that yes it would be O.K. for Sally to go back again. He also said that the other two girls had asked if they could stay with Sally until they went. He said they wanted to wander around the village a bit more and that Sally's mother would take them that afternoon.

It was still quite early, so granddad suggested that they buy some lemonade or something from the shop and then call in at the Bilk house on the way back. "There might be something we can help James with, and perhaps have another go at lifting that cover in the garden."

James was in the back orchard when they arrived there. He had another piece of paper in his hand and was studying it as he walked round between the trees.

"I think I have worked out what these holes are or were dug for," he told them. "Each hole is marked with a cross on this paper and beside each cross is a number, see?" he showed them what he meant, 'but not all the numbers are the same," he continued, "there is a six, an eight three sevens and two tens." He moved across the garden to where the cover was. There was a much larger X right where the cover was marked. Beside the X a forty-one, was written. This total equaled the rest of the numbers they could see. "I think, my father had been using this diagram to dig in certain places and that he had found something each time. He made a note of whatever it was he had found. I also think that if we can lift this cover, we may just find what it was he found. I think he stored them in here away from the prying eyes of those birds."

Granddad agreed with him saying that seemed to be the logical conclusion, and suggested they find something to lift the cover. Pedro said he and Paul would go and look in the shed round the other side of the house. His dad told them to come into the house if they found anything so they could all have a drink before they started.

The boys came back with a long metal bar with a pointed end. Granddad told them that should do very nicely saying they could lift the cover with the bar and then push the garden fork under the gap to help them lever it up.

It didn't take much effort for them to lift the cover. There was quite a deep hole under it. There was also a short ladder leaning against the side of the hole. Whatever was down there was well covered with a large piece of metal. James asked Paul and Pedro if they would like to go down and lift the metal and see what was underneath. When they got down into the hole they placed themselves either side of the piece of metal and lifted one end of it. It was very easy to lift so they moved it completely and stood it on its end against the other side of the hole. There was now a large piece of sacking covering whatever was hidden there and with a nod from James they began to move that also. Under the sacking was a pile of funny shaped rocks. In fact they were the same shape as the rocks Sally's father had brought home from the mine. "The ones she gave to granny, remember dad?" he said looking up at his father. His father told him yes he did remember.

"How many are there?" asked James.

Pedro and Paul counted the rocks loudly so they could all hear.

"Sixty four," the boys said together.

"That's twenty three more than on this piece of paper," said James. "There must be another plan somewhere of the other part of the garden."

"What shall we do with them do you think?" asked Tom.

"I think we should take a few back with us to your house and open them up and see what is inside."

"Good idea James, but before we do open them we had better check with mum to see if she knows anything about this shaped rock. I know she was most anxious that Sally should not open hers, which is why she asked Sally to give them to her."

"O.K. we will take just ten and leave the rest here." James called down to the boys to pass ten rocks up to them then asked them to recover the rest with the sacking and the metal before they came back out of the hole. When the boys were out, the men put the cover back over the hole and tried to make it and the surrounding area looks as it was before their arrival. They divided the rocks between them, two each and put them in the pockets of their trousers. Granddad suggested they leave the metal bar in the house for next time, and asked Pedro and Paul to take the garden fork back to where they found it. After having another drink each, they locked up the house and headed for home.

Halfway down the hill Tom's attention was drawn to a bush on the right of the pathway. He looked closer and saw that a bird was sitting in the foliage. The bird held up his middle foot showing he had a pebble in it. Tom moved closer to the bush and as he passed Kirkum told him that 'She' was leaving the next day so could the children please be sent through the bush the next evening. Tom told him that could be arranged and that including the two girls who would be returning, there would be nine children coming through the bush. Kirkum told him that would be fine and would pass on the message to Joshua. He flew away assuring Tom that he would keep an eye on them for him. Tom caught up with the rest of the party and told them what he had been asked by Kirkum. He added that he would go back into the village later in the day to inform everyone what was happening.

CHAPTER THIRTY-EIGHT

NEARLY THERE

Pedro's granny had just finished reading the paper she had found in the last envelope and was sitting relaxing when they arrived home. Both Pedro and Paul were keen to tell her what they had discovered, but his father suggested that they let her rest for a while so they went into the kitchen where they quietly told his mother. Tom also told her the parents were quite happy for their children to go through the bush.

"I have to go back into the village later to ask them to bring them here tomorrow afternoon," he said, telling her about his meeting with Kirkum on the way home. He mentioned as well that he had invited the parents to stay after the children had gone to the bush so they could be brought up to date with what was happening.

"In that case, you had better call in the shop when you go back to the village and get some bread and cakes," said Mary, "we can't invite them without giving them something to eat."

Joan came into the kitchen at that point and in answer to Tom's question she said that she was quite rested now and ready to hear how the 'menfolk' of the family had got on.

When they were all settled in the other room, the older men let the boys do most of the talking telling her about what they had found in the hole in the orchard. Granny asked if she could see the rocks they had brought back with them. They all removed the rocks from their pockets, and laid them on the table.

"Those are the very rocks I have been reading about today," she said, "have any of them been opened?"

When they told her no, she said that was good and for them not to do so until they were ready to use them.

She then went on to explain what she had been reading that day, telling them that the marbles inside the triangular rocks were the most powerful of all the marbles, and their magic was to be used very, very carefully.

"They can be used to do much good, but in the wrong hands could also cause great damage and distress. They should not be taken out of the rocks until just before they are to be used. You can open the rocks ready, to check there is a marble inside, but keep the rock closed after that. It would appear that the best way to crack the rocks open is for one to be hit with another.'

"Do you know how we have to use them?" asked her husband.

"Yes, you have to have at least three people present if you are making a moderate wish using just one marble. Two of the people hold hands with the marble held between their palms. The third person, who must be the 'Custodian of the Records', which at the moment is me, makes the wish saying it quietly. The other two people nod in agreement to what has been wished for and then they join hands with the third person. When they do that the wish is granted. Should one of the people holding hands with the other be not entirely in agreement with the wish, then it will not be granted and the wish will have been wasted. In other words all participants in the wishing process must be in full agreement before they start as to what they are going to wish for."

"Do you know what the marbles look like, and how many stripes they have granny?"

"Yes, from what I understand, they are quite large with eight dots on them instead of stripes, and as the wishes are made they disappear just like the stripes in the "Whishy Marbs." The wishes these rocks are used for are much more powerful, so that is why they have to be used very carefully, and not be allowed to be passed into the wrong hands."

Granny then showed them a piece of rolled up paper. It was tied with a red ribbon. She unfastened the ribbon and laid the paper out flat so they could all see it. As they looked at it, the paper moved round so that it was directly opposite granny. She turned it slightly towards Tom who was on her left but when she lifted her hand, the paper once again moved so it was facing her. Before any of them could say anything granny put up her hand to stop them, then in a quiet voice said, "Let James read you." Once she had said those words, the paper moved round and across the table until it was directly in front of James. She then said, "Let everybody read you." Again, the paper moved slowly round the table stopping in front of everyone in turn.

The family just sat there stunned at what they were seeing.

"Come back to your Mistress," commanded granny, and the paper moved until it was back in front of her.

She looked around at them all and told them that with the rolled up paper there was a note from Jessica to me.

"She must have written it when she realised that she needed someone to take care of the family secrets and had started giving me envelopes at different times. The note said that she had found the rolled up paper many years previous when she was looking through files and documents during one of the many times her husband had been away from the house and she had been left alone. Sensing it might be of some importance one day she opened it and read it. The paper moved around the table she was sitting at as if looking for someone. In the end Jessica used one of the 'Wishy Marbs' to wish that it would stop. When it did stop a voice came from the paper asking where Nathan was."

Granny looked at James and told him that Nathan had been his great, great grandfather, and said that from what she now knew about the paper Nathan many years ago must have been made custodian of it and the secrets it held.

"It would appear from Jessica's note that she spoke to the paper telling it that Nathan had passed away and the voice from the paper asked her to name a new custodian. For some reason in her wisdom she named me, and it is my name inscribed at the bottom, which means for the time being I am the 'Custodian of the Records'. Not only that, but she added my married name Vendell. She must have had an inclination John and I would eventually marry."

"Does it tell you anything important mum?" asked Tom.

"Indeed it does. That is where I got the information about what to do with the marbles from the triangular rocks. It also tells me what to do should I wish to pass the powers, or custody, of the paper over to someone else, but I think that can be left for another day if everyone is in agreement?"

They all nodded their heads accepting her suggestion, so she carefully rolled the paper up and put it back into the envelope, saying they would need it again when they came to use the marbles.

"So what happens now?"

"Well, from what you have told me Tom, that Joshua has requested the children re-visit him, and the fact that "She' will be paying a visit to Naggy's village tomorrow, I think that we should pay a visit to Ishe's house and tell her, and Naggy if he is there. At the same time we can put to him the suggestions we came up with for punishing the High Person and those who have treated the villagers so badly."

"May I suggest my dear," said John looking at his wife, "that you four go and I will stay here with the boys. I am sure we can find something to amuse us. And we will be here should Kirkum come by again."

Joan thought that was a good idea and left the room to fetch the map she used for the journey. When she returned, she checked with Pedro where she had to put the marbles and which way to turn them.

"See you all when you get back," said Pedro, as he and Paul and granddad left the room. As they sat in the kitchen having a cold drink they heard a small 'whoosh' and realised the others had gone to Ishe's.

On arrival at Ishe's house they were please to find that Naggy was also there. After many welcoming hugs and hellos Tom fetched Ishe from her chair and sat her on the table beside him. Joan started by telling Ishe and Naggy about developments at their end, and about Tanglen's pending visit. Naggy said he thought one must be due because the 'High Person' had been getting some of the workers to tidy up the place which usually happened before a visit. He said that when 'She' arrived then the 'High Person' went away for about three days. During his absence then 'She' was in charge and seemed to take great delight in finding fault with everything anyone did, saying it would be reported to the 'High Person'. When he did return he assembled everyone on the village green to give one of his talks and to issue any punishments he thought were necessary after hearing what Tanglen had told him.. At the end of the talk then 'She' simply disappeared.

"That seems about the best time to put our plan into operation," said Joan.

Between them they told Naggy and Ishe about the punishments they had been thinking about and asked them for their approval or any other ideas they might have. Joan told them also that she had found the paper making her the 'Custodian of the Records' and that the men and boys had found a supply of the triangular rocks containing the marbles, which would enable them to make the necessary wishes and changes.

"I think we had better plan on using at least three of the marbles to make sure we do everything at the same time. That will give us twenty four wishing dots to work with." She then asked Naggy if he knew four people who they could use to hold the marbles.

"Yes I do. I can get David and Arthur and one of their wives. Some other villages have shown a bit of an interest but are still a bit wary of committing themselves at this stage."

"What do you think about the punishments we have suggested?" asked Mary.

"I think they are very good and well deserving and letting them off quite lightly considering the pain and misery they have caused everyone," replied Naggy.

"May I make a suggestion please?" Ishe asked. "Might I suggest that when we turn Tanglen into a statue and the 'High Person' into a tree that they be made to maintain some kind of sense so that they will be able to see just how happy the villagers are after being freed from their power."

"I think that is an excellent suggestion Ishe," said Joan, adding that it would show the two of them that there could be kindness in the place.

"Would we want to make these changes to them last forever?" asked James.

"I hadn't thought about that," Joan answered him. "Perhaps we could say for a period of at least six of our years and then let a committee of villagers decide after that. Certainly that is something to think about when everything is settled.

"What do we do about the 'High Person's' helpers? I was thinking of the birds and the other men who carry out the punishments with such enjoyment." This time it was Naggy who posed the question.

"If I might make a suggestion," said James, "why not confine them to the grounds of the 'High Person's' house with no powers what so ever to interfere with the goings on in the village. Again it could then be up to a village committee to decide just how long that situation remained. Regarding the birds, we know Kirkum is a friendly bird and considering the other is his brother, I think it should be left to him to suggest what should be done with him."

It was Ishe who came back into the conversation reminding everyone not to forget Mariem. "She should also be brought back to life. And I think the village should be renamed Mariemville"

"That goes without saying," replied Joan who admitted that she had for the moment forgotten Mariem. "We must also ask Kirkum what part he would like to have when things were changed. Perhaps he might like to go back to the bird he once was before Tanglen changed him. I also think your suggestion to rename the village is a very good one."

"The last thing we have to discuss is when all this can take place," said Tom.

"Perhaps Naggy can help us there," answered Mary.

"The best time obviously is when the 'High Person' returns. As I told you, he assembles everyone on the village green to give one of his speeches. Arthur's house overlooks the green, so I suggest that we meet there. We can look out through his upstairs window and make the wishes from there without being seen. The 'High Person' stands with his back to Arthur's house so we will be safe. 'She' stands a little way away from him, usually close to the statue of her sister. We will have plenty of time to get to the house during the morning of the 'High Person's' return."

"Do you think three of those marbles will be enough?" Ishe asked Joan.

"I think so, but I will bring a few more just in case. After all, they are going to be big wishes we will be asking for, so we don't know how many spots will be used, although as long as we make the main changes, that is the tree and the statues, then the conditions on them can be set later if need be."

Finally Joan asked Naggy when he thought they should return, and he told her that the 'High Person' usually only stayed away for three days so the day after tomorrow would be fine. He asked if they would all be returning but James suggested that he should stay with John at the house while the children were behind the bush in case he should need any help.

"Are you sure?' asked Joan.

"Certainly, this part of things concerns you all more than me. I will have my time when we sort out the other place."

As they prepared to leave, Joan asked if Naggy or Ishe could please make contact with Jessica and asked if she had any thoughts about when she would like to see her daughter.

They promised her they would and let her know. With that, Joan turned the marble in the map and they were suddenly in their own home again. The map slowly folded itself up as before and Joan got up to return it to her room.

When granddad and the boys came back into the house they were surprised to see everyone back, exclaiming they had only been gone about five minutes. He asked if all had gone well and was told yes.

"I think we may be able to help the villagers out the day after tomorrow. James has said he will stay with you John in case you need help over at the 'Winter Shed' site. Things should be quiet for the children when they go through the bush because 'She' is going to the other place. Mary, Tom and myself will return to Ishe's house and stay there until we have made the necessary wishes which will hopefully end the suffering of the people back there."

"Is there anything we can do to help before you go granny?"

"Yes there is Pedro. Perhaps you and Paul would be kind enough to break open the ten triangular rocks you brought back with you. Just make sure they do contain a marble each with eight spots on them and then put them back into the rocks and close them tight. It might be a good idea to tie them with some string to be sure they stay closed."

"O.K. granny, come on Paul, we can do it in my bedroom. I think I have a box up there as well we can put them in for you granny."

After a drink Tom said he would take a walk to the village to see the parents and ask them to be at the house with the children by five o'clock the following evening. His father said he would go with him, and James said he would go with them as far as the hill to his house and pay another visit to his home and give it a quick check over. He told them that he wanted to see just how many rooms were ready to be used, adding that it could be that the house might be needed for some of the people from the place behind the bush to stay for a while should they decide to return, and their original homes not be ready. Joan told him she thought that was a very nice gesture on his behalf.

With the men gone and the boys upstairs, Joan suggested to Mary that perhaps they should make a list of things they would need to take with them on their next visit to Ishe's, saying that they had better not plan on taking too much as they didn't know if the magical transfer would allow them to carry a lot of extra items.

The men returned later in the afternoon and Tom said that all the parents would make sure they were at the house late afternoon on the following day. James was also with them and told Joan that as far as he could see, there were at least eight rooms that could be put to use in his house should they be required.

Mary then told them that tea was ready and would they like to eat out in the garden as it was such a lovely evening. She called the boys who came downstairs with a box, which Pedro gave to his granny. He told her that all the marbles in the rocks contained eight dots. He said he and Paul had tied the rocks closed as she had suggested.

After tea they all relaxed in the garden. All except the two boys of course who were too excited to just sit around talking.

"Well," said Joan, "it looks as if tomorrow is going to be quite a big day for all of us one way or the other. Who would have thought my dear," she said looking at her husband, 'that our usually quiet rest here with our family would turn out like it has.

CHAPTER THIRTY-NINE

TWO IMPORTANT VISITS

Sally and the two girls were the first to arrive the next afternoon. Although Rebecca and Elizabeth were excited about going back, they told Joan how much they had enjoyed their visit and really hoped that a way could found for them to come back to the old village one day. Joan said she could understand them thinking that way, but there was one big factor they had to consider and that was their ages. Looking at Rebecca she reminded her that at the time of her disappearance they had both been about the same age but now she, Joan was about ten times her age. "Would you want to become my age overnight, and miss out on all the fun of growing up?"

"I never thought of it that way," said Rebecca,"

"Maybe when we get things sorted out we will be able to come to some kind of compromise for you all," replied Joan, thinking to herself that she could see no reason why the power in the triangular rock marbles could not be used to help put wrongs right at this village as they were going to be used in the other.

"Oh I do hope so," Rebecca told her.

Shortly after that, the rest of the children and parents began to arrive, the children all excited about what might lie ahead for them, the adults understandably apprehensive for the same reason. It had been decided that it would be best if the children were spoken to as a group in the garden, where Pedro's grandfather and father between them could explain what they were going to be doing. The adults would have things explained to them by Joan and Mary in the house.

Pedro's father left the group in the garden to go into the house to collect the green scarves for the children to wear. As he rounded the corner of the house he saw Kirkum perched on the garden spade. "Just a quick message for you from Naggy," he said. "Could you please just stand the mirror in the living room before the children leave? Jessica will not be able to be seen by the children or their parents, but she would like to have a look at Elizabeth for a few minutes." Tom assured him he would do that. Kirkum also told him that 'She', his brother, and the other birds were all in Naggy's village so it was all clear for the children to go through the bush to Joshua's house.

"Before you leave," said Tom, "we need to have a word with you about your brother," then went on to tell him the main ideas for dealing with the "High Person" and Tanglen, "but we didn't want to do anything about Luffler before we had discussed it with you."

Kirkum thanked him very much and said he would call at the house tomorrow about lunchtime.

Tom went into the house to collect the scarves for the children but before he left again he fetched the mirror from the hall and stood it on a chair in the corner of the living room, telling, and winking at his mother in answer to her enquiring frown that being there would remind him to fix the hinge later on.

Back in the garden he explained to the children why he was giving them the green scarves.

"I know this is all very new and mysterious to you all, but you need to wear these scarves when you go out of Joshua's house. As we explained earlier, the people of the village cannot see you anyway but there may be some of the "High Person's" people in the place we don't know about. Remember we explained to you that the "High Person" is a not very nice man so it would be no surprise if he had spies living in the village."

"What do we have to do when we get to this place sir?" asked Jimmy.

"What I think Joshua wants you to do is just walk around the village in small groups and see if you can hear anyone saying anything about things in general but about the escape plan in particular. I am sure Joshua will tell you a lot better than I can when you get there. All you have to do is remember to stick together in your groups and do as Joshua asks. You will be doing all the people back there a great service, and it will all be explained to you when you get back. Now are there any more questions I can help you with?"

No one had anything else to ask so Tom suggested that they play around the garden for a little while before they returned to the house to say cheerio to their parents. "We will have some sandwiches and drinks and then Paul's dad and I will take you to the bush to start your little adventure. Speaking of which Pedro, don't forget to get the medallion from your granny before we go."

Tom and his father went back to the house leaving the children to amuse themselves and get to know Rebecca and Elizabeth, and Paul trying very hard to explain that Elizabeth was in fact his father's sister and so therefore 'my aunt'.

"Don't worry too much at the moment," said Pedro, "it really will all become very clear in a few days' time."

About an hour later, the children were called into the house where sandwiches and drinks had been prepared. The house seemed very crowded with everyone there so Pedro's father took the children in to the living room. He gave his mother a knowing look and she joined him. Sitting in a chair by the fireplace, she asked Pedro to introduce her to all his friends. They came forward one by one as Pedro said their names and his grandmother shook hands with them all. When it was Jimmy's turn, she made a joke with him about which hand would fall off if she shook it too hard. They all thought this was very funny, with Jimmy explaining it was his left arm which was false, and that he had got a new one but was only allowed to wear it once a week until he got used to it.

Pedro's granny then called him over to her and whispered something in his ear. He nodded and left the room, returning a moment later and putting something in her hand. She then asked the boys to leave the room saying she and the girls had something to discuss in private. When they had left the room she asked Sally to make sure the door was closed. She then called the girls to her. She asked them if they had understood why they been given the green scarves to wear when they went through the bush and they said yes they did.

"Well," she said to them, "I think we can do better than that." She then opened her hand showing them a marble with four stripes, and asked them if they knew what it was. They all answered no so she told them very briefly what it was, saying that in fact it was because of that particular kind of marble that the whole trouble many years ago had started. "What I think we should do on this occasion is to use the stripes in this marble for you to wish for something green to wear instead of those scarves." The girls liked the sound of that idea and got quite excited.

"Right Sally," said Joan handing her the marble, "close your hand and wish for what you want to wear, but make sure it is green."

"I wish I could have a green jumper to wear." As soon as she finished her wish there was a flash of coloured lights and a haze appeared round Sally. When it cleared, she was indeed wearing a green jumper. Joan asked her to pass the marble to Rebecca and for her to make her wish.

"I wish I could have a green skirt to wear," said Rebecca. Again there was a flash of coloured lights and a haze which when it cleared showed Rebecca wearing a green skirt. Joan again asked her to pass the marble to Elizabeth and for her to do the same.

"I wish my dress was a nice light green colour," said Elizabeth. Just as before the flashing lights and haze appeared, surrounding her. When everything was back to normal, they could all see her dress had changed to a nice light green colour. Joan then noticed that a slight hazy glow was coming from the mirror over in the corner. She thought, but was not too certain, that she could detect an image of Jessica there.

"Why don't you go and look at yourself in that mirror Elizabeth, and see for yourself how nice your dress is."

Elizabeth walked over to the mirror and looked at herself, doing a little turn so she could see how the dress looked. When she moved out the way, Jessica and Sally also had a look at their new clothes. As the girls moved away from the mirror Joan thought she detected Jessica's very faint image saying a 'thank you' before the mirror cleared again.

Joan asked Elizabeth to pass her the marble, showing the girls that there was now only one stripe remaining. She explained that because the wishes were only small ones, they had only used one stripe each. "We'll give the boys a chance to have a wish later," she said, and thought that they ought to return to the other room, as it must be nearly time for them to leave on their little adventure.

A short time later the children left the house with Pedro's father and grandfather to walk to the 'Winter Shed' site. Pedro had remembered just in time to ask his grandmother for the medallion, which he explained to his friends, was needed to operate the bush. James went with them for part of the way, saying he would spend the night at the Bilk house and then the next day sort out a few more things that needed to be done. The children's parents left later on in the evening to return to their homes. Mary promised them she would let them know as soon as the children returned, perhaps in about three days time.

Tom and his father returned home after about three hours telling the ladies that everything had gone well. He said the children had been sent through the bush in two groups because there were so many of them. Only five could go through the system at a time.

John said he had been able to have a quick chat with his friend Joshua who told him that things were going well on his side. "Those who he had discussed things with and knew he could trust were very much looking forward to their release from the only life they had known for many years. He also said to thank the parents of the children for allowing them to help them, assuring him that they would be well looked after."

It was generally agreed that as it had been a busy day and that the next day could be a lot busier an early night was called for. Tom remembered to mention to his mother that Kirkum would be calling in to see her about lunch time in the morning.

The following morning after breakfast, Joan suggested that they all sit down and work out the list of wishes and changes they would present to Naggy and his friends.

"Number one," said Joan, " change Mariem back into the person she was before, agreed." The family all said yes.

"Number two," said Joan, "turn the 'High Person' into a tree, agreed." Yes, came the answer.

"Number three, turn Tanglen into a statue, correct?" Again they agreed.

She was about to write down number four concerning Kirkum's brother when he appeared through the window John had left open for him.

"Morning everyone," he said, "I understand you wish to ask me something concerning my brother.

"Yes, we would like to get your opinion on what should be done about him when we deal with the 'High Person' and Tanglen." Joan said, and read out the list they had compiled so far.

"I know he is my brother, but he has been doing the bidding of those two not very nice people for a very long time now, including I may add a few things against me. I think he should be made to live in the tree you are going to turn the "High Person" into, and only be allowed to come out of it to get food the villagers provide for him."

"Any time limit on his punishment?" asked John.

"I would say the same time limits you may set on the others."

"And what about your good self, Kirkum, we all agree you should be allowed to make changes should you wish to."

Kirkum looked at Mary and said that he would very much like to be returned to his former self and become the pet once more of his mistress Mariem, but at the same time continue to help the villagers of both places.

"Then that will be wish number four on this list," Joan said indicating she had written it down already.

Kirkum then wished them all good luck with the visit to "Ishe's village as he had come to think of it. Before he left he asked John to make sure he left the little escape hatch in the hillside near the 'Winter Shed' open for him to use. "After all, my brother is away with 'herself" so there is no danger he will see what is going on, and if all goes well with what you are all planning, then there will be an end to all the unpleasant happenings."

Joan brought their attention back to the list and asked if they could think of anything else to go on there. John said he didn't think so. "We have covered the main topics so I think we should leave it to the good people themselves to decide what they want to do. One thing I will say though," he added. "and that is, you should advise Naggy to have a talk with David and Arthur and suggest they form a committee once everything has settled down. Give folk back there a chance to sample what life is like with the new changes. That will also give those who are intent on pure revenge time to calm down a little."

"I'll make a note of that here and remember to tell him," said his wife.

Mary made them a light lunch, then Joan went to collect the items she would need for the journey, not forgetting the box of triangular marbles they would need to hopefully perform the changes.

After lunch John wished them good luck as they moved into the other room for their journey.

On arrival at Ishe's home Naggy was waiting for them. He told them that all was going according to plan. Tanglen had arrived and taken up residence in the house of the 'High Person' who had gone off somewhere into the woods as usual. 'The only difference I can see this time," said Naggy, "is that he told Tanglen he would be back in two days' time. He normally goes for three days, but this can only be to our advantage as we won't have so long to wait for his return."

Tom crossed the room, picked up Ishe and brought her to the table. Joan then read out to Naggy and Ishe the wishes they had thought of so far. "The wish concerning Lufler was Kirkum's idea," she told them.

"Did you remember to put down my suggestion that both the 'High person' and 'She' retain some kind of feeling so they can see how happy people are without them in charge?"

"Yes I did," Joan assured her.

"Did David agree to let us use his house?" Mary asked Naggy.

"Yes, he was more than happy, and both he and his wife have made beds up in two rooms for you to use should we have to wait more than the two expected days."

"When do you think we should leave?" said Joan.

"I think it will be best if we leave as soon as it gets dark. I know we are certain we can't be seen but by going in the dark we will make doubly certain. Would you mind carrying Ishe please Tom?"

"Not at all," said Tom, then remembered to tell Naggy that Lufler had recruited two young black birds and was planning to train them in his evil ways."

"Thanks for the warning Tom but if all goes well, there won't be any more evil ways to train for."

Naggy then asked them if they would like a drink, and when they said yes, the drink of their choice was immediately in front of them on the table.

"I could get used to this type of service," said Mary.

A little while later Naggy looked out of one of the windows and suggested that perhaps it was now dark enough to make the short journey to David's house. He went into the other room and came out carrying a little box similar to the one Joan used for their journey. He explained it was placed outside the house so they would know how to find it on their return, although as he had said before, when they returned hopefully, everything will have been changed. "But just in case," he said.

A short distance from the house Mary couldn't resist a glance round but she could see so sign of Ishe's home at all.

They arrived at David's home in no time at all. Naggy approached the house from the back, which faced away from the village green where people may be wandering around. "No point in advertising our presence," said Naggy.

David and his wife Alice made them very welcome and started at once to thank them for what they were doing. Joan, after introducing everyone to them told her it was their pleasure but not to celebrate too soon, although she had every confidence things would work out O.K.

"Arthur will be along later," David informed them, saying that he made himself a sort of overseer of what happened whenever the High Person' left and 'She' took over. "He keeps out of sight but keeps his eyes well open and takes note of any strange goings on."

"Which could mean anything once that horrible woman arrives here!" said Alice

David asked if they would like to see their rooms and asked them to follow him upstairs. Joan's room was at the front of the house and was the room from which David suggested she make the wishes.

The rest of the evening was spent discussing what would happen the next day. Arthur arrived a little later and was introduced to everyone. He told David that there had been a bit of disturbance up around the 'High Person's' house and grounds but nothing more than usual when 'She' was here. David asked how many of the marbles Joan thought it would take.

I have brought eight with me but hopefully we will only need three. She then went on to explain just how they had to position themselves when the time came.

"I think," she said, addressing Arthur, David and Alice, "that you three people plus Naggy should be the ones to hold the marbles. I as custodian of the records must be the one to say the words."

"What do we have to do?" asked Alice.

"You four people have to stand in a half circle facing me but with your back to the window. I need to face the village green, to make sure that the people concerned are in my sight. There will be a small table in front of me on which I will place the 'Wishing Records Paper'. I would like you David to stand on my left, then you Alice next to him. Naggy I would like you to stand next to Alice with you Arthur next to Naggy. Maybe we could get a stool for you to stand on Naggy to make it easier for you.

Once I can see that the main people are in my sight, I will give David, Alice and Naggy one of the triangular rocks. They are tied up with string. I will ask you to untie them but not to open them. I will then read out the wishes we will have all agreed on. I will ask you all in turn if you are in agreement with them and hopefully you will all say yes. I will them ask you to each open the rock you are holding, remove the marble you will find there, give the rock pieces to Tom and place the marble in your left hand. Then I will ask you to join hands so all three marbles are being held by two hands. I will ask you one more time if you are all happy. Once you say you are, I will ask David to hold my left hand, with Arthur holding my right hand. Mary will hold up the wish list so I can read it one more time. Then I will read the wishing request as printed on the 'Wishing Records Paper' and wait for the wishes to be granted. I'm afraid you will all have to remain holding hands until the wishes have been granted so unfortunately you will not see the changes take place, but I will tell you as soon as they have happened."

Joan asked them if they all understood what they had to do and they all told her yes.

"What happens to the marbles once we have made the wishes?" Arthur wanted to know.

Joan explained they would look at the marbles to see how many of the dots had gone from each marble. "If they have not all been used on our main wishes then we can discuss if there are any other immediate changes you would like to wish for before we put them back into the rocks. If there are then we can see about carrying them out. If not then they can be kept in a safe place until you want to use them again." She told them that at the moment she was the only one who could request a wish, as she was the 'custodian of the records' but that she would be more than willing to return at any time to help them out.

Joan then asked them if there was anything else they wanted to add to the list of wishes for the next day. Alice said that the only one she could think of was that the length of the days be changed back to what they used to be, and together with that the working days be put back as they were.

Joan wrote that on the list she had made and said she saw no reason why that wish could not be granted.

They all spent the rest of the evening talking in general and getting to know more about one another.

David woke them all quite early the next morning to tell them that the 'High Person' had returned a day earlier than expected and was demanding that everyone should be at his attendance by midmorning on the village green.

During the morning, Joan and the rest watched from her bedroom window as the villagers slowly collected on the green. Eventually the 'High Person' came strutting down from his house with Tanglen by his side. Two of his helpers walked behind him carrying a small platform, which they placed on the ground when he stopped. He stood on the platform and surveyed the crowd. Tanglen as Naggy had predicted went over and stood by the statue of her sister.

"Looks as if everyone is in place," said Joan, "are we all ready?"

The others told her they were and moved into the positions Joan had asked them to be. Joan stood behind the small table Alice had provided for her. On the table was the box containing the rocks and the 'Wishing Records Paper'. As she put the paper on the table, they watched in amazement as it unrolled itself and came to rest in front of where Joan was standing.

Joan opened the box and gave a rock each to David, Alice and Naggy asking them to please untie the string. When they had done that, she then read out the wishes they had all agreed on the previous evening. She asked them all if they were in full agreement. They said one by one as she looked at them in turn that they were. She then asked them one more time to which they all answered yes.

"Please remove the marbles from the rocks, give the rock pieces to Tom and then join hands with the rocks between your palms. David and Arthur please join hands with me. Mary, can you please hold up the list." Mary did this and Joan then read out the wishes once more. She then looked down at the 'Wishing Record Paper' and read very clearly the words printed on it.

"I Joan Vendell, as "Custodian Of The Records" do hereby ask that the wishes we have requested be carried out in full with immediate effect. I also declare that none of these wishes will cause death or permanent harm to any individuals mentioned. I ask that the wishes be granted now."

They all stood there silently for a few minutes. Very slowly their hands began to shake. Joan told them to tighten their grips on one another and not to let go. The shaking got a little stronger. Joan looked over their shoulders and saw there was a commotion on the village green. People were gasping and putting their hands to their faces as if in disbelief. As she watched Joan saw that where the 'High Person' had been standing there was now an enormous tree. Looking over to where Tanglen had been situated, she saw a very young lady standing there looking quite mystified. A short distance away was a new statue. As she continued to watch Joan saw a very highly coloured bird fly over to the young lady who held up her hand to allow the bird to perch there. The hands of everyone stopped shaking and Joan informed them that all their wishes as far as she could tell had been granted and to go to the window and look for themselves. Tom was the first to spot a large three-legged blackbird sitting on one of the lower branches of the tree, and pointed it out excitedly to everyone else. "That must be Kirkum,s brother," he said, and went on to explain to their three new friends who Kirkum was. "And if I am not mistaken, that highly coloured bird perched on the arm of that young lady over there is in fact Kirkum, restored to his former self.

"What happens now?" asked Alice.

"First of all I need to see how many dots have gone from the marbles and to put them back into their protective rocks."

They all opened their hands and showed Joan the marbles they were holding. Two marbles had no spots left at all but the other had all its spots.

"That means we used sixteen wishes," said Joan. "You may as well keep the two empty marbles to remind you of this special day, but the other one we need to put back into the rock and tie it up again."

The two marbles being held by Alice were the ones with no dots left so she kept one and handed the other to Arthur. The full one Arthur gave to Tom who put it back in to the rock pieces and tied it up again.

As they started to go back downstairs, there was a loud knocking on the door. David opened it to find lots of his friends and neighbours all wanting to tell him about something 'strange' that had happened on the village green.

"The 'High Person' has turned into a tree!"

"'She' has turned into a statue!"

"The other statue has come back to life!"

"All his helpers walked backwards into the grounds of the house!"

All these things were told excitedly to David all at the same time. David held his hands up and told them to calm down. He looked back at Joan and asked her if he could tell them what had happened.

"I think you will have to David," she said, "would you like us to help you?"

"That would be very kind of you, yes please."

"I think you should ask your friends there to get as many people as possible back onto the green in about an hour and we will explain to them all at the same time." Looking at the friends still standing by the door she told them not to panic, the changes they had witnessed would be permanent and life would be better from now on. "Gather as many people as you can in an hour and we will tell you everything."

The friends left the house to get everyone back to the green. Meanwhile as David looked out of his door, he drew Joan's attention to the young lady approaching the house. She still had the bird on her arm. Without thinking, David opened the door wider and made a gesture for the lady to enter his home.

Before anyone could extend a welcome, the bird spoke and introduced Mariem to Joan, Mary, Tom, and Naggy.

"This is my mistress Mariem," he told them.

Joan said hello then introduced Mariem to Tom and Mary, then Mariem and Kirkum to David, Alice and Arthur. Speaking to the bird she said with a smile, "I take it I am speaking to Kirkum?"

"You are indeed," he replied, and thanked them all for what they had done for him and all the people.

"It was our pleasure entirely. We are all very glad we had the means to overturn a nasty set of miss deeds carried out all those years ago.

Alice invited them all to sit down and asked if anyone would like a drink. Before they had a chance to answer Naggy said, "Allow me," and once he had the list of drinks they asked for told them to close their eyes and count to five silently to themselves, then open them again. When they opened their eyes the drinks were in front of each of them. "Don't know how long I will be able to do that now everything is changing but it was worth a go."

Mariem then spoke for the first time asking them all but looking mainly at Joan what the plans were now for the village and the people.

"Well, to be honest Mariem, I think the future of the place and any plans for the future must be decided by your good selves. I would suggest that you form a working committee to begin with, and listen very carefully to the wishes of the people themselves. I am going to talk to the villagers in a little while and I will suggest that to them. I will tell them that they must select and elect the members of the committee very carefully. Having made their choice they must have faith and trust in them to do what is best for all. The first committee must also make it their duty to listen to the wishes of the people. I will also suggest that the first committee works together for a period of between six months and a year after which if so desired, elections can be held to form a permanent governing party. Of course, as in any village or town there will be some who will object to what they may hear or see, but they should be listened to very carefully and given their chance to put forward any ideas they may have, but at the end of the day I am sure even they would not wish to go back living the same kind of life they have been subjected to over the years."

Mariem thanked Joan and asked her if she would be staying on in the village, but Joan said that sadly no, she and her family must return to their own people, but told her that she would be happy to return on occasions should her help be required. She said that they only had to send Kirkum with a message and they would be happy to return.

David, who had been looking out the window, informed Joan that it seemed as if the residents of the village were all assembled and ready to listen to her.

Joan suddenly had a thought and asked Naggy if they would be able to see her, knowing how before the changes they had been invisible to everyone.

"I think you will find that was one of the changes which happened at the same time as the rest," replied Naggy, "after all, Mariem can see you."

They all made their way from David's house towards the village green. The crowd parted for them and let them pass through. On the way, they could hear gasps and questions about who they were, and what were they going to do, and would they be as bad as the others.

Joan turned around to face the crowd as she stood under the big new tree. She stepped a few paces forward from the rest of her group and introduced herself.

"Good afternoon to you all. My name is Joan Vendell and I have come here today from a place far away. For those of you who do not know the village is called Marbleville. Many of you will know it because you originated from there before you were very cruelly brought here to this place."

As she spoke Joan looked around at the crowd and continued, "In fact I can see many familiar faces from all those years ago, including some I may say who were my childhood friends"

She went on to tell them that her family has a very close but loose connection with their village. "The connection", she continued " is all to do with the marble mine back in our village. There are some marbles in that mine which have magical powers. Unfortunately, way back in time certain not very nice unscrupulous people decided to take advantage of those powers and use them for their own ends. You and your ancestors were brought to this place against your wishes and made to live the only life you have ever known. I honestly do not know how long this place or yourselves have been here, but I am sure that over the next weeks and months, records which were hitherto kept from your sight and knowledge will be found and a history can be put into place."

"I mentioned just a minute ago that certain marbles back in the mine in my village had certain powers. There are also others containing much more powerful, for want of a better word, magic. Some of those marbles I brought with me yesterday, and it was those powers I used to make the changes you witnessed this morning."

Joan turned to the tree at this point and continued, "This tree for example wasn't here yesterday, but a not very nice man you knew as the 'High Person' was. Nor was that new statue here yesterday but 'She' was. Most important, there was a statue which has stood here for many, many years but you could not have failed to notice is no longer there." Turning round, she held out her hand beckoning for Mariem to come forward. She put her arm round Mariem's shoulder and introduced her to the crowd.

"This is Mariem. She was turned into a statue by the very person who is now a statue herself. You all know her as 'She', but her correct name is Tanglen. The highly coloured bird Mariem is holding is the brother of the three legged blackbird you can see looking down on us from the branches of the tree. You need have no more fear of the black birds. In fact you need have no more fear of anything anymore. When I brought the special magical marbles with me and made those wishes today, I did so with the agreement of David and Arthur here. All I did was make wishes for the two people who have made your lives a misery all these years to be punished, and at the same time have no more hold over you. They will be punished two fold really, because in the wishes I made to turn them into what they are now, I included a wish that although they are now what they are, they will have to look down on you and suffer the pain of seeing you all living happy lives and not be able to do anything about it. You should all be able to live happy and contented lives from now on and myself and my family wish you all the very best for the future."

The crowd clapped and cheered and moved forward to shake Joan and her family by the hand. After a while Joan held up her hand for silence again. When all was quiet she looked at them all again and told them she had just two mare things to say to them.

"They are suggestions really," she continued. 'One is, that in honour of this beautiful young lady here who has suffered greatly all these years that your village be renamed MARIEMVILLE."

She let the cheers die down and then said, "The second suggestion is you form a committee to plan your new futures together and I would recommend that you let David and Arthur here head it together at least at the start."

Once more the crowd showed their appreciation and it was a very long time before they were able to make their way back to David's house to prepare for their journey home.

When they entered David's home, Alice who had asked that she be allowed to stay behind spoke to Joan in a very tearful way, telling her that Ishe had not said a word since the changes had taken place.

Ishe had asked Joan the previous evening to be left in a chair in Tom and Mary's room while everything was going on.

"Where is she now?" asked Joan.

"Still in the chair upstairs," replied Alice.

Joan asked Naggy to accompany her upstairs and together they went to see Ishe. As Alice had said, she was still sitting in the chair, but showed no sign of recognising either of them as they approached her. Joan picked her up and held her close to comfort her but the doll showed no signs of live at all.

"Whatever is the matter with her?' said Joan.

"I don't know," replied Naggy.

" I have a very nasty feeling that when the magic changed everything back to normal here, it also changed things for Ishe as well," said Joan.

They returned downstairs, Joan carrying Ishe, and explained to the others what they thought had happened.

"Perhaps she will be O.K. when she gets back to her own house," said Mary.

"I hope so Mary," said Joan, "but I am sure if she isn't, we can put good use some of the wishes we have left."

Naggy suggested that although he was certain everything would be O.K. now, it might be best to wait until dark to make the journey back to Ishe's house. "We have taken care of the evils we know about, but there may just be some elements of the place we did not know about out there somewhere."

He turned to David and Arthur and impressed on them to still keep a close vigil around the village until things settled down and to keep a sharp ear to the ground because of the very reason he had just stated.

David assured them he would. Soon after that Joan and her family bid farewell to David and his wife and to Arthur, reminding them once again, if they needed any kind of help they only had to get a message to them. They then set off for Ishe's house.

They found it quite easily; in fact it was a lot easier than they thought, because whereas before it had been invisible from the outside, now it was in plain view for all to see.

"Oh dear," commented Naggy, "that could make things a little awkward."

"I agree, but perhaps we can do something about it. The first priority though is to see to Ishe," said Joan, as they entered the house.

Knowing that the house was now visible from the outside Mary closed all the curtains in all the rooms. Joan sat with Ishe on her knee and tried to talk to her. She asked her what her name was, and if she knew who was talking to her and if she knew where she was. Ishe sat there motionless not saying a word.

"Oh dear," said Joan, "it seems as if our fears have been confirmed, Ishe has been changed back again to being a mere doll."

"Can you do anything about it mum?"

"I don't know Tom, all I can do is try. Before I do though, we had better see if there is anything else we need to change back so we can include everything in our wishes."

They all sat and thought, but apart from the fact that Ishe's house needed seeing to they could think of nothing else.

"Anyone like a drink?" asked Naggy.

"Yes please they answered."

Within seconds their drinks were on the table in front of them.

"Well at least it looks like I still have that bit going for me," said Naggy.

Joan had an idea and asked Naggy to say something to Ishe. He asked her what day it was and how she was feeling, but Ishe just sat there motionless as before.

"I think we are going to have to use a marble," said Joan, "but I think we will only need the one we didn't use at David's house. Are we all agreed on what we need to wish for?" she asked the others. They said they were so Joan asked Tom and Mary to hold the marble in their two hands. She laid the 'Custodian of the Wishes' paper on the table in front of her.

Please remove the marble from the rock Tom and place it in yours and Mary's hand. Now both of you hold my hands. She then spoke the wishes they would like performed; Ishe to be able to speak again and for Ishe's house to again be invisible to the outside world. As in David's house, Tom and Mary's joined hands began to shake but the shaking did not last as long as before. When the shaking stopped they all stood where they were for a few seconds.

"What's happening, why am I sitting on the table?"

It was Ishe asking the questions. Joan released Tom and Mary's hands and picking up the doll gave her a hug and held her tightly to her.

"Oh I am so glad you can talk again Ishe. We thought we had lost you as a friend."

Looking at Naggy she asked him if he would kindly go outside and see if the wish had worked on the house as well. When he came back in he told them that yes the house was now invisible again to the outside world.

Joan quickly explained to Ishe all that had happened, and how after the wishes in David's house she Ishe had been unable to talk to them.

Tom looked at the marble they had used and saw that only three spots had gone. He put it back in the rock and tied the string.

After a little while Joan thought that perhaps it was time for them to return to their own home.

"Will you be alright here Ishe or would you like to come back with us?"

Ishe asked Naggy what he was going to do now that things had changed in the village. He told her that perhaps he would spend more time in the village saying that now David and a few of his friends knew who he was then he didn't think he had anything to be afraid of. "But I would like to be able to come back here whenever I felt in need of some peace and quiet."

Ishe told him he was welcome to use the house whenever he wanted, and turning to Joan said that she would be more than happy to go back with them, just as long as she could return to her own home, if she felt she wanted to.

They all said a tearful goodbye to Naggy, and Joan thanked him for being such a good friend and for all his help in what they had been able to do for the people.

"It was a pleasure," he said and shook hands with them all telling them he would keep in touch by whatever means he could. He walked towards the door leading to the other room and with a wave of his hand and a wink, walked through it without even opening it.

"Bless him for making things easy for us," said Joan and unrolled the map ready for the trip home.

She asked Mary to hold Ishe and before they knew it they were back in their own living room.

Mary went to the windows to open the curtains and could see that it was quite light. She could see her father-in-law standing chatting to someone at the front gate but could not see who it was. At that moment he turned and saw her and gave her a wave. The other person walked away and John made his way into the house.

"Hello Mary, how did the trip go?

"Very well thank you, what time is it?" she asked him.

"Just after eight o'clock, I expect you are all ready for some supper."

"Supper, what day is it?"

"The same day you went, you have only been gone about seven hours I think."

John followed Mary into the other room to see the others and to hear how things went for them.

"Your dad said it is eight o'clock in the evening and we are back the same day we left," she said to her husband, "so time really does stand still back here when we go away."

"Hello dad, you come and sit down and let mum tell you everything. Mary and I will go and make us all a nice cup of tea.

They spent the rest of the evening telling John about their trip and that everything seemed to have gone to plan.

"When do you think we could expect the children back dad?" asked Tom.

"I think it might be as early as tomorrow. With what you managed to achieve back where you have just been, I should think that it might be quite easy for Joshua and his friends to start changing things in their village at once. I suggest you and I take a walk over to the site after breakfast in the morning and see if anything is happening. We can call at the Bilk house on the way and see how James is getting on."

They were about to call it a night when a faint glow started to come from the mirror which was still standing on the chair where Tom had left it before they went on their journey. As the glow died down they could clearly see the image of Jessica looking out at them.

She smiled at them and said, "I heard you had a very successful trip and managed to put a few things right. I am very glad."

Joan was pleased to see her as were the rest of the family, and asked her how she had heard about it and how had she managed to appear in the mirror again.

"I had a little place in the village where I could stay well out of site but at the same time see all that was going on. I was looking today when everything happened, and also saw and heard what you said to the people Joan. In answer to your other question, I still have a few magic marbles, which I can use to travel here to see you when I want to, but don't worry, I won't be bothering you all the time. In any case I can only visit you if the mirror is placed where it is now. The first time you released me when you read that letter determined where I should appear to you in the future."

Joan quickly explained a bit more what had happened and also showed her Ishe and told her why she was with them. Jessica was delighted to see her old doll again. She then asked when they thought the children might return, and did they think Elizabeth would return again.

"From what her and Rebecca told me, then I think she was quite anxious to do just that, although I did caution them about the fact they had stayed their young selves for so long, they may find things a little difficult, but that was something maybe we could try and solve."

"I am sure between us we can sort something out for them and the rest of the children as well as the adults."

Joan then suggested to Jessica that perhaps she would like it if they placed Ishe on a chair where the two of them could have a chat. The family was ready to retire for the night so they would have the room to themselves. Jessica thanked her very much and said she would just leave when she thought Ishe felt sleepy.

She said goodnight to the family, and reminded them that should she ever appear when other people were in the house, only Joan and her family would be able to see her.

CHAPTER-FORTY

TWO HAPPY VILLAGES

Next morning, granddad was having a walk round the garden before breakfast when he heard the excited shouts of Pedro and Paul.

"Granddad, granddad, we're back!"

He looked up and saw Pedro, Paul and Jimmy running down the road towards the house.

"Hello boys, you're out and about early," he said when they arrived at the gate, "How did things go back there?"

"It was really great gramps, we had a lovely time.'

"And we helped your friend Joshua sir," said Paul.

"And I lost my arm," said Jimmy, showing John his empty sleeve.

"How on earth did you manage that, Jimmy?" said Pedro's father, who had come out to see what all the fuss was about.

"Hello dad," said Pedro and went to hug his father.

"Somebody pulled my arm off sir," Jimmy told Pedro's father, "it was a good job Paul was with me."

"I think you had better all come into the house and tell us slowly what happened back there," said granddad.

Looking at Paul he explained that his father was up at the house, saying he had spent the night up there, making sure everything was clean and tidy in case it was going to be used by anyone.

"We can walk up there later and see him. That is what we had planned for this morning anyway."

Pedro's mum and grandmother were up and about when they got in the house and were just as shocked as granddad had been to see them home.

"Goodness, you are back early," said Granny "is everything alright back there?"

"Yes everything is just fine, Joshua asked us to come and see you and granddad to tell you thank you for what you had done in that other place and could you please go and see him later today."

"You won't have to go through the bush Mrs. Vendell," said Paul. "By this afternoon Joshua is hoping that he will have opened up his part of the tunnel so it will be easy for you to walk through. He asked that either Pedro or myself go through the bush the usual way and go to his house. Once he knows we are there he will go into the tunnel his side and take you through. So you should only have to wait a short while from when someone goes through from this side to him coming to get you."

"That is good news Paul. Certainly we can try and see him today."

"He also said would you be able to bring some of the Rocks you took with you to the other place, please granny."

"How on earth did he know about those I wonder?"

"He said to tell you Mariem had been to see him."

"She had a very pretty bird with her, and it knew my name granny," said Pedro.

"Well that explains that, but I wonder how did she got there? And that pretty bird she had with her was Kirkum. I will explain to you later."

John pointed out that Jimmy had lost his false arm and granny asked him to tell them all how it had happened.

"Well," said Jimmy, "we were supposed to be invisible to the people back there. Paul and I were asked to go down to the far end of the village where there was a sort of market and to listen to anything that might have been said. It was exciting really, just like being spies. Anyway we made our way down there and were just wandering among the people when a lady started screaming and pointing in our direction. We didn't really bother too much because we knew we couldn't be seen, so we carried on wandering. By now lots of other people were looking in our direction and pointing at us. Another lady then shouted 'look there's an arm floating in the air!' and pointed right towards us."

"I looked to where she was pointing and could see Jimmy's arm as clear as I can see you," said Paul.

"So what did you do?" asked Pedro's mum.

"We both started running as fast as we could back towards Joshua's house," said Jimmy, "but one man caught us up and grabbed hold of my left wrist and tried to stop me. I shouted at Paul to reach up between my elbow and shoulder and press the button he would feel there."

"I found it quite easily and pressed it," said Paul, "then Jimmy just sort of shook his shoulder and the man was left holding his metal arm by the wrist."

"We carried on running for a little bit, then stopped and looked back. The man with my arm was surrounded by lots of people trying to see what it was," Jimmy said.

"When we told Joshua what had happened he said that although we were invisible, Jimmy's metal arm would not have been," concluded Paul.

"I would have loved to have seen the look on that man's face," said granny.

"Joshua went out later in the day, and said people were still playing around with it. He said he would try and get it back for me when all the excitement had died down."

"What about the girls and the rest of your friends Pedro?" asked Mary, "are they coming back today?"

"I think they are going to wait until granny goes up there," said Pedro. "Oh and there is a girl there called Jennifer Stubbs, granny. Rebecca thinks you might have known her before."

"I certainly did, she was a little older than me. More a friend of Elizabeth's really. I wonder who else I will find when I get there?"

"Sure it won't be too upsetting for you mum?" asked Tom.

"I think it might be but it will be lovely to see people again.

Jimmy said he thought he ought to go home to see his parents and tell them about his arm.

"I hope they won't be too upset with you," said Pedro's mum.

"I don't think they will really Mrs. Vendell. It didn't fit very well now anyway, but it's a good job I didn't go with my new one."

Pedro's father and grandfather said they would walk with Jimmy as they were going up to Paul's home to see how his father had got on.

"That will give me a bit of time to sit and make a note of a few things before we go to visit Joshua," said Joan.

"In that case I will go with the men to the village, I need to get a few things anyway, and you can have all the peace and quiet you need mum," Mary told her.

When they reached the bottom of the hill leading up to the Bilk house, Mary said she would go with Jimmy to see his parents and then call at the shop afterwards. "Hopefully they will let him come back with me, so we will wait at the bottom here for you all to come back down again."

Her husband and father-in-law bid her goodbye and set off up the hill. The two boys had already raced ahead. When they arrived at the house James was busy sorting through a huge pile of paperwork he had found at the back of a cupboard in the old office. He had to stop for a while to listen to Paul and Pedro while they told him about their visit and about Jimmy's arm.

"Some of these papers go back years and years," James said. "Your parent's names appear in a few of them Tom, so we had better take them back with us so they can be studied carefully."

"Can't think why that should be," said John, "but no doubt my wife will be able to put her finger on it."

"Something about the old village hall, I think," James said, "but I didn't read it all."

"Mum mentioned something about the village hall when she first got here, and said she would explain it all another day," said Tom.

"Find anything else interesting James?" asked John.

"Not really, apart from another diagram of the field at the bottom of the garden past the small orchard. Looks a lot like the other one we found indicating where those holes had been dug. There are about twenty crosses marked on it but no numbers by them."

"Could be that is where more of those rocks are buried. If so then we have all the time in the world now to go looking for them," commented Tom.

Pedro came in from the garden saying he could see his mother and Jimmy waiting at the bottom of the hill.

"You two boys run on down then and tell them we will be along just as soon as we collect all these papers together," his father told him.

Back home they found Joan sitting in the garden studying more of the papers Jessica had left her. She said that the more she studied them, the more sense they made, especially now they had paid a few visits to the other village.

"That Mantel Helter, and later her daughter Tanglen really were two very evil ladies. I am glad we were able to help those poor people out."

Tom told his mother James had found a lot more old papers up at the old Bilk house. "You and dad are mentioned in a few of them mum," he told her, "something to do with the old village hall I think"

His mother said she would look at them later once they had been to see Joshua.

Pedro's granddad asked Jimmy if his parents had said much about his lost arm.

"Not a lot really sir. Dad said it was a pity I had lost it but at least it wasn't the new one." He held up his arm to show them his empty sleeve and said he hoped that when he returned Joshua may have got his old one back.

By early afternoon all was ready for the trip to the 'Winter Shed' site. Tom and James said they would stay behind this time once everyone had gone through to Joshua. James said he still had things to do at the house and Tom said he would stay in case any of the parents came calling.

Once at the site the three boys pulled a blade of grass each from granddad's hand to see who got the shortest and would stay with him and Pedro's granny and go through the new way. It was Paul who drew the shortest blade so Pedro handed him the medallion to open the bush.

Jimmy and Pedro said cheerio to them and walked towards the bush, with Paul beside them holding the medallion. It was the first time Pedro's granny had seen this part of the adventure and she just sat there staring as the bush moved away from the side of the hill.

"See you soon, granny," Pedro said as he and Jimmy crawled into the space behind the bush. As it closed her husband asked her if she would like to see the part of the shed they would be going through.

"I will show you as well the little trap door Paul and Pedro discovered which was used by Kirkum and his brother when they travelled from Joshua's place to us."

They walked a little way towards the shed when Paul held his hand up and asked them to listen. "I'm certain I heard a voice sir," he told John.

They all stood quietly to listen. Sure enough, after a few seconds they heard Joshua's voice asking if there was 'any other body there?'

"Yes we are here my friend," replied John.

"Good. Hello John, nice to hear you again. Could you please be so kind as to push that long piece of wood you have ready, through the hole you have been making and I will know just where to break through to you."

John placed the length of wood into the hole and asked Paul if he would kindly hold it steady for him.

He then used a large piece of rock to hit the wood further into the hole. Very soon they heard Joshua shout that he could see it his side and for them to please stand well clear while he broke through.

In no time at all, the whole of John's side of the wall fell away and there covered in sand and dust, and with a smile all over his face stood his friend Joshua. Both men just hugged one another for what seemed an eternity before they broke away and spoke to one another. Having greeted each other, John introduced his friend to his wife, and Mary. None of them knew really what to say for a few minutes, the relief of this moment having such an effect on them all. Finally, it was Joshua who shook hands again with Joan and told her how much everyone appreciated what she had done to help them, and for whatever help she was able to do in the future. Joan in reply said it had been a pleasure sorting through the various papers left by old Jessica, although at times quite stressful too.

"So how do we get to your side of the world Joshua?" asked John.

"Similar to how the children get through the bush really. We will all go through this hole we have made and walk for several minutes in till we come to a door. Once there I will knock on the door, and my friend Peter, who is waiting on the other side, will let us through. We go through the door, which will then close behind us. A little way further on we go through another door and there we are in my side of the mine. We will then have quite a walk until we get to the exit but it won't take us too long."

Joshua asked if they were ready and led the way through the hole he had just made. After passing through the two doors, and a quite long walk through darkened tunnels, they emerged into bright sunshine. Quite a few people were waiting for them as they came out of the mine entrance all anxious to meet the lady who would change their lives.

"I have told them all about you," said Joshua. "Ever since we got word of what you had done for the people in Mariemville, these good folk are keen to be part of a new life."

"That's very flattering," said Joan, "I only hope I can live up to their expectations."

"I am sure you will do that and more," replied Joshua. "I will take you to my house for a little rest after your long walk. After that just tell me what your requirements are and I will get things organised for you."

Joshua explained to the people who had collected to meet Joan and her party what was going to happen.

"Once the lady has had a little rest we will arrange a meeting place where she can explain to you all what will be happening."

"Shall I open the school Joshua? we can use the main hall."

Joshua looked at Rachel who was the schoolmistress and who had made the suggestion. "That would be very kind of you Rachel, thank you. If you other people could spread the word that we will meet there in about one of our hours that would be really helpful."

Mary noticed that her mother in law was looking very a little pale and asked her if she was alright.

"Yes thank you Mary, I have just had a bit of a shock that's all. That lady Rachel is I believe my old school teacher. We were told she died from a terrible accident during one of our summer holidays. I need to check with Joshua if it is who I think it is."

On arrival at Joshua's home, he introduced them to Elspeth, his wife. Joan recognised her at once as did Elspeth her. Joan knew her of course when she and Rebecca had been best friends. Elspeth had been the much older sister of another of their friends and had always found her quite a formidable person; although very nice she had been the kind of person Joan had been a little wary of. It seemed strange to Joan that now she was considerable older than Elspeth, due to the way the people who had been 'abducted' to this place had stopped getting any older.

"Please, come in all of you do. Make yourselves at home. I expect you would all like a drink after your journey." She led them into a cosy room overlooking the back garden. The doors were open and there was a nice cooling breeze blowing into the room. It brought with it the scent of the flowers, which could be seen in abundance.

As they entered the room, Joan introduced John and Mary to Elspeth, explaining that Mary was her daughter in law and mother of Pedro, who she had already met.

"Joshua has told me so much about all of you," said Elspeth. "Who would have thought that his best friend from when he was a boy would end up marrying Rebecca's best friend?" She said it felt a bit strange being the same age as when Joan knew her in the past, but now Joan was older than when she knew her then.

"Perhaps something can be done about that, but we will need to be very careful how we approach it," said Joan.

Joshua appeared then with drinks for them all. After a little more general chat he asked Joan what they needed to do as a group to be of assistance to her.

Joan explained the ritual required to make any changes. She said that as far as she could see, only a couple of major changes needed to be done at once as the rest could be carried out over a period of time.

"At the moment, I'm afraid it is only I who can carry out the wishes, although that too may be changed in the future." She went on to explain about her being 'Custodian of the Records' for the mine and that there was a certain procedure that had to be adhered to. "I will need four people to help me carry out the wishes, so you need to ask two more besides you and Elspeth."

"So what you and your fellow villagers need to do Joshua is to make a list of things you would like to be changed immediately. Can you think of any at this moment?"

"One thing that comes to mind, and I think the rest will agree with me, is that our time be put back to what we were used to before we were brought to this place."

"O.K. I will write that down," said Joan, "anything else?"

"What about being allowed out after dark again, instead of being confined to our homes?" suggested Elspeth.

"I will write that down also, but I thing we may be able to come up with a suitable way of saying it when we make the wishes, that will include all that and more. Anything else?"

"Not having to work seven days a week." would be nice, added Joshua.

Joan wrote that down as well, and then suggested to Joshua that he should go to the school room where this was all going to take place and see if anyone there had any more ideas.

"Remember, we do not need to make all changes at this time, so just concentrate on the things that will improve all your lifestyles at this moment. I must also ask you to be certain of the people you talk to, as there may be some amongst the villagers who were closely connected to the past rulers, for want of a better word, and would not be too keen on seeing changes. Most importantly, the two who will join you and your wife when we make the wishes need to be absolutely one hundred percent behind us, because if just one person in the lineup is not in full agreement, even though they may say they are, the changes will not happen and we will have wasted the wishes."

Joshua assured Joan that he knew exactly who he would ask, and said he would leave at once for the school, saying that Elspeth could bring them there in about an hour. He invited John to accompany him leaving the ladies to get to know one another better.

When Elspeth led Joan and Mary into the school hall, there was an instant round of applause for them. They both felt a little embarrassed about it all. Elspeth led them to the front of the hall and up on to the stage. Rachel was on the stage to meet them and invited them to sit down while introduced them to everyone. She gave a knowing look and a smile to Joan as she greeted her. Joan knew then she had been correct in what she had told Mary.

"Ladies and gentlemen," said Rachel, "may I please introduce you to Joan Vendell and her daughter in law Mary. Most of you have already met her husband John. I am sure she won't mind me saying that I first knew Joan when she was a young girl in my class at the old school in Marbleville. I knew her then as Joan Meaker. Now it seems she and her family are going to teach me and all of us a thing or two." Turning to Joan she told her that she and her family were very welcome to their village and everyone was looking forward to what she had to tell them. Again the audience applauded as Rachel invited Joan to speak to them all.

Nervously, Joan stood up to tell everyone who she was and how it was she and her family were able to hopefully put an end to the only way of life most of them had known for so many years.

"I won't bore you with all the details at this time as I am sure you are all very anxious to get on with things. I can tell you that I as 'Custodian of the Records' have been given powers to carry out this task."

She then went on to briefly explain what would happen.

"Joshua has given me a list of the things you want to change immediately, and I can see no reason from looking at it, that it can't be done. Lots of other things I am sure you will think of can be done at a later date."

Joan then read out the list and asked if they were all in agreement with what was on there. When the people said they were, Joan said they could proceed, and asked for Joshua and Elspeth to please come on the stage together with the two other people who would form the group. She told the audience that they were not to be alarmed at what might happen or what they would see. "I can assure you all, nothing bad will happen to any of you, but I do ask that you all remain as quiet as possible during the procedure"

Joshua and his wife came on the stage accompanied by two friends Michael and Pamela. Joan asked them to stand on front of her with Joshua on the left, then Elspeth, then Pamela and finally Michael on the right. She asked Tom to remove the marbles from the rocks and give one each to Joshua, Elspeth, and Pamela and them to hold them in their right hands.

"Now please all join hands holding the marbles tightly in your palms," said Joan. She then read out the declaration, after which she asked Mary to hold up the wish list for her to read.

"I Joan Vendel, do request that the wishes I will request on behalf of the people of this community be carried out immediately and safely. I also declare that no one will be harmed as a result of these wish requests."

She then read out the wishes from the list being held up by Mary.

"Number one, that the days and nights return to the normal, that is back to a twenty-four hour system.

Number two, that the good people be no longer confined to their houses after working hours.

Number three, that the good people have all restrictions on their lifestyle lifted to enable them to live normal lives.

Number three, that all persons who helped the previous rulers in any kind of capacity have all their powers removed, and have no recollection of previous activities.

Number four, that the village now be known as Kirkumville in honour of the bird who helped make all this possible.

Joan then asked if everyone was in agreement with the wishes she had just read out and they all said yes. She then asked each person before her individually and again got all yeses. She then asked Joshua and Michael to take and hold her hands. As they did so she asked that the wishes she had requested be made to come into force immediately.

Nothing happened for a few seconds, and then just as in the other place, all their hands began to shake quite violently. Joan whispered for them to keep tight hold of one another. After a short time the shaking stopped and all went very quiet. Joan told them they could now release their hands, and asked Tom to collect the marbles and return them to the rocks.

The people in the audience sat there in silence until someone looked out of the window and gave a little shout, "It's gone dark outside! It's gone dark outside! What have you done?"

"Please don't worry." shouted Joan, holding up her hands to try to calm people down. When they had and she had their attention again she reminded them of wish number one, and that was to return the days and nights back to normal. "That is obviously what has happened and the proper time has caught up with this place and it is obviously night time. We will now have to wait until sunrise to put all clocks to where they should be."

Joshua then stood facing the audience and proposed a vote of thanks for Joan and her family for what they had done for them all. This was taken up by everyone clapping and cheering. Joan thanked them and suggested that they all meet on the village green later in the day in the sunshine 'as free people' to have a discussion as to what to do next. She said there were a few things she had to tell them all before she and her family left them to enjoy their new life.

By mid afternoon the next day, there was an even larger crowd waiting for the visitors on the green. Joshua introduced Joan and her family to those who had not been present the previous day.

Joan stepped forward amid more applause.

"Thank you all very much. I won't keep you every long but there are just a few things I need to say to you all. The first one is, welcome to you new life." This brought another round of applause and a few cheers. "The changes we made yesterday were the immediate ones requested by Joshua here and a few of the villagers. Hopefully what we achieved then will put you all on the way to a much better way of life than most of you have known for a good many years. As far as we know, we have eradicated all bad persons from the scene, but you, and us will need to stay on our guard to make sure others who we were not aware of, show themselves in the future."

"There are still changes that need to be made and some you may all wish for as you get used to your new life. What I suggest is that Joshua here heads up a temporary committee who will be available for meetings where you can all have your say on any changes you would like to see. Should any of the changes require the use of a special wishing marble, then Joshua can contact me and I will be more than happy to return to help you out. At this moment in time I am the only person who can use these marbles but I am sure in time that can be sorted out too."

Joan asked if anyone had any questions. The one that seemed uppermost in people's minds concerned their ages and would they stay as they were or could they be altered.

"I thought that one would be on your minds," said Joan. "What I would advise for the immediate time is to please be a little patient and continue as you are. I still have a lot more old papers to read through and study and that is the main item I will be looking into. What will be uppermost in my mind will be how, if some of you want to go to the age you would have been, will it affect your health suddenly putting on all those years." There were a few nods of understanding as the people heard this.

"Just a couple more things then I will leave you to your new life. As I look around you all, I think I can see a few familiar faces in the crowd, but at the same time I have to remind myself that when most of you were mysteriously removed from Marbleville I was only a young girl. It really is a strange feeling to look at you all now knowing I have past you all by many years."

"On the subject of returning to Marbleville at a later date, I can tell you that a lot of work is being carried out by the villagers back there to restore your homes to a good living standard so you have no need to worry on that score." Again there was applause and thanks shouted to Joan.

"Finally, I will tell you that the owner of the mine that a lot of you will have remembered, Cedric Bilk, sadly passed away recently. His son James has returned and I am convinced he will run things in a very fair way." Again there was a small round of applause.

"All that remains for me to say to you all, is enjoy your new life. My family and I will be returning to our home later today but should you require any help, let Joshua know, and I will be happy to come back."

There were more cheers and applause as Joan and her family left the schoo;l and headed for Joshua's house. It took them quite a while to get there as many of the people wanted to chat to them as they left. Finally they made it and sat down to a very welcome cup of tea.

The girls returned a little while later and asked what time they would going back. Joan told her very soon and did they know where the boys were. Sally told her they were on their way also. Sally then asked if Elizabeth and Rebecca could return with them. Joan told her that it was up to their parents but they were welcome as far as she was concerned. Joshua said he had no objections to Rebecca going for a while but they would have to speak to Elizabeth's step mother about her. Elspeth said she would nip round and see her and ask.

The boys returned a little while later, with Jimmy proudly holding up his false arm. He said he had found it lying in the grass by the market, which is where it had been pulled out of his sleeve.

Elspeth came back saying that it was alright for Elizabeth to return with the family for a visit.

"All that remains now is to escort you all back through the mine tunnels and your way out of here," said Joshua, "but what I suggest is that at least three of you children go back via the bush. We have no one to fear now, so it will be quite safe to use that way and leave things in place for a return journey back through to this side."

Joan and her family and the boys said goodbye to Elspeth, and followed Joshua to the mine entrance. When they arrived there, a crowd had gathered to say goodbye and thank them once again for what they had done. There was a large bunch of flowers each for Joan and Mary.

Joshua led them all back through the tunnel with instructions as to what to do to let themselves out at the other end. He wished them all goodbye saying that he was sure they would all meet again soon.

When they arrived at their side of the tunnel, Rebecca, Sally and Paul were waiting for them, having returned via the bush.

It was a very happy bunch of people who returned to Pedro's home.

Sally's mother arrived at the house a little while later and was delighted to see they had all returned safe and sound. Sally asked her if it would be alright for Rebecca and Elizabeth to come home with her and stay for a while.

"I don't mind as long as it is acceptable to Pedro's grandmother," she replied.

Joan told her it would be perfectly fine. Secretly Joan was pleased to let her go with Sally and her mother because she needed to contact Jessica to check with her how she felt about seeing Elizabeth and it would be a lot easier if she were not in the house.

Tom said he would walk into the village with Sally's mum and the girls, and return the boys safely to their parents. Pedro and Paul went along as well, Paul saying he would go up to the house to spend the night there with his father.

When they had all gone, Mary remarked on what a very busy two days they had had, and how nice and peaceful the house seemed.

"I will enjoy the peace and quiet for the next few days," said her mother in law. "I need to study the rest of the papers Jessica left me and also there are those papers that James found up at the house. I think they will open up a few secrets too."

CHAPTER FORTY-ONE

MORE DETAILS FROM THE PAST, PLANS FOR THE FUTURE

Over the next few days the family, at her request, left Joan on her own to study thoroughly all the paperwork she now had in her possession. She told them she would let them know when she was ready to reveal all. Meanwhile Pedro and his father and grandfather spent a lot of time up at the Bilk house helping James to give it a good clean and tidy up. It was decided to leave the triangular rocks buried where they were. As granddad said no one else but themselves knew they were there so they should be safe for the time being. "Although," he warned them, "we will need to move them somewhere safer eventually. As far as we know we got rid of the baddies but they were only the ones we knew about. We will have to put that on the list of things to discuss when we start to settle things."

James suggested, for the very same reason that all evidence of the diggings his father had done in the garden and orchard should be removed, so the boys were given the job of filling all the holes in and removing all the ribbons and tapes from the tree trunks.

Following breakfast on the fifth day after their visits to the two villages, Joan announced she was ready to tell them all just what she had found out from both sets of papers.

It was decided that the garden would again be a nice place for them all to sit and listen to what Joan had to tell them. They waited for the arrival of James and Paul who had said they would be down that morning.

"Do we have to stay Granny, or can Paul and I go into the village."

"You two run along to the village. I think I heard your mother say we needed some more milk anyway."

Mary gave them the milk containers and said to make sure they were back by lunchtime."

"O.K. mum we will," said Pedro and off they went.

It had been decided that the village was now a much safer place so the boys had been allowed to go there unaccompanied.

"Right," said Joan when they were all settled, "what I have found out will change the way we think of our village. It appears that our family by way of my maiden name Meaker, had an awful lot to do with the marble mine way back in the past. By way back I mean over one hundred and fifty years ago. From what I can make out my four times great grandfather was once in partnership with the original Bilk family. In fact it appears that it was a Meaker who discovered the secret of some of the marbles. As in all families and partnerships there came a falling out and in this case it seems as if the Bilks won out and took control of the mine completely. What exactly happened I have no idea. What I do know is that our family does in fact still own the old village church. I knew we owned the village hall, which if you remember Tom, I said I was going to tell you about during this visit, but I had no idea we owned the village church as well. It seems James, that when the big falling out happened it was decided the Bilks should have the old manor house and the Meakers would have the church and hall. The Meakers also have the right to the village green. The village shop is owned jointly both families. At least the shop that was in place at the time." She looked at James and said that she was sure that the two families were not going to argue about that.

"Certainly not, Joan," he said, 'there had been enough bad feelings around here to last a lifetime.

"As regards to the school, because it was originally held in the Manor House then old Nathan Bilk took it upon himself to continue to support it and eventually it just sort of belonged to him. He provided the teachers and their accommodation and everyone seemed happy with that arrangement. Your father continued with it on the death of his father. Now I suppose it will fall on your shoulders if you are prepared to take it on as a commitment."

James assured her that he would, saying it would give him an interest in life and hopefully allow him to repay to the community some of the wrongs his father had carried out.

"Getting back to the marbles," said Joan. "It would seem that the ones we know as 'Wishy Marbs' are not the only ones with magical powers, or any other powers. I believe some marbles have coloured dots, which fit into marbles with a sort of dent in them. Those seem to have some kind of healing properties. It is probably those marbles the 'High Person' and the one we know as 'She', were trying to get hold of. They probably thought they could get everlasting life or something by using them. We will have to have a closer look at just what marbles are found in the mine and what use they are. We must also make sure they do not get into the wrong hands. I know we think we have got rid of the wrong doers but they were the ones we knew about."

"That is just what dad was saying today," said Tom.

"We should also make a list of all the designs and patterns of the various marbles and just what if anything they can do."

"What I propose is that sometime in the very near future we call a meeting of all the villagers and tell them what has happened, although I do think we should keep anything highly sensitive to ourselves at this time, just until we are sure everyone is with us, agreed?"

They all said yes they were in agreement.

"We can introduce James to everyone and explain he will be taking over from his father as the owner of the mine, although I suspect there will be a different atmosphere there from now on."

"You can be sure of that, and I will tell them so," said James.

"I don't think we need to change the 'Custodian of the Records' at the moment but I do think that our two families should maintain the right to hold that position. We must certainly before too much longer name a successor to me for when I can no longer carry out the duties expected of the position."

"I'm sure that won't be for a long time yet," commented James.

Joan gave him a smile saying she hoped he was right. Joan looked at Tom and said that she and his father had decided before they came on this visit that they would like to look for a house back in Marbleville. "Now it looks as if I have a very good reason for us to settle here," she said.

Tom said he was delighted at their decision and added they could stay with them as long as they needed while they were looking for a house.

Before Joan had a chance to thank him, James butted in by saying he knew of a certain very large house on a hill with plenty of room to spare, far more than one man and a boy could use.

Joan smiled and thanked him saying she would keep the offer in mind.

"One thing we do need to concentrate on is how the people back in Kirkumville can return here without there being any effect on their health should they wish to get to the age where they would have been. I am sure we can come up with a way to help them using the marbles in the triangular rocks, but it will need very careful thinking. But that," she concluded, "will be a task for another day in